Image & Likeness

by

Derek Olsen

Aurora Books, an imprint of Eco-Justice Press, L.L.C.

Aurora Books
P.O. Box 5409 Eugene, OR 97405
www.ecojusticepress.com

Image and Likeness
by Derek Olsen

Library of Congress Control Number: 2020951085
ISBN: 978-1-945432-42-2

This book is dedicated to the people who have inspired and taught me as I traveled, trained, researched, and wrote this novel:

To all who have taught me about the Orthodox faith and iconography: Fr. Seraphim of St. Nicholas Orthodox Church in Tacoma; Fr. Climent and Fr. Simeon of Zographou Monastery; and Dr. Dimitri Conomos of Oxford, whom I met on Mt. Athos, Greece;

To all who have taught me about Taoism and Taoist martial arts: Dr. Mei-Hui Lu and Master Wuna Chang, my instructors during 2 years at Wudang International Martial Arts Academy in Seattle; and the venerable monks Renjie Cao and Li-Yi Yin of Mt. Hua, China;

To Mr. George Pirotis, my Greek teacher in Tacoma; Ms. Diya Peng, my Chinese teacher in Xi'an; and Mr. Barry Linn, my 9th-grade English teacher, who first led me to read The Odyssey and the Tao Te Ching and who has since been my mentor for nearly 20 years;

To my friends, Alex, Sky, Victoria, and Jen for their feedback and cultural perspectives;

To my parents, grandparents, and brother Kevin for their continued support, inspiration, and suggestions;

To the collective unconscious; to the Tao (known as "the Way"); and most of all, to God.

Thank you all.

Chapter 1

Adrian Loukas, the artist, stood bedazzled. He leaned his eyes as close to the glass as he could without tickling his lashes. Behind the glass was the *Sinai Pantocrator*, the icon he revered more than anything. It was an icon of mystical persuasion, painted in the sixth century by a Byzantine priest. Through the icon, the solemn eyes of Jesus of Nazareth gazed back at him, enchanting his heart and stirring up the passion of his spiritual yearning. Icons were meant to do this, Loukas reflected. His Orthodox faith had taught him that icons were not merely paintings on wooden canvases but gateways to divine knowledge, windows into the spiritual world of the saints. Their crisp lines and sensational colors were meant to light up the depths of the soul like Paschal candles in the darkness. As the artist stood silently, loving the *Sinai Pantocrator* with all his being, he took refuge in this inner world. The hours faded away like a setting sun.

"Mr. Loukas," called a voice, "we are closing for the night."

Loukas blinked his eyes without breaking contact with the icon. The voice came from Father Feyzal, the chief librarian at Saint Catherine's monastery. Feyzal wore a brown, cotton cassock tied with a gray sash. It was coarse and economical, yet clean and well cared for. On his head was a brown, flat-topped hat typical of what a monk might wear. One could say that the monastery and all its holy treasures—including the *Sinai Pantocrator*—represented a kind of cloister on Mount Sinai, in which faithful devotees maintained a shelter from outside turmoil.

"Give me one more minute," Loukas requested. The artist touched his lips reverently to the glass as if to kiss the holy face of Christ.

"I tell you, I have never seen any visitor stand and admire an icon for as long as you have," remarked Father Feyzal, joining Loukas in front of the *Pantocrator*. "It is clear that you love the Lord dearly."

As Loukas nodded politely, he wiped his sweaty hands on his pants. They were faded blue jeans nearly worn out with holes emerging in the knees and at the buttocks. Together with his unkempt hair and ratty, old gray t-shirt—stained with drops of paint and wine—the artist lacked any sense of a formal appearance. He realized now, this made Father Feyzal uncomfortable, but he didn't care. The librarian was too restrained by his pious manners to mention it, and besides, the artist had been far too engrossed in the images that now surrounded him to be bothered with his own appearance. He was too captivated by the beauty of the icons to even return Feyzal's invitation to answer.

"You must be well-versed in iconography," added the gray-bearded librarian, trying to elicit a response. "I can tell by the way you are studying the *Pantocrator*."

Loukas came to his senses at last. "I suppose. But I am an artist, not a scholar."

"Of course, of course. I have met countless academics who can discuss the origins and symbolism of religious pieces, but you are different. Your eyes speak of something different, something deeper."

Loukas looked up at the *Pantocrator* again and smiled inwardly. It took the eyes of an artist, he believed, to experience the full beauty and rapture of Orthodox icons. He knew that their images were not meant to look realistic. On the contrary, icons stylistically embraced crude dimensionality and imperfect proportions. They did this to captivate the observer with their stunning color and austere beauty. The icons' faces were solemn like those of ascetics held up in monasteries and detached from worldly pleasures. Yet, once the beholder was able to see through the veil of an icon's imagery and symbolism, then the austerity of the form would transmute into a sublime comfort known only to the mystics, those wholly devoted to the Orthodox way. The secret to making this transformation, he understood, was not to worship the icons or analyze them; both of these approaches would defeat their purpose. Rather, it was to let oneself be seen by them, to bare one's naked soul before their painted eyes. Then, if one looked on in just the right way and with the right intention, the solemn faces would appear to smile.

As Loukas's gaze deepened, he felt warmth and love inside. He felt a personal connection to Christ through the icon's artistic form. As an artist, he knew that everything about Christ's iconographic form was intentional: the eyes were dark like the bark of a black pine, intensified by their contrast to the pale, oily tones of the face and neck; the hair was slick and chestnut brown, while the beard and mustache were lighter and scraggly; and beneath the mustache was a set of pale, pink lips. By outward appearances these lips were still, and yet something mysterious about their depiction made Loukas feel that they were perpetually moving, whispering to him from behind the withered paint and varnish, pronouncing the journey of his soul from start to finish. As he looked even deeper into the icon, his eyelids quivered. He could feel the lips moving closer to him, hovering over his eyelids as if to kiss them tenderly, just as his own mother and father had done at his hour of birth.

"Of course, this is only one of our many fine icons here at Saint Catherine's monastery," Feyzal persisted. However, he failed to get a response. It seemed the artist was swept away again in his inner world. "I can only imagine what thoughts must be going through your mind."

One last time, Loukas surrendered his soul to the eyes of the *Sinai Pantocrator*. The icon was worn with time and yet eternally reminiscent of all holy things. Being near this face and its gold-painted aura made Loukas lose sight of all worldly attachments and trivialities. It made him laugh at the tiny blunders and regrets that had weighed so heavily on his mind, it made him lament the lost souls who would never feel God's love, and it let him escape—temporarily—the woes of his impending divorce, which had prompted him to make the pilgrimage to Mount Sinai alone.

Indeed, beholding the *Sinai Pantocrator* made the treacheries of his lonely three-day camel ride across Egypt to reach Saint Catherine's monastery vanish from his thoughts completely. Seeing the icon in person, he thought to himself that such a masterpiece should not be hidden away in a remote monastery but shown, studied, and experienced by all. Its image and likeness should be reproduced everywhere by the world's worthiest painters. How he burned with passion to become such a masterful painter!

"Mr. Loukas?" Feyzal called, waving his bony hand in front of the artist's face.

"Sorry. I'm coming."

Feyzal escorted the artist through the winding room of icon displays, which ended at a small, tidy corridor. He pulled a rusty lever to turn off the lights inside the icon chamber, then turned to address the artist:

"You were in quite a rapture, I think! I quite admire your ability to understand art."

Loukas squeezed his eyebrows.

"Are you an artist, Father?"

"No, no," Feyzal answered, scratching his head. "I have not been made for that."

"Then how would you know how an artist understands art? Or that he understands it at all?"

"Well, I—"

"Form and symbolism are like a language that must be learned and studied over time. A painter who has not mastered the language of the artform cannot truly be called great."

"No?"

"I don't believe so." Loukas buried his hands in his pockets, trying to keep his erratic body language controlled. "I believe scholarship cannot be properly divorced from artistry. The iconographer must follow the rules of the artform." Though he didn't show it, Loukas's heart raced with enthusiasm. He rarely discussed art with anyone, much less with a casual acquaintance. He was unsure if Father Feyzal understood his words, but nevertheless, being able to express them right then and there made him feel free from inhibitions, free from judgment, if only for a moment.

"But isn't there something deeper than the rules?" questioned Feyzal. "Something beyond mere form?"

"Of course, there is. But don't we also rely upon technique and scholarship in order to get there? How can you expect to have freedom of expression without a clear set of rules to define it? That would be like having a house without walls, or a country without borders!"

"So says the American," the librarian retorted, his brow and chin swooping downward.

The artist didn't know if the remark was careless or meant as an insult.

"What?"

"Isn't that what your country does—build walls to keep people out who don't fit within the borders? Bah!"

With some effort, Loukas refrained from presuming the worst intentions in this remark. He returned his mind to the image of *Sinai Pantocrator*—those soft yet penetrating eyes, those pale, delicate cheeks and that swarthy, well-attended hair—and focused on the light within his heart, waiting for Father Feyzal to clarify what he meant.

"Never mind that," the librarian finally said, shaking off the emotional residue of his hasty political assertion. "I only meant that as an American you have an outsider's perspective that is different from those of us here who have lived with this iconography most of our lives. Just look at our pilgrim log—you are the first American we have hosted in quite some time!"

"Well, Saint Catherine's monastery isn't exactly easy to get to," Loukas said as he sharply rubbed his outer thighs, which were still sore from the camel ride. "But the pilgrimage is important to me. I was brought up in the Orthodox church. My parents were immigrants."

"From where?"

"From Thessaloniki, Greece."

"When I saw your name in our log I wondered if you were Greek!" Feyzal's eyes glowed.

"Greek-American."

"My mother is also from Thessaloniki!"

"You don't say!"

"When I first met you I knew—I knew it!—that we were like brothers somehow." Feyzal clasped the artist's hands and shook them cordially. "Brothers from three different continents. Welcome again to Egypt!"

"Thank you, Father."

"Not that Greece is any better than America these days, what with their movement to ban all immigration. Can you believe it, Mr. Loukas? 'Keep Greece for the Greeks,' they are saying. 'Immigrants go home!'"

"I'm trying not to think about that."

"Yes, yes, as an artist you have more creative matters to attend to."

Loukas nodded and breathed in heavily. "I should be getting to bed now. I'm hoping Mount Sinai will not be too crowded tomorrow morning. I plan to paint the sunrise from the top, and I want to be well rested for my first impression."

"You mean, you haven't climbed the peak yet? Ah! You will find it inspiring, I am certain! Just be sure to start very, very early so you can reach the top before sunrise. There are plenty of guides. Better yet, I will take you myself! I know the perfect vantage point from which you can paint the miracle of the sunrise. What do you say, my brother?"

The artist accepted the offer, and the librarian clasped his shoulder. But before they could say anything more, a faint crash sounded from behind them. Then, without warning, all the lights in the monastery went out. Loukas jerked his shoulder away from the librarian's delicate hand and ran toward the sound.

"Where did you go?" Feyzal called out.

The artist rushed back toward his beloved *Pantocrator* like an eagle protecting its nest. It was pitch-black, but his eyes of faith (or, more accurately, his impeccable visual memory) allowed him to round the corners of the iconography display cases without peril. Feyzal fumbled around to find the rusty lever, but when he pulled it the lights in the icon chamber would not turn on. He then reached for his keychain flashlight. Once he turned it on, he moved around the displays and aimed it at the *Pantocrator's* case. The light revealed a jet-black cloak positioned on the wall above, covering what he presumed to be an intruder.

"There she is!" exclaimed Loukas, who was already in front of the *Pantocrator*.

"She? How can you tell it's a woman?"

Swiftly, the cloaked woman readjusted herself and flew onto the floor. She skidded along the side of the far wall and retreated into a corner, shaded by a tall shelf. Then, she was still.

Loukas moved his eyes around. His fingers traced the air as his photographic memory summoned images of the layout of the icon chamber. The details lit up in his faithful eidetic mind; he could visualize every nook and cranny, every blemish on the wall and every dusty footprint on the floor. Now, too, there was the added outline of a form that did not fit in with his memory.

"I see her!" the artist shouted as he ran towards her.

As he neared the shelf, the intruder's shape took a more defined form in front of his eyes. She was fast—unfathomably fast! And she moved without a sound.

"Do you taste smoke?" shouted Feyzal. The air was thick with black fog.

"It must be a smoke bomb," Loukas reasoned. "Look!"

"I'd look if I could see anything!"

"Get back to the *Pantocrator!*"

Loukas reached his arms up like a bear trying to extend

his reach. But it was no use. The cloaked intruder shoved his chest forcefully. Then, with a fluid motion she wrapped her ankle around the back of his leg like a hook, making him trip and fall backwards onto the floor.

"Mr. Loukas, what's happening?" Feyzal turned around again and again, aimlessly, unable to focus his flashlight on anything.

The black plume of smoke continued to pour its darkness across the whole floor. Squinting to see, the artist stood up and widened his search. His eyes patrolled the spaces between the icons, starting from the shelf in the far corner, until finally he came to the *Pantocrator*. The fog was still thick, but through it the artist beheld the phantom intruder climbing upon the glass that protected his favorite icon. Feyzal took out his smartphone, thinking its flashlight would be more powerful than the one on his keychain. When he got it turned on, the intruder became somewhat visible. She was suspended in the air, perfectly motionless, with her arms spread out like the wings of a crane. They both could make out her round face and athletic physique. In fact, she wasn't wearing a cloak at all, only dark clothing that billowed out from her slim yet muscular frame. And then it became clear why she kept still and did not try to run: she was caught inside the glass display case.

"How did she get in there?" the artist marveled as the fog cleared. Feyzal turned off the flashlight as soon as the glass started to reflect its light back to them.

The artist examined the woman's face behind the glass. Her elliptical eyes were shut, gazing inwardly. Her firm face and unshakable brow glowed with an aura of grace. Like a martial arts master patiently awaiting an enemy, she kept still. She even resembled a kind of still portrait in the way she meditated. Behind the glass she hung like a chrysalis from a leaf, as if frozen in time, waiting to come to life.

"She's so still," noticed Loukas. "You can't even see she is breathing."

"We must open the door under the case and apprehend her," ordered Feyzal, taking out a piece of rope to tie her wrists. "But be careful! "

The librarian inserted his key into the trap door below the glass case and counted to three. In an instantaneous movement—perhaps, to Loukas's secret admiration—the cloakless woman ejected herself through the trapdoor and sped across the slick floor like a field mouse evading an owl. Almost invisibly, she slipped into the shadows, taking the *Sinai Pantocrator* with her. The two men grasped at her to no avail.

Loukas was hysterical. "She has the icon! Stop her!"

To the artist and his gifted eyes, nothing was so hellish as the sight of a sin being committed right in front of him. And though it was the darkness that gave the thief her winning advantage, it was the light that cursed the artist more, for his eyes were such that they could never forget what they had witnessed. If anything, the dimness of the room only made his focus on the thief especially pronounced. It also made his clinging to the disappearing face of the icon especially desperate. Fortunately, an emergency generator came on, making a loud whirring sound. Lights gradually began to illuminate the room. A low hum in the background indicated that the air filtration system had powered up, and gradually the fog disappeared leaving no trace.

"Are you okay, Mr. Loukas?"

"I think so," he answered, patting his humble clothing, disoriented. When he turned back around, the intruder was nowhere in sight. Surprisingly, nothing looked out of order except for the *Pantocrator's* absence. He wiped the sweat from his neck and chin, closed his eyes, and took a deep breath. Father Feyzal saddened his eyebrows and adjusted his brown cap. Then, with a terrified yet guarded disposition, he shook his head. After a moment of silence, he spoke:

"I'm sorry Mr. Loukas, but I must ask you to leave."

"But what do we do?" The artist's heart raced. "How do we

catch her?"

"I'll put in a police report. I doubt we can catch her ourselves."

"But we have to!" He threw up his hands erratically.

"How? She is clearly an experienced thief. Do you think she would let herself be followed?" A trace of spittle from the librarian's aged lips indicated, perhaps, that he shared the artist's anger. "We must be patient."

Loukas placed his hand on his own heart. It felt cold, dark and abandoned. The image of the beloved *Pantocrator*, like the sweet imprint of a kiss from the Divine, was fading from his eyesight. Those eyes of dark pine, those pale, oily cheeks, that scraggly beard, that golden aura—all of it was growing dim. And though the icon itself remained perfectly constructed in his memory, the living presence of Christ that had come through the icon to stir his heart seemed to grow more distant with each passing thought.

"I wish I could." Loukas's agitated hand trembled along with his speech.

The librarian cupped the artist's shoulder again and nodded. He escorted the artist up to his room and did his best to console him.

"Get some rest, my brother."

"How can I sleep? I have to find that thief and get the *Pantocrator* back!"

"You have a very important pilgrimage tomorrow. You will paint the sunrise from atop Mount Sinai! Who knows? Maybe you will find some other kind of spiritual image to admire."

"That still won't bring back the *Pantocrator*."

"Then consider this, Mr. Loukas. In the scripture it is written that we are created in the image and likeness of God. That means every one of us, without exception, carries that image and likeness within. Why do intruders penetrate our walls and take what we hold most sacred? I don't know. But surely the Creator has an answer, a vision, a plan, one that even your eyes cannot yet see."

With a speechless nod, the artist retired to his guest chamber in the monastery. The image of the *Pantocrator's* golden aura faded in his mind like stars at daybreak.

Chapter 2

Cassandra Yin and her nephew Jason were playing backgammon at the table in the breakfast nook. The busy sounds from the kitchen provided the perfect background noise for their afternoon game.

"One. Two. Three. Four. Five. Six. Seven. Eight!"

Jason moved his white backgammon piece excitedly around the board and captured the black piece eight steps away.

"Ha-ha! I got you, Auntie!"

"Jason!" scolded his grandmother, coming out of the kitchen with a wet skillet and a green drying towel. "I told you to speak Chinese at home!"

"But...but," the boy stuttered, trying to obey.

"Greek is for out there!" She pointed with the skillet. "Not in here!"

"I...trying," Jason managed with his infantile grasp of Mandarin.

The grandmother scowled at him as she dried the skillet with her towel. Her drying motions were sharp and automatic, acquired from decades of practice. She was dressed in black, well-laundered clothes from head to toe and wore a gray bandana, which was wrapped so firmly around her head that not a strand of hair could deviate from the rest. Her disposition was similarly unyielding, and the deep creases in the skin around her eyes marked her as the Yin family matriarch.

"Please, mother, speak lightly to him," pleaded his aunt Cassandra from the breakfast nook. "He was born here. Greece is all he's ever known!"

"What a disgrace!" the matriarch criticized in a voice that echoed generations of scowling, tight-fisted elders that came before her. "It's his mother's fault. With his head so filled with Greek, what room is left for us?" She turned her shoulder coldly and returned to the kitchen. Angry pans clamored and clanged as she resumed her labor. "We never should have left Xi'an," she muttered.

Jason rolled his eyes at his grandma, not entirely sure what her fuss was about. Cassandra, meanwhile, knew it all too well. She knew her mother had never fully adjusted to life in Athens. In China, life was familiar and safe. Neighbors were dependable, worry was unproductive, and hardship was shared. Farming had been toilsome work, but it was a life of vitality and virtue. Until coming to Greece, the Yin family had never known anything different. China was home, without any question. However, ever since Jason was born, the rich legacy of their Chinese way of life had grown steadily diluted, ill-revered, a burden to an ungrateful half-Greek heir.

Startled by the clanging of the pans, Peony, the household cat, scampered out of the breakfast nook and into the living room to find Daphne, Jason's mother, reading a newspaper on the couch. Peony wove her way between Daphne's thin legs and brushed her fur against rough designer jeans. Cassandra knew Daphne had detected her mother's insult from the kitchen. But she suspected Daphne didn't care. Ever since marrying into the Yin family, hearing callous remarks in Chinese—none of which she could understand—had become a normal event. Cassandra also knew her mother was not oblivious to Daphne's feelings but simply disregarded them.

As usual, following the matriarch's outburst, a thick, numbing silence settled in the apartment. Daphne buried her head in the newspaper, while Jason studied the backgammon board waiting quietly for his aunt Cassandra to take her turn. After a minute, Cassandra smiled and adjusted her glasses. She picked up the dice and shook them in her hands, and then paused.

"How about I tell you a story?" she asked the boy.

"What kind of story?"

"It's a very old myth, one I think you'll like very much."

"Is it Jason and the Argonauts?"

Cassandra kept quiet and rolled the dice.

"Double threes!" Jason laughed, trying to sound sarcastic. "You are so lucky, Auntie!"

"Maybe, maybe not. Time will tell. Now listen closely! Long ago in China, in a mountain village just east of Xi'an, there lived four brothers. The oldest brother, Yang, was chosen to train as a warrior under the emperor. His parents were proud of him, but his brothers were jealous. They knew that Yang was learning the secret Way that gives warriors their strength. And yet Yang was warned by the emperor never to speak about the Way or to reveal any knowledge of it. Yang could see that his brothers desperately wanted to learn, so he decided to make riddles for them. 'I will give each of you a riddle,' he told them. 'And if any one of you can solve it, I shall show you everything I know about the Way.'"

Cassandra reached for her first black backgammon piece.

"Yang turned to the first brother and told the first riddle: 'I am seen in the dark but hidden in the light. What am I?'"

She picked up her first black piece and moved it three spaces, tapping it loudly upon the felt of the board at each space.

"'You are fire!' answered the first brother. But Yang said, 'No, I am not fire, for how can fire be hidden in the light?'"

Then Cassandra reached for her second piece.

"To the second brother, he gave his second riddle: 'Fools doubt me, but the wise believe in me without question. What am I?'"

She moved her second black piece three spaces, tapping it loudly like she had done with the first one.

"'You are truth!' answered the second brother. But Yang said, 'No, I am not truth, for how can the wise not question the truth?'"

Cassandra grabbed her third piece and let it hover over the board. Jason watched closely.

"The third brother was very clever. Yang gave him the

hardest riddle: 'Newborn children bring me into the world, and the dying take me with them as they leave. What am I?'"

Cassandra placed the third piece back upon the felt and slid it silently into the pocket at the end of the board.

"'I don't know,' admitted the third brother. 'I can think of nothing.' To this, Yang said: 'My brother, you have spoken correctly. The answer to all three riddles is the same: *nothing*. Nothing can be seen in the dark, and nothing is hidden in the light. Fools doubt nothing, while the wise believe in nothing without question. Newborn children bring nothing into the world, and the dying take nothing with them as they leave.'"

She moved her fourth piece three spaces, capturing one of Jason's white pieces and placing it in the center of the board.

"'Unfortunately,' Yang confessed, 'the answer to what I know about the secret Way is also the same: *nothing*.'"

Jason furrowed his eyebrows. "If it was *nothing*," he remarked disparagingly, "then what was the point of the myth?"

Without warning, the grandmother burst into the breakfast nook. "How can you sit there and play games when I am sick and dying?" She pulled him up from his seat by his ear and dragged him into the living room, then plopped him down onto the couch next to his mother, who paid little attention. Peony tiptoed frantically into the hallway. Jason pressed his throbbing ear with his palm, trying with all his might to keep a stoic face.

"Never forget what I've told you!" his grandmother cried.

"I'm sorry, Grandmother," he said in Mandarin.

Jason knew to obey. His eardrum pounded with the voices of his ancestors ruling his conscience. These were voices of conscience that Cassandra, too, had acquired from her upbringing, though she felt them much more profoundly. She had lived in Xi'an until she was twelve years old, the same as Jason was now. Though now she was twenty-eight, memories of her early childhood in China still shimmered nostalgically within her heart like light inside a crystalline jewel. Looking at her half-Chinese nephew often rekindled those memories;

yet paradoxically, his image was unknowably distant to her, his face a stranger to the distant home she treasured. As Cassandra packed up the backgammon pieces and closed the board, her mother's futile cries for home echoed through her pensive ears.

"Good," the grandma said, holding her hand on her chest as if to catch her sickly breath. "Now, do your math homework. Auntie will help you. She's a doctor now!" The matriarch stomped out of the room, shaking her head and mumbling further disapproval of Jason's Greek mother.

"She means, I have a doctorate degree," Cassandra clarified as she moved to the living room. "You have to have a degree in mythology if you want to be a professional *mythologist.*" She grabbed a book for herself: *Symbols and the Interpretation of Dreams* by the renowned analytical psychologist Carl Jung. "Don't worry, we can finish our game later."

"It's okay, doctor. I like math. It's probably my favorite subject."

Jason dove into his math book with the singular concentration of an Olympic diver plunging into a pool. Cassandra, the mythologist, admired how the boy took to his studies, sometimes forgetting to pay any attention to the outside world. She could relate to this state of intense focus. As a child her shelf was full of books of myths, both Greek and Chinese. Mythology was a world where her imagination could run free. She could distract herself from problems by meeting up with legendary gods and heroes and pretending to join them in their adventures.

Each myth was its own colorful, fantastic universe. Some explained the origins of things, like how Prometheus created humankind out of clay and gave them stolen fire from the gods. Others contained compelling romantic plotlines, like that of the lovers Zhinu and Niulang, who were banished to opposite sides of the galaxy and only allowed to see each other once a year. But all myths had a lesson to teach, and they appealed to different parts of her own psyche.

Unlike Jason, however, Cassandra's tendency to get lost in

her inner world had been motivated by the need to escape from difficult problems. Her parents would argue constantly, mostly over issues regarding her older brother George. The most bitter argument had taken place on the day they discovered George was not accepted into the University of Xi'an.

Cassandra hid in her room in order to tune out the deafening discussions of George's 'permanent stain' on the family's good name. But, in the end, George turned out fine. They all moved to Athens so George could go to a Western college. They started a laundry business in Chinatown, which George inherited after their father died. The real stain, it seemed, was the ill effect those constant arguments had had on Cassandra's upbringing, leaving her to hide in her room and prefer ancient myths over real-life events.

"Cassandra!" her mother called from the kitchen. "Did you pick up the suckling pig for our dinner?"

"I'll pick it up later tonight."

"Okay. Don't forget."

Cassandra's mother had become much kinder to her after her father died. That was the turning point, when Cassandra's interest in mythology became deeper and more academic—a way of detaching herself from the pain of loss. She discovered that myths of the gods represented deep psychological tendencies laden in humanity, like the wrath of Ares and the charm of Aphrodite. Myths of heroes like Odysseus the Ithacan warrior and Sun Wukong the Monkey King spoke of universal archetypes seen in all cultures. Through the study of mythology, one could access what Carl Jung had called the collective unconscious, a common ancestral memory from which all patterns of human nature and belief were derived. As Cassandra Yin had proven in her doctoral dissertation, there was even a mythological framework explaining the modern immigrant experience in Greece. Myths were not mere stories; they contained the power to unite people in a journey of self-discovery. The problem with this journey, however, was that it revealed both the positive and the negative traits of humanity.

As Cassandra sat in the chair opposite the couch, she watched Jason work through his math assignment, occasionally glancing down at her book to hide the fact that she was observing. She hoped math, for him, could be a refuge from life's more complicated struggles, just as mythology had been for her.

"Mom, what's a negative times a negative?" Jason asked, keeping his eyes on his book.

"A negative?" Daphne thought out loud.

"Nope, it's a positive. Ha-ha!" Jason laughed snidely. "Negative and negative cancel each other out. Didn't you know that?"

By now, all the Yin family noticed Jason's penchant for playful deception. His mother found it annoying, and to his father it was worthy of a smack on the head. But to Cassandra, it was charming. It was one of the dark yet necessary elements of adolescent nature, a right of passage reinforced by all sorts of legends: Zeus and his brothers defied their father Cronus to take over the heavens; Emperor Taizong's sons plotted to kill him at the start of the Tang dynasty in China. Tales of adolescent rebellion—whether of ordinary or extraordinary proportions—were a fascinating aspect of humanity's dual nature. Though Cassandra did her best to help encourage Jason's respectability, she secretly wished him to explore both the good and the deviant tendencies emerging within him.

The dual nature of the human mind was a theme Cassandra contemplated often. Lately, she thought of how it related to her family's immigration. Some Greeks were friendly and welcoming to them, while others—even neighbors—treated them like invaders. Some Athenians were keen on helping Chinatown thrive, while others started riots in the name of Greek ethnic nationalism.

And yet, Cassandra asked herself, what was the difference between those who embraced foreigners and those who disparaged them? Nothing. People who were loving and hospitable towards most could at the same time have prejudiced or even racist inclinations towards certain groups. All people had a dual nature, she recognized, just like the mythical two-headed snake called *Ouroboros*. All people were like *yin* and *yang* mixed up and tangled within each other in a messy stew of sociopolitical convictions. Mythology was a means by which these dualities could be told as stories, staged as dialogue and channeled into a productive common good.

"Jason, what are you reading in your history class this week?" she asked a few minutes later.

"Nothing," he stated snidely as if answering one of Yang's riddles.

The evening sun made the whole apartment hot. A thin yellow curtain dangled in front of the window, blowing gently in the soft breeze. Yellow light filled the living room, enriching the paleness of the white stucco walls and their sepia trim. Framed displays of Chinese calligraphy and stylized, amateur watercolors filled the wall spaces, reflecting and amplifying the evening glow. If not for getting lost in mental concentration, the momentary beauty of the room might have been admired, or else the heat might have been a nuisance.

Suddenly, Daphne threw down her newspaper and shouted at her son.

"Jason, look at the time! You need to get your uniform on for *Kung Fu* practice!"

"You remembered!" he answered sardonically. He closed his math book and went to his room to change. Irritated at her son's acerbic attitude, Daphne turned to her sister-in-law and made a request:

"Cassie, will you take him? I have plans this evening."

Cassandra skimmed the remainder of the paragraph she was feigning to read and took her time to answer. Slowly she inched the book closed, as if to linger on every letter before answering Daphne's plea. Daphne twisted her curly, strawberry blonde hair, until finally Cassandra forced the book closed to make a crisp popping noise.

"Fine, I'll take him," Cassandra sighed. "It's not like I have a job."

As she grabbed her jacket from the arm of the sofa, a disturbing headline from Daphne's newspaper caught her eye: *Two Chinese Killed in Anti-Immigrant Riots*. She squeezed her fists and hardened her lips. "Has Jason seen this?"

"Seen what?" answered Daphne.

"The riots! Have you even paid attention to what's going on?"

"He's a boy, Cassie. What's his concern?"

"What's his concern?" She snatched the paper from Daphne's long, manicured fingers and waved it at her. "Two Chinese killed in anti-immigrant riots! Right here in Athens!"

The mythologist couldn't comprehend Daphne's apathy toward the riots. It peeved her, too, that her brother George acted just as aloof regarding the issue, as though it was better for the whole family to pretend nothing was happening. She figured he did this mostly to shelter their mother from grief. But for Cassandra, the riots were the last thing she could ignore—they were the epitome of all that was wrong with the world. 'Greece for the Greeks!' the rioters were saying. 'Immigrants, go home!' These were not just remote political statements heaved into the headlines for sensationalism; they were personal, egregious, and now apparently a threat to life. As Cassandra snatched the newspaper to scan the article, she felt her lifelong anxieties about survival in Greece—about the dark side of humanity, about her family and her future— being turned over in agony in the soils of her heart.

Jason emerged from his room stuffing his foot into his shoe. His uniform was black from head to toe, except for a white logo on the shirt of his school's name. "Are you taking me?" he asked his aunt.

"When does it start?" Cassandra asked, squeezing the newspaper's corners with her fingertips and then letting it fall back onto the table.

"In twenty minutes. Hurry, Auntie! Master Nikos will be upset if I'm late again."

Without another word, Cassandra and Jason flew down their four flights of stairs and into the car.

"I don't like *Kung Fu*," the twelve-year-old complained as he fastened his seatbelt.

"Why not?"

"First of all, everyone thinks I'm Chinese."

Cassandra was outraged. "You are Chinese!"

"But I've never even seen China! It's so annoying. Plus, I'd rather learn something useful like music or art."

"Give it another chance, Jason." Cassandra sighed as she took the wheel and pulled out of the driveway. "Even I took *Kung Fu* when I was your age."

"You did?"

"Of course, back in Xi'an. But I stopped when we came here."

"Why did you stop?"

"I didn't have time, I guess. Life was really chaotic when we first got here."

"But now it's great, right?"

"Yes, Jason," she said to reassure him, though she knew it was not fully true. "We're very lucky."

"Why yes, *doctor*, we are!" he said playfully.

When they arrived at the school, Jason escorted his aunt into the gymnasium. Master Nikos shook his finger perfunctorily at the boy before inviting him to warm up. Jason bowed and then joined his place at the end of a row of boys ordered by height. Cassandra relaxed her shoulders and found a seat in the far corner of the bleachers. *Greece for the Greeks. Immigrants, go home. Two Chinese killed.* She tried to stamp it all out of her mind.

Nearby sat an old man with an expressionless face. He was completely bald, and to Cassandra's fascination, his head was nearly spherical in shape. It was shiny like a porcelain statue and lacked any trace of facial hair. As she observed longer, she noticed the elegant curves of his wrinkles. His round face revealed no emotion except for the general impression of fatigue that comes with age. Around the edges of the man's loose-fitting, dark-blue martial arts uniform, there was a continuous pattern of circles resembling the *yin-yang*, only much more elaborate. Curious, and yet careful not to be noticed, Cassandra realigned her glasses and angled her vision to get a better look at his uniform. Then, with a turn of his eyeballs only, the man looked at her.

Instinctively, Cassandra massages her kneecaps as an excuse to break eye contact. But just as she looked down, she noticed the man's stealthy, black shoes right beside her own—he had moved almost instantaneously and was sitting right next to her! Cassandra was slightly unsettled, but she tried to drum up a polite conversation:

"How are you, sir? Jason *Yin* is my nephew. He's on the far left. Hasn't quite hit his growth spurt yet."

The man angled his gaze slightly downward but didn't respond.

"As you can see, I'm still working on that myself."

She could tell he was listening deeply—more deeply than most people tend to listen—but he didn't speak. Instead, he waited for Cassandra to pour out the rest of her thoughts. Yet his silence was not unsatisfying. It gave her an opportunity to assess whether the man was Chinese. Her intuition, as well as her genuine desire to make a connection with him, told her to switch to Mandarin.

"I hope I'm not being too impolite," she began, "but I was only looking at you because of your uniform."

The man continued to listen, taking in each word as if he were breathing it into his lungs, drawing it effortlessly into the heart of his being.

"Forgive me, we don't know each other. My name is Cassandra Yin. I'm a mythologist. Well, not professionally yet, actually. I just graduated with my doctorate. Who are you, sir?"

The man looked down for a moment, and then quietly introduced himself as Master Zhang. He bowed his head to her, and Cassandra was struck by the way his elevated status carried no pride.

"It is a great honor to meet you," she said.

He nodded, half-smiling.

"So, which boy are you here to see?"

Master Zhang pointed his eyes toward Master Nikos.

"Master Nikos? Are you his *shifu*?" she asked, using the Chinese word for master teacher.

"I am his *shifu's shifu*."

"Based on your uniform, I figured you must be a very advanced *shifu*."

He inclined his head to one side, almost in a shrug, as if to dismiss her supposition.

"How old are you?" the man asked.

"Twenty-eight," she answered. She knew this was not an uncommon question for a stranger to ask a younger person in China.

"You were born in the year of the dragon?"

"Yes."

The man nodded his head with a hint of enthusiasm.

"Is that good?" she asked.

"Yes. Very good. Everything adds up."

"What do you mean? What adds up?"

"The universe has joined our paths at this precise moment in history." Master Zhang lifted the palm of his hand to Cassandra's eye level and used it to accentuate his speech. "Now is the time for you to discover why you are here."

Cassandra was baffled by this man. Everything about him seemed surreal, as if he were a character straight out her mythology books. But this also intrigued her. She was captivated by the grace of Master Zhang's moving hand. If the uniform hadn't been a clear sign of the man's superior ranking in martial arts, then surely the artful way he moved was definitive proof. His hand was still and yet not so still that it lacked vitality. The gentle way his wrist and elbows arched as he bent and unbent them was a perfect expression of the eternal give and take of nature. Mythologically, she knew that this give and take were represented by the light and dark halves of the *yin-yang*. But she wasn't sure what he meant by implying that there was some kind of force in the universe that had brought her to him, but whatever his story, she wished enthusiastically to know the rest of it.

"The world is aching," he finally said.

"Are you talking about the riots?"

"Yes. But not just in Athens—the whole world is aching."

"I wish I could explain these things to Jason, or even just make him feel what the rest of us feel. Two Chinese were killed in those riots! How can I keep calm in a situation like this? My mother struggles with it more than anyone—she's sick, and she doesn't even know Greek well enough to understand her doctors. Can you imagine? And have you heard the rioters' new slogan? They are saying '*Greece for the Greeks! Immigrants, go home!*' They have the whole country looking at us like we're outsiders, like we're some kind of threat to the Greek way of life. I wish we didn't have to divide ourselves into tribes like this."

Master Zhang lowered his hand, and Cassandra watched his sleeve land upon the fabric of his pants like a feather on a soft bed.

"Humanity has always divided itself into tribes," he explained, and then began tracing his index finger along the curvatures of one of the *yin-yang*s on his sleeve. "If there were no dark, nothing would appear light; and if there were no light, nothing would appear dark. All things find their nature in opposition to each other. It is natural and healthy to have opposing elements."

"Then what did you mean when you said that the world was aching?"

"Light and dark exist in opposition, but they don't struggle against each other. They alternate with each other in balance. That is the nature of things. Light and dark give into one another and recede like the natural passing of the dynasties.

Struggle is what people are doing out of fear, especially in the West. And that is why the world is aching."

"But what can we do about it?"

Master Zhang gestured toward the boys as they punched in unison: "Ha!"

"You mean, fight? You want to start a war to end conflict? That seems counterproductive to me."

"Not a war," he clarified. "A training."

The mythologist caught herself biting her cuticles.

"I told you," the round-headed *shifu* continued, "that the universe has joined our paths together. Well, there is more. It can also show you where you are going."

"Are you some kind of Taoist Immortal?" she said, making a joking reference to the mythical sages of Chinese folklore. This made Master Zhang smile nearly up to his ears, sending deep wrinkles across the hairless contours of his face like ripples across a pond.

"No, I am not," the *shifu* finally confessed. But I have trained with them. My sister has trained with them too. And so shall you!"

"I don't know about that," she said abruptly before entertaining the *shifu's* words. She wondered how this could be true, but she suspended her disbelief. She felt herself becoming wrapped up in his intriguing chronicle, unable to resist seeing where it would lead. "Why would the Taoist Immortals train me?" she asked humbly.

"You could be a great warrior."

"How? My size doesn't exactly intimidate."

"Do you think being a warrior has anything to do with size?"

"There's also the fact that I haven't practiced *Kung Fu* since I was twelve."

"I disagree. You have practiced every day of your life."

"With respect, Master Zhang, I have not—"

"*Kung Fu* means any discipline you commit to and become a master in. Your training is not in fighting, but in mythology, in storytelling. A mythologist knows how to speak to our hearts and join together in our universal journey of self-discovery. Don't you think you've waited long enough to learn to apply your knowledge?"

"How do you mean?"

"Your skills are very advanced by now. Your work on the mythological framework of the modern immigrant experience places you at the top of your field."

"You've read my dissertation? You mean, you knew who I was already?"

"But your knowledge is still incomplete. By training with the Taoist Immortals, you will learn to apply the wisdom of myths toward the greatest humanitarian advantage on earth."

"And what is that?"

"Ending conflict," he answered. "Ending the struggle between East and West, light and dark. The time is now, Cassandra! The universe's timing is unmistakable. Your precise combination of knowledge, experience, and passion is exactly what we need in order to bring an end to these riots. That is your *Kung Fu*." He lifted both arms into the air with the same graceful fluidity as he had done before. "This is precisely why the universe has chosen you. It brought you here to me on this day in this gymnasium at this exact minute. That is why it is you who will train with the Taoist Immortals and show all of Greece...*the Way*."

Cassandra's jaw dropped. The Way was a central concept in Taoist philosophy; it stood for the ideal of balance and harmony in nature, a dual-natured path of goodness in moderation and simplicity as represented by the *yin-yang*. She knew it well from reading classics like *The Art of War* and the *Tao Te Ching*; however she had never considered the Way to be more than an abstract concept. It was an interesting philosophy, and maybe there was some truth to it, but there were no heroes or conflicts, and no legendary plotlines to make it worthy of a chapter in any mythology book.

"What does the Way have to do with it?"

"The Way is everywhere. It is the pattern that underlies all inner workings of nature—that is, for those who learn to read it. The Way is the secret knowledge of the changing of the seasons, of the turning of wheels and tides, of human conflict and resolution and all the archetypes of our evolution. The Way is hidden from those who do not study it—like a vast collective unconscious—flowing like a river with everyone and everything naturally following its course. In a sense, the Way is the root of all mythology. Don't you think?"

In that moment, Cassandra's ever-inquisitive heart opened to a new theory. If the Way was the root of all mythology, she thought, then it was worth investigating. Despite how surreal she felt in the presence of Master Zhang, she longed to know more. The boys in the background continued sparring with each other, heaving grunts of exertion and play.

"But it will not be easy," the *shifu* continued. "First, listen to me. As part of my dealings with the Taoist Immortals, my sister and I vowed to safeguard an ancient marble tablet on which was painted a portrait of an immortal called Zhen Wu. This is how we maintained our relationship with the Taoist Immortals. But recently, this painting was stolen. Those thieves! Now that we have lost it, we dare not contact the Taoist Immortals. Even if we tried, with our honor compromised, they would not teach us anything more. We fear that the painting of Zhen Wu has been destroyed—or worse, that it has fallen into the wrong hands. And if this has happened," he sighed, returning to his stoic disposition, "then Greece, China and everywhere in between may be in grave danger."

"So if we find the stolen painting, will we find the Taoist Immortals?"

"If we find the painting, then they will find us."

Master Zhang placed his strong, gentle hand on Cassandra's back, and instantly she had a vision: first, a piercing, white light appeared, which brought her feelings to a slow, still calm. She even felt a faint warmth on her face from the light, which resolved into an enormous image of a dozen concentric *yin-yang* circles drawn with immaculate precision. Within each *yin-yang*, dark and light colors of all shades commingled along lines and curves and tangents, each one pulsating with the vitality of life. The entire design was continuous, and yet dark remained dark and light remained light, each opposite finely distinguished from the other. In this vision there was no trace of struggle, no trace of conflict—the nature of the universe was order and balance. That was the Way of all things.

Then, at the center of the image, a blemish appeared. It sent chills down her spine and made her shiver. The blemish was neither light nor dark but an indiscernible void, growing larger and larger, tearing a hole in the splendid *yin-yang* from the inside out. As the hole ripped open wider, Cassandra felt the world ache and moan as if impaled at the heart by a razor blade, cutting it swiftly, violently and irreverently. She could feel the laws of both cosmos and psyche—the order of the collective unconscious—folding inward and breaking down in front of her eyes. Through the hole, she could see nothing but eternal oblivion. She watched the hole rip open from the center in all directions like an unstoppable cancer, perverting each *yin-yang*, one-by-one, into a meaningless, mangled mess until nothing remained. The truth was shattered. The Way was lost.

Cassandra came out of her vision both frightened and awestruck. Though her reasons to trust this strange, round-headed man were few, everything seemed to make perfect sense. "All myths reflect stories in our collective unconscious," she thought to herself. "And if the collective unconscious itself were to be represented as a myth, then it must be what the Taoists call *the Way*. And if we can bring peace to our homeland by telling this myth, then I must learn the Way. I must train." At that moment, she decided she would follow Master Zhang's lead.

"Will you let me help you find Zhen Wu's portrait?" she asked.

Master Zhang nodded.

The world is aching.

Chapter 3

Adrian Loukas trailed Father Feyzal up Mount Sinai, carrying an easel, a small stool, and a satchel with paints and brushes. He had put a light-brown collared shirt over his white t-shirt and an auburn silk scarf around his neck. Feyzal, meanwhile, carried an oil lamp and a backpack with the day's provisions. The morning was dark. Neither sun nor moon shown above.

"Here you will see the kinds of weeds and brush that would have carpeted the desert during Moses's time," explained the librarian. "Why, it was right in this vicinity the Lord descended to him in a fiery cloud to give him the ten commandments!"

"I've often wondered," Loukas shared, "if Moses had been a painter, what would he have painted after witnessing such an event?"

"I suppose we must leave that to our imaginations."

Loukas watched his shoes collect reddish-brown dust from the ground of the holy site. But there was still that one image he could not clear from his mind: the sight of the thief running out of the monastery with the *Sinai Pantocrator* under her arm. She had stolen it right before his eyes! He latched onto his memory of the icon as tightly as he could, recalling the rugged gracefulness of Christ's bearded face and the warm, glowing aura that circled His head. But he felt the *Pantocrator's* absence sorely in his heart.

"We are taking a back route," the librarian explained. "This way you'll avoid the other pilgrims."

"I appreciate it."

"I'm sure you are feeling great inspiration for your painting by now!"

"Well, I confess, I have not felt inspiration yet. It's still so dark! Can't we use a flashlight, or at least a brighter lamp?"

"Bah! For centuries pilgrims have ascended Mount Sinai before sunrise with nothing more than a dim flame. If you want to be genuine in your spiritual ascent, you will do the same. Besides, didn't you already prove last night that you could see in the dark?"

Loukas chuckled. "No, I can't see in the dark."

"Then how did you manage to chase after our intruder last night without running into any of the icon displays?"

"I worked out the appearance of the room from memory."

"A photographic memory! And of such precision! Truly, truly, my brother, I have never met anyone who could see in the way that you do."

Loukas kicked over a rock that had caught his shoe. A handful of scorpions scattered from the place where the rock had been. The soft stirrings of lizards and moths animated the otherwise still terrain and sky. The night was pulsing with life. Soon, they reached the summit. Dawn was breaking, and Loukas wasted no time in setting up his easel and preparing his paints. Feyzal stood by and pondered.

"I've been thinking," Feyzal began, "about what you said about Moses. You know, about him not being a painter."

The artist nodded, acknowledging the comment as he busily equipped his palette.

"I believe there is a cruel irony to art," the librarian continued. "The greatest seers among us don't paint, and the greatest painters never see God directly. Don't you think that is tragic?"

Loukas put down his brush and raised his brow at the old man.

"Have you suddenly become an artist, Father?"

"Not unless you have suddenly become a seer, Mr. Loukas."

"I suppose you're right. I'm no Andrei Rublev."

"Of course, of course!" Feyzal exclaimed excitedly, striking his palm to his head. "I stand corrected! If you count Saint Andrei, then clearly the artist may be a seer after all. Saint Andrei was no mere painter but a visionary, if I do say so.

Did you know? He was the only painter ever canonized as an Orthodox saint only for the miracle of his iconography."

The artist darkened his canvas with a layer of greenish gray as he thought up his response.

"I have no doubt Saint Andrei's icons were divinely inspired," Loukas explained. "But to be perfectly truthful, I don't consider iconography to be proper art."

The librarian was flabbergasted.

"But you spent all of yesterday admiring the *Pantocrator!* What on earth do you mean?"

"What I mean is that iconography has many rules, and there is not much room for interpretation. There are strict specifications for how each saint must be depicted. I'm referring to the composition of their faces, the colors of their clothes, the objects they hold and so on. These rules are carried through the ages, and the iconographer is obliged to uphold them."

"But how does that make it less than proper art?"

"Consider this: what if the iconographer doesn't uphold the rules? What if, instead, God inspires him to paint what he sees in his heart? How can he not abandon those rules for the sake of divine inspiration? Or, if instead he resists this inspiration for the sake of following the rules, then how can he call it 'art' when the inspiration that defines art is the very thing he has betrayed?"

"Now you are contradicting yourself," Feyzal contended. "Yesterday you said that the study and scholarship of these rules was necessary for expressing God in art, and yet now you are saying that rules inhibit their expression. You can't have it both ways!"

"Make no mistake, I adore icons. Maybe, through their rules, they are actually superior to proper art. I don't know. I'm not a scholar." He sighed, wishing he had just avoided the question. The sun was rising, and the chirping of crickets crescendoed in the distance. "But I know that when I paint what comes naturally, without considering the rules, I feel connected with the unseen world. Think of it this way: the world we can see, like the world of the icons and their beauty, contains both light and dark. It contains shadows and dimness, against which light and color make a profound impression. But the unseen world contains everything beyond what the shadows can cover. The unseen world is revealed when all the darkness disappears and all light and all images are revealed at once. For that you have to go deeper, beyond what the icon is showing you. You have to go behind the veil, to the unseen world from which all its images and shadows were derived. It's more about the essence than the form."

"And how do you expect to paint what you can't see, hmm? At least with icons, you know what the form is supposed to look like."

"I said I don't know!" Loukas erupted. His brow stiffened. "Can't we leave it at that?" With a jerking motion he turned away and returned his brush to the canvas. Paint dripped clumsily onto his tennis shoes.

Feyzal scoffed at the artist's sudden change in temperament and then sat down to relieve himself of his pack. He snuffed out the oil lamp and set it aside. The sunrise was forging its brazen beauty across the skies.

Meanwhile, Loukas rolled up his sleeves, flung the silk scarf over his shoulder, and entered deeper into his creative element. He invited the crisp desert air and the soothing wind to fill his lungs. Then, channeling his breath, he made strokes of bright red on the canvas. His brush caressed the painting like a sweet morning kiss. Reds then curved into grays, and yellows spotted the orange glow of the sunrise. And although Loukas's depiction of the sunrise was fluid and impressionistic, he strove to capture its unseen essence—that eternal feeling of the God's divine presence rising with the sun. If he could illustrate this essence, he thought, then his Sinai Sunrise would come to life.

After a time, Feyzal lost interest. He stood up and grabbed the oil lamp from the dirt. Then he called out to Loukas saying that he was returning to the monastery and was leaving the backpack there beside him. The artist ignored him.

"God help any pilgrims who make it to the summit and disturb your peace," Feyzal muttered as he began his descent.

But in truth, nothing escaped Loukas's notice. He was present yet aloof, as though his eyes had become the sun, the earth his touch. And all of the anger, the passion and the devastation that had stricken his soul while witnessing the *Pantocrator's* capture—these feelings filled him with a passion far greater than he had anticipated. He dipped his brush in brown and struck the canvas harder than before.

"Uh oh," he muttered. Anxiously he tried painting around the erroneous brown stroke to make it blend in. But it stood out like a tree in a desert. The more he tried to paint over it, the worse it looked. He yanked off his auburn scarf and threw it on the ground.

"Damn. I've ruined it."

Frustrated, he laid three more brazen strokes haphazardly upon the canvas. Aesthetically, this made it a little more balanced, since now the brown lines at least looked intentional. But it had lost the essence of the sunrise. It had lost the feeling of love that inspired it.

"Just like my marriage," he thought. "How can I paint without love? How can I ever paint again?"

Loukas picked up a jar of black paint and heaved its contents at his Sinai Sunrise.

"Done. Now no one has to see it."

Loukas set down his brush and wiped his brow. He patted his forehead with the silk cloth and looked up at the sun, which had risen significantly since he started. From behind, he heard a soft whisper. His aching heart jumped with panic.

"What?"

But as he turned around, no one was there.

He heard the whisper again, only louder. It was a deep female voice. He spun his head around, and he extended his senses in all directions.

"Who's there?"

"Adrian," she called in a slightly raised whisper.

The artist turned back toward his painting, from which the voice seemed to proffer.

"Look at me!"

Loukas turned around again and beheld the impossible. The same mystifying thief he had seen in the monastery the night before was standing right in front of him! She was petite yet muscular, dressed in a lightweight, black robe. He could see by the weightiness of her nose and ears that she was much older than looks and physical stamina would have suggested. Her hair was curled into an infinity-shaped bun, and her black shirt bore a faint embroidered design of the *yin-yang*.

"It's you! You stole the *Pantocrator!*"

"Don't speak."

"But how did you get up here?"

"Don't ask questions. Just look at me. I need to see your eyes."

The stealthy old woman leaned into his face and grabbed his head, drawing his forehead uncomfortably close to hers. Her elliptical eyes were as black as the River Styx.

"Who are you? And where is the *Pantocrator?*"

"I told you not to ask questions." She turned away and began moving down the mountain. "Follow me, Adrian."

The artist tried to object. He tried to demand answers. But the old woman moved in front of him with a mirage-like gait—making her seem to float above the ground—and he was powerless to resist following her, leaving everything behind. He was under her spell.

As he followed her, the sun grew hotter. Time wore on, and before he knew it, it was night again. The woman's smooth, viscous walking drew him forward like a powerful river flow. Loukas's shirt became drenched in sweat. Soon, the red-brown terrain beneath his feet gave way to gray rock, and before him lay the entrance to a cave.

Loukas fell over at the cave's entrance, out of breath. The spell was broken.

"Where are we? How——?"

"Remember what I said! No questions."

He looked around. Only rock surrounded them, and it wasn't even clear from which way he had arrived. They entered the cave slowly. Curiously, the interior bore the sweet smell of incense reminiscent of the inside of an Orthodox church. However, this was not much comfort for Loukas's otherwise tormented senses. The more he analyzed his circumstances, the more aware he became of his discontent.

"My painting!" he cried, suddenly remembering it. "My Sinai Sunrise!"

"Your painting is not important compared to the reason I have brought you here," she stated abruptly. "Come quickly. You need to see something."

She led him into a smaller cavern, where two men and a second, younger woman huddled, all dressed in similar black robes. They greeted her in their native Mandarin.

"Look at this, and tell me what you see."

She shoved a tome-sized marble tablet in front of his face and dusted it off with a dry brush. The artist gasped for air and coughed.

"What is it?" he asked.

She grabbed the collar of his shirt, shaking him violently.

"No questions!"

"Okay, I'll give it a look."

His eyes moved around the tablet, perusing what he gathered to be a very old depiction of a male elder with a goatee wearing a robe.

"What am I supposed to——?" He stopped his question before she could assault him again.

"Answer us now," the old woman ordered.

"What do you see?" asked the younger woman.

"It's very old. I would guess, Chinese. It's probably painted with lac tree sap, maybe from an early dynasty. But I'm not sure. I'm an artist, not a scholar."

"Look harder," suggested the shorter of the two men, whose broken English took Loukas a second to process.

"It appears to be authentic. However, you would need to do a chemical analysis of the marble and the ink to know for sure."

"That is not the issue!" corrected the taller man in much better English. "This painting depicts one of the greatest teachers who ever lived."

"A Taoist Immortal!" chimed the shorter man.

"A teacher of the Way!" exclaimed the younger woman.

"Look into his eyes," commanded the *Pantocrator's* captor. Her face was as still as stone. Her grainy voice deepened. "Tell us everything that you see." She clasped the back of his skull with her fingertips and eased his nose closer to the painting. This made Loukas wince uncomfortably.

"Well, I suppose—"

"Don't suppose!"

"Okay, I think—"

"Don't think either!"

The artist sealed his lips and observed the portrait with his full artistic capacity. It showed an old Chinese man—who the others in the cave called a Taoist Immortal—with an elegant nose. A white robe draped over his knees as he sat upon a stone. From the immortal's chin, a long, pointed black goatee reached all the way down to his heart. Around his head was a faint, circular halo that indented slightly into the marble. The top half of the background was filled with smooth, textured clouds, while the bottom half consisted of dark, jagged mountains and valleys. The artist imagined how the painting would have originally looked, with its deep red drawn upon a much lighter marble white. He traced the painting's rough texture with his eyes and imagined feeling its chiseled indentations and detailed brushwork.

The longer Loukas studied the portrait, the more the details intrigued him. The immortal's hands were dark and slender, his shoulders poised yet relaxed. He held out a scroll with three Chinese characters, which Loukas could not read. In the sky on the right side, a trio of tiny birds flew overhead;

next to them, a temple stood on the highest mountain peak, nearly concealed by the clouds. But the strangest detail in the picture was a distant pair of animals at the foot of the mountain on the left side: a red turtle with a round shell, and a faceless, black snake, which coiled its tail around the turtle's shell three times. Not fully aware of the symbology of this strange animal combination, Loukas took his attention back to the immortal's face. Dark, linear eyebrows suggested a serious demeanor, while the plumpness of his cheeks indicated generosity. Each eye was barely a centimeter wide, and yet the detail was so precise as to capture the refraction of light in the immortal's retinas. These eyes were so ancient, Loukas imagined, they had seen a world vastly different than the one that presently existed.

Then, all at once, he saw and felt something extraordinary. He couldn't explain it, but he sensed it, as though the man inside were somehow alive. The portrait gave Loukas a feeling that this man was not some long-departed historical figure but a sage whose presence could be felt here and now. There was much more to the marble tablet than its form suggested— the immortal's saint-like essence was somehow captured and preserved in the brush strokes and in the fine engravings on the tablet. Though it was not clear how or why, this painting revealed some kind of wisdom from a higher power. It appeared to be a genuine expression of a man made in the image and likeness of God.

For a moment, the artist shuddered at the thought. The only paintings through which he had come close to knowing God were Christian icons. They portrayed venerated Orthodox saints, angels and biblical prophets, not to mention Christ. None of the icons he knew in his heart had any relation to a Chinese teacher.

Loukas felt it a betrayal of his faith to look at a foreign painting as he would an icon. His every intuition, his Orthodox upbringing, his deep connection to God through art—all of these things begged him to look away. But he couldn't resist! As he gazed into the immortal's eyes, he felt an inner peace that only a saint could bestow on him. The painting stirred up the yearning within him to bear his soul to the Divine.

"This painting reveals God," Loukas whimpered with a sadness that seemed to emanate from the Taoist Immortal himself. "But it can't—"

Just as the artist was about to explain what he meant, a shout came from the front of the cave.

"We need to leave now! It's not safe here anymore!"

To Loukas's surprise, this flawless Mandarin came from a tall and hefty white man wearing purple suspenders. He was a Bulgarian named Leon Brazhnikov, and he held out a leather carrying bag in front of Loukas's chest. Brazhnikov addressed the artist sternly in English.

"Adrian Loukas."

Loukas nodded.

"Put Master Yan-Mei's painting in this sack and bring it with you."

"Master Yan-Mei?"

"Do as Mr. Brazhnikov says," ordered the woman who had brought him to the cave. From her tone, it was clear that she was Master Yan-Mei, thief of the *Sinai Pantocrator*, and the apparent leader of the assembled group.

By watching the agile and intentional way her body moved, Loukas was reminded of the highly trained martial artists he had seen in movies. Master Yan-Mei passed Loukas the sack, which was made of dense animal hide and had a shoulder strap and thick strings to fasten it. Loukas placed the marble tablet carefully inside and tied the strings. It weighed immensely upon his shoulder.

"Now hold out your hands."

Master Yan-Mei slapped a pair of rusty handcuffs onto the artist's wrists. Loukas hadn't even noticed she had them in her hands.

"Good. Stay behind me."

She gave the rest of them a few instructions in Mandarin, and they all followed her through the cavern and out of the cave. The artist was under her spell again.

The air was dusty, and soon Loukas heard the sound of a helicopter approaching. Brazhnikov clapped his shoulder and consoled him with a show of camaraderie that seemed suspiciously feigned.

"On the bright side," the Bulgarian remarked, "you won't mind leaving Egypt with us. It's better than sitting on a camel."

The muscular Brazhnikov heaved Loukas, now a prisoner, up into the back of the helicopter. The others climbed in the front, where the shortest man took the pilot's seat, and moments later the helicopter leapt into the air.

As they skimmed over the nighttime desert landscape, Loukas peered out the window, trying to remain calm. He thought of his distant wife and missed her a little. Then, with bitter amusement, he realized that the familiar sourness of his pending divorce did not seem quite so unpleasant compared with his present situation. Now there was a new menace: the thief who had pirated his beloved *Pantocrator*—this Master Yan-Mei—was there in the seat in front of him, and yet he was powerless to stop her. Loukas looked down at his leather carrying bag while the tumultuous chopping of the helicopter blades numbed his mind. In the seat next to Master Yan-Mei, he noticed a large, silver, metallic-looking rolling suitcase, which her dark eyes never left. Its dimensions looked to be exactly suited to fit the *Sinai Pantocrator*. Loukas felt certain that the sacred icon must be inside it. The artist began visualizing a plan to reach the suitcase and escape with it.

This was the only way out he could see.

Chapter 4

Cassandra and Jason came home to find Grandmother lying unconscious on the couch. Peony paced back and forth across the living room with her tail tensely coiled. The matriarch was still breathing, but her stillness was frightening.

"Grandma?" cried Jason, ignoring his cat. He knew his grandmother was prone to dizzy spells, and yet the shock of seeing her in such a state left his mouth dry.

"Go get her a glass of water," Cassandra said to Jason. She ran to the medicine cabinet to get her mother's pills. When each of them returned, Cassandra stuffed a pill in her mother's sagging mouth and poured in the water Jason had brought. By reflex alone, the old woman managed to swallow. After a few minutes, she regained consciousness.

"Cassandra, is that you?"

"Yes, mother. We are here for you now."

The front door creaked open and in sauntered Jason's mother.

"Daphne, call George!" Cassandra shouted. "Tell him to come quickly."

Daphne entered the living room and saw her mother-in-law lying in pain upon the couch. "What happened?"

"I'm dying, you selfish louse!" the grandma screamed in Mandarin, though her speech was too quick and emotional for Daphne to understand. She pulled herself up off of the couch and dusted off her pants. "It's these damn pills!" she grumbled, coming to a full stand. "They're killing me!" She threw the pill bottle at the cushion of the couch, causing Peony to flinch. Then she pushed the palm of her left hand flat against the wall as she bent forward and massaged her right temple.

"Are you feeling better?" Daphne asked in slow Greek, as if speaking to a child.

"She is now," answered Cassandra, consoling her mother with touch. Peony cuddled Cassandra's lower leg with her skull.

"Better be covered with sickly warts than to have a pretty face without a soul," muttered the peevish grandma to her daughter-in-law. Then she retreated to the kitchen to make tea.

"Jason, go change out of your uniform," Cassandra told him. The boy obeyed his aunt.

As Jason left the living room, Daphne pulled Cassandra into a guilty, defensive hug. "I'm so sorry I made you take Jason and left your mom here alone! I never should have put my own selfish things ahead of you. Can you forgive me?"

"It was no trouble taking him," Cassandra replied. "In fact, other than mom's bad luck, I'm glad I went." She bent down and took Peony into her arms. "Where is George, anyway?"

"Oh, who knows." Daphne pulled out her phone and began writing a text message. "He's worse than the boy sometimes."

Cassandra did not appreciate Daphne speaking of her brother that way.

"Oh, but Cassie!" she exclaimed. Her eyes lit up with a thirst for gossip. "Tell me about Stavros. Have you given him your answer yet?"

Daphne was referring to a marriage proposal, which Cassandra had put off answering for nearly three days.

"Ugh...that's the last thing I want to think about right now."

"You're crazy! Just tell him yes already!"

"It's just...it's such an unstable time. And then there's Mother's health!"

"Take it from me, Cassie, call him now and give him an answer. Seriously. You're not getting any younger." Daphne turned to the mirror on the wall and began inspecting her eyelashes. "Besides, cute men like Stavros aren't going to wait around forever."

"There's something else," the mythologist said. "I had a

vision.”

"A vision? About Stavros?”

"A vision of the *yin-yang*," Cassandra explained. "And it was getting torn apart by all the world's suffering.”

"Oh, quit being dramatic." Suddenly Daphne's phone buzzed. She checked the message and rolled her eyes. "George is on his way," she said. "Now, what are you talking about?”

"The riots going on all over Greece!" she said, irritated. The gray cat leapt from Cassandra's arms.

"You had a vision about the riots?”

"It was more of a dream, I guess. Symbolic, like a myth.”

"Ha-ha, you and myths," Daphne muttered, simultaneously texting another message to George. "What do you think it means?”

"I don't know," she lied. Inside, she felt anxious about what Master Zhang had told her. *The world is aching. It is you who will teach all of Greece the Way*. It was as though she had entered into her very own myth, not even knowing where it would lead. "But first I have to help Master Zhang find an old painting.”

"Oh," Daphne responded with a disinterested tone. She shook her head at George's text message and sighed. Then, Jason came down the stairs. "Jason, what are you doing in your pajamas?" his mother shouted.

"They're comfy.”

"Go change into real clothes!" Daphne ordered. "There's still three hours till bedtime! Do you want to waste the rest of the evening?”

"Three hours till bedtime," the boy repeated as he skipped back to his room. "That's sixty times three, which is one-hundred-eighty minutes till bedtime, times sixty, which is... ten thousand eight-hundred seconds!”

The evening air was beginning to cool down. The curtain's yellow glow had gone, leaving Peony to clean her fur in the dim living room light. Cicadas began serenading the moonless evening with their constant drone.

"You're right. There's no point in wasting time." Cassandra decided. "Mother!" she shouted, "George is on his way. I am going out."

......

Cassandra put on her shoes and went to her bookcase before leaving. On the middle shelf, next to an old photo of her with her father, were some of her favorites: a well-worn copy of Homer's The Iliad, an anthology of Tang Dynasty poetry, a Greek mythology compendium, and many others. After a moment of deliberation, she grabbed the *Tao Te Ching* by Lao Tzu. She hadn't read it in several years, but from what she remembered it described the ancient philosophy of the Way just as Master Zhang had presented it to her.

"Is the Way really the root of all mythology?" she wondered. "And if so, can the power of myth really bring about changes in society's consciousness?" Wasting no time, she stuffed the book in her bookbag and set out on foot. Cassandra crossed the street and reached her favorite city park, the archaeological site of Plato's Academy. During her undergraduate years, she used to sit on the large square stones on weekends to study. She had brought Stavros there many times also, though it was not where he proposed to her. How much more convincing of a proposal that would have been!

More than any other place, Plato's Academy Park had a personal meaning for her. It was where Greece's greatest thinkers had studied myth and rhetoric and even trained in athletics. Yet despite its historical significance, this park was largely unmanaged, abandoned and far removed from the flow of passing tourism. Pushing thoughts of Stavros aside, she figured this would be the perfect place to brush up on her knowledge of Taoist philosophy.

The mythologist sat down upon an unassuming block of stone amidst the ruins and opened her book to the introduction, written by the University of Athens' own East Asia scholar, Hermia Antonaki. Cassandra had highlighted key phrases and written notes in the margins to make reviewing it more efficient. As she scanned each paragraph, she imagined herself encircled by scholars like Plato and Aristotle during the Academy's glory days, reading the book aloud with them, discussing its philosophy. One passage, which she had marked with a green highlighter, felt particularly relevant:

"In ancient China," the book said, "the Way existed before any philosopher had ever discussed it. The Way was practiced even before people had a name for it. It was not only a philosophy that could be preached, it was a lifestyle and a consciousness. This is why Lao Tzu taught that knowledge of the Way could not be explained using words. It could not be told through proverbs or demonstrated in parables. Any attempt to describe the Way or give it a name would get in the way of a true understanding. But the unnamable, unspeakable Way, Lao Tzu teaches us, is infinitely powerful. When we practice the Way, anything is possible."

Cassandra read the last line out loud for emphasis. "Anything is possible." She nodded to assure herself. "Even stopping anti-immigrant riots." When she finished, she noticed a familiar pair of black shoes beside her feet. Filling those shoes was Master Zhang, adorned in his dark-blue martial arts uniform.

"You're here!" she exclaimed.

Master Zhang nodded his spotless, spherical head.

"Are you ready to begin your training, Cassandra?"

"I think so," she answered. "Do you have any ideas about where to find the painting of Zhen Wu?"

"Before we start looking, I need to give you your first lesson."

"You? But didn't you say I would train with the Taoist Immortals?"

"Not until you become worthy. You have to understand who the Taoist Immortals are and what they expect of you."

Cassandra nodded and listened.

"The Taoist Immortals," he continued, "trace their lineage to the dawn of time. They were wise sages, like Lao Tzu, who once advised the rulers and philosophers of all great nations in this world—spanning East to West on all continents—

opening them up to the power of the Way. But they worked in secret so that no one would question their wisdom. Most of the time, they lived on high mountains and remained recluses. Sometimes, they communicated with the world through art and symbols."

"And through their myths," she added.

"Myths are told using words, Cassandra. But what does the *Tao Te Ching* say about words?"

"That trying to describe the Way makes it less powerful?"

"Less powerful indeed. To get at the root of all myths, you must learn to be without words. This is what the Taoist Immortals will expect of you. It is also why you must have a physical image linking you to them. Something symbolic, but without words."

"Like your painting?"

"Precisely. That painting of Zhen Wu has been our link to the Taoist Immortals ever since we came to Greece."

"Then let's find it! You said it was painted on a marble tablet, right? Where did you see it last?"

"Be patient, Cassandra. Like great teachers, art and symbols appear at the exact moment in your life in which you are ready to receive them. The key to attracting an image is to hone your awareness. This is why you need a lesson from me."

"I understand. Tell me where to begin."

"You begin with what you are reading," suggested Master Zhang. "What does your book say?"

Cassandra opened to the page her finger was marking.

"It's the fourth chapter."

"An excellent chapter!" exclaimed the round-headed *shifu*. "Can you interpret it?"

Cassandra read the verses:

......

The Way is like a well:
Used, but never used up
It is like the Eternal Void: filled with infinite possibilities
It is hidden, but always present

......

"I interpret this to mean—" she began, setting down the book.

"No!" shouted Master Zhang. He grabbed the book from her and threw it on the ground. "A proper interpretation does not require words. Didn't you learn that already? You must not describe it. You must put it into practice."

Cassandra picked up the book and put it in her bookbag. "What? How?"

"By doing what it says: learning to draw from the hidden well, to draw infinite possibilities from the Eternal Void."

"Okay, but I don't even understand what it means. How do I do that?"

Master Zhang looked at her as if to say, *do you think I can explain it using words?*

"Okay," she said. "Don't tell me. Show me."

The *shifu* stood still, then began to pick up his foot. He raised it so slowly and gradually that it didn't even appear to be moving, but she could not deny that its position was changing. He lowered his foot down, and then picked up his other foot. Again, his movement was so subtle that she could not even sense the change of weight in his legs. Then, with the grace of two traveling stars, he placed his feet together and looked at Cassandra. By watching him she understood that stillness was the source of his movements, just as Lao Tzu's Eternal Void was the wellspring of the infinite possibilities. The stillness and subtlety of his movements was what made them potentially powerful.

"I see," she said. "So, the lesson will be a kind of Tai Chi exercise?"

"What do you know about Tai Chi, Cassandra?"

Cassandra closed her mouth tight. She knew he was testing her.

"Nothing," she finally answered. Her lips pressed together decisively with a soft smile.

"Good. Watch closely."

Master Zhang took four slow steps away from her and turned around. He stood tall, bent his knees slightly and lifted his arms slowly to draw a perfect circle in the air. His head moved in a circle concentric to the one suggested by his fingertips. Cassandra stood and watched, amazed. She could see in his movements and in his face exactly what the book had described: *anything was possible.*

"Tai Chi is the foundation of many Chinese movement arts. This is because it trains you to concentrate your power in even the smallest movement directed outward."

Cassandra nodded and relaxed her stance.

"But because Tai Chi is based on movement and change," he continued, it will always be finite. Movement may not use words, but it is still a kind of expression, and for that reason it is incomparable to the Way, which is both nameless and formless."

"But everything has form, doesn't it? Nothing is formless!"

"Correct, nothing."

She nodded and waited for her *shifu* to continue.

"That is why we have a second practice: Wu Chi."

Cassandra's eyes widened.

"Wu Chi," he continued, "is an exercise of complete stillness, not exerting energy or expression in any outward direction. This is the state in which your movements are not yet formed, not even in your thoughts! It is a stillness that is so profound and indescribable, that it transcends the limits of form and name and reaches into the Eternal Void, like it says in the *Tao Te Ching*. When you practice Wu Chi, you even transcend time! When you transcend time, you are no longer subject to change. And because you are changeless and timeless, you gain the power to change anything."

Cassandra's heart skipped a beat. What he explained was too abstract for her to comprehend. Instead she focused on learning from his movements rather than his words.

"Anything!" he repeated.

Instantly, Cassandra's mind was wrenched into another

vision. This time, the vision was of a riot in the streets of Athens. The people had no faces, but the outlines of their bodies were completely distinct. Furthermore, they were full of jagged edges, and when the people marched around, holding up picket signs, their movements were jerky and full of friction. As Cassandra studied the crowd, she realized that she could control their movements by waving her arms. The faster she moved, the more convulsive the crowd moved, but the slower she moved, the more those jagged edges eased into curves, and the people began to move more harmoniously. Cassandra, too, felt easiness in her stance and her breathing. She stopped worrying, stopped judging, and simply opened her eyes.

"That was incredible! It was like I could affect the movements of everyone else just by making my own movements smoother."

"That is the power of stillness, of non-movement."

"But can I do that in real life?"

Master Zhang smiled and received her excitement without answering the question. He instructed her to stand up straight.

"Now, let me adjust your posture a little," he whispered. "First, plant your feet into the ground like roots, and you're the tree. Squat down just slightly. Hold your arms out in a circle so that your fingertips point at each other and your palms face your torso."

The mythologist did as he instructed.

"Now, close your eyes. Be still."

She closed her eyes.

"Don't strain yourself," the *shifu* cautioned. "To practice Wu Chi, you must relax into the stillness, like mud settling to the bottom of a lake. The more you tense, the more you stir the mud. And you don't want that. Now sink lower!"

Cassandra relaxed her muscles and sat down a little lower in her stance. Standing in this way was immediately tiresome and made her sore.

"Also, don't listen to that voice within that says you are uncomfortable. Remember, in the Wu Chi state, time does not exist."

"I think this will be more easily said than done," she grumbled.

"Nothing needs to be done! Just be still."

"Okay."

The grueling seconds ticked by.

"Can I stop now?"

"Have you no discipline? Not even a full minute has passed!"

"How long do you want me to stay like this?"

"Until I tell you to stop. Understand?"

She didn't reply. She tried not to internalize his words. She tried to block out the sensations that came at her from the outside world—the sweat on her face, the stench of the air, the buzzing of the electric lamps that lit up the park.

"Don't squeeze your eyes closed!" Master Zhang told her. "You aren't trying to shut out the world. Imagine you are the well of infinite power, like the Way, and all the universe is drawing from you."

Cassandra tried her best to relax, but the more she worked at it, the more tired she felt. Her muscles began to shake. She felt she would collapse at any moment.

"How long has it been now?"

The mythologist listened for Master Zhang's voice, but there was no reply. Even the birds had abandoned her. A cool breeze tickled her face and made the nose under her glasses itch. She was hungry and tired. She must have been keeping the posture for at least five minutes, she guessed.

"Master Zhang?"

As she called his name, the petite mythologist fell over backwards. She rolled onto her left side and pushed herself up to a seated lotus position. She massaged her chafed hands and cheek. She picked up her fallen glasses from the ground and lifted them up to the streetlamp to check for dirt. Then, she noticed a man running towards her.

"Master Zhang?"

But it wasn't her round-headed *shifu*. This man's head

was scruffy and asymmetrical. Moreover, he was dressed in red jogging clothes, and his movements were hasty and uncoordinated.

"Is everything alright?" she called to the man, wiping her glasses with her sleeve.

The man charged at her with an unrelenting glare, breathing and panting like a madman. Cassandra wished she had not made eye contact and her heart began to race as he drew closer. She tried to stand, but she was off balance, and the anticipation of what this man was capable of kept her in a powerless trance.

"Help!" she screamed. "Somebody!"

Cassandra tried to stand again, but fear paralyzed her. Her palms sweated and she struggled to breathe. When the man reached her, he struck Cassandra viciously in the chest with the toe of his boot. She fell upon the dry, dark soil with the air knocked from her lungs in a way that made her gasp.

"Uf!"

Before she could defend herself, or even react, the man snatched her bookbag and screamed in her face.

"Go back to China!"

Then he leapt away, taunting her with that menacing refrain: *Greece for the Greeks! Immigrants, go home!*

After he had gone, Cassandra sat up, reeling in pain and disbelief. The bruise on her chest throbbed intensely for several minutes, and she still struggled to catch her breath. But what haunted her most was the memory of the hatred in his eyes, the agony of knowing that there were people in Athens— even some powerful people—who would target her for being Chinese, for being an immigrant, an outsider. They would see her that way no matter how much she tried to conform. Sometimes, as she had just experienced, they would attack.

"Master Zhang, where are you?" she wondered.

Slowly and feebly she climbed to her feet and tottered back across the street to her apartment. She took the elevator, trying to get a grip on her movements so no one would notice anything wrong. And when she got home, she locked herself in her room and cried her soul out. Her bookbag was gone, and inside it was her only copy of the *Tao Te Ching*.

So many questions swirled inside her head. How could Master Zhang have deserted her without a word? How would she explain to her family what had happened?

On the nightstand next to her bed lay her phone. It rang.

"Ugh!" she groaned loudly, covering her ears and digging her nose into her pillow. After the fourth ring, she picked up the phone and glanced at it. It was Stavros. "Ugh!" she groaned again, falling back onto her bed, unable to answer. Even if she had picked up, she knew she could not have given him the response he was hoping for. Her mind was filled to the brim with problems, and no thoughts of marriage could enter.

"Greece has lost its way," she said to herself. "Now I feel it in my bones." Everything she had written about in her dissertation about the modern immigrant experience and its mythological foundations was coming to pass in its most extreme form. News headlines everywhere portrayed the Chinese as thieves, as indigents, and even as instigators of violence. As a result, the Greeks reinforced that image by treating them exactly so. The power of the news to shape the myth and amplify attitudes was measurable and, unfortunately, robust. Cassandra kicked the air angrily and screamed, letting her legs fall limp back on the bed.

"The world is aching," she said out loud, trying to calm down. She lay still and stared blankly at the ceiling. "I hope we can find our Way."

Chapter 5

When the helicopter landed, Adrian Loukas was asleep, unconscious. The sky was dark, and the air was still.

"Wake up!" barked a deep voice. Leon Brazhnikov, the large Bulgarian patted Loukas's face with his hand. "I think he's out cold, Master Yan-Mei."

"It's shock trauma. You will have to carry him."

"Why? A dog can walk."

"He needs his rest."

"What rest? He's had plenty of that all night!"

"Listen to yourself, Leon!"

"I always listen to myself."

"Then you hear your arrogance. Do not forget! This arrogance is why Li-Kuo refused to be your *shifu*."

"And yet you took me on as your student anyway," he sneered.

"Only because Li-Kuo is my brother."

"Is that the only reason?"

Master Yan-Mei reached up and squeezed Leon Brazhnikov's muscular shoulder with her hand like a claw. "Yesterday you lifted a sack of cement weighing four hundred pounds, and yet now you resist carrying a slender man on your back!"

Brazhnikov shook his head. He hated it when she pointed out the inconsistencies in his words. Even after three years of training under Master Yan-Mei and her brother, there were still subtle weaknesses he struggled to overcome. Wincing with irritation, he nodded in her direction.

"The mind is a real devil sometimes," he said without sincerity. Then he picked up the artist by his handcuffed wrists and hoisted him up on his back. At such a height, the artist's legs dangled half a meter off the ground.

"That is why you never stop learning from your *shifu*."

Brazhnikov nodded and picked up Loukas by the arms.

"Thank you, *shifu*, I will try."

Master Yan-Mei took the silver suitcase from the helicopter and commanded her three compatriots to take off. Brazhnikov carried Loukas and followed his *shifu* to a van with tinted windows. Waves from the mighty Aegean Sea beat upon the edges of the helipad as the van took off.

It headed for Athens.

......

When Loukas woke up he found himself in the backseat of the van. It was daytime, and the van sat parked in front of a tall, gray apartment building. The artist's wrists were sore and his shoulder ached.

Master Yan-Mei startled Loukas by grabbing his wrist.

"Whoa!" he recoiled.

She removed his handcuffs.

"We have a job for you," she said, eerily calm.

"Will I have to...?"

"Enough questions!"

Brazhnikov turned around from the driver's seat and pointed a solid jade dagger directly at the space between the artist's eyes. Loukas shivered. He had never looked at a blade from quite that angle before. Then again, he had also never been kidnapped and threatened.

Caught in an instant of sheer panic, time seemed to stop. He examined the dagger, easily making out the shimmering red and yellow jewels at the base of its pale green blade. Farther down the handle, there were four muscular fingers and a brutish thumb, all soiled with the elements, gripping tightly to cast their intent. And that intent was, as far as Loukas could gather, to penetrate his skull if he refused to comply. He had no choice.

"This is a public place. Follow us upstairs, and do not make a scene."

Presuming the artist's cooperation, Master Yan-Mei opened

the door and pulled Loukas out of the van. The image of the jade dagger with its terrifying jewels persisted in his mind like a vivid nightmare. When they entered the apartment, Brazhnikov pushed Loukas down onto a well-worn, maroon leather sofa. He reached into a white, cube-shaped mini-fridge and pulled out a can of Coca Cola. Loukas blinked, and resisted the temptation to rub his eyes.

"Welcome to Chinatown," resounded Brazhnikov. He took a sip of his Coca Cola and burped.

"Chinatown? Which Chinatown?"

Loukas observed what he could of the room with his peripheral vision. It was a tiny living room with a large oak desk in the center, which seemed to dominate the entire space. On top of the desk was a marble tablet similar to the one he had seen with the Taoist Immortal's portrait, except it was blank and much whiter. The walls of the room were bare and lackluster, revealing several hideous cracks of wear and tear. He was afraid to look down at his own body, worrying he would notice an injury. But to his relief, he was unharmed. His hands were free. He gave his eyes one last forceful blink.

"I'm sorry, where did you say we are?"

"Welcome to Athens," answered Master Yan-Mei. She opened the faded, pink curtains, revealing the urban metropolis. "Chinatown district."

"I wasn't aware Athens had a Chinatown."

"Every town has a Chinatown," whispered Brazhnikov as if beginning a horror story. "The Chinese are everywhere." Then he took another swig from his can.

"But what are we doing here?"

Brazhnikov released another enormous belch. "Are you a fool? She doesn't like it when you ask questions."

"Sorry."

"She also doesn't like it when you apologize."

"That's enough, Leon." She gave the artist an emotionless stare. "Sit down."

The artist sat at the table and laid his eyes upon the portrait of the Taoist Immortal, which Master Yan-Mei had placed in front of him.

"Here, have a Coke." Brazhnikov planted a cold, damp can on the table next to the marble tablet.

"He doesn't need a Coke."

"A dog needs a treat."

"We don't have time for this."

"I am NOT helping you," Loukas interrupted. "Not until you show me that the *Pantocrator* is safe. Those holy icons belong to the church, and may God smite you for all you have stolen, including that Chinese painting!"

Master Yan-Mei stood quiet and still. She turned her neck slowly towards him, signaling with her eyes a warning even sharper and more cutting than Brazhnikov's jade dagger. Her face was at once wise and ferocious, beautiful and pernicious, momentary and yet somehow timeless. Her expression was serene on the surface, almost stoic, but he knew it contained something fiercely energetic underneath.

Under less threatening circumstances, the artist might have admired her for this face, perhaps even tried to record its essence on canvas. After all, he believed, the greatest portrait was one that could reveal contrasting aspects of human nature coexisting in a single expression. In a purely aesthetic sense, Master Yan-Mei's face would have been the perfect one to represent the glorious and terrifying duality of the human condition. But in person, it was sheer terror.

"Good," she finally uttered. "You have stopped asking questions."

In spite of her words, Loukas felt no relief. He was perplexed. He had expected her to berate him for his outburst, and anticipated Brazhnikov's jade dagger coming at him with a vengeance. But instead the artist found his kidnappers unmoved, leaving his heart to throb inside his chest like a gong struck repeatedly, counting the harrowing beats until Master Yan-Mei spoke.

"I did not steal the portrait of Zhen Wu," she finally added, without elaborating further. She grabbed the silver suitcase, which Loukas had not seen since the helicopter ride. "But I understand that you are upset about the *Pantocrator*." She handed him a soft, white towelette for him to dab his forehead. "Adrian, listen carefully. I will tell you why you are here."

"Good. I'm listening."

"First of all, you must understand my position. I am Greek Orthodox, just like you."

"You are Greek Orthodox?" From the violence of his capture to her heartless seizing of the *Pantocrator*, everything about her seemed as unorthodox as he could imagine. "But you...can't be."

"Why not? Because I'm Chinese?" She squeezed the towelette in front of his face with her energetic fist until suds oozed from between her fingers.

"That's not what I meant."

"Our religion extends far beyond the borders of Greece."

"Of course, it does. I never meant to imply that—"

"Then listen to me. Open your narrow mind. This is a crisis of faith, Adrian. The Orthodoxy is in danger! I am saving these icons, not stealing them."

As she pointed to the silver suitcase, Loukas clenched his fists in anger. He had not imagined there were other stolen icons inside too.

"Saving them from what?"

"From decay." She opened the suitcase and pulled out an icon of *Saint Macarius*. "You have seen and venerated many icons, I am sure."

"I have."

"And you understand that an icon is not merely a portrait but a window into the life and divinity of the saint that is depicted."

"Icons are precious windows into the soul of God," he added precociously, trying to suggest that his knowledge was superior to hers. "But only for those who know their hidden meaning."

"Look at Saint Macarius," she directed. "Look at any

ancient icon. Through the centuries, icons fade. They break and crumble. They remind us that our windows into the lives of the saints are slowly, perpetually closing. They are dying!" She held the Saint Macarius up to the artist's face.

"But the saints cannot die. They continue to live in heaven. Besides, iconographers are also constantly making new icons of old saints."

"That is not enough," she continued. "The saints live on, but only in the realm of the unseen. That is why we pray with icons, as you well know. But still, only one in many thousands of iconographers can capture the true essence of a saint. This icon of Saint Macarius, for example, is from the fourth century. It was one of the first ones ever painted of him. He lives here, visible to our eyes, thanks to the genius of the painter who captured his essence. But do you see how the icon is decaying? This means he is dying to us; our link with the real person Macarius is fading away. See now! In order to keep our communication with the saints of the past and gain their wisdom, we need these icons in perfect condition."

"Are you saying you want me to restore the icons? I'm an artist, not an art restorer."

"Of course not. You will repaint them from scratch."

"Nonsense! How could I hope to accomplish such a task?"

"I have seen your eyes, Adrian! You have the holy gift of sight. You are the Orthodoxy's best hope for restoring our connection with the saints of the past."

From the depths beneath the artist's fear, a swell of pride emerged. He imagined what it would feel like to use his gift of sight for the noble cause of replicating the world's greatest icons and saving the saints from dying—such an honor might bring him the fame and recognition he had worked so hard to achieve! It might bring him closer to sainthood, closer to the oneness he longed for with his Lord and Savior. It might even someday forgive the fact that he was coerced into the job, not to mention that he was involving himself in an unforgivable act of theft. Those were minor details in the scheme of his proud fantasies.

"And as you are doing this," she continued, setting the *Saint Macarius* carefully on a chair beside the desk, "you must do one more thing." She gestured to the portrait of the Taoist Immortal. "You must also replicate this icon of Zhen Wu."

The artist recoiled in his chair. "That is no icon, Master Yan-Mei!"

"Listen to me," she said calmly. Her voice became tender like the cooing of a mother eagle to her eaglets. She folded the moist towelette and laid it upon Loukas's knee. "Most people, when they see a portrait of a venerated immortal, see only a painting." She held the portrait up, next to the blank marble tablet and waved her hand over its surface as if casting a spell. "But when you looked into Zhen Wu's eyes, you saw into his soul. You saw the world within him. You beheld eternity in your gifted eyes!"

"Are you trying to flatter me?"

"That was not a compliment. It is your calling. Look, there, into his eyes again and tell me what you see."

In the instant Loukas's eyes met the time-worn marble tablet, the immortal's eyes returned the glance. Zhen Wu's expression suggested he was about to speak. His lips appeared puckered, his tongue flexed and his eyelids sagged. It was an expression of yearning, indeed, of the yearning to be freed from imprisonment.

"He's crying," the artist observed.

Suddenly a water droplet appeared in the marble crevice right where the immortal's eyes were etched. Loukas shuttered and grabbed his moist towelette. He had read about icons that miraculously emitted tears, but he had never witnessed it with his own eyes.

"It can't be! Only Christian icons are allowed to weep!"

"Christian icons are quite powerful," Master Yan-Mei explained. "They have taught us many secrets!"

"Secrets? You? But it's not...this can't be..."

Loukas didn't know whether to be relieved that she purportedly shared his faith or angered that she had gained its secrets so undeservingly.

"Some of these secrets, like the secret of sight, you already know. And that is my point, Adrian. We need you to restore these icons, not just for me but for the Orthodoxy."

"But what does your Taoist Immortal have to do with the Orthodoxy?"

Yan-Mei frowned at his question and answered abruptly.

"He has to do with me, and I am Orthodox." Agitated, she broke her eye contact and threw the leather carrying sack on the ground. "If you want more connection than that, use your eyes. You have felt him, seen him weep. You have proof of his sainthood!"

"This is not right."

"It is perfectly right."

"No, it's not. First of all, I am not a proper iconographer!"

"Get rid of your concepts, Adrian!" She slapped both her hands on his knees at once to motivate him. "Icon or not, you know how to paint. More importantly, you know how to see. That is what you must do."

"I may be a painter, but not—"

Brazhnikov's phone rang to the tune of the Russian ballad, Ochi Chernye. He answered it and began shouting in Russian. Then he moved quickly into the other room.

Master Yan-Mei rolled her eyes at her student. "He's enjoying himself too much." Then she picked up the *Saint Macarius* and showed it again to Loukas.

"Perhaps this will convince you," Master Yan-Mei redirected. "As you know, icons have a power to reveal to us the personalities of the saints. But they also have the power to transport us into their own realm."

"What do you mean?"

"Saint Macarius will be your first lesson."

"Lesson?"

"You have already shown me your eyes can see in the dark. Your eyes can recognize God in iconography. But your training is incomplete."

"Training?"

"Fate is a fine line, Adrian, like a knife's edge. Keep to it, and do not resist your fate."

"Okay, fine," he conceded, remembering the threat of Brazhnikov's dagger. "Tell me what to do."

"First look into Saint Macarius's eyes just like you did with the portrait of Zhen Wu. Saint Macarius is alive inside, though his icon has almost fully decayed. This means we may not be able to communicate with him in a way that he can understand us perfectly."

Loukas did as he was told.

"Breath with me," instructed Master Yan-Mei. "Hold the icon up to the light from the window. Let it shine on Saint Macarius's face. But do not shine it too directly. You don't want to blind him!"

"Now what?"

"Enter the presence of the saint. Bare your soul to him beyond the veil. Feel the Holy Spirit in this icon, and feel it also within you. Know yourself to have the gift of sight."

The long-bearded Saint Macarius glowed with an aura of sublime wisdom. As Loukas looked closer, the icon's background grew crisper and more textured. A horizontal line separated a solid, blue sky from the yellow desert sands. The saint's eyes lit up, and a jolting sensation surged through Loukas's senses like an electromagnetic pulse. The artist's consciousness quaked, then stilled. A warm light dawned on his outer eyelids and faded as he breathed out.

For a moment Loukas could no longer feel his own heartbeat. He was like a ghost, a tiny shadow in time and space, floating back to a bygone century. He was a drop of paint upon the infinite canvas of creation, which absorbed him, mixed him round amidst shades and colors and formed his image anew. Then, the desert appeared in front of him. Each grain of dusty sand was as real as he was. The pristine, blue sky towered above him in all directions. And in the distance a shadow formed and, like a ghost, meandered towards him. It was Saint Macarius.

The icon was a window into another world. And the artist

had climbed through.

Chapter 6

It was a peaceful morning, but Cassandra Yin could not relax. She slipped on some gray sweats and a light-blue athletic jacket before brewing a small cup of coffee. She slathered butter and jam on a piece of whole wheat toast, which she ate with her eyes barely open.

Every time it occurred to her to call Stavros back, she put it off, trying not to think about him. She also avoided waking her mother, not wanting to burden her with the news that she had been attacked in the park the previous night. As she chewed her toast, her bones trembled as the man's menacing voice echoed in her mind: *Greece for the Greeks! Immigrants, go home!*

Sometimes it took dramatic incidents to shock her back into the reality that she was still, above all things, Chinese. As much she prided herself on having assimilated to Greek culture, the things she inherited from her mother and father—language, learning styles, etiquette and emotional sensibilities—would always mark her as a product of Eastern civilization. And yet, at the same time, her life and her education made her unquestionably Greek. Her mind was forged by a pantheon of ancient Greek thinkers who were as relevant to her life as any Chinese ancestor. There were also times when she felt neither Greek nor Chinese but an out-of-place wanderer, ravaged by a dual identity. She was unable to bring *yin* and *yang* together without a struggle.

Shaking her head to rid herself of the memory, she collected her breakfast dishes and dropped them into the sink, letting them clang against the stainless steel basin. She wiped her hands on the towel and let out a heavy sigh. Whatever it might take, however challenging it might be, the time to learn how to fight for a better world was now. There was a Way, and it was up to Cassandra to find it.

The voice of Cassandra's mother interrupted her thoughts: "What are you doing?"

"I'm just about to leave, mom. I have things to do."

"Did you get the suckling pig for dinner?"

"Oh, shit. I forgot," Cassandra thought to herself. She would never curse in her mother's presence. Instead she cast her face down and apologized.

"Give me a hug," her mother said.

As much as Cassandra's mother favored her, she was not an affectionate person. A hug from her mother, especially without a specific reason, was a rare occurrence.

"Mom, what are you doing?"

"Don't worry, my little flower," said the mother. Cassandra relaxed and invited the hug. She alone knew how much she needed it. "You'll be okay. You'll get a job. You'll get married. You'll be happy. That's all I want. My happy daughter."

"Xie xie," she thanked her.

Without giving into tears, she handed her mother her pills and promised to call her later. Then she left the apartment and hopped on a bus. Cassandra's thoughts were still anxious and her chest still hurt, but ut her mom's hug had helped. As she rode the bus she imagined those motherly arms embracing her once more, extending their healing power all the way back into her childhood.

Despite the Yin household's unharmonious moments, Cassandra's mom had always been there for her. Every expression of love Cassandra had ever learned could trace its origins to her mother's love for her—in a way, she had been like the mother of all her myths. A mother's love did not ask questions or try to change things, it only accepted what was, even when it did not understand. Now, just when she needed it, this acceptance reached her and provided just enough healing to get her through the moment.

The bus eventually rounded the Acropolis, and Cassandra

decided to get off. Looking up at the ruins, she spied Athena's Temple, which gave her an idea. "I have to continue my training," she said to herself. "And if Master Zhang won't be there to guide me, then maybe the goddess Athena will." Cassandra did not actually believe in the Greek Pantheon. In reality she didn't believe in most of the myths she studied, or even a god at all.

For the twenty-eight-year-old mythologist, the gods were symbolic rather than factual. Athena the goddess of warriors, crafts and wisdom represented not a person or a divine force but a state of mind, a way of reconciling the warring factions of her mind. She had dreamt of Athena many times. When she had trouble making the right decision, sometimes she would imagine the goddess coming to her, drawing her into a giant blue cloud and revealing the answer. From her mother she could get love and comfort, but when it came to getting focused clarity and inner guidance, she needed Athena's blue cloud.

The petite mythologist climbed the Acropolis and made her way to the front of Athena's Temple. She closed her eyes and imagined Athena's blue cloud appearing in the sky and offering her the answers she sought. As she inhaled, she imagined Athena's wisdom filling her lungs, invigorating her with the cunning and craftiness that had guided Odysseus home and won the Greeks the ancient war. But the value of the myth was about more than just receiving wisdom. It was also about activating her own intuition, the true and formless source from which all wisdom originates. She now had a name for this source: the Way. When Cassandra opened her eyes, she felt Master Zhang's hand on her shoulder. Unsurprised, she recoiled and faced him. She had rehearsed this confrontation.

"How nice of you to finally show up."

The *shifu* was dressed in the same stately, dark-blue martial arts uniform. He scanned Cassandra's appearance from bottom to top, from her white running shoes to her black hair, which was squeezed back into a ponytail. He waited for her to speak.

"Why did you leave me in the dark?" she began. "Do you know that I was attacked? What am I going to tell my family? Do you know my mother is sick?"

Master Zhang showed no reaction. She had predicted he would act this way, and it infuriated her all the more to be proven correct.

"For someone as wise as you, that was incredibly cruel. Didn't you anticipate the danger of leaving me alone in the park, defenseless?"

From his silence, she could stir up a myriad of hypotheses about his motives.

"What good is your knowledge of the Way if you won't use it for common decency?"

Master Zhang lifted his brow.

"Or is this how you teach? Is this how the Taoist Immortals teach? Just throw the Chinese girl into the prairie like a zebra to get torn apart by lions? Don't you know right from wrong?"

"The knowledge of right and wrong is not as black and white as a zebra," he replied.

"Is that supposed to be funny?" His continued tranquility only inflamed her anger further.

"I can see that I wasn't much use to you."

"Is that all you have to say? *Not much use?*"

"The Way is only as useful as you make it."

"How? Please explain, oh, *great* Master Zhang. How could the Way have protected me from that attacker, hmm?"

The *shifu* absorbed the force of her rage like a branch swaying in a disquieted breeze.

"You could have used him."

"Used him?"

"For all you know, he could have been a Taoist Immortal."

"Seriously? What kind of Taoist Immortal would accost me in the middle of the night and take my bookbag? My *Tao Te Ching* was in there!"

"A book is just a book."

"He wasn't even Chinese!"

"You have to empty your mind, Cassandra. That's what the exercise of Wu Chi was about. And that is why you found it difficult. When you fell, you let your mind fill up again with all those fears and preconceptions."

"Wait a minute—how did you know I fell? Were you *watching* me get attacked?"

"I saw no attack. Only opportunity."

"Opportunity for what? For me to feel pain?"

"Look at that vine." Master Zhang pointed to a small vine that was sprouting through a stone on the side of the temple. "That vine was able to conquer the stone because it used the stone to its advantage. The vine didn't curse at the stone just because the stone got in its way. What good would that have done? Instead it listened to the stone. It gave way, adapted, and that is why the vine could penetrate the stone."

Cassandra pondered his analogy, trying to shift her thinking.

"When you rid yourself of your fears and preconceptions like this vine, Cassandra, you will be invincible—you will rise up beyond all obstacles. You will be able to act in any environment according to what is useful."

"But the attacker—"

"There is no attacker. 'Attack' is a concept, and not a very useful one."

She rubbed her bruised chest with the pad of her thumb.

"It didn't feel like a concept."

"The only real things are your raw senses. You must do as Lao Tzu taught: empty yourself of these concepts and sense things as they are."

"So you *did* want me to feel pain!"

Master Zhang laughed.

"Everyone feels pain!" he said. "You must feel the pain. But do not fight it. Do not even think about it. Instead, experience it."

"And that's Wu Chi?"

"No, that is common sense," he said. "Remember, Wu Chi is the practice of complete stillness."

"Then how do I get *common sense?*"

"You don't get it, Cassandra. You use it."

This technicality made her even more frustrated.

"But how?"

"By learning to fight the most powerful adversary on earth."

"Fight? But you said this was a training, not a war!"

"A training, yes," the *shifu* said as he stroked his shiny chin. "A training in how to handle our arch enemy."

"Doesn't sound like much of a difference."

"Some say we are foolish to fight him. And yet we pick this fight every moment of our lives!"

"Who is it?"

"If I tell you, then you may never view reality the same way again!"

"Tell me, already!"

Master Zhang restrained himself from toying with her impatience any longer. In her face he could see not only emotion but also a studiousness that made her determined to learn. He knew that with more information he could change her mind.

"Very well. The adversary is called *the mind*."

Cassandra rolled her eyes.

"The mind?"

Master Zhang recited a passage from the *Tao Te Ching*:

......

Knowing others is intelligence;
Knowing yourself is true wisdom.
Mastering others is strength;
Mastering yourself is true power.

......

"Are you saying that in order to change the world, I have to first change *my mind*?"

"I could not have said it any clearer."

"Somehow I don't think you're saying I was right."

"When you truly know yourself—when you've mastered your temptations, your ego, and that inner voice that tells you certain things are impossible—then you can reach out to others using the full power of the Way."

The *shifu* clasped Cassandra's shoulders and drew her into another vision: This time, she was standing on the stage of the Theater of Dionysus in downtown Athens. The ancient theater's seats were filled with spectators, and Cassandra herself was facing them all, giving a speech. She felt something warm in her belly, like a steady heat radiating from within her. Her head was cool, and her tongue was gifted by Calliope, the muse of eloquence and epic poetry. As she spoke, her movements were smooth and powerful, and words left her lips like the breath of a god.

Though she couldn't understand her own words exactly, she knew she was telling a myth. And she knew this myth was calling to a deep yearning in the collective unconscious. As the myth came through her, she saw images of different gods and heroes of all cultures appearing as rays of light, pouring out from her body and filling the auditorium. As the light reached the people, everyone stood up in their seats offering thunderous applause. Then the vision ended.

"How are you doing that?" Cassandra demanded.

"I am not doing anything," the *shifu* answered humbly. "It is you who are beginning to unlock the depths of your imagination."

"But that's just it. These are only dreams. They're only imagination. How can such a power be real?" Cassandra rubbed her belly, finding nothing unusual. The visions were strange, but something in them felt deeply authentic, even though she couldn't explain why.

"I suppose you need the Taoist Immortals to show you."

"Right. Let's find that painting!"

"Don't get ahead of yourself, Cassandra! You still have your lesson for today."

"Oh, right. The mind."

"First, get into the Wu Chi position like we practiced yesterday."

Though skeptical, Cassandra removed her glasses and adjusted her posture. She took off her jacket, under which she had on a lightweight, white blouse. Her white Nike shoes were comfortable and breathable. She was ready.

She bent her knees slightly and reached her arms outward to form a circle, just as she had done last night in the park. Minutes flew by, and Cassandra managed to keep firm in her pose.

"Sink deeper," instructed the round-headed Master.

She lowered her stance.

"Relax," he advised. "Imagine your mind is like a flowing river. Your thoughts are like water flowing through you, sinking deeper and deeper into the ground." He pressed down on her shoulders with his palms. "Feel yourself heavy with thoughts. Sink deeper!"

She squeezed her buttocks and sank even deeper.

"Yes, that's it." Master Zhang let go of her shoulders. "Now let the river go. Let the mind empty its thoughts into the earth."

She breathed slowly and visualized her racing thoughts dripping off of her like rain water and sinking into the soil.

"Now, let go of your tension. Ease your shoulders. Be completely empty, like a bathtub drained of its fluids."

As Cassandra Yin relaxed into her Wu Chi pose, a strong magnetic force pulled her to the left several inches. She snapped out of the meditative state with a cry of surprise.

"What was that?"

"That is what we call the first movement."

"The what? I thought the Wu Chi required complete stillness."

"Complete stillness isn't permanent. When movement returns, there is always a first movement, which comes from the purest state of your being. You might know this movement as your intuition."

Cassandra pointed to the left and gazed as far as she could see.

"You mean, we have to go that way? Is that where Zhen Wu's portrait is?"

"That is where your intuition is pulling you to."

"It's not a very specific direction."

"Then let me help you."

The round-headed master grabbed her shoulders again and pulled her into yet another vision, which lasted no longer than the blink of an eye.

"What did you see, Cassandra?"

"I saw a blue cloud like the one I used to dream about with—" she stopped before mentioning the goddess Athena. How peculiar would that have sounded to Master Zhang! "Below the cloud was a man with a gray beard and mustache. Then there were two rows of columns—Corinthian columns, I think."

"Did you see anything else?"

She closed her eyes to recall the vision.

"There was also a number: three hundred fifteen. I guess this means we are looking for a man somewhere with three hundred and fifteen columns. Or for a man whose address is 315. Or for some kind of—"

"Don't analyze it, Cassandra. And try not to look for anything specific. Just keep your eyes open and let your subconscious make the associations."

"Okay," she agreed, still unsure that she understood what she was learning but willing to follow Master Zhang's teaching. She grabbed her jacket and glasses. "Let's go this way."

......

Cassandra led Master Zhang down the hill of the Acropolis and into the center of downtown Athens. They crossed north through Syntagma Square, where two trained national guards in uniform stood perfectly still, letting crowds of tourists take their photos. The late morning's heat was already sweltering, and yet Cassandra raced in the direction of her intuition like the swift-footed god Hermes. When her lungs got tired, she stopped.

"I think my intuition moves faster than my legs," she remarked.

But Master Zang was no longer behind her. He had disappeared.

"Master Zhang? Oh, not again."

Cassandra caught her breath in front of the church of Saint Demetrios. To her chagrin, the church's address was not 315, nor did it have Corinthian columns in its architecture. From all sides, Greek Orthodox churchgoers poured into the temple gates. The smell of incense hung in the air, almost like a cloud, and penetrated her gasping lungs. She doubted the church had any connection to Zhen Wu, but her intuition told her to follow them inside, and so she did.

"Are you lost?" asked a robust, middle-aged woman with curly hair and a golden-yellow shirt.

"I'm just resting."

"Are you here for the liturgy?" she probed, squinting at the petite Chinese mythologist.

"No, I'm not religious."

"Not religious?"

"I'm a mythologist."

"Eh?"

"A mythologist."

"A schoolgirl?"

The words in Greek sounded vaguely similar amidst the clamor of incoming worshippers.

"No, a mythologist." She scoffed inwardly, unsure if the woman had simply mistaken her for someone much younger or was being intentionally obtuse.

"Oh." The woman pretended to understand. "You have come from very far to study here. So, come in with me! My name is Hariklia. All are welcome to attend the liturgy. Just don't take the communion if you're not Orthodox!"

Cassandra nodded and followed Hariklia into the narthex, still frustrated with the woman's presumptions about her age and status. Her proud mind searched for ways to boast that she had a doctorate degree in comparative mythology.

However, good manners kept her mouth shut.

Hariklia led Cassandra into the nave of the church. It had been a decade, perhaps, since the mythologist had set foot inside an Orthodox church. Her friend Maria Stournari had invited her once. She could recall colorful frescoes on every wall and ceiling, icons mounted and propped up in every corner and a beautifully painted iconostasis erected to honor the saints. She could recall feeling safe inside the church walls, as though they were protecting her somehow. It was the kind of safety she didn't particularly crave, nor had she remembered it before the sights and sounds that now surrounded her provoked her memory. Like so many scenes from her colorful past, the church visit had faded, but now, she was about to become reacquainted with all of it.

Straight ahead, an icon of Saint Demetrios greeted her. Hariklia, whose golden-yellow shirt and brown, curly hair seemed to complement the bold tones of the icon itself, leaned her lips into the icon and kissed it. But this was no superficial kiss! To Cassandra, it almost seemed like it was the kind of kiss that might occur between old friends. Everyone else, too, it seemed, was kissing icons of the different saints, of the Virgin Mary and of Jesus.

Hariklia smiled affectionately at her beloved Saint Demetrios and proceeded into the worship line. Though Cassandra did not kiss the icon herself, she offered a polite bow and a closed-eyed grin. It suddenly occurred to her that all the other Greeks were thinking of how Chinese she looked as she bowed, and she grimaced, sure she had just reinforced a stereotype.

The liturgical singing had already started; however, the priest had not yet appeared from behind the iconostasis. Cassandra now remembered the music being the most pleasant thing about the Orthodox church. Choir singers chanted from opposite sides of the room, calling and responding to each other like a well-rehearsed orchestra. There was a certain droning quality to the singing that attuned the mythologist to her inner thoughts, almost pulling her into a meditative trance.

The dim lighting of the church's interior made all the gold-plated wood carvings glow like candelabras. Then there was the presence of countless icons and mosaics depicting the saints. All these things made the entire church feel alive. She was hardly religious, and yet strangely, they also made her feel at home.

"You stay standing," Hariklia reminded her.

"Okay," the mythologist answered.

As she took in the visual grandeur of the iconography and the timeless melody of the choir, Cassandra let her mind wander. She looked around, counting the objects around her. There were ten candles in the majestic chandelier above her, twelve points on the star inscribed within the circular floor mosaic, four gospel writers painted in full color on the ceiling dome, and forty speedy repetitions of the phrase *kyrie eleison* by the deacon.

Soon, the clean-shaven priest entered through the iconostasis, dressed in a white cassock with fine, gold sashes. He began shaking the silver incest burner and spouting its plumes of scent in every direction. Cassandra's mind continued counting. *Seventy-six, seventy-seven, seventy-eight...* She kept track of how many puffs of scented air had been wrung from the embers, wondering what it was all adding up to.

After an hour or so, the priest's attendants pulled out a pedestal and placed the Holy Scripture upon it. The scripture was a gold-plated, medieval-looking manuscript, though its pages were crisp and uneroded. As Cassandra listened, the words didn't catch her attention as much as the general cadence and timber of the priest's speech. Then, finally, the priest began his sermon.

"We all want love. Don't you want love? Many of us search for it, and find it. But some of us are impatient and don't trust that love will find us. We want to know the future. But who can know the future? The scripture says: 'If I have the gift of prophecy and can fathom all mysteries and all knowledge, but do not have love, then I am nothing.' First Corinthians 13:2."

The mythologist's knees began to shake with exhaustion from standing. Running had fatigued her more than she realized. As her restless arms struggled to find a comfortable position, she squeezed the jacket she carried in her hands. To occupy her mind, she tried counting again—the number of words the priest was saying, the number of syllables, the number of times the letters alpha or omega were pronounced—anything to make the time pass faster until she could get to a chair and sit. She became annoyed with herself for thinking so many negative thoughts: that standing there for so long was impossible, that she was wasting time and wished she could leave. The mind was, indeed, a worthy adversary.

"My dear brothers and sisters," the priest continued, "if you want to have love, you must show faith. And if you want to have faith, you must show love. Faith and love are like two rows of columns holding up a house. If you have all the columns of faith but none of the columns of love, then your house will not stand."

"Two rows of columns!" Cassandra gasped under her breath.

The clean-shaven priest went on. "If we are to live in God's household, we must build our understanding upon the twin pillars of faith and love. But how can we learn to build strong pillars? Fear not, for there is a Way. Jesus shows us the Way to love through our faith and the church. That is why his disciples were called *followers of the Way*."

Cassandra's eyebrows rose as high as they would go. She thought his mention of the Way was too much of a coincidence. How could Taoism and Christianity both teach the Way? And were their teachings related? She didn't understand the meaning, but she was suddenly certain her attention was in the right place. Through her dusty glasses she fixed her vision upon the robed priest, looking for the next clue that would lead her to Zhen Wu's portrait, to the Taoist Immortals.

"When we know the Way, then everything we are looking for will find us. When we live in the Way, then we build a strong foundation for the temple of God within ourselves. As the scripture says: 'This is the church of the living God, the pillar and foundation of truth.' Timothy 3:15."

"Three fifteen!" she blurted out.

"Eh?" responded Hariklia.

"Uh, nothing. I'm just very glad to be here. Thank you for allowing me into this temple." She bowed goodbye.

"You are always welcome, child!"

The mythologist pulled a clump of straying hair strands back behind her ear and turned toward the door. Instantly, her eyes met those of a man with the gray beard and mustache—the same man from her vision. But he was not physically present inside the church. Rather, he was the man depicted in the icon of John the Revelator. The man from her last vision was Saint John! The icon was mounted to the rectangular pillar in the middle of the nave. In it, Saint John was holding a parchment and quill, reading from the scriptures. However, his eyes were not pointed at the scripture on his desk. Instead, his head was turned toward a blue cloud that appeared in the top-left corner of the icon. Seeing this image gave Cassandra goosebumps.

"It's the blue cloud!"

Though the cloud shown in the icon was not identical to the one from her childhood dreams about Athena, her intuition told her it had to be the same mythological symbol. Saint John looked to the blue cloud for divine wisdom, just as Cassandra had looked toward Athena for guidance. She paused to contemplate the man in the icon. How peaceful he must feel, she mused, to receive guidance directly from the heavens without needing to decipher its meaning. But at second glance, she realized that Saint John's expression was not one of peaceful reflection. His face was frightened, as if troubled by sudden danger.

In an instant, the image of the blue cloud triggered a new vision in Cassandra's mind. She saw Jason studying at the kitchen table. Her mother and Daphne were quarreling about something trivial, and then a crack broke out in the ceiling above them. Through the crack, the blue clouds poured into the apartment. She looked up and noticed that the ceiling was supported by a pillar of rocks, which were then shaken by an earthquake. The column was breaking apart right above them, but none of them noticed! Instantly, the column collapsed and the ceiling caved in, burying them all in dust and ash.

"Jason!"

Cassandra came out of her vision in a sweat, uncomfortably shifting her legs. Without thinking, she hurried toward the exit of the church.

"Sorry. Sorry," she said as she pushed through a line of worshippers receiving communion.

Something was about to happen, and she could feel it. Jason was in danger, and maybe her mother as well. She needed to get home and make sure they were safe. Though she hoped the danger was not connected to the riots, she tried not to analyze what she had seen in the vision. Whatever it meant, she would just follow the feeling: the world is aching. Her intuition, like an arrow, was pulling Cassandra into the center of everything.

Chapter 7

"Saint Macarius?" Loukas called as he gathered his senses. He felt like he was on a different planet, as if there had been a change in atmospheric pressure making it difficult to breathe and to speak.

"Who is it?"

The voice he heard was distinctly male.

"Are you a demon or an angel?" asked the man.

"What?" answered an astonished Loukas. "Neither!"

"Then I am truly lost in the desert, for I am imagining company for myself."

Macarius polished his black, jeweled cross and prayed silently. Loukas looked around for Master Yan-Mei, who was nowhere in sight. Like the scene in the icon, all that surrounded them was sand and sky.

"Are you Saint Macarius of Egypt?"

Macarius laughed.

"A saint? Is that how I imagine myself? Bah! My damned vanity. I am no saint."

"Where are we?" asked Loukas.

"That's exactly what I am trying not to think about, no thanks to you!"

"You mean, you're lost in the desert?"

Macarius threw down his walking staff down on the sand and pointed his cross at Loukas.

"Demon! Go away!"

Loukas put his hands up and froze.

"But I—"

Behind the terror in the Egyptian's eyes, the artist could see sincerity and holiness glowing from within him. Even the golden halo portrayed in the icon could be seen faintly radiating from Macarius's head.

"I know who you are," Macarius said as he clutched the cross in his fist and waved it at Loukas, "I have seen you many times. You are the demon within my mind trying to make me lose my way. Now I must leave you in this woeful place and never return."

"But that's not true!" the artist tried to proclaim.

Instead of hearing him, the saint turned around, picked up his staff and dusted off his robe. Then he proceeded into the desert, leaving Loukas to watch him go.

"Adrian," spoke a grainy female voice. It was Master Yan-Mei, who had appeared at his side.

"What's going on? Why does he think I'm a demon?"

"Because we have come here in an unholy way."

"What? How did we come here? Where are we exactly?"

"Watch your questioning, Adrian. It makes you weak." She got closer to the artist's face and whispered. "Listen. We have entered Saint Macarius's world by using the icon as a window."

Loukas looked up at the sky, which was blue and lacked any trace of clouds or imperfections. Yet at the same time, the sky seemed faded, as if the entire environment were disappearing right in front of him. It was as if all the light were being sucked out of the air as he breathed.

"It feels like...we are not just inside the icon," the artist realized. "It feels like we are inside Saint Macarius's mind."

Master Yan-Mei smiled. "You are very perceptive. We are inside the world as he saw it. Right now, it is the middle of the fourth century."

"You mean, we have travelled in time?"

"Differences in time are merely differences in perspective. To view the world from Saint Macarius's perspective, we must be in another time."

"But we can't *actually* be here. This must be some kind of dream."

"To us, it is a dream, yes. We will wake up and find ourselves drooling in our seats. But to Saint Macarius, we are very real!"

"You mean, when I spoke to him, I became a part of

history? Could I have said something to change the outcome of his future? Could I touch him, or even kill him?" His heart cringed and regretted proposing such a sinful test of proof.

"Throughout history there have been saints who could see what no one else could see. You might call these things ghosts, demons or angels. They exist in the physical world, but they vibrate at a frequency undetectable by normal eyes."

"Meaning that Saint Macarius is the only one who can see us here."

"Correct."

"Because we are ghosts."

"No. We are real people. Look at the footprints you have made!"

"But...that's impossible!"

"Not impossible," Master Yan-Mei assured him. "What you see here, you see with your real eyes."

Loukas looked around the yellow-sanded desert again, trying to comprehend Master Yan-Mei's explanation.

"Here is the problem, Adrian," she continued. "If you look closely, you will see that the icon is decaying around us. That is why the air is thick and stale here. That is why Macarius thinks we are demons!"

"So, you're saying that we're inside the icon, and the icon is decaying," Loukas summarized. "But if the icon were restored, and we came back to this world, Saint Macarius wouldn't mistake us for demons?"

"You are correct. He would not. And more importantly, we would not see the side of him who struggled with demons. We would see only Macarius painted in his best light, living in the immortal wisdom of his sainthood."

Behind them, Macarius's form grew fainter and more distant. Soon the saint was nothing more than a black dot nearly eclipsed by the dusts on the horizon. In the instant they could no longer see him, the end came.

"Brace yourself," advised Master Yan-Mei.

The air pressure returned to normal, and Loukas could breathe more easily. The heat of the desert was replaced with a different kind of heat—the kind that condenses while in a crowded space with unwanted company. The artist opened his eyes.

......

"Good boy," Brazhnikov sneered as Loukas and Master Yan-Mei came out of the *Saint Macarius*. The number of cans on top of the mini-fridge suggested the Bulgarian was on his sixth Coke.

"Did that really happen?" asked a curious Loukas. "How much time has gone by?"

"Look at your watch," the Bulgarian answered.

"About thirty minutes."

"The time should not concern you," advised Master Yan-Mei.

"But how could that happen?" Loukas demanded. "I mean, how did you do that? Was it just a dream?"

"It was very real. Remember your footsteps?"

"It just doesn't make sense. How can people simply appear in another place and time and become physically real?"

"How can you not believe?" Master Yan-Mei protested. "You saw Zhen Wu cry!"

"A tear appearing miraculously on a painting is one thing. Christian icons shed tears and sometimes even fragrances. But to say that our entire bodies travelled centuries back? God wouldn't allow that to happen. There's no need."

"Art is the need," she argued. "Isn't that why you paint? You see images in your mind, which are ideas not dependent on space or time, and then you move those images into the physical world. Like passing through a veil. Think of the miracle of our travel like the miracle of art - matter is simply being moved between the seen and unseen worlds like images from your mind onto a canvas. That is how tears appear upon the icons, and that is how we appear inside them. All of the saints understood this. That is why restoring the ancient icons is so important. Icons are the gateways through which we access their realm."

The artist tried to open his mind to what she was saying, but he couldn't. On the surface it sounded coherent. In fact, the idea of images passing through his mind from the formless world into the physical world was exactly what he had tried to explain to Father Feyzal on Mount Sinai. But on a spiritual level, there was no convincing him. "It can't be more than a dream," he thought to himself.

One by one, Master Yan-Mei placed painting supplies on the table in front of the artist. Just the sight of these familiar objects helped ease his tumultuous feelings. He still couldn't decide if what he experienced was a dream or not. In front of him there was a set of small chisels with a hammer, a pair of brushes and two elegantly decorated bowls of lac tree sap. One bowl contained a deep red color, nearly the color of blood, which the artist found himself excited to use. The other contained a sap so black and lightless that it was difficult to look at. Loukas surmised that it somehow contained a shade of ultraviolet invisible to the eye, which would explain why it was hard to tell its exact color.

"Tell me if there is anything else you need."

"White acrylic. And a palette."

"Done." She pulled out a slick, wooden palette and a tube of white acrylic paint from a chest of drawers beside the table.

"And how about some privacy," Loukas requested, still not sure if he could trust her.

"Fine." She turned to Brazhnikov and pointed to the army of empty cans on top of the mini-fridge. "Clean those up!" she shouted in Mandarin and then retired into the bedroom.

Brazhnikov made a feigned movement toward the cans, but as soon as Master Yan-Mei was out of sight, he changed course and plopped down on the leather sofa, heaving a cathartic sigh.

"Some privacy?" Loukas repeated.

Brazhnikov pulled the straps of his purple suspenders off of his shoulders and adjusted himself so he lay facing the ceiling. It was quite a large sofa, and its boxy frame was a perfect fit for the man's broad shoulders and ample hindquarters.

"Americans," he muttered in Bulgarian as he closed his eyes.

Loukas turned away from Brazhnikov and examined Zhen Wu's portrait, but he couldn't get Saint Macarius off his mind. "It had to be a dream," he thought. "It's impossible to enter an icon and travel in time."

Loukas looked down at the blank, marble tablet and tried his best to put the question out of his mind. He fixed his eyes intently upon the marble's clean surface, as if beaming a holographic projection of Zhen Wu upon it. He could see the immortal's final form, finished, completed in his mind. All that remained was for him to bring the essence of that form from the unseen world into the seen world.

Behind him on the sofa, the Bulgarian started to snore. Loukas lifted the chisel in his right hand and traced it over the marble tablet in the shape of his intended incisions. His left hand held the hammer gently as he prepared to strike. The artist's concentration was so expertly honed that there was no need to trace it in pencil first. There was no possibility of error.

As he began to chisel the textures of the clouds and mountains, other thoughts overtook him. First, he thought of Father Feyzal's comments about art and artistry. They were puerile comments, he felt, and yet he could not help but be grateful for them, for they had created the space for Loukas to derive new insights. Surely, there was value in discussing matters of artistry, even with those who didn't understand art.

He thought of how Feyzal must have felt as Master Yan-Mei stole the *Pantocrator* right before his eyes. What a burden of shame he must now be facing in explaining its absence to the other priests! And what a pity, too, that they all were unaware of the danger the Orthodoxy was facing due to the decaying of the icons.

Loukas's inner voice grew even more emotional as he chiseled in the inscription of the three Chinese characters written on the immortal's scroll. Though he could not decipher their meaning he knew that each line and stroke needed to be replicated with the utmost fidelity.

The chiseling continued, and Loukas's thoughts shifted to his estranged wife, Sharon. Thinking of her ignited painful feelings of longing. However, he knew that what he longed for was not his wife but the vibrant feeling of love that once existed between them. That feeling was gone, never to be revived.

Getting divorced was like experiencing a kind of death, or, at least, it felt like a terminal sickness of the soul. As he bore this sickness, he felt he could understand all deaths, even physical deaths. Death was the irreplaceable loss of some vital image of love inspired from within. Sharon's love was an image that he had cherished until the very last possible moment. But alas, thinking of her now only spoiled the purpose of the pilgrimage that had first brought him to *Pantocrator*: to reorient himself back toward God and art. Fortunately, he was making progress. Zhen Wu was looking much better than his shamefully unsuccessful Sinai Sunrise.

Finally, once he had finished chiseling the background, he textured in the outline of Zhen Wu's body, head and halo. After sweeping off the debris with his hands, he lifted the tablet to try and blow off every last bit of dust, as though by purifying the tablet he was also purifying his heart. He set aside the hammer and chisel and picked up the wooden painter's palette, then used the white acrylic to create a continuum of shades for the red and black lac tree sap. The black and gray, he decided, would shade the mountainous background and provide highlights to the immortal's form. As he completed his palette, the image in his mind grew more detailed and even gained a bit of character, which he focused on replicating exactly as he saw it on the marble canvas.

Hours passed. Loukas lost himself to the flow of his artistry. He painted the rough edges of the mountains and the cascading curves of the clouds before adding the finer details in color, including the birds in the sky, the temple on the mountain and the mysterious red turtle with a snake coiled around it. As he painted, time ceased to contain him, and his thoughts, worries, joys and wisdom coalesced in a singular moment. All of his energy was channeled into the artistic expression of the Taoist Immortal's essence. Indeed, Master Yan-Mei had understood it perfectly. Painting was an act of drawing images from the unseen world and bringing them into form in the physical world. The image he was forming on the marble tablet was as timeless and divine as the world from which it came. It was the essence of a saint, made in the image and likeness of God.

Loukas set his brush and palette down and paused for a moment. The entire portrait was complete with the exception of the face. In traditional iconography, he knew, the face was the last thing to be painted. This was not to suggest it was the most difficult thing to paint, but rather that the face was the final capstone to complete the image. In the case of the Taoist Immortal, though, Loukas's Orthodox sensibilities made him resist painting the face of a non-Orthodox man in a halo for as long as he could. And yet aesthetic curiosity, more than anything, inspired him to wonder how it would feel to bring the face fully into form from the unseen world.

As Loukas waited for his paint to dry, he stood up and went toward the window. Through the dusty glass, Loukas saw a kind of Chinatown he had never seen before. Grimy and unmanaged, the dark, crooked alleyway was lined with what looked like pawn shops and run-down used clothing stores. Graffiti of all kinds and colors filled every square inch of a concrete wall. And like much of struggling Athens, several buildings were crumbling down, abandoned. From what view of the city the small window offered, he could see that streets like this were not uncommon.

A closer look at the graffiti revealed that it had been sprayed on and covered up many times over. Some of it consisted of intelligible phrases and characters. A pink, wavy letter *pi*, outlined in white, began the name *Porphyrius*, which Loukas figured must refer to the graffiti artist rather than the saint.

Other parts, like a series of green and gray boxes, contained Chinese characters he could not read. Others, still, like the wavy blue squiggles in the shape of cheese puff snacks, had no meaning at all. Then, a phrase hit him that was shocking indeed. Its Greek letters were in all capitals, as if speaking an assertive edict: *Chinese, go home.*

Then, at once, he remembered that the silver suitcase stood next to the table. The *Pantocrator*, as far as he knew, was safely concealed inside. How he longed to see that holy icon once more! How he longed to cast his eyes upon the solemn, loving face of Christ again! Then he had a disturbing yet intriguing idea.

"What if his meeting Saint Macarius wasn't a dream," he thought. "What if it really is possible to enter an icon and meet a saint? After all, mysticism does allow for a certain alteration of the senses beyond what can be explained. And even if it was just some kind of vision, it had to be *spiritually* real. At least, it felt real."

At this thought the artist leapt towards the suitcase. He tugged on the zipper, but it was locked, and as he discovered this, Brazhnikov stirred and mumbled in his sleep.

"I have to escape," Loukas decided. He grabbed the silver suitcase and rolled it carefully towards the window. Looking out, however, he realized that he could not carry it down without risking damage to its holy contents. "I will tell the police about these icons," he resolved. "They can recover them later."

However, since he could not escape with the *Pantocrator* himself, he figured he would take the next best thing: the ancient portrait of Zhen Wu. He moved toward the window again, hearing Brazhnikov stir a little louder. Then, without much thought he also grabbed his own painting, in which only the face of the Taoist Immortal remained blank, and stuffed it in the leather carrying bag along with the original. Hastily he threw in as many of the painting supplies as he could. The sack was unbearably heavy, but the sturdy strap was enough to keep him from dropping it. Furthermore, the weight of the bag on his shoulder appeared insignificant next to the possible danger to his life if he stayed.

......

Carefully, Loukas maneuvered out of the window and climbed down a sequence of loose bricks, which led him to the floor of the alleyway. There, a restless crowd of protesters emerged and startled him.

"Greece for one, and Greece for all!" they chanted. One of them threw a pamphlet at Loukas's feet. The entire page was written in Chinese characters except for the title in large, bold print: "Democracy leaves no one behind!"

It seemed to be a peaceful protest, but Loukas didn't let himself be too careless. He was aware that riots had been going on in Greece. Nationalist organizations had been targeting immigrants for years. They claimed that their homeland was 'for the Greeks', and blamed the Chinese and other groups for coming in and taking up space, taking jobs, and diluting the purity of their ancient culture.

Loukas didn't like politics and rarely got involved. No doubt, he observed, the Chinese Greeks feel marginalized by the new immigration ban proposal. But being in the middle of such a scene challenged his more conservative sensibilities. Upholding traditions was as important to social life as it was to religious life. If immigration were not restricted, how could Greece hope to remain Orthodox?

As he thought these things he tried to remain open-minded. Whether Greece's borders opened or not, it was in God's hands, not his own. He had no time to dwell on these matters any further. The bag he carried was heavy, and he had to escape the vicinity as quickly as possible. He folded up the pamphlet and stuffed it in the dumpster beside the brick wall.

Next to the dumpster, a small boy stood with a camera. He wore slightly faded, brown khakis and a green t-shirt with a picture of a tiger. It was Jason Yin.

"Who are you?" asked Jason intrusively. He snapped a

photo of Loukas and his stolen carrying bag.

"I'm nobody."

"What's in the bag?"

Loukas looked up at the window, fearing Brazhnikov's wrath and his jade dagger. Fortunately, no one looked out.

"I have to get out of here."

The artist set out walking briskly, and the boy with the camera followed him.

"Wait! What's in the bag?"

The intrigue of the bag's contents was too enticing for Jason to resist. And Loukas, despite his hurry, sensed as much. So, he decided to make a friend. He stopped, and the boy bumped into him.

"Ha!" cried Jason, punching Loukas in his left rib cage in self-defense.

"Uf!" reacted Loukas.

"Do not touch me!"

"You bumped into me!"

"Ok, but why did you stop?"

"Tell me your name," the artist demanded.

"You tell me yours!"

"Fine. It's Adrian."

"I'm Jason."

"We have to get out of here, Jason."

Loukas moved the carrying bag to his other shoulder and ran as fast as its weight would allow. Jason, who was much quicker, caught up and ran beside him.

"Who's chasing you? Did you steal something?"

Jason knew that his questions could only be answered if he helped his new friend. The boy sped up and turned a corner, heading home.

"Where are you going?" called Loukas.

"We're taking a shortcut!"

The shortcut was not easy for one carrying two heavy marble tablets. It involved winding through narrow paved stairways whose steps were uneven heights, sliding upon cracked pavement and pushing one's way across streets of heavy traffic. At last, the boy arrived at his building's front gate. He used the key tied around his neck to unlock the gate.

"Is this where you live?" Loukas asked.

"Maybe," Jason paused before answering, as it dawned on him that he was about to let in a complete stranger. Quickly he thought up a way to test Adrian's trustworthiness. "I'll let you in only if you can answer my riddles."

"Believe me. This isn't the time for riddles."

"The first riddle is—"

"I'm serious! Athens isn't safe right now, especially for you and me."

"THE FIRST RIDDLE IS," he repeated. "I am hidden in the light but seen in the dark. What am I?"

Loukas guided the boy through the gate and closed it behind them. The building's front door, however, remained locked.

"If you let me in, I'll show you what's in this bag!"

"Okay." Jason grabbed the sack and tried to sneak a peek.

"*First* let me in, *then* I'll show you."

"Aren't you being chased?"

"I can't show you out here!"

"I AM HIDDEN IN THE LIGHT BUT SEEN IN THE DARK. WHAT AM I?"

"Okay, fine." Scanning his surroundings, there was no sign of Brazhnikov or Master Yan-Mei following his tracks. He let Jason see into the bag.

"That's all? Engravings of a Chinese guy? And why doesn't that one have a face?" Jason cringed self-consciously, trying not to let himself show any interest in the portraits. He hated having the Eastern half of his identity shoved in his face.

"Now I've shown you. Let me inside."

"I AM HIDDEN IN THE LIGHT BUT SEEN IN THE—"

"Please! I'll tell you once we're inside!"

"Answer my riddle now! What am I?"

"What are you?"

"That's the riddle. What am I?

"I can't tell you."

"Why not?"

Loukas quickly crafted an answer:

"My reason is a secret. It's a secret so ancient, it must never to be shown to anyone else!"

"I'm not interested in your stupid secrets anymore."

"But that's the answer to your riddle, Jason: a secret. A secret is never shown where everyone around can see; it is *hidden in the light.* A secret is only revealed when nobody else is watching; it is *seen in the dark.*"

Jason was flabbergasted. It wasn't the answer he thought was correct, but it fit perfectly. He looked up and smiled cautiously.

"Okay, you can come in. But you can only stay for one hour, okay?" The small boy held up a decisive finger to emphasize his point.

Jason let Loukas in and took him up the elevator and into the apartment.

"Grandma! Is Auntie home?"

As Jason signaled for his new friend to take a seat on the living room couch, his grandma shouted back grumpily that she was napping and didn't want to be disturbed.

"That's my Grandma," he whispered to Loukas. "She yells a lot, but when she sleeps, she is quiet as a cat."

As if to defy the boy's comparison, Peony raced into the room and pounced on Jason's left shoe with a flamboyant hiss, clutching it with her paws and licking his ankles. Jason bent down to greet his cat.

"And this is Peony!"

Loukas unloaded his heavy sack and sat on the couch, exhausted. He rubbed his eyes.

"You have a nice house, Jason."

"Are you Greek?" Jason asked. He let go of Peony, who, having successfully upstaged the grandmother, lost interest in getting any more attention than was absolutely necessary. Jason took out his camera and absent-mindedly scrolled through his photos of the protest.

"My parents are Greek," the artist answered, "but I was born in the United States."

"Do you want tea, Adrian? We Greeks are known for our hospitality!"

"Yes, please. But you seem only partly Greek."

Jason grunted, trying not to dignify the comment. "I'm more Greek than you are." He raced into the kitchen and started the kettle.

Loukas looked around the living room for Peony, but her gray fur seemed to lose itself in one of the room's many dark corners. In the lighter spaces of the room, frames of Chinese art and calligraphy lined the walls. Though the artist could not read them, they suggested an environment of peace, and indeed, of hospitality. Jason's math book rested on the coffee table in front of him, next to a coaster with a black-and-white image of a rooster. From the kitchen, Loukas could hear spoons and porcelain cups clanging together as the boy fixed the tea.

The artist leaned into the sofa, trying to rest his body. So many things had happened to him in the short time since the *Pantocrator* was stolen, and his mind could not get still. But the most intriguing thing was how Master Yan-Mei had made him enter the icon of Saint Macarius. Like a mysterious power, she was able to lead him from the seen to the unseen world. It was a surreal and mystical experience, akin to the most sublime bursts of creative inspiration he had ever known.

In a way he could not fully comprehend, Master Yan-Mei was his teacher. She possessed a power and a knowledge of the world of iconography that he struggled not to revere, especially now knowing she was Greek Orthodox. It was clear she was not a criminal at all, but a kind of renegade believer with an unmistakable connection to the saints. At the most basic level he hated her for kidnapping him, and yet, part of him felt a strange allegiance to her. Though he supposed he had now broken that allegiance by taking Zhen Wu's portrait.

Perhaps it was still his duty—even his destiny—to restore the icons she had stolen. He worried he might never find out.

Jason peaked his head in and spoke in the deepest voice he could manage. "How much sugar do you want?"

"Make it half-sweet, please."

Loukas reached for the leather carrying bag. Slowly, he removed the ancient portrait from the bag and set the portrait on his knees. Carefully he studied it with his eyes, looking for remnant tears.

Jason burst into the room, clumsily clanging two tiny, full cups together as he carried them. Startled, Loukas set the painting on the cushion next to him and covered it with the leather carrying bag containing his own unfinished replica.

"Here you go!"

The artist looked at the tea.

"Um...Jason...you forgot to strain it."

"What do you mean?"

"I mean, there are bits of leaves floating in the water. You can't drink those. Don't you have a strainer?"

"I think—"

An impatient key turned the lock of the door. It was Aunt Cassandra.

"Quick, Adrian! Get into the bathroom!"

Loukas frantically grabbed his leather carrying bag and stepped into the bathroom as his host advised. Jason closed the door and held his breath.

Then, Cassandra rushed in.

Chapter 8

Cassandra Yin knew something was wrong. In her vision, she had seen blue clouds seeping into her home and causing the pillars to collapse on Jason and the rest of her family. Though she didn't understand the meaning of the vision, she followed her intuition home, hoping she wasn't too late for whatever was about to happen.

"Jason, are you okay?"

"Why wouldn't I be okay?" Jason answered. He noticed she was out of breath, but his eyes cautiously guarded the bathroom, where Loukas hid. "Where have you been?"

"I've been out." Cassandra breathed heavily. "Is Grandma okay?"

Jason's eyes shifted mischievously away from the bathroom door. "She's sleeping. Everything's fine."

"Is someone else here?"

"Absolutely not!" the boy lied.

"Then why do you have two cups of tea?

"I was practicing."

"And what is that?" She pointed to Zhen Wu's portrait, which now lay out in the open on her living room sofa. "Oh my god!" she exclaimed, nearly falling to her knees in disbelief.

Cassandra sat down beside the portrait and took it carefully into her hands. She leaned her face to it as close as she could while still being able to see the whole image at once. Her intuition told her instantly who was depicted in it: Zhen Wu, the Taoist Immortal.

While seated in meditation, Zhen Wu radiated his mysterious knowledge of the Way. Mystified by this knowledge, Cassandra smiled and wondered. Only twenty-four hours ago she had believed the Way was only an abstract philosophy; now, it felt not only symbolic but also real. Master Zhang was the first step on her path to follow the Way, and this painting was her next. And as soon as she could find the Taoist Immortals, she would train with them to use the power of myth to end the world's aching. She held her face up to the portrait again and trembled with excitement. Then she thought of how pleased Master Zhang would be when she could show it to him.

Jason took a sip of tea and didn't pay much attention to Cassandra's fascination with the painting. He was more worried about getting in trouble for letting in a stranger.

"Peony!" Jason whispered, calling his cat.

"Jason, where did this painting come from?"

The boy put down his teacup and puffed up his chest.

"I got it from a guy in the alley who jumped out of a window. He was tough but I fought him off." He made *Kung Fu* punches in the air to show his strength.

"You fought him?" cried the mythologist. Her maternal instincts honed in on him like a fly to a lamp. "Did he hurt you?"

Jason realized his half-lies were getting his aunt overly worried, but he couldn't stop. Instead, he decided to try and get Aunt Cassandra on his side by giving up Loukas.

"No, but I think he still might."

Cassandra's mouth swung open. "Where is he? Is he downstairs?"

"He's in the bathroom."

The mythologist looked at the bathroom door, not entirely sure whether to believe the boy.

"Is somebody in there?" knocked Cassandra.

"I'll defend you, Autie!" he said from across the room.

Meanwhile, Loukas didn't know what to do. He was trapped in the Yin family's bathroom with his unfinished portrait of Zhen Wu, and he could hear the entirety of the conversation leading up to their ambush. Fortunately, the bathroom door had a lock, which he turned in the nick of time.

"If you're in there," she tried to say firmly, "we need to know who you are. Come out and explain yourself."

"Adrian!" called the boy.

"How do you know his name?" she whispered.

"I'm Adrian Loukas," the artist answered from behind the door. "I brought you the painting on your sofa."

Cassandra was speechless. She couldn't understand how this man knew the painting was meant for her. Perhaps, she surmised, it was another case of the universe joining two paths at a precise moment in history. Still, her warning of danger did not afford her much room to trust without questioning.

"Why did you jump out that window?" Jason interrogated, trying to sound firm and in control. He pounded on the bathroom door.

Loukas realized he would do well to match wits with Jason's half-lies. "Jason, you promised me Greek hospitality! Why did you lock me in the bathroom?"

Cassandra jumped defensively in her stance. "Jason, we must never let strange men into the apartment."

"He solved *your* riddle!"

"What riddle?"

"I am hidden in the light but seen in the—"

"Will you please let me out? I only want to explain the paintings. I need to go after the thieves who have the rest of them!"

"Yeah! The thieves!" Jason leapt about, doing kicks in the air in sequence.

"Jason, quit doing *Kung Fu* in the living room."

Cassandra invited Loukas to come out, promising peace. After taking a deep breath, the artist emerged from the bathroom with his leather carrying bag and asked politely to resume his tea. The mythologist agreed and joined him by taking Jason's cup.

"As I said, my name is Adrian, and I am a painter. And this," he pulled out his unfinished painting from the carrying bag, "is my replica of the painting on your sofa. The original is Chinese, probably very ancient."

"It's a replica?" she said, comparing the portraits and pretending not to know who was depicted on them.

"But where is his face?" Jason interrupted.

"I couldn't finish it. I had to leave, and that's when I ran into Jason taking pictures of the protest."

"What!?"

Jason knew his aunt would overreact. What he hadn't anticipated was his new friend giving him up so quickly.

"What's the big deal?" He took out his camera and displayed it defiantly.

"Go to your room! Your dad will deal with you when he gets home."

"But I'm entertaining a guest!" he whined.

Loukas did not look up to gratify the boy's manipulative attempt at camaraderie.

"Go. Now."

Jason snatched Loukas's cup of tea and unleashed an angry stare.

"And leave me your camera."

He obeyed his aunt and went to his bedroom.

The living room became still. Then Cassandra spoke:

"Was there really a riot going on?"

"I think it was just a peaceful protest. But it was right here in Chinatown. I can see how you would be upset at him participating."

"He was participating?" Her shoulders raised.

"Well, maybe not. I only saw him taking pictures."

"Hardly the same thing!"

"How was I supposed to know?" Loukas asked.

"Haven't you read the papers? Two Chinese were killed during the riots!"

"That's awful. I'm sorry I didn't know. I only woke up in Greece this morning."

Cassandra clasped her hands and took a deep breath. "We are all a little wary of the danger." To fill the silence, she picked up Jason's camera and took a quick glance through its pictures. Then she reached her hand out and offered the artist a handshake. "I'm Cassandra Yin, by the way. A mythologist."

"A mythologist?" Loukas's eyebrows shot up with surprise. "What does a mythologist do?"

"Well, I've only just graduated. I guess we'll find out."

"And you're Jason's sister?"

"Aunt," she corrected.

Loukas nodded. "I knew you were too young to have children of your own."

She crossed her arms. "I'm twenty-eight!"

"Oh, well I'm forty," Loukas countered quickly. He relaxed his brow and smiled, then extended his hand again. "Pleased to meet you."

Cassandra eased her shoulders and laughed, then shook the artist's hand a second time.

"Are you a dragon?" she asked.

"Excuse me?"

"I mean, your zodiac sign."

"I don't know."

"It's okay," she said, worried she might have offended him. "It's just a Chinese superstition. I was born in the year of the dragon, and since you are twelve years older, I thought you must be a dragon as well. The zodiac is a cycle of twelve years."

"I see," Loukas nodded. "You really are a mythologist, aren't you!"

"If only I could get paid for it," she grimaced.

"You're unemployed?"

"Jobs in Athens are a little scarce, in case you didn't know. Even for people with advanced degrees."

"I wouldn't know. I'm not much of a scholar."

"But you love painting, right?"

"More than anything. I paint every day. It's a creative outlet for me."

"That's exactly how I feel about mythology!"

"Really? How?"

"Mythology can also be a creative outlet."

"How is mythology creative?"

"Myths are the stories we tell ourselves so that our lives

make sense. They're like building blocks that come from the universal story of humanity. When we live out our own stories, we combine these building blocks in new ways and see where life takes us. How is that not creative?"

Loukas could see the passion in Cassandra's eyes as she spoke.

"I've never thought of it that way," the artist confessed.

"Most people haven't." Cassandra put down the camera and took a seat.

Loukas scratched the back of his neck. Surely by now, he imagined, Master Yan-Mei and Brazhnikov would have realized he had fled with the paintings. Making small talk with Cassandra relaxed him a bit. His palms were sweating heavily. He counted the seconds as they ticked by on his watch, hoping that each one made it less likely they would find him. He sat on the sofa and picked up the teacup Jason had prepared for himself. Though he didn't intend to drink any, as the floating leaves made it awkward, holding it was somewhat comforting.

"So," Loukas began, "how long have you lived in Athens?"

"For most of my life. My brother George and I came here when we were teenagers. Well, I was only twelve. But we came with our parents."

"Where did you come from?"

"From Xi'an, China. George married a Greek and had Jason."

"I am guessing he is quite a handful."

"It's like pulling teeth to get him to speak Mandarin at home."

"I don't understand a word of it," Loukas confessed.

"But your Greek is very good, for a Greek-American."

"How did you know I was American?"

"Intuition," she answered, dismissing his question. "What city do you live in?"

"Seattle," the artist answered.

"Is your family there?"

"Yes, both my parents are there. And I have a sister in

Vancouver."

"Are you married?"

"Yes, but—" Loukas bit his lip. He didn't want to get into the topic of his divorce. "My wife and I have separated."

As the artist confessed this fact, a novel yet obvious truth dawned on him: this was the first time he had yet uttered these words to anyone. *My wife and I have separated.* Now he had said them. However, saying them didn't help sort out his feelings, nor did it grant him any sense of relief to finally admit he was getting divorced. If anything, it made it feel more real, which was much worse and made his stomach tie up into knots. Cassandra didn't seem to know how to respond, and remained silent. Loukas scratched his neck again, then polished the face of his watch with his thumb. The seconds ticked by.

"Are you married?" he asked.

"No," she answered awkwardly. "I mean, I could be if I wanted to, but I'm not."

Loukas spent a moment trying to understand this cryptic answer, but quickly gave up. He swirled the tea around in his cup and watched the tea leaves move around.

"Do you paint professionally?" Cassandra asked to try and break the silence again.

"Yes, I do." He looked down at his faceless painting, then at his shoe. "But this one has been a particular challenge."

"What is the challenge?"

"They wanted me to paint a replica of this ancient portrait, but to paint it like an icon. You know, like in the Orthodox churches."

"Oh!" she exclaimed. "Christian icons are so beautiful!"

"Are you Greek Orthodox?" Loukas asked, trying to keep an open mind.

"Just Greek," she answered.

"Of course." He smiled, amused.

"But I am wondering," she continued, "why did you bring the paintings here? Why didn't you finish your replica?"

"Because I had to escape. I was forced to paint it against

my will."

"What do you mean, forced?"

"I was kidnapped and held at daggerpoint, believe it or not."

Cassandra couldn't believe it. "Who would do that?"

"Thieves, that's who. They've stolen icons from all different monasteries, including Saint Catherine's in Egypt, where I was just yesterday. I suspect they also stole this Chinese painting."

"I think I know who they stole it from!" Cassandra interjected.

"Really? Who?"

"From my *Kung Fu* teacher, Master Zhang."

"You practice *Kung Fu*!" Loukas exclaimed.

"Well, kind of. It's not what you're thinking. I started recently."

"Still, that's impressive."

"Master Zhang is looking for a painting that was stolen from him. He says it's a portrait of a Taoist Immortal called Zhen Wu."

"That's exactly who this is!" he shouted, unable to contain his excitement.

"Who did you take it from?"

"She's called Master Yan-Mei. A highly skilled martial artist. She has a bodyguard called Brazhnikov, and they have an apartment here in Chinatown right where the protest was."

"And Jason was there? Are they after him too? I assume they're after you."

Loukas massaged his neck and refrained from scratching. It was a relief to confess his predicament.

"No, Jason never saw them. I had to climb out the window to escape." Loukas turned the painting so he could look at it face-on. "I guess that makes me a thief too," he said facetiously.

"Let me see your replica," the mythologist said, grabbing the portrait from Loukas's hands. "This is stunning. How long did it take you to paint this much?"

"Maybe, two hours."

"And you are sure this is Zhen Wu?" she asked.

"It will be, as soon as I can finish the face."

"Why is there a red turtle with a snake coiled around it?"

"How should I know?"

"You painted it!"

"I only copied it from the original."

"Oh, right."

"Shouldn't you know who Zhen Wu is? You're a mythologist!"

"I didn't specialize in Taoist myths. But Adrian! You have quite an eye for reproducing ancient art!"

"Thanks, but it almost got me killed."

"What do you mean?"

"Didn't I mention the Orthodox icons? Master Yan-Mei wanted me to replicate them."

"I thought you said Master Yan-Mei stole them."

"She did."

"And you had nothing to do with it?"

"Of course not." the artist protested. "Didn't I mention the dagger? I was forced! Besides, I didn't steal anything."

"I understand. It was just your Master Yan-Mei, then."

Curiously, Cassandra's suggestion that the fearsome woman was his Master Yan-Mei made Loukas feel honored rather than ashamed. Indeed, he reflected, if there was one thing he knew for certain about the old woman, it was that she understood icons. He could not deny that she had given him a vivid experience of the world inside the icon. It was even possible—dare he admit it—that his meeting with Saint Macarius was real. And even if it wasn't, the spiritual feeling was real. The experience with the icon had opened up a possibility within his soul he had never considered.

"Master Yan-Mei stole the icons," Loukas explained. "But the thing is, she did it for a reason. She is Greek Orthodox. She took the icons in order to save them from decaying and being lost forever. She says that I am the only one who can replicate them correctly, and I have to do this before the images fade away."

"Do you believe her?"

"I'm still not sure. But I am sure this must be the painting your Master Zhang is looking for."

Cassandra smiled to think of the wise, round-headed man as her Master Zhang. The coincidence of the painting showing up in her living room had to be a sign that she was connected to him, and that Loukas was connected to them too, somehow. But how could she explain this to him? How could she tell the artist that she was studying the Way in order to use its power—the source of all myths and storytelling—to bring peace to the riots in Greece? As her first encounter with Loukas continued, it was clear that these were secrets to be seen only later, in the dark.

"Then let's go and return it to him," Cassandra suggested.

"Now? But we haven't finished our tea," he joked.

Cassandra laughed, and then stood up to go make more tea. "Just give me a moment."

Loukas nodded and thanked her. While waiting for his tea, he thought about all that had happened within the last day. He thanked God for letting him escape and prayed for guidance. He was sure that God wanted him to get the *Pantocrator* back, and yet he wasn't sure how to go about it or if he even had the strength. Then, as Cassandra brought in a teapot and two clean cups, it dawned on him. He now had a potential ally with possible connections to a martial arts master. Unlike Master Yan-Mei, whose character was questionable, Cassandra Yin appeared genuine. Maybe it was the childlike quality of her voice and smile; he didn't try to analyze it. He simply felt he could trust her—not with everything, yet, but he could trust her well enough for the moment.

"This is an oolong tea," she said, handing him a cup and filling it. "I sweetened it a little bit."

"Thanks."

She sat down next to him and poured her own tea.

"So, Adrian, what is your sister's name?"

"Jeanne."

"How old is she?"

"She's thirty-five."

"So, five years younger than you. Are you close?"

"Well, she comes down and visits on holidays and brings her kids. Her husband is an evangelical preacher. Actually, that makes holidays a little difficult since we're Greek Orthodox."

"Aren't the evangelicals also Christian?"

"By name, yes. But we're not the same. The Orthodoxy doesn't try to force people to convert. We honor God using the same traditions of music, incense and iconography that the original disciples used."

"I don't believe in God," Cassandra stated bluntly.

"Not any god?"

"Nope."

"But you're a mythologist! Surely you've learned about God."

"Hey! You said you weren't going to convert me!" she joked.

"Ha-ha," he said perfunctorily. "I only meant that as a mythologist you must know myths about God from all sorts of religions. I just think it's interesting that you don't believe in any of them."

"Myths aren't about what is real or what we should believe in. They're symbols for something deeper in the human psyche. The truth behind the myths comes to us through our dreams. Carl Jung called it the collective unconscious. It influences how we understand the stories of our own lives and the choices we make."

"That's a nice philosophy," Loukas responded. "But it doesn't really answer the spiritual question. If you're only listening to your own stories without God to guide you, how do you know what is right and wrong?"

"Not just your own stories, everybody's stories. Myths are *universal* stories."

"I only mean that, just because something is universal doesn't mean it's right. Sometimes we have to fight our unconscious tendencies and not give into them. Dreams can deceive us."

"So can religion," Cassandra retorted. Loukas looked down at his tea and took a sip. It was time to change the subject.

"How old are Jeanne's kids?" This made Loukas smile.

"There are three. The oldest, Kira, just turned twelve."

"The same as Jason!"

"Kira's a soccer player. Then there's Susannah, who will be ten soon. She plays the piano. The youngest is a boy, Saul, who is seven and a half."

"Do you have a picture of them?"

"Yes, I think so." He reached into his wallet and took out a photo of the entire family. "Here."

Cassandra took the photo and read over it with her eyes.

"You have such a big family! Why are you traveling alone?"

"Uh…"

"Saul is so cute!" she added before he had time to answer. "And your sister looks like you!"

"We get that a lot."

"Are those your parents?"

"Yes, they're both from Thessaloniki."

"Your wife is pretty."

Loukas's heart jumped. "That photo is a couple years old." He grabbed it back and put it away.

"I'm sorry. I didn't mean to—"

"Let's just forget about her, okay?"

"Okay, sorry."

"We fell out of love, that's all."

The mythologist poured them each some more white tea. Then she sprung a question on him with unexpected enthusiasm.

"How do you know if you're in love? In general, I mean."

"Hmm." Loukas took a large sip of tea and swished it around in his mouth before answering. "For me, I suppose, it was the way Sharon looked at me. I could see it in her eyes that she loved me and saw that I loved her back. Then I knew."

"Don't you have a story for how you fell in love?"

"No story. It was just a feeling. Something you take on faith."

"But which came first? Did you love her, or did she love you?"

"Why are you so curious about love?" he teased. "Does it have to do with the person you could marry but haven't?"

Her blush revealed the truth.

"Ah-hah! I knew it."

"Do you want to see his picture?"

"Maybe some other time." The artist looked at his watch anxiously. He set his cup down, then looked towards the door. "But I'm thinking we should probably do something about these paintings before the thieves have a chance to find us."

"Oh, yes, the thieves. What was Master Yan-Mei's bodyguard called again? Something Russian?"

Loukas shuddered just thinking of the man. "Brazhnikov. It could be Russian, I'm not sure. But he's the one with the dagger."

"And where did you see the icons last?" Cassandra asked.

"They kept them locked in a silver suitcase. But somehow, I think it wouldn't be wise to go after them without help. Didn't you say Master Zhang was a martial arts master?"

"Oh! I know exactly where we can go!"

"To find Master Zhang?"

"Don't worry about finding Master Zhang. When the time is right he will find us. I meant that I know where you can finish your replica."

"Finish the painting? Why does that matter?" He joked about it, but truthfully he longed to paint the face of Zhen Wu and complete his work.

"If we are going to work together, Adrian, then I need you to trust my intuition."

"Your intuition?"

"You do want to finish painting it, don't you?"

"Yes, of course!"

"Then I will help you. Mythologists have a highly precise intuition. You're lucky you've met one."

"I don't believe in luck, Cassandra."

"My friend Maria Stournari works in the art restoration room in the basement of the public library. She can let us in to work on it there."

"That sounds perfect," agreed Loukas.

"Just put the paintings back in your leather bag and—"

The artist coughed and rubbed his shoulder, which was still sore.

"You don't want to carry both paintings because they're heavy," she surmised. The artist's silence affirmed her guess. "Very well. You take your replica, and I'll take the original." She went over to the living room closet. There, she retrieved a large, square, black backpack from the very back.

"What's that?"

"I used to deliver pizzas to pay for my graduate school. I'm sure it will fit." She delicately slipped the ancient portrait of Zhen Wu into her square backpack and fastened it shut. "Are you ready?"

Loukas smiled to hide his anxiety, and placed his unfinished painting in the leather carrying bag before swinging it over his shoulder. "You should make sure Jason knows we are leaving."

"Oh, don't worry about him. If he thinks I'm still here, he'll stay out of trouble. Besides, my mother is in her room if he needs anything."

"Okay. How long will it take us to get to the library??"

"It's not far to walk," Cassandra assured him with a gentle smile. She pulled Loukas outside and locked the door behind her. "Just be careful."

Chapter 9

It was late afternoon and the protesters were gone. The mythologist led the artist through the backstreets of Chinatown, where dingy import clothing stores brought traces of life to otherwise vacant buildings. Some buildings were run-down and abandoned altogether. Roofs had collapsed, concrete corners had chipped away, windows had fallen out and walls became too dusty even for graffiti. Loukas could not help but turn his head every few seconds to make sure he wasn't being followed. Cassandra, too, hurried forward with a sort of impatience. "Athens seems to be doing worse than the last time I was here," Loukas observed.

"Tell me about it."

"Are other neighborhoods as rundown as this one?"

"Some of them are struggling," she lamented with a slight edge in her voice. "But I think we're the worst. It's a real shame. We came to the West to improve our standard of living. But look at the ghetto they've put us in! So much for the famous Greek hospitality."

Loukas looked up and beheld an abandoned, gray, eight-story building. Its unadorned concrete frame gave the impression of a parking garage, and yet the openings where windows should have been were sized for either residence or rental units. Lifelessness dusted the entire structure. Death kept it crumbling.

Leaving Chinatown was like escaping from the desert and being swept away all at once by a river of tourists and busy locals. Cassandra took Loukas to Panepistimio Street, where the central library was located. Sweltering sunbeams fell upon the city center like a rain into a valley. She led Loukas to the main desk to ask for Maria Stournari, who soon appeared.

"Hi Maria."

"Cassie!" Maria whispered with bubbly, breathy enthusiasm. "How have you been? How's your mother?"

"Mom is not doing too well, but she has her good days."

"And your school? You just graduated, right?"

"Yes, except I can't find work."

"Oh my gosh! I heard Stavros finally asked you to—"

"What?" Cassandra interrupted, looking at Loukas as though it were making him feel awkward. "Is this all over the news?"

Maria studied Loukas's appearance from head to toe. His dirty, light-brown collared shirt gave the impression he hadn't changed his clothes in a while. His blue jeans had traces of red dust at the bottom. His socks and shoes were likewise stained with the dusts of Mount Sinai. His palms, fingers, nails, and even forearms bore traces of all colors of paint, while his wavy, black hair was attractively erratic, as if blown by a favorable wind. The one unusually clean aspect of his appearance was his wristwatch, which had not a smudge on it. Loukas could sense that Maria was noticing him, but he chalked it up to the fact that Cassandra wasn't giving her much attention.

"I'm Adrian," said the artist. "Pleased to meet you, Maria."

"Likewise."

"Maria, we need your help," the mythologist said with urgency. "And we're actually in a bit of a hurry."

"Sure," Maria said, slightly deflated by her seriousness.

"Adrian needs a place to finish his painting." She turned to the artist. "Get it out and show her!"

Loukas showed Maria the portrait with the unfinished face, and was charmed by her reaction.

"Such form! Such texture!"

"Well, it's not done yet," said the artist humbly.

"You are so talented, Adrian! And I love the little red turtle with the—"

"Do you think you can help us?" Cassandra interrupted.

"Of course." Maria broke her eye contact with the artist and her smile faded. "Let me take you to the art restoration room. It's in the second basement."

Without further ado, Maria took them to the elevator and pulled out a circular key ring with two dozen keys on it. She shuffled through them until coming to each one she needed. First, a tiny, bronze key controlled the elevator that took them to the second basement. Then, a much larger, older, leaden key opened the art restoration. Finally, a cheap-looking silver key unlocked a wall of drawers inside the art restoration room.

"These drawers have paints and brushes and so on," Maria explained as she met Loukas's eyes and her smile returned. "Adrian, you can set up your painting over here."

"Thank you," the artist nodded, though he quickly diverged from the smile they shared.

He found the sweet, feminine likeness of Maria Stournari particularly pleasing. Her hair was curly, like his wife's, though her face was softer and more innocent. Her green, teardrop-shaped earrings were nearly long enough to touch her shoulders, which were round and huggable. Her curving waistline gave way to perfectly formed hips and agile thighs. Indeed, the more Loukas admired Maria's physique, the more her image seemed to glisten in his mind like a siren on the rocks. Maria's hazel eyes lit up his heart with a raw, youthful zest that he remembered quite well—it was the glow he used to see in Sharon's eyes when they were younger.

Cassandra and Maria continued talking for a while longer as Loukas set up his painting palate, lost in his own thoughts. It saddened the artist a bit to think how much he and Sharon had aged in only a decade. At forty, the glow in their eyes had already faded. In Maria's likeness he saw some aspects of his wife: the way she could wear a straight-laced shirt provocatively, the way she held her hands confidently on her hips as she spoke, and the way she smiled and laughed wholeheartedly, regardless of what she felt inside—which had been Sharon's natural tendency for many years—were all things that had attracted him in his youth.

At this stage of his life, however, seeing this kind of playful smile was exhausting to him. He could recognize it as a mere projection, a show of outward pleasantries that would be unsustainable over time. On the surface, he liked Maria's smile very much. He might have even confessed to having a romantic inkling towards her. But the circumstances of his divorce made any such attraction unquestionably futile.

Eventually Maria left. Loukas was too involved in his brooding thoughts to say goodbye.

In a parallel inner world, Cassandra found herself sitting on the floor in the art restoration room holding the ancient portrait of the Taoist Immortal in her lap. The further she examined the exquisite artifact, the more she felt sad. From close up, it looked as if Zhen Wu was about to shed tears. She moved her fingers along the engraved contours of his eyes, which felt strangely damp, adding to the impression that Zhen Wu was crying. His were tears that she, too, knew all too well. They were her mother's tears, crying for Jason and for the fading of her culture before her eyes. They were the tears of her father, she imagined, if he had been alive to grieve for how far they had strayed from their ancestors' ways. Chinese tradition was a kind of sacred bond she was only just beginning to appreciate, now that its threads were unravelling at an accelerated rate.

It aggravated her that Jason didn't seem to care one bit about his Chinese heritage. It was as if he wished to bury that part of his identity within himself like a dusty relic beneath the dirt. At times, Cassandra worried that soon Jason's Greekness would overtake his Chineseness in a deadly coup. *Greece for the Greeks! Immigrants, go home!* It was the inescapable refrain of his upbringing and also, she feared, the cruel destiny of the Yin family: they would be forced into exile, not in the sense of removing themselves from Greece, but in the sense of removing the Chineseness from themselves. Their Chineseness, she felt more strongly than ever before, was as precious as the living artifact that lay on the table before her, since it was alive and breathing! The artifact she beheld was a symbol of her Chinese identity. The more she studied it, the more alive she felt.

"Cassandra, I'm going to need that portrait back."

"It's not stone!" she blurted out.

"You're right, it's marble."

"No, what I mean is…it's almost as if…"

"What is it?"

"It's as if Zhen Wu is crying, as if he is alive inside this painting."

Alive, Loukas repeated in his head. He didn't want to believe it. When Master Yan-Mei showed him Zhen Wu's painting, an actual tear had manifested, which should have been impossible—only a Christian icon could bear such a miracle. He could not accept that the painting could be an icon. It puzzled him that Cassandra seemed to see the tears too. He couldn't explain it, so he let out a vague response:

"Well, maybe he's somewhat alive. Now give me the painting."

"What do you mean, *somewhat*?" she asked, placing the painting on his table. "How can a person be somewhat alive?"

"I guess, maybe, the idea of him is still alive. You understand, right? Like a myth."

A myth, she wanted to repeat. She could tell by the way the artist fumbled with his words that he saw something more than he revealed. The crying was, if not real, then symbolic. Art, like myth, could open our hearts to a deep, primal emotion that was universal to the human experience. A painting could beget a thousand stories; it was a gateway to a myriad of myths, and, as Master Zhang had told her, this one could even connect her with the Taoist Immortals. Her intuition told her that Adrian was key to opening up this passageway. So, like the goddess Athena she crafted a way to prod him further.

"Do you like myths, Adrian?"

"I prefer to paint in silence."

"That wasn't my question."

Loukas looked up from his painting and came out of his inner thoughts.

"I like the histories of great artists and saints. But those are not myths."

"Perhaps you will change your mind about this one. It concerns art."

"Fine. Indulge me."

Loukas looked down and dabbed his brush in the paint to begin Zhen Wu's face. Meanwhile, Cassandra told the story:

"The King of Thebes had four daughters, and the youngest one was called Semele. Because the King was a great hero, his daughters grew up with everything their hearts desired. But he was also a proud king, and he had given his first three daughters only to worthy princes and heroes of other kingdoms. And so, hoping to find a worthy prince to inherit his own kingdom, he vowed not to let any man marry Semele unless he could give her the finest gift *the eyes could see*." She redirected her voice to catch Loukas's attention. "The eyes could see."

"I get it," dismissed Loukas, who didn't look up at all. "It's about art."

But the artist's apathy didn't discourage the mythologist, for she had chosen this story very carefully. She knew that it would speak to the artist's heart and maybe even persuade him to trust her.

"One day, the King decided to call in three suitors for his youngest daughter. He told them, 'If you can give Semele the finest gift the eyes can see, then you can take her as your bride, and all of Thebes will be yours.' Hearing this, the suitors became very excited. The first suitor, who was a wealthy prince from the south, approached Semele and said, 'I will give you this chalice of gold, laden with three dozen precious stones, for this is the finest gift the eyes can see.' But Semele shook her head and said, 'I do not accept your gift. A chalice can be sold for a price and soon forgotten. It is not the finest gift the eyes can see.' And so the first suitor, sad and disheartened, went on his way."

Loukas listened as he colored in Zhen Wu's elegant nose

and cheeks.

"To the second suitor, who was a mighty conqueror from the north, the King repeated his decree: 'If you can give Semele the finest gift the eyes can see, then you can take her as your bride, and all of Thebes will be yours.' This suitor decided that no man-made treasure would do, only something found in the natural world. He approached Semele and said, 'I will give you gardens of heavenly delight filled with the most beautiful flowers you can imagine, for that is the finest gift the eyes can see.' But Semele shook her head and said, 'I do not accept your gift. A garden withers in the winter. It can be neglected and left to overgrow. It is not the finest gift the eyes can see.' And so the second suitor, even more upset than the first, went on his way."

Loukas switched to a smaller brush to shade in Zhen Wu's neck and dimples.

"The third suitor," Cassandra continued, "was a nobleman from a nearby city, and he was also very clever. He commissioned the most skilled artist in Thebes to paint a portrait of Aphrodite, the goddess of beauty, and he presented it to Semele. He said: 'Dearest Semele, I know that you value what is priceless and what is timeless, and so I give you the gift of the Goddess of Beauty herself as shown in art, for its beauty is the finest gift the eyes can see.' When the King saw the painting of Aphrodite, he wept and invited the third suitor to take Semele's hand in marriage."

"Your ending is a little storybookish, don't you think?"

"I beg your pardon?"

"Surely you don't think art can be reduced to something so trivial as a beautiful gift, do you?"

"There is more, Adrian!"

Loukas wanted to call into question what the mythologist truly knew about art, whether she really understood its beauty, or was just reciting a hollow narrative. But apparently her story was not finished. And as he examined his own words, he realized it might be prudent to say nothing more. Cassandra was his only ally, after all, and he needed her help to get the *Pantocrator* and the other icons from Master Yan-Mei and Brazhnikov. And anyway, he still needed to apply Zhen Wu's eyebrows and long, pointed goatee. He switched to the smallest brush as Cassandra continued:

"Although the King was impressed with Aphrodite's portrait, Semele was not. 'Art is dear to me,' she said, 'but it also fades with time. It is not what my heart desires.' When she said this, the third suitor was infuriated. He raised his voice: 'This is a portrait of the most beautiful goddess painted by the most talented painter in the land! How can it not be the finest gift the eyes can see?' To this, Semele answered: 'You are very wise to ask me. Beauty can be expressed in gold and in flowers, and it can be expressed in painting. But even a painting of the Goddess of Beauty is not beauty itself. Art represents beauty, yes. But it only *represents* it. Therefore, it cannot be the greatest gift the eyes can see.' The third suitor stormed off and took his painting with him.

"Now, the King was also angry. He said to his daughter: 'What is this you are saying about beauty? Have you become a philosopher? Or do you simply not want to be with a man at all?' 'Oh, I do wish to be with a man,' Semele answered, 'he just doesn't exist.' 'Then since he does not exist,' said the King, 'you will settle for the next one I choose.' 'Fine,' she said and crossed her arms. 'But since you wish to deprive me of the finest gift the eyes can see, I will never open my eyes again.' She tied a yellow fleece around her head as a blindfold and went up to her chamber in tears."

Loukas found himself listening intently. He considered that Cassandra knew more about art than he had first realized. After all, she too recognized that Zhen Wu was alive and crying. Moreover, the intrigue of the myth gave him exactly the stimulus he needed for the final stage of his painting—adding fine shadows to the Taoist Immortal's illustrious face.

"Up on Mount Olympus," she continued, "Almighty Zeus heard about Semele and her suitors. He, too, knew that no mortal man could give Semele the beauty she truly desired to see. And so, in his lust and vanity he disguised himself as a mortal man and seized her in her bedroom. 'Who are you?' cried the blindfolded Semele. He answered: 'I have brought you what your heart desires.' 'No, you have not,' she presumed. 'You know nothing of what my heart desires.' 'O, but I do!' proclaimed Almighty Zeus. 'You want the finest gift the eyes can see. You want beauty itself!' 'And you, strange man,' she answered, intrigued by his seductive voice, 'how will you show me beauty?' To this he said: 'Take off your blindfold, and you shall see. But be warned! I am a god, and no one can see the true form of God and live to tell the tale!' It didn't take Semele more than a few seconds to decide she was ready. She believed only the gods could show her true beauty, and to behold it directly was her heart's greatest desire.

"Keeping her eyes closed, Semele pulled the blindfold down across her face. 'Okay, strange god, I am ready. Show me beauty itself in its true form!' 'Okay,' answered Zeus, 'as you wish.' Then Zeus emerged from his disguise as a mortal man, and when Semele opened her eyes she beheld the god with her own eyes. His body appeared as a human figure, and yet its grandeur was beyond anything seen on earth. He was double the size of an average man, and his head radiated a golden aura of power. Semele shivered in awe when she saw him, but then she crossed her arms and sighed. 'I am still not satisfied,' she told the god, 'for still what I see is your form. You are still only a representation! O, almighty god, show me beauty itself!'

"When Zeus heard this, his booming voice became vengeful. 'Who are you to belittle my form?' Storms of lightning and thunder filled the entire bedroom. And before Semele could speak or even think, Zeus shed his form and became pure light. This light was formless, and yet she could see it with her eyes. It was the brightest, most beautiful thing her eyes could ever see! Then, instantly, as the full splendor of a god was too much for any mortal eyes to witness, she fell to her face and died."

Loukas was speechless. He used his breath to dry a little of the paint.

Finally, he asked, "Was that a real Greek myth?"

"Somewhat," she smiled cryptically.

"It was quite profound. Truly, thank you." He winced with uncertainty about what he was about to say. "It also makes me think of…"

"It makes you think of what?"

"A dream I had recently."

"Tell me!"

"Master Yan-Mei showed me one of the icons she had stolen. It was of Saint Macarius of Egypt. Then, she did something to me that made me feel as though I was falling into the icon. When I landed, I was talking with Saint Macarius right there in the desert."

"Did you notice any symbols?"

"Cassandra, this wasn't a sleeping dream. I was awake. But yes, he held a black cross in his hand. He also called us demons."

"It was a vision, then."

"Maybe."

"The cross is a symbol of religiosity," Cassandra explained, "but also a symbol of unjust condemnation. The fact that he called you a demon may mean that you are condemning yourself for some reason. Maybe you are blaming yourself for something you shouldn't."

"Blaming myself?"

Cassandra paused before responding. She didn't want to presume to know too much about the artist. She decided to use questions instead.

"Didn't the Orthodox saints have visions that guided them?"

"Of course, they did. But they weren't myths laden with symbolism. They were moments of divine inspiration."

"How do you know you weren't experiencing a moment of divine inspiration too?"

"Because I'm not a—"

Suddenly, Cassandra was overcome with a rush of excitement, and she couldn't help but interrupt him.

"Adrian, I have an idea." She began looking around the art

restoration room for an icon to experiment with. "I want to see if it will work. I mean, to see if you really have visions." She pulled a dusty tarp off of a pile of old paintings stacked behind him and sifted through them.

"What are you looking for?"

"Sometimes I have visions too," she shared while searching. "I don't understand them, but the feeling they give me is real. And I have to trust them."

"Like you trust your intuition?"

"Yes. Ah-hah!" The mythologist rescued an icon of an empress stuffed between two obscure reproductions of works by the painter El Greco. "Isn't she beautiful? She will be your next adventure!"

"I'm not sure what you're getting at."

"You said that when Master Yan-Mei showed you the icon of Saint Macarius, you 'fell into his world', right?"

Loukas scratched his chin and clarified, "It was more like entering through a window. The icon was a window and we climbed through to the saint on the other side."

"Try it again with this icon!" she proposed.

Loukas's eyes settled into the icon of the empress without breaking contact. Instantly, his heart melted. Her wise, knowing smile and firm brow had shot through the air and pierced his forehead like a fishhook, reeling him in to take a closer look.

"It's beautiful," remarked the artist. He read the description: "Saint Theodora, the Empress. Ninth century."

"Don't you want to meet her?" she prodded. "All you need is to have a vision!"

"I don't know." Loukas took his sleeve and carefully wiped the dust off of the face of the Empress. "Look at the profoundness of her face! Can you see the exquisiteness of her brow and the wisdom in her hands?"

"Her beauty surpasses all the others," she concluded.

Loukas considered it a moment, and then opened up. "Let me tell you something I wouldn't normally share. I think I have felt the kind of beauty you described in your myth. In fact, I feel it every time I paint. You could say that each painting is a different vision. And when I enter into the creative process—like I have done with Zhen Wu's painting—I feel as though I am bringing beauty from a higher reality into this one." His hand made brush strokes in the air without him realizing. "I can't explain it, but I can see what hasn't yet been formed, and then I paint what I see."

"Hmm...I think there's a myth about a painter named—"

"Cassandra," he interrupted. "You're right that mystic visions are a part of the Orthodox tradition. But they're not actually visions! They are experiences of physical reality seen through your real eyes. Look at Theodora."

"What am I looking for?"

"In the Orthodox religion, we don't worship icons; that would be idolatrous. We use icons as windows, so to speak, to see the Divine on the other side, which is what we truly worship. Now, what I'm asking you to do is not to see her, but to be seen by her." He paused for her to process the suggestion. Then he whispered: "The saints are alive. The empress is alive, and she is living on the other side of this window."

Together they gazed at the *Empress Theodora*. Within a few seconds, Loukas saw the empress smiling back at him. She was alive. Inside her world, the Saint Theodora sat upon a throne of gold wearing silks of red and purple. Two angels looked upon her from above, while two phoenixes sat near her feet. An icon of Mary and Jesus rested on her lap—an icon within the icon—as well as an old, green book with Greek inscriptions. Seeing these images, Loukas knew that not only the icon's painter, but also Saint Theodora herself, had eyes powerful enough for visions of the Divine. Cassandra, too, must have these discerning eyes, he reasoned. How else could she have told the myth of Semele and the formless beauty of God so masterfully?

Suddenly Cassandra saw it too. The empress was smiling at her. The mythologist couldn't explain it, but in this icon, Saint Theodora's face was not simply an artistic rendition. It was not something abstract or symbolic, it was real! On the other side of the iconographic window, the empress's cheeks were soft and her nose was drawing breath. Her golden earrings adorned ears that were sensing everything around them. And what was even more convincing was that the empress's smile felt personal, as if it were made especially for her. She was smiling for Cassandra the mythologist, at this very moment, in order to invite her into a new way of observing the world.

Without another word between them, they leaned in. Cassandra's feet trembled. Loukas felt himself becoming weightless. The majesty of Saint Theodora's golden aura and regal crown lit up in front of them, nearly blinding them for a moment. At first, Cassandra resisted. She shuddered and held her breath. Loukas was surprised. He thought he had been the more skeptical one. But soon they both surrendered with eyes closed. They beheld Saint Theodora sitting on the golden throne in her palace. They could taste and smell the fragrance of a new realm. They had entered the world of an empress and saint.

......

"Welcome, angels," greeted Theodora from her throne.

Cassandra bowed, not fully believing she was there. It didn't feel like one of her normal visions. Beside her, Loukas excitedly widened his eyes.

"Let the angels witness," Saint Theodora continued, "that I will not let the Eastern Roman Empire fall into darkness at my husband's death. His rulership was misguided and full of sin. O, Heavenly Father! Have mercy on his soul!" The empress closed her eyes and made the sign of the cross with her right hand.

Loukas watched with amazement. His memory of Byzantine history was hazy, but Saint Theodora's next prayer was detailed enough for him to catch on:

"Dear Father, forgive my husband Theophilus for falling under the influence of the iconoclasts. Forgive him for burning the icons of the church and setting them ablaze. Forgive him for imprisoning and torturing the iconographers whose visions have led us to divine knowledge. Let me repent on his behalf!" The empress held the icon of Mary and Jesus up in front of her and kissed it. "Please grant me the strength to rule my empire and restore the icons to their rightful places. Despite what people may say, I have seen Your heavenly face! My eyes attest that icons are not idols but windows into the heavenly realms beyond this world!" She kissed her icon again and set it down on the floor.

From across the room, Cassandra stood still and tried to get a glimpse of the icon Saint Theodora was venerating. Her knowledge of Christian theology was mostly guesswork, and she wasn't sure she could name the woman and the child depicted. Whoever they were, their heads were inscribed within perfect circular halos. There even seemed to be an invisible, spherical halo surrounding *Empress Theodora*'s head, though Cassandra's eyes could not discern it definitively.

Loukas, on the other hand, could see Theodora's halo perfectly. His eyes were sensitive to its light vibrations, which tickled his retinas like little hairs upon the skin. Being present to this great saint during such a pivotal moment in the history of the Orthodox church brought him unspeakable joy. If Emperor Theophilus had not died, Loukas reflected, then all icons throughout the Roman Empire might have been destroyed. Theophilus and his armies would have raided the churches and burned them all! But with Theodora as empress, the icons would be saved, and the Orthodoxy would cherish them for centuries to come. Never had Loukas appreciated Saint Theodora's role in preserving the world's icons as he did now. And perhaps, he secretly hoped, she would be his inspiration to save the icons himself, if he could get them back from Master Yan-Mei.

"Adrian," whispered Cassandra.

"Shush! She's praying!"

From Theodora's lips came an repeating string of prayers in Greek: Κύριε Ἰησου Χριστέ, Υἱέ του Θεού, ελέησον με τον αμαρτωλόν.

"Do you think we are dreaming?"

Loukas smiled ecstatically. It wasn't a dream, he now understood. It was a mystic vision happening through his real eyes. It was exactly as Master Yan-Mei had tried to convince him—his body had moved between the seen and unseen worlds just as images do through the imagination and into reality. Everything was real!

"How do we get back?" Cassandra whispered.

All sensations lifted the artist's soul in rapture. Everything in the throne room was irresistibly beautiful. There were frescoes painted on the walls in blue, yellow, orange and white, and icons adorned the empty spaces. Even the golden light coming through the windows felt magical. His eyes were as close to Heaven as they had ever been. And he suddenly realized why this experience was so different from his visit to Saint Macarius—the Egyptian's icon was decaying. To that saint Loukas had appeared as a demon. But to the *Empress Theodora*, whose icon was restored to perfection, he was a kind of ghostly angel. The Saint Theodora trusted him and even prayed to God before him. He knew from the depths of his faithful soul that the beauty and divinity of the Orthodoxy must be saved. This was his proof that the image and likeness of sainthood could be rendered in art.

"How can you want to go back?"

"I'm not Orthodox!"

"Cassandra, this is it. What more proof of God do you need?"

Cassandra looked around the throne room. Above the throne was a curved, stylized archway supported by Corinthian columns on each side. The columns were painted a rich red, matched in boldness only by the tips of the empress's royal shoes. Brilliantly glowing icons lined the walls stretching from the throne at one end to the room's entrance at the other end, which had an archway above it similar to the one above the throne. Both arches were supported by ornately carved red columns. But it wasn't the columns that drew Cassandra's attention; instead it was a marble bust that stood on a pedestal beside the entryway.

It was the bust of Homer, the ancient bard who immortalized the myth of Odysseus and the Trojan War. Cassandra recognized him in an instant. Homer had used his skills as an orator to captivate his audience in the world of myth. His storytelling was capable of creating visions of heroes and deities in everyone's minds, revealing the journey of their own lives. His myths tapped into the collective unconscious, leading people throughout the centuries to recognize the forces of nature within them. These forces of nature were, as Master Zhang had explained, related to the Way and to the visions she was experiencing. Everything was connected. All these visions made up the story of her destiny.

"Zhen Wu!" Cassandra exclaimed, even louder than her last outburst. "Adrian, we have to get back!"

"Calm down. You don't want to lose concentration."

The phoenix at Theodora's left foot cocked its head and looked at her.

"But I figured it out! I know what to do now!"

Before Loukas could react, the phoenixes let out an alarming squawk. The sound echoed from the archway above the throne all the way to the bust of Homer above the entryway.

"Please, Cassandra, you have to concentrate." He tensed his brow and made an irritable gesture with his arms. "Otherwise she might get upset at us. You wouldn't want that, would you?"

"What are you talking about? We have to go back," she insisted.

Both of them were losing their concentration. The ominous squawking of Saint Theodora's phoenixes grew louder and louder, and their sound ran like pitchforks through the ears.

The empress raised her eyebrows and paused her prayer and commanded them, "Go, now."

Saint Theodora winked, and that was the last thing either Loukas or Cassandra saw before their vision came to an end. The artist and the mythologist were about to return through the window of the icon back to their own world.

Chapter 10

Master Yan-Mei sat cross-legged on the living room table with her hands clasping her knees. Her thumbs nestled into the soft spaces just next to her kneecaps. Her spine was perpendicular to the floor and impeccably straight, and her hair was pulled up into an infinity-shaped bun. Her eyelids were closed like clamshells repelling the tide.

Next to her, on the floor, was Brazhnikov practicing a similar meditation. His spine curved slightly to compensate for the robustness of his gut; however, as he had learned from thousands of corrections from his *shifu*, he kept his chin tucked in toward his chest. The top of his head, which Master Yan-Mei called the *baihui* point, stretched continually upward as if being raised by an invisible string. Together, their stillness produced a monastic-like silence that, like a black hole, absorbed even the faintest sounds around them into perfect and uninterruptible concentration.

Soon, a soft knock struck the door twice. It was the kind of rapping that didn't draw attention to itself, and yet its intention reached into the silence and invited an answer. Brazhnikov's eyes peaked slightly open as he sensed who it was.

"Your brother is here."

Master Yan-Mei rubbed her knees and pressed into her eye sockets with her palms. She knew her brother, Li-Kuo, was infinitely patient, but convenience urged her to get up and answer the door. When she did, her round-headed brother entered carrying a book. He wore his dark-blue martial arts uniform and greeted Master Yan-Mei with a taciturn smile. Then he turned to Brazhnikov and probed him with his eyes.

"Hello, Master Zhang," uttered Brazhnikov, followed by a nervous cough.

Master Zhang gave Leon Brazhnikov a half-smile and indicated for him to take a seat on the sofa.

"Thank you for coming, Li-Kuo," said Master Yan-Mei. She put her palms together in front of her heart. "The worst has happened. Not only have we lost our artist, but he has taken Zhen Wu's portrait with him."

Master Zhang nodded sternly, giving no words. His sister Yan-Mei accepted his silence like a fern receiving sunlight. For what seemed like minutes, the conversation was without words.

"You're right, Master Zhang," Brazhnikov said from the sofa, mocking his lack of response. He found those silent moments unbearably awkward. "We need to find Adrian Loukas, take him by force, and get it back."

"Your presumptions make you weak, Leon," his *shifu* said. "As does your need for talking." She took out a map of Athens and laid it out on the living room table. "Li-Kuo, tell us where we should go in order to find him."

Master Zhang set down his book and leaned over the table to view the map. He furrowed his eyebrows and grunted softly.

"We don't need to look for him at all. Mr. Loukas will come after us." He turned the map over to the back side, revealing a map of Greece, and pointed to Thessaloniki. "He will follow us here."

"Excellent," Brazhnikov said. "I have connections in Thessaloniki. What time is the train?"

Master Zhang squinted his eyes at the Bulgarian, but he was not in the mood to question him. Instead, he addressed his sister.

"There is something else. Mr. Loukas has a friend helping him."

"Who is it?"

"A Chinese girl. I have seen her. She is small, and not as young as she looks."

"Like you, *Shifu*," smiled Brazhnikov.

"But who is she?" asked Master Yan-Mei. "Where does she

come from?”

"I don't know. But we will soon find out. They will both draw near to us like lodestones."

"Excellent," Brazhnikov repeated, holding his jade dagger in his hand.

"Put that weapon away!" shouted his *shifu*.

"This weapon? The one that got Adrian to paint Zhen Wu's portrait?"

"Yan-Mei is right," said Master Zhang.

"No need to be condescending," snapped Brazhnikov.

Master Zhang feigned a smile.

"Leon, you must keep vigilant. Do you know what happens when you blink?"

"Master Zhang, I don't need your advice. You are not my *shifu* anymore."

"You are right, forgive me."

"Don't patronize me!"

"Enough, Leon!" ordered Master Yan-Mei.

Brazhnikov bit his lip. "Yes, *Shifu*." He sat up straight on the sofa and reached for the map.

"What my brother means," she explained, "is that your sleeping allowed Adrian to escape. Vigilance is your training."

"Understood."

Master Yan-Mei invited her brother into the kitchen, where she prepared three cups of tea. Brazhnikov remained on the sofa. While he waited for his tea, he studied the map of Greece and found the train schedule written in fine print below it. Careful not to wrinkle the map, he rolled it up into a scroll and tied it with a weathered piece of leather string. His large hands tapped it rhythmically against the table while he continued to wait for his *shifu*. His lips curved upwards in satisfaction.

The plot to catch the thieves was set.

......

On the other side of Chinatown, Jason Yin sat on his living room couch, stroking the fur of his gray cat. In front of him stood his grandmother, red with anger. She held his camera in her tight fist and shook it as she scolded him. Her words came at him like darts through the air to shame and punish him. Though they were words that Jason could barely grasp, most of the meaning was clear: the streets were dangerous and forbidden, and if he was ever caught near a protest or riot again, then his punishment would be severe.

Meanwhile, Peony's fur stood on end as she listened to the grandmother's reproach. But she kept her head sunk low and her eyelids barely open, hiding her disdain until the grandmother was out of sight and the boy left alone. The feline then stood up on Jason's lap and rubbed the side of her head against his shoulder. Jason was not in the mood for this kind of play, but he massaged her anyway, rubbing her gray fur like an agitated inmate fidgeting to pass the time.

"You're on my side, aren't you, Peony?"

The feline meowed, which he took as an affirmative reply. From the kitchen came sounds of angry ceramic lids clinking against the jars where sugar and spices were kept.

"Come on. Let's play a game."

Jason took the cat into his room. The room was so small and cluttered that hardly any of the floor remained visible except what was necessary for walking. A bed with a red frame rested in the center of the room, while a child-sized desk and chair stood against the far wall below a narrow window. Along the other three walls were shelves of games, clothes, art projects, school awards and paraphernalia to keep him materially stimulated. He didn't particularly like the clutter, but everything in his room had a place, a memory. There were no useless decorations. Every object and souvenir he had acquired over his twelve years was sacred to him, as was his freedom to retreat into his personal space when needed.

In the sanctity of his room, Jason set up a backgammon board on his bed and leaned against the headboard using a pillow. He tried not to think about his family. He knew there were things about them he didn't understand, and perhaps, also things they didn't want him to understand. His father, George, more than anyone, was the force of condemnation that kept Jason in the dark, despite being old enough to learn. And yet, though part of him rebelled and longed to know, another part of him felt a certain contentment being sheltered from the complexities of the family's past. He had never been to Xi'an or any part of China; not a single book on his shelves could have fostered a picture of China for his imagination. Instead he was free to imagine it for himself, to choose for himself how to see that part of the world and everyone in it, rather than have his family choose for him, so long as he acted correctly around them.

Jason made sure the backgammon board was flat. He put the black pieces in their designated columns and the white pieces in theirs. Each circular piece was smooth and shiny from the oils of his frequenting fingertips. He took the dice in his hands and shook them fiercely. Peony watched closely as the boy ejected the dice onto the board.

"A three and a one. What a dumb roll."

He plopped himself stomach-down on his bed and contemplated his move. He hovered his hand over one of the white pieces and examined all the options. As he did this, Peony dug the skull of her forehead into the tender crevice opposite his elbow.

"Hey!"

He held the board secure enough not to let any of the pieces move, but let his hand deviate slightly. When he looked back, he saw his fingers hovering over one of the black pieces instead. He considered how he could apply his roll to the black piece directly across from him.

"It's the same move. I could play the black side just as well."

Then an idea came to him. Since he was alone he would have to roll the dice for both sides and play according to each color's best possible move. He would have to play both white and black. Fortunately, his skill at backgammon was good enough that he could make a coherent strategy for each side without letting bias for either color influence his decisions. For the black side, he played more cautiously, making pieces travel in pairs whenever possible. For the white side, he took more risks sending single pieces traveling across the board for the advantage of distance. Each time he rolled, he genuinely wished for that side to get a good outcome. Yet simultaneously, he hoped for that side's strategy to give way to loss. When the black pieces appeared more symmetrical, he delighted himself to see that symmetry broken up while the white pieces evened out. And when the white pieces appeared further advanced around the board, he relished a secret desire for the black pieces to capture them.

Jason found that great joy could come from playing against oneself. However, this was not the joy of one side decimating the other in a thirsty frenzy. Instead it was the kind of satisfaction of orchestrating the game so that both sides had roughly an even chance at winning. The art of solitary play was to maintain a ruling balance of allegiances to both sides, so that whenever one side appeared at an advantage, the other side would catch up; whenever one side would suffer a defeating capture, or many captures, it would soon recover by getting an extraordinary string of doubles; whenever one side was close to winning, a playful error would stifle its own success and leave an opening for weakness. Like the balance of all things in nature, the solitary game was a lesson in the necessity both forward and backward, gaining and losing, never forgetting that both sides depended on each other for the game to make sense and give the player pleasure.

Eventually, however, one side would always win. That was the conundrum. No matter how closely the scales were balanced the whole way through, one side had to reach the finish line first. This ending had to come! If it did not, then what would be the point of the game? What pleasure would it bring the orchestrator to play himself at all? What reason would he have to create these beautiful alternations of winning and losing if there was no ultimate measure that they could add up to?

After about six games, he lost count of how many each side had won. He used his palms to swish the shiny, circular pieces around the board, first slowly and methodically, then quickly and frivolously. Some pieces clashed with others so strongly that they stood upright and fell over. Other pieces drifted into the pockets at the ends of the board. Those that remained in the center of the board formed a constantly changing design, like a swirling mosaic of black and white circles against a green, felt background. Shuffling the pieces in this way was relatively fun. Jason had lost track of the time. At the sign of his first yawn, he closed his eyes and began ruminating.

"Peony, do you realize how lucky you are? You're gray. Do you know what that means? It means nobody asks whether you're white or black. Gray is its own color, but what is gray? Gray is made of both black and white. Do you understand? By being gray, you are neither, but actually you are both!"

Jason didn't actually believe his cat could understand him, but he continued.

"But I am different. People see me and only see my black side, my Chinese side. I have a white side too—it's called being Greek! Sometimes I feel my black side getting too much attention, and so I make my white side win. Especially with these riots. Greece for the Greeks! Yeah, right. What color are the true Greeks? And why do I have to be Chinese? Why can't I just be gray?"

Jason stood up at the foot of his bed and ran his hands through his black, buzz-cut hair. Peony could feel his speech getting passionate, and she lifted her head like a hero awaiting a call to war.

"I don't know which side I'm on, little gray one, but I'm not going to sit in my room and stay out of the fight. Who does that? The two sides have to fight each other. That's the point. Someone has to win!" He swooped down and lifted Peony into his arms. "I have to find out if I'm Greek or Chinese. I have to play both sides, white and black."

Jason went to the window, carrying his cat, and opened

it. Cool, nighttime air wafted in, and yet the air carried with it a warm lingering resonance from the hot day. From the window, the urban noises stirred his fearless enthusiasm. Jason felt the streets of Athens calling his name. Which side would he take? The punishment of being locked in his room, he reasoned, could only be counteracted by making an escape far away. It was risky, yes, but it had to be done. His life was like the solitary game he played from both sides, and it had to be brought into balance.

"If I don't fight for something, or against something, or at least figure out what it's all about, then what's the point of being anything? What's the point of being a Chinese Greek?"

He adjusted Peony in his arms and looked up out the window. High in the sky was the constellation known as the Great Bear. In school he had learned the story of the Great Bear, which was really the goddess Callisto transformed into a bear by Hera, who was jealous of Callisto's love for Zeus. It was a silly myth, he thought, but at least it was something. It was a conflict, a fight to win. The constellations were not simply random stars; they had a story to tell, a purpose.

"Being something is the only way to live," he told himself. "I've got to find out who I am."

With that thought, Jason snuck out the window and onto the fire escape with his cat. The riots were just getting started.

Chapter 11

Cassandra Yin patted her shirt and pants to make sure she was really back in the art restoration room. She was still awake, and Loukas was there next to her. Both were sitting down in front of the *Empress Theodora*.

"Cassandra?"

"Yes?"

"What did you experience just now?"

The mythologist hesitated to speak. Despite her passion for storytelling, it seemed somehow wrong to try and describe it. Instead she looked wide-eyed at the artist and grinned. Returning her gaze, Loukas was sure she had experienced the same thing.

"Are there any side-effects?" she finally blurted out.

"To what?"

"You said you had done this before, correct? Are there any side effects?"

"To be honest, I'm not sure," admitted the artist.

"Then there won't be a problem if I do it again. You can come with me!"

"What are you talking about?"

"While we were visiting *Empress Theodora*, I figured out what I am supposed to do."

"I remember you saying that. That's what broke your concentration and made us come back too soon!"

"Listen. I told you that Master Zhang asked me to find the portrait of Zhen Wu, correct? That it had been stolen from him? Well, he said he needed it back in order to get in touch with Zhen Wu. He said that the painting was his connection to the Taoist Immortals, and if we found that painting, then the immortals would find us. Do you know what I think?"

Loukas rubbed his eyes and shook his head no.

"I think I need to enter the painting so I can meet Zhen Wu!"

The artist was flummoxed.

"Well, that won't work. It's not an icon."

"But Zhen Wu is a saint, just like *Empress Theodora*."

"He's not the same kind of saint. Listen, Christian icons may have a mystical power to them, but it's not the kind of thing you want to mess around with."

"What could go wrong?" she pleaded.

"Didn't I tell you what happened with Saint Macarius? The icon was faded. That means when we tried to enter it, Macarius thought we were demons. Even if that painting were an icon, it wouldn't work because it's too decayed."

"Then we'll use your replica!"

"No! For the last time, Cassandra, it's not an icon!"

"Please, just let me try! I need to meet Zhen Wu so I can begin my training!"

Loukas stood up and returned to his painting. It was now fully dried. It was as spectacular and beautiful as anything he had created, perhaps even more so due to the element of mystique involved. Like every one of his paintings, it was hard for him to look away from it immediately. It brought him supreme gratification to retrace it and repaint it in his mind as he studied his own creation and how it had come to be. He didn't want to let go of the connection he had forged between the seen and unseen worlds during the brief interval of time it took him to paint Zhen Wu's portrait. Like Narcissus beholding his inner beauty in the pond, Loukas could have done nothing more than admire his own art until the end of time. Fortunately, having Cassandra with him was enough to keep him present.

"What training are you talking about, Cassandra?"

"My training with the Taoist Immortals."

"I thought you were unemployed," he joked.

She raised her voice. "And I thought you were going to go

after Master Yan-Mei and the stolen icons! But no, you had to work on your painting. Why couldn't you just leave the face blank, hmm?"

Loukas looked around the art restoration room, avoiding Cassandra's question. The room smelled musty and lacked windows; he wanted to leave it as soon as possible.

"I thought so," Cassandra chided. "Either you admit there is something more to Master Yan-Mei than your Orthodox religion will let you admit, or you only finished it out of vanity for your own work!"

The artist had no defense; the Narcissus in him was exposed. He had willed his painting to completion without even a thought of why. It simply felt so natural and so divine for him to do it. But that is how his inspiration had always worked: God would implant in him the seed of a divine image, and there was no room for anything else in his mind until it was nurtured and brought to fruition. There was not even room for his wife, sadly, but that was another issue altogether.

Before hearing Cassandra's words, he had never considered this to be vanity, only a calling to which he was both morally and spiritually obliged to fulfill. But how could it be spiritual if it was outside of Orthodoxy? Or, even if he could accept that Master Yan-Mei was truly serving the Orthodoxy, how could he have trusted her to tell him what to paint? A knot formed in the artist's gut, and he felt like it was eating him from the inside. The mythologist sensed it and immediately regretted her critical tone.

"I'm sorry, Adrian, I didn't mean to upset you."

"Didn't you?"

The musty air of the library basement was taking its toll. Cassandra sighed and coughed into her elbow. The mythologist weighed her options and decided to compromise.

"As much as I want to meet Zhen Wu, I also promised to help you track down the real icons."

"Then let's get out of here." He packed up his painting into the leather carrying bag and moved toward the door.

Cassandra knelt down and placed the heavy, ancient

portrait into her backpack. While struggling, she gasped and half-mockingly made a suggestion.

"Hey, while I'm training you could go and meet Jesus!"

Loukas froze in his steps. He was within an arm's length of the door, and yet he could not continue. "Of course!" he thought to himself. "How did I not think of that? When I find the *Pantocrator*, I can use it to have a vision of Lord Jesus. It's so clear!"

The prospect of visiting Jesus of Nazareth in his own historical place and time had a swift and intoxicating effect on him. He immediately started to fantasize this encounter in his head. He visualized the colorful details of the *Sinai Pantocrator* in oil, and let out a yearning sigh. How torturous it would be for him to concentrate on anything else now that he had that thought! Every icon of Christ he passed, potentially, could be a chance to meet his Savior in person. And yet, maybe, he wasn't ready.

"I have to recover the *Pantocrator* before I can enter it," he reminded himself.

As Cassandra zipped up her bag, her cough grew worse. She tried to stand up, but her head was growing foggy and weighed her down. Fortunately, it was not dizziness that overtook her, but a vision. She closed her eyes, and her eyelids fluttered like a movie reel.

"Are you coming?" asked Loukas, still romanticizing his meeting with the *Pantocrator*.

The mythologist didn't respond.

"Cassandra, what's wrong?"

He set down his carrying bag and took the backpack from her hands. Cassandra stared down at her shoes. Her breathing sped up. All Loukas could think to do was take hold of her arms to catch her if she fell. At last, Cassandra opened her fluttering eyelids and made contact with the artist.

Then she came to and spoke. "I...I've gotten visions like this before."

"Visions? I thought you said you'd never entered an icon

before."

"They come from my intuition. Not from the icons."

"What did you see?"

"I saw train tracks leading up into a tall mountain."

"Is that all? What does it mean?"

The mythologist responded without thinking. "It means we need to go north. To Thessaloniki."

"What? Just like that?"

"I told you to trust my intuition!"

"But it's almost sunset!"

"There's an overnight train."

She walked past him and opened the exit door.

"Aren't you forgetting your backpack?"

"It will be fine here. The door will lock behind us. And Maria is nearby. Now, hurry! I think our train will leave soon."

"Suit yourself," said the artist. He wasn't about to leave his precious painting behind.

......

The library's exit led them back to Panepistimio street, where they noticed the sky was gray and cloudy.

"I hope it doesn't rain," sighed Loukas.

"You don't like rain?"

"It's ruined more than a few of my paintings." He wasn't sure how waterproof the leather back was, nor did he want to find out.

Cassandra took on a brisk pace as she headed towards Syntagma square. She led Loukas past the Hellenic Parliament building and the tomb of the unknown soldier, which they could see through the fence that lined the sidewalk. To Loukas's relief, the streets were crowded enough for them to blend in, making it unlikely that his captors would find him unless they knew specifically where to look.

Cassandra, on the other hand, couldn't stop thinking of being assaulted in the park. No public place could offer her relief anymore. She still felt the fear of that moment imploding within her. Each time she passed a stranger who seemed to stare at her, she pressed a palm against her bruised chest and proceeded forward.

From Syntagma square, they caught the subway to the train station. A dozen others got on at the same time, but Loukas and Cassandra found a pair of open seats. Despite being in an enclosed space, Loukas's anxiety returned as they sat down. The mythologist noticed his knee bouncing rapidly.

"You seem stressed. Are you okay?"

"I'm just exhausted. Maybe a little traumatized from the whole kidnapping incident, that's all."

"I forgot about that. I'm sorry I wasn't more sympathetic."

"Even though I escaped," he continued, looking vigilantly around the subway car, "I won't be fully relaxed until we're on the train."

"Why are you so willing to go with me?" she asked suddenly.

Loukas didn't know how to answer. The question was abrupt, and he had too much on his mind to try and justify what he considered to be a surrender to the will of God, wherever that might take him.

"It seemed like a real adventure," he finally said. "The kind that doesn't ordinarily happen."

"An extraordinary adventure!" she exclaimed.

"Plus, you're lucky." He wasn't sure what he meant by that, but he thought she would understand.

"But do you think we should go to the police?"

He laughed. "I don't think so."

"Why not?" She massaged the place on her chest where the bruise had been.

"You're a mythologist. Think about it. Was there ever a legend or myth in which the heroes stopped their journey and let the police do their mission for them?"

She smiled. "Not one. The heroes always persevere. Or, they run in the opposite direction. But they never just give it over to someone else."

"Exactly."

Soon the subway car stopped, and they ascended the stairs into the train station. The waiting room was filled with lines of yellow plastic chairs facing a long, windowed wall.

"Here's a seat," Loukas offered. "Why don't you rest while I get our tickets?" As a show of trust, the artist set his leather carrying bag beside Cassandra's feet and smiled. "Take good care of Zhen Wu, okay?" he said.

Cassandra nodded. As the artist walked away, she observed the movements of his lanky, slightly clumsy form. His asymmetrical gait made him limp slightly on his right foot. His right arm was tenser than his left with a higher, tighter shoulder. His was the body of someone sedentary whose posture was molded to fit one specific task: painting. She imagined him sitting at an easel, hunched over, lifting his brush and letting it fly over the canvas with beauty and ease.

Indeed, though she was fitter and more coordinated than he, there was something strong about Loukas that she admired. Unlike Master Zhang, whose perfect movements suggested a kind of infinite power, Loukas revealed his artistic gifts through his physical limitations. It was precisely this imperfect combination of tension and atrophy that allowed him to be his true, authentic self.

When the artist was out of sight, Cassandra sat down and pulled out her phone. Her duties, she reflected, were practical rather than creative. She had to call Daphne to make sure Jason was home safe, to make sure her mother had gotten her pills, and rest and regain her energy. Wasting no time, she dialed Daphne's number. After that, she called her mother just to hear her voice again. With everything changing so rapidly in Cassandra's life, she felt grateful to have a mother who cared for her, who knew her history and could always give her what she needed. Once her conversations with both of them were completed, she rubbed her phone screen in circles with her thumb as she pondered, neglecting the obvious third phone call she would have been expected to make.

It was nearly an hour before the artist returned.

"Sorry to take so long. I had to find a place to wash up. Also, I picked up some toiletries. And a phone charger."

"Thank you," answered the surprised mythologist. "But

how did you know which charger to buy?”

“I saw your phone slip from your pocket for a moment while we were sitting on the subway.”

“And you knew the make and model just like that? Does anything escape your eyes?”

“Here. We have toothbrushes, shirts and towels.”

“And something to carry them in, I hope.”

Loukas nodded and handed her a light blue backpack he had bought. Just then, the loudspeaker announced that the train to Thessaloniki was boarding.

“Don’t forget Zhen Wu!” Cassandra whispered.

“This can’t be good,” Loukas said, looking across the room. Goosebumps broke out on his arms and neck.

“What?”

“They found us. That’s Brazhnikov, with the purple suspenders.”

The Bulgarian was clean-shaven with his hair slicked back. Even from a distance away, they could sense a shiftiness in his eyes. Furthermore, Loukas noticed that his boots were larger than the ones he had worn earlier. Were they concealing the jade dagger? The artist shuddered at the thought.

“You mean, we found them. We’re trying to get the icons back, remember?”

“Right.”

“What should we do?” whispered Cassandra.

“Just try to blend in.”

Cassandra nodded, looking for any groups of travelers that they might be able to cling to without drawing notice, but then she saw something that brought her immense relief.

“It’s Master Zhang!”

Her *shifu* wore a similar dark-blue martial uniform as before, except there were no *yin-yang*s in the design, only a solid color. He was standing next to Brazhnikov at the far end of the waiting room. The two men were still and silent, like pillars standing parallel to each other, unaware of the other’s presence, or so she assumed.

While Cassandra and Loukas observed them discreetly, another announcement came on for all passengers to board the train to Thessaloniki. They grabbed their belongings and proceeded as nonchalantly to the platform as they could. To their relief, Brazhnikov did not appear to notice them. If they were to make it to Thessaloniki, they would need to keep it that way.

Just before they stepped inside, Master Yan-Mei appeared on the platform, wearing a pink, satin martial arts robe and white low-cut shoes. Loukas's heart skipped a beat when he saw that she was wheeling the silver suitcase. She greeted her brother, Master Zhang, with a hug and a kiss on the cheek. Brazhnikov bowed to his *shifu*.

"Who is she?" Cassandra exclaimed, nearly breaking her whisper.

"That's Master Yan-Mei" answered Loukas. He had an uneasy feeling there was something important that they didn't know, though he tried not to let on that he was anxious. "She's a highly skilled martial artist. I would not have thought pink was her color."

"How do they know each other?"

"I have no idea," Loukas gulped. Master Yan-Mei was full of contradictions to him. She was wise in the ways of Orthodox philosophy and understood iconography in ways beyond his comprehension; and yet her manners toward him had been abrasive, immoral, and downright scary. Seeing her warmly embrace the man that Cassandra seemed to hold in high esteem only added to the mysterious picture that she represented in his mind. Then again, he felt, if even Master Yan-Mei could be kind, then anything was possible. "Should we run?"

"No. Let's get on the train."

Chapter 12

Adrian Loukas and Cassandra Yin entered the train car and eyed their seats in the twentieth row. Cassandra decisively maneuvered through the other passengers to take the window seat, which faced the train platform, leaving Loukas with the aisle seat. Across the aisle, in the opposite window seat, sat a middle-aged woman with eyes that darted back and forth between the other passengers rapidly. She wore a tan, checkered cap and a shabby, navy blue shirt. Her trousers, ragged and soiled, suggested she had not changed clothes in a while, as did her unpleasant smell. On the empty aisle seat next to her was a green backpack, from which a curly strand of headphone cables connected directly to her ears. After a moment, she seemed to allow her eyes to close, though the way her body stiffened as the train took off suggested she was far from sleeping.

The train slowly rolled out of the station. Loukas felt somewhat relieved that they sat in the middle of the car, since it allowed him to keep an eye on both of the exits equally. The doors were open, making it possible to see into the chambers between cars and detect anyone entering the one where he and Cassandra sat. Unfortunately, being able to see danger coming didn't mean he was prepared to face it.

"Be careful with that!" commanded the deep, grainy voice of Master Yan-Mei. Loukas couldn't see her, but he could see Brazhnikov rolling the silver suitcase onto the train car from the exit chamber.

"Of course, *Shifu*." the Bulgarian answered.

Again, Loukas could tell that something was off. Brazhnikov's face was concealing something. The artist could read it in his eyes and his sinister smile. He found it peculiar that Brazhnikov seemed to block the pink-garbed Master Yan-Mei from getting into the train car. Li-Kuo Zhang muttered something to his sister Yan-Mei, and as he did so, Loukas and Cassandra both spied his spherical head peeking around Brazhnikov's muscular arm.

"They're coming!" Cassandra exclaimed under her breath.

"Try not to panic," Loukas said, more for his own sake than for hers.

A loud ringing blasted from Cassandra's phone.

"Turn that off!" shushed the artist.

"Ugh, I really have to answer. I'll be quick!" She accepted the call and folded her face down between her knees. She abruptly spoke: "I'm so, so sorry, but I can't talk now...Yes, I know it's been four days, but...I'm in danger!...No really, there's a...I'm on a train...Thessaloniki...listen, I'll call you back tomorrow, I promise...I love you too."

To Loukas's relief, Master Yan-Mei did not appear to notice Cassandra's agitated phone conversation. As other passengers were entering, Brazhnikov continued to stall for time, holding the silver suitcase in front of her and looking in the opposite direction. Then, instead of loading the suitcase onto the overhead rack, he pulled out a can of Coke from his bag and opened it. The air fizzed out.

"Will you hand me my duffle bag, *Shifu?*"

Master Yan-Mei reached for Brazhnikov's duffle bag. But without warning, Brazhnikov turned back and squeezed the Coke can, spraying it into his *shifu's* eyes. He rammed his shoulder into the blue-garbed Master Zhang, who deflected his momentum and sent the boxy-framed Bulgarian flying into the door of the train.

"Leon, what is the meaning of this?" cried Master Yan-Mei. Both *shifus* stepped toward Brazhnikov and covered him from both sides.

But the force of the hefty Bulgarian hitting the door was enough to bust the door locks. Quick-moving air rushed into the train, but Brazhnikov kept the crack small enough to not draw anyone's attention to it. Then, in one swift motion he sunk down onto the floor and grabbed Masters Zhang and Yan-Mei by the ankles. He kicked the door open behind him and let his legs dangle outside the speeding train. Master Zhang reached for his sister's hand in order to ground them both. However, instead of holding ground with her brother, Master Yan-Mei reached in vain for the silver suitcase. As such, Brazhnikov's weight was too much for the two to escape. All three of them fell out of the train and disappeared.

"What's going on?" asked Cassandra, bewildered as to why no other passengers seemed to notice the brawl that had just occurred. "Are they gone?"

"The silver suitcase!" exclaimed the artist. "They left it unguarded!"

At that moment, however, a brawny arm appeared at the base of the opening that Brazhnikov had created. The Bulgarian pulled his way back up into the moving train, but he was alone. He slowly stood up, brushed himself off, and closed the door behind him. A crew member, yawning and half-asleep, arrived and asked him if everything was okay.

"Yes, sir. I only spilled my Coke, that's all."

Brazhnikov stood in front of the door so the crew member couldn't see that the latch was broken, giving him no reason to suspect that anything was amiss, let alone that two of his passengers were thrown out of the train in a swift act of betrayal.

"Good," the yawning man responded. "Enjoy your trip."

As the crew member disappeared into the opposite car, Brazhnikov took his duffle bag and the silver suitcase and stuffed them into the overhead compartments. Then he tossed his Coke can into a trash bin and made his way towards Loukas and Cassandra. It was clear that he knew they were there. It was also clear that Leon Brazhnikov had his own agenda.

"Adrian Loukas," called the Bulgarian in a less menacing tone than he had used before. Brazhnikov stomped his heavy boots as he walked towards them.

The woman with the checkered cap rubbed her eyes

dramatically as he approached her row. But instead of respecting her feigned sleep, Brazhnikov wrapped his fingers around the bulk of her green backpack and chucked it onto her lap in order to steal the adjoining seat. "Hey!" the woman exclaimed, but then she simply hugged her green backpack and turned to lean her head against the window. Brazhnikov sat down in the aisle seat next to her and stared straight at Loukas.

"Introduce me to your friend, Adrian."

Cassandra wasn't fazed by the Bulgarian's presence. She was more preoccupied with trying to figure out how they all knew each other. Master Zhang and Master Yan-Mei had embraced like family on the train station platform. And though Loukas had said Brazhnikov was an ally of Master Yan-Mei, he had thrown her, along with Master Zhang, out of the train.

"Master Zhang!" she called, banging her fist upon the window in vain. She could find no assuring sign of her *shifu's* survival.

"Leave us alone," Loukas answered. "We don't have the portrait of Zhen Wu."

"Relax, boy," the Bulgarian answered. He held out his hand for Cassandra to shake it. "I'm Leon Brazhnikov. From Bulgaria."

She shook his hand reluctantly. "I'm Cassandra Yin."

"And I hope you really do have that painting," the Bulgarian said.

"Why?"

"Because I'm actually on your side, as you can plainly see!" He pulled out a Coke can from his large vest pocket, opened it and took a swig. "I'm trying to help you steal it."

"Steal it?" challenged Loukas. "Like you stole that silver suitcase? Do you even know what's inside?"

"The question is, do *you*?"

"The only thieves here are you and Master Yan-Mei," Loukas contended.

"Why is Master Zhang helping her?" interrupted Cassandra.

The Bulgarian squinted at her. "You really don't know who Master Zhang is, do you? It took me many years to get Master Yan-Mei and her brother to make me an inner-door disciple." He took another sip from his can and set it in the cup holder at his seat.

"They are brother and sister?" exclaimed Cassandra.

"His given name is Li-Kuo, and he was my *shifu*."

"I thought Master Yan-Mei was your *shifu*."

"They both are—or, *were*. The Zhang family works as a unit."

"If that is true," argued the mythologist, "then why did Master Yan-Mei take Zhen Wu's portrait from Master Zhang without telling him?"

"You took it!" barked Brazhnikov. He reached his muscular arm under the seats and grabbed the carrying bag from under them. He shook it excitedly in front of their faces. "We took it!"

"No, no, no!" Cassandra objected. "Master Zhang was training me to help him find it. It was already stolen, and we were stealing it back!"

"Stealing now, stealing then—it is all the same." Brazhnikov set the carrying bag on Loukas's lap. "But we can rest for a while. The train is a safe place." He reclined his seat and put his hands behind his head.

The train shot out of the Greek metropolis and into the countryside like a bee from a hive. After a few moments of processing what had happened, Loukas broke the silence.

"Mr. Brazhnikov, let me see inside the silver suitcase."

"When we get there, sure," Brazhnikov promised.

"Fine." Loukas nodded. He thought it prudent to avoid pressing the issue, as the threat of the jade dagger was still weighing on his mind. "But if the *Pantocrator* is damaged at all, I mean, if I can see even the slightest scratch, then you'll be sorry you ever—!"

"I will return the *Pantocrator* as soon as we are done here. You have my word. The *Pantocrator*, the *Saint Macarius*—I will return them all." Brazhnikov reached behind his left purple suspender and revealed a charm with a small wooden carving of the Orthodox cross attached. He was trying to show a symbol of good faith, Loukas gathered.

"What other icons are there?"

"Ah! The best icon of all! It is an icon of *Saint George*, which belongs to *Moni Zographou*, our monastery on Mount Athos. After we get to Thessaloniki, I must go to Mount Athos and return it to them, first thing. You should come with me." Brazhnikov switched the subject urgently and pointed at Cassandra. "Is she Greek Orthodox?"

"Just Greek," the mythologist answered. Loukas was disappointed to discover that this witty clarification was a routine response for her.

The Bulgarian smiled. "Just as well. The subject of Orthodoxy is where Yan-Mei and Li-Kuo always disagreed. The Zhang family has one of the longest lineages in China, going back to the sixth century before Christ, the time of the great Taoist teacher, Lao Tzu. I am not sure exactly when Master Yan-Mei became Greek Orthodox, but to her brother, this conversion was a betrayal of their ancestors. She, on the other hand, believes that Li-Kuo is 'trapped by a veil of innocence', whatever that means." Brazhnikov switched to Mandarin and asked Cassandra a question: "So you're not Orthodox. Are you a Taoist?"

Cassandra sat up straight and relaxed her skeptical brow. She was impressed with his masterful Chinese pronunciation, though she answered in Greek for Loukas's sake.

"I don't follow any religion. I'm a mythologist. But as Master Zhang—I mean, Li-Kuo—taught me, the secret Way of the Taoist religion is very much like the power of mythology. Taoism expresses the underlying order and nature of all things, and yet most people don't realize it consciously. Only the experts really understand it."

"Are you talking about mythology or religion?" asked Loukas.

"Both."

"They hardly seem similar to me. Religion deals with truth—at least, the Christian religion does. Mythology only disguises it."

"That's exactly why we need mythology."

"I'm not following. You'll have to explain it better."

"Unfortunately, Adrian, I cannot explain it," she answered. "No one can. Listen to what Lao Tzu wrote in the first verse of the *Tao Te Ching: 'The Way that can be explained is not the true Way'*. It's a classic riddle of Chinese thought. Nothing can truly be taught; one must undergo the learning for oneself. And the power of myth is the same: one cannot discover the meaning of life by hearing a teacher's words. A teacher may give us clues, but in the end the student can only find the Way through self-discovery, which is what myths are used for. That is the value of Taoism as well—understanding human nature."

"That is one interpretation, yes," explained Brazhnikov. "Throughout history, Taoists have set off to live simple lives alone in the mountains in order to contemplate the Way and learn from nature. According to the legends, some of them became so spiritually advanced that they attained immortality. Others returned from the mountains to become great martial artists. But like you said, this is a path that cannot be taught, not even by the Taoist Immortals, and not even by Lao Tzu. It was futile for him to teach about the Way using words. So, at the peak of his old age, Lao Tzu took his ox and headed west into the mountains, never to be seen again. Some say he still lives in the mountains with the other Taoist Immortals. Me, I'm not so sure. I think it's not the human lifespan that achieves immortality but the legacy that the great master leaves behind, a presence that we can connect with on a personal level."

"Lao Tzu's legacy is the *Tao Te Ching*, right?" Cassandra clarified for Loukas's benefit.

"Part of it, yes," Brazhnikov answered.

"That is what Master Zhang was explaining to me this morning," the mythologist commented. "He wants me to train with the Taoist Immortals so I can develop the power of myth."

"Yes, that is what Li-Kuo used to teach me too. But years ago, Yan-Mei grew discontented with the traditional teaching. She wanted even greater power. So, she went to the mountains and meditated deeply, until she had a revelation about the Way. She realized that most people learn by seeing, not by reading or hearing explanations. So, she reasoned, even though the Way could not be described through words, it might still be shown through images. And that is what led her to study Greek and Russian iconography, and after that, to convert to the Orthodox religion." Brazhnikov took out a miniature, hand-painted icon from his pocket and polished it with his thumb. It was of a white-bearded man robed in white with green geometric designs. Under the man's arm he carried a book, the cover of which was laden with stones of white, blue, and red. "This is Saint Leon, Pope of Rome, my name saint."

"Name saint?" asked Cassandra.

"In the Orthodox tradition," Loukas explained, "all children are named after past saints and spiritual leaders. You celebrate your name day on the day of the saint that shares your name."

"That is not the point," redirected Brazhnikov. "When I use this icon to form a personal connection with the saint, he becomes immortal to me. I don't mean in an abstract or symbolic way as he would if I studied his writings, but in a way that I can see, touch and feel. That is the genius of icons in the classical Greek tradition."

"Classical Greek?" questioned the artist. "Don't you mean, Byzantine Greek?"

"Icons were a tradition long before the Byzantine empire. In fact, long before the birth of Christ. Early Christians may have formalized iconography, but the concept of forming an image, or *ikona*, to connect us with the divine was already an ancient practice in Greece. And this tradition drew Master Yan-Mei to the Orthodox church. She has spent decades of her life searching for a way to use icons to obtain direct knowledge of the Way."

"But that goes against the spirit of Taoism," Cassandra argued. "If the true Way couldn't be taught through words, then how could it be shown through images?"

"How could it not?" argued Loukas.

"It just doesn't make sense."

"Didn't you feel it when you saw *Empress Theodora* in the flesh?"

"Feel what?"

"The power of the icons!"

"I'm not sure I understand."

"The power to see the truth."

Cassandra shook her head. "I believe that truth is something ineffable and abstract. You can think about it mythically, but surely you can't touch it. You can't get at the truth through something as mundane as an image."

"Mundane as an image?" Loukas' nostrils flared and his body became rigid. "Then what's the point of art? Or have you forgotten about our shared excursion, Cassandra? Do you think art is just a waste of time?" Brazhnikov grabbed the artist's shoulder to calm him down, but the artist resisted. "The reason for icons is clear, I should think. There is no secret Way that hides behind riddles and archaic myths. Just look at the *Pantocrator!* Or have you forgotten about that icon, Mr. Brazhnikov? Do you think Jesus is looking back at us to express some sort of Zen metaphor? No. He is showing the way to eternal life, and when you look back and feel the love in his eyes, the way is clear. The image in the icon *is* exactly what it represents: Christ the person, the son, the most perfect image and likeness of God."

On the other side of Brazhnikov, the woman with the checkered cap and green backpack sat up and stretched her arms.

"Master Yan-Mei would agree with you, Adrian," Brazhnikov explained, trying to calm him down. "The Zhang family has been using ancient art to connect with the Taoist Immortals for nearly a hundred generations. But until recently, they did not have the power of Christian icons to help them. Now you have experienced the power of the icons first-hand! You can see how Yan-Mei would get the idea to enter the icon of Zhen Wu just as she enters the icons of the saints. Meeting him in person in his own world could mean finding a shortcut to immortality. Then she could become an all-powerful Taoist Immortal herself."

"I had that same idea!" exclaimed Cassandra. "I mean, the idea of meeting Zhen Wu, not of trying to become an immortal."

"No! This is too dangerous," the artist riled. "You are playing with matters that should be reserved for God. What good can come of that? This is why religions should never mix. Zhen Wu's portrait is *not* an icon and never will be, if only for the fact that I painted it myself, and I am not an iconographer!"

"How can you deny that this is iconography?" she protested, grabbing the painting from the carrying bag and shoving it under Loukas's eyes.

"Calm down, my friends," directed Brazhnikov. He took the painting from Cassandra and held it up to his eyes. "Impeccable work, Adrian."

The artist nodded his thanks but maintained his ire.

"Both of you are forgetting why we are here," said Brazhnikov.

"I don't know about *him*," Cassandra stated haughtily, "but I am here because my mind is actually open enough to learn something."

"Holding onto my faith doesn't make me closed-minded." Loukas argued.

"Listen to yourself! Religions should never mix? Next thing you'll say is, *Greece for the Greeks!* Why can't we coexist?"

"Coexisting isn't the same as mixing," the artist said,

defending his statement.

"Then why do you mix colors together, hmm? Why not paint every shade as separate?"

"This is ludicrous!" shouted Loukas. His throat was becoming hoarse with anger. "Fine. Experiment with my painting. But I will have no part in it. What you're trying to do will never work anyway. You can't use it like an icon, because it isn't one." He stood up precipitously and adjusted his belt. "Excuse me, but I am hungry." Loukas made his way to the dining car. As he left, the rest of the train got quiet.

Brazhnikov sized up the woman with the checkered cap beside him. She was wearing headphones, though she didn't appear to be sleeping. But just when the Bulgarian was about to interrupt the woman's peace, Cassandra stole back his attention.

"What was the name of the icon you have in the silver suitcase?"

"You mean, the *Sinai Pantocrator*?"

"No, the other one. Did you say Saint George?"

"I did. Are you familiar with it?"

"Only by name. The Saint George Cathedral is where my friend Maria Stournari used to go. I remember Saint George distinctly because his icon has a picture of him taming a wild dragon. I was surprised when I saw it because Chinese culture is full of similar dragon myths."

"That is true," said Brazhnikov.

"The dragon is also my zodiac sign. I am very much a dragon."

"Then it may sadden you to know that Saint George slayed the dragon in the end."

"Oh, I guess I forgot that part."

"The most important part! Many churches have taken Saint George as their patron saint for his heroic conquest. And artists throughout time have paid homage to the great saint through their iconography."

"I imagine they have."

"But the icon Master Yan-Mei and I recovered is particularly significant. To tell the truth, it may be the most significant art piece in all of human history."

"Why?"

Brazhnikov leaned in and proffered an eerie whisper.

"Because it was not painted by human hands."

Cassandra held her breath, not sure what to believe. Her imagination could only bend so far in such a short time.

"Let me explain," Brazhnikov continued. "*Moni Zographou* was built by the Bulgarians of the ninth century. They came to Greece because they believed Mount Athos was the most remote, pristine place to escape worldly life and contemplate the path to God."

"Kind of like the Taoists escaping to the mountains."

"Yes, more or less. But the Bulgarians did not want solitude; they wanted to build a monastery and form a community of monks. And so, they ascended Mount Athos, carrying brick after brick, and completed their construction. However, they had not chosen a patron saint for their monastery. They were waiting for a sign from God. Now, the bishop of the Eastern Orthodox Church was impatient with them. He demanded that they create an icon to represent their patron saint immediately. 'What should we do?' the Bulgarians asked each other. The head priest reminded them: 'We can't paint an icon of our patron saint until we have chosen who it will be, and we can't choose our patron saint until we receive divine guidance!' But then the clever deacon had an idea: 'Maybe, while we are waiting for our sign from God, we can create an icon with a blank face. That way, the bishop sees that we are complying, and we can fill in the face just as soon as God gives us His sign.'

"'That seems most clever,' answered the head priest. Then he turned to the iconographer, who was already at the monastery awaiting instruction, and asked him to paint the body and background of a saint without a face. By nightfall, he finished the icon, except for the face. All the monks then went to their chambers to pray and then to sleep. The next morning, when they went to look at the icon, they saw that the face was miraculously filled in! It was the face of Saint George. 'Who did this?' asked the iconographer. He was furious that anyone would dare tamper with his work. But the monks had eyes that could see beyond the material world of paints and textures. They knew that it was God Himself who had finished the face. 'Behold!' exclaimed the head priest, 'God has used His own hands to paint us the sign. He has chosen Saint George as our patron.' And because of this, too, the Bulgarians decided to call their monastery Zographou, meaning Painter."

Cassandra listened intently. She thought Brazhnikov was an excellent storyteller, but she wasn't convinced that his story was true. Humans could do anything, she believed. The Taoist Immortals were teaching her that. But she didn't believe in God, and so it was certainly not possible for a supernatural force to paint an image on a canvas. She smiled politely and decided to test him.

"I think you need to show me the icon so I can understand it."

"I'm afraid I can't. Not here, anyway"

"Why not?"

"Because the icon painted by God is still at Moni Zographou. It's far too large to remove, and besides, we have no power to improve upon it. It bears the perfect image and likeness of the saint. The Saint George I have in my suitcase is a mere human rendition of the icon, and it is in desperate need of restoration. That is where Adrian Loukas comes in. Yan-Mei and I took this Saint George so that Adrian could replicate it as a painter."

"But why is it so important to restore the icons?"

"Because icons are windows into the world of the saints," Leon Brazhnikov said in his deep voice. "When your eyes meet the eyes of the saints in just the right way, then—"

"Then you enter the icon. I already know this."

Brazhnikov glared at her. "You know too much," he said sarcastically.

Cassandra laughed. "Was that a reference to Taoism? The more one claims to know, the less one really knows?"

"It's a reference to you, here and now. If you want Taoist instruction, I suggest you go to Zhen Wu himself."

"You mean...enter the icon right now? Is it safe?"

"Don't worry. It's an overnight train ride. I'll watch over you until you come out. I'm just as curious as you whether you will be able to enter it, especially since Adrian painted it under duress." The Bulgarian laughed and pulled out another can of Coke from a pocket in his vest. He cracked the seal just as he heaved a heavy sigh. On the other side of him, the woman with the checkered cap adjusted her position and resumed leaning her head against the window.

"Are you sure?" Cassandra asked. She wasn't entirely sure she could trust Brazhnikov. On top of that, she also worried she was not yet ready to meet the Taoist Immortal. "You'll protect me until I come out of it?"

"You have my word."

Cassandra nodded. His offer piqued her curiosity too much to let the opportunity pass. She pulled a hair tie out of her pocket and fastened her hair tightly into a ponytail. Then she emptied her mind and prepared herself for a new round of training. She clutched Zhen Wu's portrait with both hands and pressed it onto her lap. Then she curled her stomach inward to bring her eyes close to the immortal's face. A shiver went down her spine. She couldn't imagine where this legend would take her.

"It's okay," Brazhnikov comforted her as he patted her shoulder with his monstrous hand. He directed her to hold the painting closer to her eyes.

As Cassandra leaned in even further, she felt the train's vibrations getting fainter and fainter. The rich colors of Loukas's painting glowed in her imagination. She imagined the Taoist Immortal looking up and listening to the birds overhead, smelling the sweet pine-scent of nature in the mountains around him. She imagined him holding up the text with three Chinese characters and instructing her what they meant. She focused all her attention and energy on these colorful details until all physical sensation left her, and her body relaxed into a deep sleep. Her limp head rolled over and hit against the window.

Everything went dark.

Chapter 13

It was a wild and tempestuous time for Greece. For decades, the country had toiled in economic hardship. High-paid professional jobs were scarce, and most educated people could only find secure employment beyond the border. Naturally, the immigration waves consisted of working class people, some displaced from Syria and other war-torn nations, others simply seeking community in a more amicable corner of the world. Some started up restaurants, others opened import stores.

The Yin family ran a local laundry business, which was now headed by Cassandra's brother George. Like all foreign-run enterprises, Yin Family Laundry had weathered both the rising and the falling tides of fortune. Business in Chinatown thrived when it could appeal to the Greeks' adventurousness in trade and marketship. Unfortunately for all Chinese Greeks, the present moment fell amidst a wave of public intolerance and discord.

Since the age of ten, Jason Yin had been trained to pick up and deliver laundry to customers all over Chinatown. He learned to load laundry bags on his father's square, wooden pulling cart, which sat on plastic wheels that clattered even on the smoothest of sidewalks. His father taught him punctuality, good manners, and how to navigate his route in the most efficient way while avoiding the alleyways that were deemed 'too dangerous'. It was these alleyways that intrigued him most, now that he was setting out on his own, defying the rules and charting his own course.

Jason Yin climbed out his bedroom window and descended the fire escape carrying Peony in his arms. By the time his feet reached the ground, he was panting like a lion. The small feline leapt from his arms and took to the street beside him. Jason wasn't sure what he would find, but he knew he needed to confront the chaos of Athens alone. The riots were forbidden to him. He knew that if he were caught in any danger his grandmother would punish him severely. And yet, his stronger impulse led him to risk it all in order to discover his true identity among the Greeks and the Chinese. To discover himself, Jason knew he would have to defy his family's code and set out from his home like a warrior braving the darkness, like a hero into the unknown.

The irony, however, was that when one looked for danger it sometimes concealed itself too well. Not every dark alley was the proverbial meeting place of cloaked hoodlums he had imagined. In fact, the maze of corners and passageways throughout Chinatown seemed to act as a shelter to Jason, a protective labyrinth wherein no harm could reach him. He found wanderers, but no mischief makers; smells of liquor and tobacco smoke, but no dirty dealings; loud music, but nothing frightening. Even the dirtiness of the streets appeared less sinful now that he was there by his own power. Everything had its rightful place within his familiar neighborhood.

As Jason calmed his breathing, he wiped his sweaty hands on his sleeves and listened to the noise in the distance. It was a kind of modern jazz band with a saxophone, a guitar, drums and a traditional Greek *bouzouki* thrown in. He didn't recognize the song they were performing but the style appealed to him, and so he followed the music until he could see where it was coming from: Nero's Lounge, an Italian restaurant which, according to his friend Petros, was where men took their wives to fancy dinners. Outside of the door, a female hostess with short, brown hair stood behind a podium to greet hungry passers-by.

"Excuse me," Jason addressed the hostess.

"Are you looking for someone?" she asked the boy.

No one was watching him. There were no rules. So, he decided to play a trick.

"I...not sure," he answered with a thick Chinese accent.

"Who are you looking for?" asked the hostess, this time in English.

"I...hungry."

"You're hungry? Are you lost?"

"I...so hungry!" he said, persisting with his charade. He grabbed his stomach and winced as if in pain.

"Where are your parents? I can't let you in without your parents."

"O...kay," Jason answered, looking up at the woman and dropping his arms to his side.

The woman glanced at Jason a moment longer and then asked: "Where are you from?"

"I'm from here! Where do you think?" Jason snapped, this time with perfect Greek pronunciation.

The hostess rolled her eyes. "Get out of here, you prankster!"

Peony hissed at her and sauntered away. Jason followed.

"Peony, where are you going?"

The feline led Jason away from Nero's Lounge and toward a metal bench across the street. The bench was spray-painted with blue and white diagonal lines, though Jason could not gather why. Above the bench was a street light that flickered dimly.

"Come on, let's sit down."

He took the cat into his lap and rested on the bench. He rubbed the spray-painted line back and forth with his fingers, which he kept lined up together like boards in a sturdy plank. Thanks to his *Kung Fu* practice, even a simple movement like rubbing made him feel strong and coordinated.

As his eyes moved to the blue lines, his mood turned thoughtful. Blue was his favorite color. It always made him think of bright summer skies and placid Aegean seas. But it also reminded him of the little blue ribbons his piano teacher used to tie around his wrists while practicing so she could yank them up if his hand posture ever sagged. He rubbed his left wrist with three right fingers as the memory came to him.

The pressure from his fingers left brief white marks, which delighted him to watch vanish before his eyes.

As he eyed the painted lines on the bench again, it occurred to him that white and blue were the colors of Greece's flag. Maybe it was a coincidence, or maybe it wasn't. Jason wasn't sure he believed in coincidences. There must be a reason, he told himself, why he was sitting on that bench at that exact moment, hearing music from Nero's Lounge across the street, sitting beneath a street lamp that didn't light up fully, playing with his hands.

"You!" a raspy, male voice exclaimed. "Little boy!"

Jason looked up to see a raggedy, old beggar in gray clothing. The beggar looked familiar, and he certainly seemed to recognize Jason.

"Who are you? What do you want?"

"Give me my coins!"

Suddenly Jason remembered where he had encountered this man. It was last Saturday at the Marathon Street market, and Jason had been on his way home from school. He was bouncing a hacky sack on his knees as he pranced about the street, so oblivious and carefree that he bumped into a fruit stand, causing a row of ripe, yellow and red peaches to fall onto the pavement. The boy apologized, but the vendor demanded he pay for the peaches in the amount of three euros.

Not knowing what to do, Jason nodded his head and kept quiet as he picked up the peaches from the ground. The vendor held out a bag for him and smiled, saying it was okay and that a little dirt wouldn't spoil the fruit. But Jason panicked. He turned to the side where a beggar was sitting and stuck his hand into the beggar's cup. To his amazement there were exactly three euros in the cup. Before the beggar could realize what was going on, Jason threw the sack of peaches on his lap, placed the coins on the counter for the vendor and ran off. The memory was vivid, and it was now coming back to life.

"Not until you give me my peaches!" Jason shouted back, standing up slowly.

"You owe me," the beggar demanded, then he reached

down and scooped Peony up from the bench.

"Hey! She's mine!"

The beggar's gray clothes were soft and stank of fish and saltwater, which may have explained why Peony seemed unfrightened. But Jason was not at ease. Though the man was Asian, he was clearly not Chinese—his accent was sharper and his tone less melodic than that of Jason's dad and grandma. Nothing about this man felt warm or familiar.

"Three euros. Or I keep her for good."

Jason fought his urge to strike the man with his fists. Master Nikos had taught him that the mark of a good warrior was to use violence only as a last resort. Instead, the warrior was to stand tall with a calm attitude, and in most cases, this would make people listen to him. And if that didn't work, then he was to walk away and alert the authorities.

"You can't very well give her a home, now can you?" Jason spoke calmly. He kept his feet together, his knees slightly bent and his body as still as he could.

"What do you know, little boy?"

"Nothing," Jason answered, giving a half smile. "How about we play for her? Backgammon, I mean."

The beggar scratched his nose and looked around. After blinking a couple times he set Peony down and sniffed. Then, without warning, he lunged toward Jason with his arms, trying to reach into the boy's pants pockets for coins.

"Gimme my coins, you trickster!"

But Jason stood firm and deflected the man's attempts to grab him with a simple *Kung Fu* block.

"No. Leave my cat alone."

With that, the beggar spat on Jason's sneakers and walked away empty handed.

"Ha!" Jason gloated to himself. He thought about how proud Master Nikos would have been. He couldn't wait to tell Aunt Cassandra he had defended himself and saved Peony from a foreign man! Except he realized he could never admit to being out in the streets at night alone.

"Wait a minute! Where's Peony?"

The cat was nowhere in sight. The wind suddenly howled in his ears.

"Peony!" he shouted "Here, kitty!"

Jason ran around the corner to Alexandros Street. His calm was lost.

"Give her back to me!" he shouted into the wind that blew against him. But all he could hear was the flapping of a Greek flag billowing in the breeze. "She has a home, you know!"

The night wind was cool, and goosebumps appeared along Jason's arms. Above him was a flag just like ones he would see out in front of many people's homes. It was as large as a kitchen table and hung from a diagonal pole at a 45-degree angle. The flags people wove in the riots were similar, only smaller, and the poles they held were narrower and much more agile. How fun it must be to chant and wave a flag, he thought.

Suddenly an idea dawned on him If he was going to investigate the riots, perhaps he should have a Greek flag with him for protection, so he could prove he was a patriot. He could borrow that flag while no one was watching and take it with him—this was a plan, at least. He studied the flag's position and determined it could be done.

After the wind died down, he climbed onto a nearby trash can and reached up to feel the flag. The blue and white stripes of the fabric folded softly in his grip. Reaching higher, he traced the stripes up the flag's diameter with his fingers and saw the blue and white lines intersecting at the corner to represent the Christian cross. He didn't know much about religion, except that his mother hated going to church. She had told him that Greece was an ancient country full of old relics, and that religion was one of them. But Jason wasn't sure. He saw more than just history in the cross and in the flag; Greece was also his present reality, the world that kept him alive in that very moment. Most of the country was foreign to him, like all the history he had learned in school, and yet its traces were alive within him, flowing through him like blood in his veins. Greece was his home.

"Pssst!" whispered a faint female voice from a nearby window.

Jason shivered and let go of the flag. He looked up and to the right. "Sorry!" he whispered back. "I just really love my homeland!"

The girl leaned farther out the window and gasped, "I know you!"

"You do?"

"You're the boy who picks up our laundry."

Jason lifted his chest and looked proud.

"I knew it!" she said. She examined his green t-shirt with the tiger image. "Aren't you cold without a jacket?"

"Nope."

"What's your name?"

"Jason."

"How old are you?"

"Twelve."

"And what are you doing out there?"

"Maybe you could try answering questions instead of asking them." Jason crossed his arms and shifted his weight to keep his balance atop the garbage can.

"What questions?" she said with a sarcastic flare. "You want to know about the flag above our kitchen window? Okay, I'll tell you. That is the flag my father brought home with him from the army."

"Oh."

"Aren't you going to ask me my name?"

"Fine. What's your name?"

"Sophia."

"Want to come down and help me find my cat?"

"Aren't you going to ask me how old I am?"

"Fine. How old are you?"

"Well, I was born twelve years ago, but my soul has been around much, much longer."

"What's that supposed to mean?"

"Some of us are old souls. Do you believe that? Do you believe we have souls?"

"You're not making sense. If you're twelve, then you're the same age as me. What else is there?"

"Ugh. I guess you're just a laundry boy after all."

"I'm also good at math!" he protested.

"It's late. Why aren't you sleeping?"

"I just told you. I am looking for Peony, my cat."

"Do you want to know why I wasn't sleeping when I saw you?"

Jason found Sophia's leading questions annoying.

"Do you ever let me ask my own questions?"

Sophia looked up at the sky for a moment, then she disappeared into the shroud of her bedroom leaving the window open.

"Sophia? Where did you go?"

He looked around to make sure no one had caught him talking to her. Seconds later, after he had climbed down from the trash can, the girl appeared in front of him.

"I climbed down the fire escape outside my parents' bedroom window," she explained.

Jason paused for a moment to examine the girl. She was a forehead taller than he, and she had on a royal blue gabardine coat with a hood covering her pulled-back hair. Her cheeks were round and full, and her nose was long and pointed, giving her somewhat of a cartoonish face.

"Your parents aren't sleeping?"

"They're working," she explained.

"Oh."

Jason continued to study Sophia's appearance. Her coat came all the way down past her knees and had more buttons on it than he could count all at once without getting distracted by counting. Quickly she uncovered her left wrist and showed him her silver watch with a leather strap.

"It's a quarter past eleven," she said. "That means I have a little over an hour till my mom gets home. I can help you for that long."

"What about your dad?"

"He's away." She crossed her arms and looked up, aloof.

"But I'll help you find your cat."

"Thanks."

Jason led Sophia back around the corner to the bench across from Nero's Lounge, but the gray Peony was nowhere in sight.

"This has to be the ugliest bench I've ever seen!" Sophia exclaimed.

"It's not so bad. Blue and white!"

"I forgot. You're a patriot."

"Is that such a bad thing?"

"I'm not even Greek," she confessed using a bragging tone.

"You're not?"

"Nope. My dad's Greek, but my mom's Chinese."

"I'm Chinese!" Jason exclaimed, immediately regretting saying it. Never had he been so quick to claim the foreign half of his identity.

"I thought you were Greek!"

"Behold! A Chinese Greek, in the flesh!" He held out his arms in a sarcastic gesture.

"And in the soul," she said mysteriously.

"Whatever that means."

Jason took Sophia down Alexandros street in the other direction. This was one of Chinatown's busiest mercantile areas. Six full-sized vendor carts were covered with enormous tan tarps and tied down with ropes to shield them from animals, rain and thieves. Farther down was a row of boarded-up buildings with vines sprouting from their walls in all directions. The street fed into a larger boulevard, marking the end of the Chinatown district, where there stood a monument of the beloved mythical character, Icarus. The monument was made of coarse marble and depicted Icarus falling to the ground and crashing in his legendary show of hubris.

"Do you really think Peony could have gone this far?" asked Sophia.

He shrugged. "She probably went home. I don't think we'll find her out here."

Sophia was furious. "Then why did you bring me here?"

"To find out if you're Greek or Chinese."

"What?"

"Do you know about the riots?"

"Of course, I do. Do you think my head is buried in the sand?"

"Look!" he pointed. "Omonia district is that way. That's where those riots were!"

"Don't you think I know that? Why do you think my dad says never to go to Omonia?"

"All the more reason we should go!"

"You're crazy!" Sophia protested. "People were killed there!"

"Then the police will be all over it. They'll protect us."

"But what if they chase us?"

"Trust me. I know *Kung Fu*. I can defend you!"

"That doesn't make me trust you. Actually, that makes me distrust you."

"Then listen to my heart." Jason grabbed Sophia's hand and placed it on his chest. Startled, she gasped noticeably, then relaxed with a faint, warm smile as she listened to his heartbeat. Then Jason held her hand to his chest with both of his and looked into her eyes. "Sophia, I'm your neighbor and your friend. You can trust me."

Ashamed, she broke eye contact and withdrew her hand. She looked out across the boulevard towards Omonia and then back at the boy who had appeared under her window. "But what are we going to do? Do you have a plan?"

Jason skipped three paces ahead and held out his arms with enthusiasm. "Don't you see? The future has no plan. We make it as we go! Come on!" He galloped down the sidewalk toward Omonia. Sophia squeezed her elbows and ran clumsily to catch up with him. A sudden chill made her shiver. She tried to convince herself to trust Jason, but this was not where she wanted to be.

"Hey, laundry boy!" she called.

"What!" He stopped and rolled his eyes. Her choice of name for him was almost as annoying as her slow pace.

"You should slow down. Pace yourself. Don't be like Icarus."

"Icarus?"

"I'm saying, don't fly too close to the riots," she said with a timid smile. "Didn't you study mythology?"

"Listen!" he said to her, lifting his hands to his ears.

"I don't hear anything."

"Exactly."

"So?"

"Don't you know? From the greatest silence comes the loudest thunder."

Sophia considered his statement and briefly admired its poetic merit. "Then let's stick together."

Jason nodded. As they continued walking, the forbidden Omonia district looked exactly as Jason had pictured it: dark like charcoal, filthy and aesthetically repulsive. Instead of familiar carts and tarp-covered wagons, there were boarded-up newspaper stands. Instead of elegant graffiti made of Chinese characters, there were hideous caricatures of Greek politicians, none of which he knew by name but could recognize from the television. With a calm chill, Jason realized he was no longer in Chinatown's protective labyrinth. He was on the outside, exposed, far from home.

Even if there was danger, he had a mission. Between the Chinese and the Greeks there was a living game to be played, a challenge to be had, a lesson to be learned. He could no longer ignore the yearning in his heart to understand the conflict, nor could leave alone the questions his parents refused to discuss. He could not accept silence as his final answer.

For all of Greece, that night, the silence was about to end.

Chapter 14

Cassandra Yin blinked and looked around. The air was fresh and damp, and the sky was filled with towering clouds of all different shades. Black trees with crisp, green leaves surrounded her. All the colors seemed too bold to be real. The sun in the sky was a deep red, while the dirt beneath her feet was an unnaturally uniform mocha color, almost like clay. However, everything around her was also pulsating with life. As a gentle wind greeted her face, a trio of small, pink butterflies fluttered by. They were so graceful and gentle that they barely needed to move their wings to glide on air. Cassandra observed everything without moving and she listened without thinking. She was alive and breathing in the world of Zhen Wu, seeing China as he saw it four hundred years ago.

As the butterflies glided out of sight, Cassandra closed her eyes to experience the wind on her face. In the distance she could hear the cheerful chirping of sparrows greeting each other. The breeze tickled the hairs on the back of her neck as if to tease her. She smiled, feeling laughter bubble up, though she remained silent. The benevolent, red sun shone brightly above her like a hot lamp. Perceiving these things so vividly made her feel like a child again. It emptied her of all expectations and opened her to a sense of wonder not felt since she had left China all those years ago. Slowly she began to shift her legs. The dirt ground beneath her feet felt mutable and uneven, a refreshing contrast to the mostly artificial, paved grounds of her birthplace, Xi'an. Finally, she had returned.

After a few minutes taking everything in, she decided to practice the Wu Chi posture Master Zhang had taught her in the hopes that such a tranquil environment might strengthen her ability. She bent and relaxed her knees and allowed her arms to float up in front of her, trying to empty her mind of the pressures and distractions of her own world.

After a long minute, she could feel the discomfort again. Her mind begged her to stop. But she persisted and forced herself to concentrate on the posture, remonstrating herself, "have you no discipline? Not even a full minute has passed!" But the discomfort in her legs and arms gradually devolved into pain. Her limbs trembled from the strain of staying in Wu Chi position for so long. Her mind was defeating her once again.

Abruptly she exhaled and stood up straight, then turned around. There, sitting on the ground, was Zhen Wu, exactly like he appeared in Loukas's painting. His long, black goatee shot down from his chin like a one-pointed waterfall ending decisively at heart level. He was even holding the scroll with the three Chinese characters that Cassandra could read: *jing, qi*, and *shen*. She knew these characters had some significance to Taoism but was unsure of their specific meaning. In order to receive the lesson from her new *shifu*, she knew she would have to keep her mind open and not presume to know anything. At least, that is what she imagined Master Zhang would have told her.

As Cassandra calmly squatted down to take her seat in front of the Taoist Immortal Zhen Wu, she could feel his powerful aura. Sitting at eye level, she felt his gaze to be even more penetrating than before. Yet she did not feel threatened in his presence. She felt safe, curious, wide-eyed, and inspired to begin her training.

"Good day, *Shifu*."

Zhen Wu paused and held the scroll close to his navel for a moment, then he looked up and waited for her to speak.

"Do you know who I am?" she asked him.

The immortal gave a nearly imperceptible fraction of a nod. Cassandra checked her posture, which had just begun to slouch. She tried to relax and sit tall as much as she could to show she was ready.

"I have a few questions for you, *Shifu*," she began.

"First, sit correctly," snapped the immortal.

"I thought I was," she answered, disappointed.

"You think too much."

"Right." She made her back as straight and perpendicular to the ground as she could "Master Zhang said the same thing."

"Fortunately, there is a remedy for thinking."

Emptying the mind, she thought, must be the remedy he was referring to. With this in mind, Cassandra focused on her peripheral vision and tried to become mindful of her surroundings. In the distance beyond a curtain of mist she saw a great mountain peak, just as there had been in the painting. On the mountain's highest peak, a temple stood between two giant stone walls like a small book sandwiched between two tomes. Above the mountain was a sea of ethereal, wave-like clouds. Some of the clouds looked like curvy blankets covering the landscape with proud layers of blue and white; others looked like steps leading from the mountain peaks up into the heavens. And there again, in the distance, was the mysterious red turtle with a snake coiled around its shell. Those two animals appeared to gyrate and dance. Then, at once, they vanished, leaving an ominous shadow in the space where they had been.

"The Taoist Immortals have cultivated herbal remedies for thousands of years," explained Zhen Wu. "They possess infinite healing properties."

Cassandra looked down and noticed that he had put down his scroll and was holding a round, seaweed-green tea cake the diameter of her hand's length, partially wrapped in white tissue paper. Also, a white ceramic teapot and two jade-green cups had appeared in front of them along with a rectangular, beige lacquer serving tray.

When she saw these things, she inwardly lamented that she had failed to notice him setting them out in front of her. "So much for being mindful of my surroundings," she thought to herself. But she brought her attention quickly back to the tea cake. The wrapping paper was marked with the Chinese character *shou*, meaning longevity. She knew this to be the kind of tea cake that was aged for long periods of time—sometimes years—and drunk only on special occasions, like a fine Greek wine.

"Mount Wudang has many mysteries, Cassandra." With his adept hands the immortal broke off a crispy piece of the teacake and placed it into the teapot. The smoky smell of aged tea filled the air. "Would you like to know why you are here?"

"Well, Master Zhang said the world was aching and asked me to help him find a painting of—"

"No, no," the immortal interrupted. "Your teacher is of no concern to me."

"But then how do you know my name? Aren't you connected to Li-Kuo Zhang and his sister Yan-Mei?"

"Many ancient family lineages are connected." Zhen Wu lifted the teapot and poured out the first strain of tea into a nearby receptacle, as was customary to do in order to make sure the tea leaves were thoroughly cleansed before drinking any tea. Then he refilled the teapot with hot water, waited a few seconds before filling both of their cups. Cassandra politely tapped her finger on the stone as a sign of respect for receiving tea. "It is true the Zhang family comes to train with me from time to time. But you haven't come for training, have you?"

"Yes, *Shifu*, I have."

The immortal squinted at her. His long, pointed beard wiggled as his face turned skeptical.

"Telling myths is my skill," she added, trying to prove herself. "I have passed all my examinations and achieved the highest degree possible. But now I wish to learn the Way. Teach me to use mythology to heal my country of its conflicts. This is my *Kung Fu*. My destiny."

"Very well," he said. He took a quick sip from his teacup and wiped his goatee. "But I warn you. Self-cultivation is not easy on Mount Wudang.”

“I am ready for the lesson, *Shifu*,” Cassandra affirmed. She took a sip of tea but immediately recoiled. It was still boiling hot.

“Maybe you are too ready,” the *shifu* muttered.

“Too ready?” she said, blowing on the tea in her cup.

“How can a cup be filled when your cup is already full?”

“With respect, the tea is too hot to drink.”

“You are the cup, Cassandra. The Way is the tea. How can you learn anything if you come to me full of skills and readiness?”

“Hmm,” reflected Cassandra. She took a tiny sip of the scalding tea and tried to hide feeling the burn on her tongue. The aged tea left a smoky taste in the back of her mouth.

“But that is beside the point,” he added. “Yan-Mei and Li-Kuo have decided to send you to train here on their behalf, it seems.” He took a sip from his own teacup and wiped his goatee. “Come. First, I will take you to the monastery and show you where you will stay.”

“Stay?” She immediately thought of the world she came from. In Greece, there was a train headed for Thessaloniki, where her body lay sleeping next to Brazhnikov. “What do you mean, *Shifu*?”

“Training takes time. Did you think you could learn from me in only one day? One lesson?”

“How long will it take?” she asked.

“That is up to you.”

As the *shifu* stood up, his head and shoulders ascended smoothly and evenly like an elevator. Cassandra set down her teacup and stood up also. She had trouble seeing through her glasses, so she took them off. To her amazement, her vision without them was perfectly clear.

“I can see! But how?”

“Infinite healing properties.”

Cassandra placed her glasses in her pants pocket. Zhen Wu led the speechless mythologist to a path leading up to the temple.

"After you complete your work here," he explained, "not much time will have passed in your world."

"But the training could take days, no?"

"Arrogant girl!" Zhen Wu shouted. His booming voice seemed to echo throughout the hills. "Monks train with us for many years and still do not master their *Kung Fu!*"

"Years!?"

Without reacting, the *shifu* took to the ascending path in front of them with quick-footed, leaping strides. The mythologist followed him. The path was steep and required stepping upon large rocks and tree roots. Her legs and feet did their best to keep up, but soon she was gasping for air. The immortal was so far ahead of her, she could barely see his white robe. She worried that if she didn't keep up, she would vanish from his world altogether.

"Wait for me, please!" she shouted, looking down at the ground as she tried to catch her breath.

"These paths were made long ago by—"

"Ahh!" the mythologist screamed, startled to find Zhen Wu standing directly behind her.

"As I was saying," he continued, grabbing Cassandra by the waist and proceeding to push her up the path, "these paths were made by our ancient master Yong-Le, a disciple of Lao Tzu. Yong-Le came to Mount Wudang to cultivate the Way in solitude. But he had to make his way through its thick brush and harsh terrain in order to reach the summit. Yong-Le was the first Taoist to climb the mountain and survive. Everything that we have built on Mount Wudang began with Yong-Le's success."

Cassandra's legs still hurt, but she kept up her pace. Zhen Wu released his hands and let her climb the rocky path without help.

"How long did it take Master Yong-Le to reach the summit when there was no path?"

"Many months, according to the legend. Yong-Le started

from the foothills. There was no civilization nearby, only rivers, trees, and rocks. And these things were not always so friendly to him. Sometimes he had to stave off his appetite for days at a time. He also had to make shelter from the snow as winter came."

"That sounds like an excellent way to train," said Cassandra, trying to show that she understood something about the austerity of the Way.

"Cultivating the Way is about getting in touch with the physical aspects of ourselves, even if it means battling nature's harshest elements and nearly dying in the process."

"That is exactly what I am learning," she explained. "There is a physical side to the Way in addition to the philosophy."

As she spoke, her tired breath regained its vital rhythm, and she increased her speed.

She continued: "For example, I have learned to tap into my intuition and let it guide me in the right direction, like a vision."

"Do you know what our intuition is made of?"

"It never occurred to me that intuition could be made of anything."

"It is made of energy."

"You mean, physical energy?"

"Energy inside you is awakened by your knowledge of the Way. It enlivens your body and makes it pulse with light. You want to access the source of myth? You must cultivate energy within yourself. By the way, do you know what this energy is called?"

"Isn't it called *qi*? The second word from your scroll?"

"It is indeed," he affirmed. "*Qi* is the bioelectric current that flows within us, allowing the body to perform all its functions."

"Bioelectric current?" She knew the ancients of her culture had wisdom beyond their time, but she never imagined an 17th-century monk would use such modern-sounding vocabulary.

"To build strong *qi*, you need to keep the bioelectric current flowing constantly inside you. See? You can feel it in your fingertips."

It was a kind of tingling sensation, yet it didn't come with the numbness of having cut off the circulation. This sensation felt strong and energetic, and yet also vulnerable, receptive as well as active.

"Is that why Master Zhang had me practice holding my arms to form a circle?"

"*Qi* is not a mystery like you think. We can observe its creation quite well. *Qi* comes from *jing*, the seminal fluid of creation. *Jing* accumulates in the kidneys. We all produce *jing* naturally, and we choose what to feed it to. If we use *jing* to nurture our body through proper exercises and herbal supplements, then the core of our being becomes a reservoir of *qi*, and it enlivens us forever. But if we let *jing* grow stale, our *qi* becomes stifled. When *qi* is blocked in a particular location in the body, poor health results there. When we master our *qi*, our entire body develops an aura of radiance called *shen*."

"*Jing, qi, shen*," Cassandra recapitulated, recalling the three words from the scroll.

"If we look closely at an enlightened person, we can see their *shen*. It hovers around their head like a round halo."

Cassandra could not resist her curiosity to turn around and look back at him. She found if she squinted her eyes, she could manage to see a faint circular halo around him—the halo of his *shen*—just as he had described. At first it seemed too surreal for her to believe. She thought about whether Loukas, with his ingenious eyes, would be able to see it too. But she knew the artist would never allow himself to enter Zhen Wu's portrait. He would never betray his Orthodox faith by considering it an icon. And yet everything around her appeared to be as real as their surroundings had been when they entered the icon of *Empress Theodora*. Zhen Wu had a halo like the saints in the Orthodox icons, which surely proved that his teaching of *jing, qi* and *shen* must be true? And who other than a Taoist

Immortal could have mastered these things? The questions, her surroundings, all of it seemed to be inviting Cassandra further into the legend.

As master and student continued up Mount Wudang, their conversation tapered off into occasional words interspersed with introspective silence. Slowly, the red sun descended beneath the foothills, and the sky went dark. Zhen Wu led Cassandra up more stairs and into a small hut. There, next to an altar with a stone statue of Guanyin, the goddess of compassion, she would get a temporary bed to sleep the night.

"Rest, Cassandra," the immortal said with gravity. "But don't rest too much!" Those words stayed with Cassandra throughout the night. Taoism, as she understood it, was a philosophy of moderation. Anything could be taken to an unhealthy extreme, even rest.

Sleeping felt bizarre in the world within the painting. Cassandra's visiting body was in a state of inactivity, and yet her mind was not fully unconscious. She remained alert to her duty, even excited, despite the immortal's stern warning about the difficulty of monastic life on Mount Wudang. As she slept, visions of the peaceful moonlight shining upon the mountain filled her eyes.

The next day, as her training began, she realized how unprepared she was. Being a lifelong academic had furnished her a sense of discipline; however, she was not used to applying it to a physical training. Zhen Wu took her to a spot at the summit of Mount Wudang he called Heavenly Pillar Peak. This was a giant, rocky land formation that jutted out of the mountain like a pillar ascending toward the heavens. The mind, she suspected, would need to be conquered again.

"This is your first task," explained the *shifu*. "Find the quickest way to climb Heavenly Pillar Peak."

"Okay," she said. "First let me practice Wu Chi."

"No!" scolded Zhen Wu. He placed his hands on her back near the kidneys and pushed her forward. "Climb it now!"

Cassandra did her best to take to the task with an open

mind. First she circumnavigated the base of the peak looking for the smoothest incline. However, she couldn't avoid needing to use her hands to climb over rocks and fallen logs. It was a dense, vertical wilderness unlike any place she had seen before. She carved switchbacks into the trails, circling up the peak over the course of about three and a half hours, with periodic pauses to catch her breath and massage the soles of her feet.

When she reached the top, she congratulated herself. But when she turned to find Zhen Wu had beaten her to the summit, his expression suggested that any celebration would be premature.

"You have failed."

"What? How?"

"Your ascent was slow. Too much meandering!"

"But I was searching for the quickest way up!"

"When you search, you do not find. In order to find, you must give up the search. Follow your intuition, remember!"

"Right," she remembered. "Empty the mind."

Before she could finish the thought, the scenery transformed around her. She and Zhen Wu were standing once again at the base of Heavenly Pillar Peak. Without further words, the *shifu* prompted her to try her ascent again. This time, she was invigorated. She tried not to think, just to follow her intuition. Each time she observed a potential path, she decided not to judge its ease or its difficulty; instead she kept her attention on how to use the natural landscape. She hurdled branches that she had previously avoided, and when her intuition told her she had reached an impasse, she backtracked to find a different path. When she reached the top for the second time, she was much more tired than before, though she also felt even more accomplished.

"Yes! That was so much quicker." she boasted.

"No!" the *shifu* screamed. "Have you learned nothing?"

Instantly she found herself at the base of the peak again, her heart discouraged and her spirits crushed. Once again she felt a sense of the surreal, and it disappointed her. She had not even managed to appreciate the view from the summit.

"But I followed my intuition!" she protested. "I shaved at least two hours off my time."

"Two hours or two minutes, the time is irrelevant."

"What? How can the time be irrelevant? You told me to find the quickest path!"

"I have not contradicted myself, Cassandra. It is your mind which struggles against itself."

Her chest ached with frustration.

"Please, just tell me what to do!"

"Listen to yourself, young one. Do you hear the sound of failure?"

"I mean no disrespect," she pleaded, "but how can I do what you ask if I don't understand what you are asking?" Her chest was pounding, and this made her whole body ache. She bent over and placed her hands on her knees to catch her breath.

"Stand straight when I'm speaking to you."

She obeyed.

"Did you not ask to be trained? Did you not accept my instruction and claim it as part of your destiny?"

"I did, *Shifu*."

"Then get rid of your need to understand. Listen to what Lao Tzu wrote in the *Tao Te Ching*:

......

Not-knowing is true knowledge
Presuming to know is a disease
First realize that you are sick;
Then you can move toward health

......

"You are weak with disease, Cassandra. Your impatience, too, is a disease. Quickness, for an immortal, has nothing to do with time."

Cassandra lowered her head, nearly in tears. Her mind and body had been stretched too much. She wanted to go back to reality.

"I thought so," chided the *shifu*.

The look in his eyes was heart-wrenching. In it she imagined herself having not only failed this teacher but also her culture, her legacy as a Chinese native. She worried that her logical Greek sensibilities had robbed her of the ability to internalize Zhen Wu's teaching, for to do so would mean surrendering all she knew, her entire education. Even her vast knowledge of mythology was just a 'disease' to him. Cassandra sank to her knees and sobbed. She felt impotent and worthless. She felt hopelessly unworthy to accomplish all that Master Zhang had invited her to. Her soul, she lamented, like her homeland, might remain forever divided.

When she opened her eyes, Zhen Wu's face had changed. It was hard to describe, but in that moment, he looked more like a snake than a man. His eyes glowed red with ferocity. His round cheeks bulged with a kind of reptilian gluttony that fed on the weakness of unsuspecting prey. Standing in front of him was like cowering beneath a cruel and indifferent beast, which she could not understand. It was worse than her vision of the *yin-yang*—at least, in that vision, the destruction was symbolic and not immediately in front of her. But in Zhen Wu's snake-like visage, she could see the reflection of a beast within herself, a fierce and wretched nature within her own soul that she could never hope to tame.

In the blink of an eye, Zhen Wu's face returned to its normal, human appearance. Peace once again flowed from his dark eyes and soothed Cassandra's aching heart. She cleared her face of errant tears as the *shifu* redirected her attention.

"Take a look at this tree," he said. "It is a plum tree. They're very common here. Plum trees bear fruit every year."

Cassandra nodded and observed. The Immortal's sudden, brief transfiguration had been so inexplicable that she struggled to think, much less form an intelligent reaction.

"Do you notice this branch? It has grains entirely different from the plum tree. Do you know why? We grafted this branch onto the plum tree just before you arrived. The branch comes from a betel nut tree, not a plum tree. Do you think it will produce betel nuts? Of course, it is the nature of a betel nut branch to produce betel nuts as its fruit. But we may be certain, Cassandra, if you can train with discipline for as many seasons as come to pass until this branch produces plums for its fruit, then you shall call yourself Master."

"But that's impossible," whispered Cassandra. "How can you change a plant's nature by grafting it onto another plant?"

"Do you think all things keep their nature forever? The nature of all things is to change. Even your own nature, as you have been grafted like a branch and planted in this new environment. What matters is not the time it takes one to change, but the path before them that leads to transformation. When you commit yourself to that path, anything becomes possible, even the impossible."

"I think I understand. I'm like the betel nut branch, and Mount Wudang is like the plum tree. After I spend enough seasons practicing the Way on this mountain, my nature will transform and I will be able to produce the fruits I seek in life."

"Do not seek the fruits!" Zhen Wu cautioned. "Keep them far from your mind. The fruits are a distraction! We may seek a certain result, but the result must not be your motivation. It is only feedback as to whether we are making progress. We cultivate the Way for the sake of the Way, not because we want something from it."

"But how long will it take? Years?"

"We cannot know. Now, go quickly. Climb Heavenly Pillar Peak."

Cassandra attempted the climb a third time. This time, she attacked the peak at its straightest and steepest point. Sweat and tears dripped from her face as she grappled the earth and stones with her hands to pull herself up. With each climbing footstep she let out a hopeless groan. Her knees smashed and bruised themselves against the dusty forest ground. Even her forehead sagged and pounded upon the soil, until she could no longer press forward. She had to give up. It was too steep. She had failed the training.

Chapter 15

When Adrian Loukas returned to his seat on the train, he found Leon Brazhnikov sitting with the unkempt woman in the tan checkered cap. From the looks of it, they were engaged in a flirtations dialogue, stroking each other's hands and cheeks like two teenage lovers. The sight of the rough and stocky, middle-aged Bulgarian cuddling and cooing romantically was enough to make the artist question reality. Loukas couldn't decide who was more enigmatic—Brazhnikov or Master Yan-Mei.

Without disturbing them, he took his seat next to Cassandra, who was sitting slouched with her eyes closed and her hands to her sides. The marble slab lay face-down on her lap. It bothered him to see his painting lying there so carelessly. However, not wanting to disturb her sleep, he left his painting alone and began eating the deli sandwich he had bought. Half-way through the sandwich, the compulsion finally got to him. "Art should not be placed face-down," he thought. He carefully lifted the painting off of the sleeping mythologist's lap and turned it face-up, then set it back down on top of her. He couldn't help himself. Fortunately, his movements didn't seem to wake her.

The high-speed train connecting Athens to Thessaloniki was nicknamed the *Silver Arrow*. It shot through the Greek countryside like a meteor in the night. From the window, Loukas admired the rocky hills and fertile valleys of the heartland. He recalled how, in ancient times, many Greek city-states were completely isolated from each other—connected only by seafaring routes by way of the coast. Now the *Silver Arrow* made it possible to zoom from the south to the north of the country in less than a day. It was a perfect vehicle for escaping the menaces who hunted him, except that they knew his intended destination: Thessaloniki. How else could he explain how they knew to find him at the station in Athens? They must have known it. Like the *silver arrows* of Artemis, goddess of the hunt, Loukas was sure Masters Zhang and Yan-Mei would lock onto him like homing missiles and chase him down no matter how far away he tried to get.

Cassandra, he presumed, was getting much-needed rest. Her eyelids flickered, indicating she was in REM sleep rather than a quick doze. And yet, to the keenly observant eye, something about her body suggested discontent. The knuckles in her hands were sharp, and her fingers seemed to fidget and grip her seat cushion like a bear clawing at a tree trunk. Her legs pulsed with subtle undulations which moved her knees slightly forward and backward, alternating a millimeter or so at a time. In her dreaming face, too, he sensed an expression of disturbance. But, he figured, since he had only just met her, nightmares might be her usual pattern, so he tried not to worry himself.

What was more concerning was Brazhnikov. Loukas wondered what the Bulgarian's personal motive could have been for throwing Master Yan-Mei and Master Zhang off the train. Surely, the artist considered, if his Orthodox faith was sincere, he would have a compelling reason to betray them. Then again, given all of Brazhnikov's surprises since his capture on Mount Sinai, Loukas wasn't about to place his confidence in the fellow any more than his and Cassandra's safety required. Beyond that, there was still his unfinished business of retrieving the *Sinai Pantocrator* from its silver suitcase. Loukas decided that the time was now or never. While Brazhnikov was busy in his amorous dialogue with the woman to his left, the artist would sneak a peek, just to make sure the icon was inside. He gripped the arm rests of his seat in order to stand.

"Hey, you!" barked the surly Bulgarian before Loukas had even set foot in the aisle. Without turning his head, Brazhnikov placed his generous index finger on the woman's worried lips, saying, "*Da. Da.*" Then he turned to face the artist, who fell back into his seat immediately and returned eye contact. But the Bulgarian's eyes spoke more of sarcastic pity and derision than anger.

"What's the matter?" asserted Loukas, not wanting to appear weak or subordinate.

Brazhnikov laughed. "If you're thinking about grabbing my suitcase, quit it." He turned to the woman and muttered something in Bulgarian, to which she also laughed like a schoolgirl.

Loukas softened his guard and tried to laugh with them. "Aren't you going to introduce me to your *girlfriend*?"

"Adrian, the stars have been very kind to us tonight." He reclined his seat so the woman could see Loukas a bit better. "They have delivered to me an angel!"

"I can see that." He extended his hand. "I'm Adrian."

"My name is Devora," she answered, removing her checkered cap. "I don't normally dress like this. I just came from a dig."

"Devora is a renowned archaeologist."

"Actually, I'm just a digger."

"And Bulgarian, too!"

"A match made in heaven," commented the artist.

"My angel," cooed Brazhnikov, "tell him why you're going to Thessaloniki. Adrian, you won't believe it!"

"Why?" Loukas asked.

"My brother Svetan lives in a monastery on Mount Athos."

"Tell him which monastery, my princess!"

"*Moni Zographou*, of course. There is only one Bulgarian monastery."

"You mean, he's a monk?"

"Not only is he a monk," Brazhnikov interjected, "he is the head caretaker of the entire monastery. That means," he explained as he made a key-turning gesture with his hand, "he can open for us any door that we may choose."

"Svetan is a good man," Devora said, defending him

preemptively. "He will help you restore the icon of Saint George."

"Adrian doesn't need any help with that," Brazhnikov assured them both, looking directly at Loukas's gifted eyes. "He's already proven himself as an iconographer."

"Actually, I'm not an iconographer!"

"Splitting hairs."

"And that painting of Zhen Wu is not an icon!"

"Then how was your *girlfriend* able to use it, hmm?"

Ignoring Brazhnikov's silly joke, Loukas glanced abruptly at Cassandra. She was still quivering in her sleep in the seat on the other side of him. But now, Loukas saw a frightening expression on her face, as if she was struggling with possession by spirits. "Cassandra?" he called, failing to get a response. He wasn't sure which to fear more: that she was merely dreaming and Brazhnikov was messing with him, or that his painting had actually succeeded in transporting the mythologist to the historic time and place of Zhen Wu. Either way, he dreaded finding out.

"She's not my girlfriend. I'm married, you know," Loukas retorted, sustaining the half-sarcastic tone which, apart from being annoying to maintain, actually helped him forget about the danger he was in.

"Oh? Where is your wife?" asked a smiling Devora.

"Sharon is…" Loukas held his head up high. For his second time pronouncing the news, he wanted to own it as his own decision rather than look like a victim. "Well, she and I are separated."

"Ah." Brazhnikov winked at Loukas and delivered an awkward, conniving smile. "I see how it is."

"You don't see anything."

Devora whispered something flirtatiously to Brazhnikov, making him erupt in a jolly laughter that seemed to shake the whole train. The *Silver Arrow* slowed down as it approached the town of Larissa. A handful of weary passengers began shuffling for their baggage.

"You're a serious type, aren't you, Adrian?" commented Brazhnikov. He reached across the aisle and placed his large hand benevolently on the artist's shoulder. "You'll fit right in on Mount Athos."

Loukas recalled what he knew about Mount Athos. It sat isolated from the rest of Greece on a peninsula accessible only by boat, and was one of the holiest mountains in the Orthodox Christian world, after Mount Sinai. Monks from Greece, Serbia, Russia, and Bulgaria had built a total of twenty monasteries on its placid peaks. The entire mountain carried a certain mystique about it, as if to go there would be to pass from one world into another. He recalled once seeing black-and-white photos of Athonite monks smiling radiantly as they did their daily monastic chores: weeding the gardens, fixing up weathered cracks in the walls, drawing water from rustic-looking wells, and praying before icons. From what he could tell, it was a peaceful, fulfilling lifestyle.

Despite the artist's penchant for pilgrimage, practical reasons had stripped him of any previous inclination to visit Mount Athos, even during his visits to Thessaloniki when it wouldn't have been inconvenient. Athos was a province dominated entirely by men. Even into the 21st century, women were prohibited from even entering. Loukas had loved his wife. Since she couldn't go with him, there was no point in going. Whether or not the rule made sense, he didn't question it. Instead he worked around it, which meant avoiding Athos and turning to other focal points for his faith.

It is true that the Athonite monks had made an exception once: during the Nazi invasion women were allowed to take refuge on Mount Athos for the safety of their lives. After that, the ancient rule was restored. Since then, some of the Orthodoxy's most faithful spiritual seekers privately criticized the rule, asserting that women's spiritual presence was not only worthy of Athos but also necessary. They argued that both male *and* female make humankind complete; therefore, the holy mountain was incomplete without an equal monastic presence of women. Loukas might have agreed in principle, though his rule-following mind prevented him from challenging the order in any meaningful way.

"Mr. Brazhnikov, I think you're forgetting something."

"What's that?"

"What about Cassandra? Mount Athos hasn't admitted women for a thousand years. I don't think they're about to start now."

"Have faith, Adrian. We know the gatekeeper now. Besides, the Orthodoxy has never had a problem with women, per se, nor has it denied that women could attain the highest state of spiritual enlightenment."

"Then what's the reason for the rule?"

"That's simple. The rule was made because men feared that women would disturb the peace of Athos. They feared that the so-called 'feminine energy' would bring an imbalance by arousing men's sexual desires. But those men never acknowledged one basic fact: both male and female energies make up the balance of spiritual perfection. Both men and women are needed in order to perfect the soul. Think of it as *yin* and *yang*."

"What do *yin* and *yang* have to do with it?"

"*Yin* and *yang*," Brazhnikov explained, "are how all opposing forces in the universe mix and mingle. Dark and light, warm and cool, male and female—these are all aspects of *yin* and *yang* in Chinese philosophy."

"That's interesting, but it has nothing to do with Orthodoxy."

"Orthodoxy may not use the words *yin* and *yang*, but do we not also understand the essence of what is male and what is female in God's universe?"

"Of course, we do."

"And do you remember your comment to Cassandra earlier? You told her that religions shouldn't coexist."

"I said they shouldn't *mix*, not that they shouldn't coexist."

"Maybe in your mind there is a difference. But how can two things coexist without mixing? That is the lesson of *yin* and *yang*. Opposite forces like male and female tend towards each other and mix together. That is why in the image of the *yin-yang*, black spirals into white and white into black, and the two colors even penetrate the other from the inside."

"But isn't that the point? That they are opposite forces? Maybe the rule was made so male and female could be known separately before they mix."

"The rule was made because the men of the times were not yet spiritually advanced enough to recognize the truth of the matter."

"The truth? What truth?"

"Adrian, do you think that you are only a male? Do you think Cassandra is only a female? Why, the truth is, we all have elements of both. We're all made up of both light and dark, both *yin* and *yang*, so to speak. We're born from both a mother and a father."

"That sounds like a philosophical argument divorced from reality."

"Who are you trying to defend?" said Brazhnikov shaking his head. "Think about it. The monks of Athos made a rule to exclude women not because they wanted to rid the place of all feminine energy—how could they do that when they themselves were born of women?—but because they wanted to perfect the balance of male and female within themselves. And in fact, there is one woman who has always been essential to monastic life on Athos."

"Who?"

"The Virgin Mary, of course."

"I suppose so. But—"

"Try to expand your mind, my friend. We are all a mix of both *yin* and *yang*. No one is completely one or the other. We're all womanly at times and manly at times. We're all somewhat dark and somewhat light, partly rational and partly emotional, a bit male and a bit female. Cassandra has just as much *yang* energy as you and I do. Can't you perceive that? And for this reason, I assure you, when we enter Athos, as long as we don't draw any attention to her sex, no one will stop us. They won't sense anything in her to disturb the spiritual balance of the Athonite tradition. She will be fine."

"There's also the problem that she's not Orthodox."

"Ha-ha, yes, there is also that," the Bulgarian replied as if it were hardly a concern.

"I just hope you're right," sighed the artist. He didn't want to incur trouble with the monks. but his desire to avoid arguing outweighed his impulse to question Brazhnikov's reasoning any further.

As the train pulled out of Larissa station, the artist and the Bulgarian prepared to sleep the rest of the night until the train reached Thessaloniki. Devora had already dozed off, folding the brim of her checkered cap over her dirty, green backpack and resting her forehead upon it. She clutched the bag in her sleep like a rugged pirate guarding her bounty.

Loukas closed his eyes and pictured the *yin-yang* that Brazhnikov had referred to. He imagined the faces of male and female saints mixing together in the light and dark sides of the figure. Strangely enough, the mixing in his mind felt harmonious and natural rather than defiant. He slept without dreaming and without shifting in his sleep even once.

Brazhnikov took up his usual nocturnal mumbling, though it was quiet enough not to disturb the peace. Cassandra slept more soundly than the rest, filled with the slumber of four hundred years past.

......

Outside the train windows, the sun dawned, filling the dark, receptive sky with light. Beneath this celestial meeting of *yin* and *yang*, the two women and two men awoke in their seats and greeted each other.

"Adrian, where's your painting?" asked Cassandra, making sure she still had her glasses. "You will not believe what I experienced!"

"Oh no!" he snapped, picking it up from the floor and checking to see it wasn't damaged. "You dropped it in your sleep."

"How long was I asleep?"

"For most of the night. You must have had a dream," said Loukas disparagingly.

"Your painting is very nice," commented Devora as she tried not to yawn. "Leon showed it to me earlier while you were getting your sandwich."

"Did he show you what's in his silver suitcase?" asked Loukas.

"The Saint George, remember? The icon we're taking to Zographou."

"But did he show you what else?"

"You'll see your precious *Pantocrator* later," interjected a grumpy Brazhnikov with pungent morning breath. "Right now, we need a plan for getting past our *shifu*." He pointed out the window on Cassandra's side as the train pulled up to the platform. Sure enough, both Master Yan-Mei and Master Zhang were waiting there.

"How did they make it here before us?" Cassandra's heart began to pound and she wondered if the Bulgarian was the ally he claimed. "What if they see us?

"We should try and avoid that." Brazhnikov reached into his seat pocket and grabbed a can of Coke he had stashed there. "Now that we've broken our relations with them."

"*I* haven't broken anything," the mythologist asserted. "And neither has Adrian. I still don't understand why Master Zhang didn't recognize me. He has no reason to think we stole Zhen Wu's portrait. If anything, we were trying to return it to him."

"I see," answered Leon Brazhnikov. "So, you brought it with you to give to him, then?"

"Well, no," Cassandra admitted. "But it's in a safe place."

"A safe place, I'm sure. Hidden from the people it belongs to, while they chase us down to get it back."

"That's not fair!" she argued. "Zhen Wu told me himself that I was training on their behalf."

"Hmm, training on their behalf, behind their backs. That seems like stealing to me." Brazhnikov caressed Devora's thigh with his hand. "Don't you think, my angel?"

"I've seen many precious artifacts," the digger answered. "Some even Chinese, like your painting. They always seem to switch hands in the middle of the night."

"What does that mean?" asked Loukas.

"I mean, people will obsess over any old discovery. They take things for all sorts of reasons. They buy them, pawn them, lose them. But does anyone really own an artifact?"

"Not individually, no. But I think, as a culture we own them," Cassandra reasoned. "Like your Saint George. Was it wrong to take it even when your intentions of restoring it were for the good of many?"

"I never said stealing was wrong," the Bulgarian clarified. He winked and took a giant swig of his Coke.

"That's right," Loukas attempted to joke. "Sometimes Mr. Brazhnikov even steals *people*."

"Look here, you devil," snapped Leon Brazhnikov. He raised his hand as if to slap the shorter man's face from a downward angle. But then he felt Devora rubbing the back of his neck as they spoke. He lowered his tone, though his anger remained. "I did what I had to do. I played a role. Isn't that what we're all doing?"

"Now who's the serious type?" the artist commented snidely.

"You're a temperamental bastard, you know that?" He swished his Coke and sniffed it, then took another sip.

"Quickly, my prince," Devora said soothingly, pulling Brazhnikov to his feet. "Let's get your bags."

Relishing his mental victory over Brazhnikov, Loukas leapt out of his seat and led the rest of them off of the train. He carried his painting of Zhen Wu in the bag over his shoulder, while the Bulgarian toted the silver suitcase and held his duffle bag with a single hand. Fortunately, the train had pulled up far enough that Masters Zhang and Yan-Mei were out of sight.

"This way!" called Devora. "Svetan parks his car in the south lot."

"Keep it soft, my dear," shushed Brazhnikov as politely as he could.

A cool breeze poured through the platform. It was the kind of breeze that made Cassandra think of her father. During her childhood in Xi'an, her father used to take Cassandra up into the foothills in the summer to watch the butterflies. It was one of her favorite memories. The Yin family farm sat on the outskirts of town, just beneath Camel Hump Hill. A dirt trail embossed by unbridled grass led straight up between the two tall humps of the hill, where the wind would speed up due to the narrowness of the crevice. It was also the shadiest part of the hill, which made for a spectacular phenomenon: for about forty-five minutes each day, the sun would reach just high enough in the sky for light to fill the space between the peaks. Butterflies would then flock to glean the hidden nectar of flowers that revealed themselves only at that secret, magical moment.

Now, feeling the wind being sucked through the narrow channels between train platforms, Cassandra gave into the pull of her memory. She reached her hands up into the air in front of her as if to form the twin peaks of Camel Hump Hill. Slowly, her footsteps halted. Her hands formed fists, the knuckles of which now resembled the hills more clearly.

"Cassandra?" called Loukas.

But she didn't respond. Just as her name dissipated into the wind, a pink butterfly descended from the heavens and landed on her right thumb. It was the same shade and character of the ones she had seen on Mount Wudang during her brief training. Feeling the tingling from the little insect on her skin, she smiled and gently opened her hand, lifting it up into the air like an offering to the gods. But as she was caught in this wistful moment, a deep, grainy female voice spoke to her.

"Don't think of running away from us."

Instantly, the butterfly vanished, and Cassandra's eyes fell upon the person in front of her.

"Master Yan-Mei?" The *shifu* made no reply. Even the wind died down in order to mark the ambient silence. "Is Master Zhang really your brother?"

"Your Bulgarian friend," Master Yan-Mei responded, ignoring her question, "has taken something very valuable from us."

"Leave her alone!" cried Loukas. About thirty meters away, Brazhnikov was holding him back, refusing to let him come to Cassandra's aid.

"Where is Master Zhang?" The mythologist tried to keep her voice from shaking.

The round-headed Master appeared behind his sister. As Cassandra looked at him she noticed something strange. In Athens, Master Zhang's round face had been completely shaved and had a shiny glow. Now, it was spotted with stubble and boasted a silver goatee. Something was different about him.

"You should choose your friends wisely," Master Zhang said to her coldly. "It is easy to dodge an enemy's arrows, but difficult to evade the spear of one close to you."

"I have nothing to give you!" she protested. She pulled the light blue backpack off of her shoulder and opened it in front of them.

"Wrong," corrected Master Zhang, using a menacing tone that surprised her. "You have everything to give us."

Cassandra could feel Master Yan-Mei's lethal hands grab her right wrist and twist it against her shoulder blades, and yet something inside her told her not to resist. Master Zhang—the Master Zhang she remembered—had taught her to visualize herself sinking all her energy into the earth, like a river, emptying all thoughts from her mind. If that *shifu* were here, she thought, he would have instructed her to give into the movement instead of fighting it. As she gave in, she could feel the tingling sensation of *qi* in her fingertips, the energy from which she was made. Her body felt dense and still, like a stone. Then, as if to release the energy, she pushed all of her weight back into Master Yan-Mei, forcing her to recoil. Then, once Cassandra's hands were free, she held them out in front of her with her palms facing up.

"Don't you know who I am?"

"What is she doing?" Master Zhang asked his sister.

Not fully aware of the source of knowledge from which her movements came, the mythologist held her arms into a circle with her fingertips just slightly apart. She could feel *jing* stirring up inside her kidneys and *qi* flowing through the circular formation of her arms. Then, in a sequence the Taoist Immortals would have called the *double-bumping palm*, she turned her palms to an outward pushing position. She could feel bioelectric energy pulsing up and down her spine. Like a tractor, she pushed through air with her palms facing forward, keeping her arms in a circle to keep up the flow of *qi*.

She ran as fast as she could, not even minding the direction, just maintaining her energy and trusting her intuition. An intense aura of light seemed to form around her palms, then around her whole body, then around the entire train platform. The aura of light felt vast, powerful, and yet empty, like a universe contained within a vacuum.

Unable to control herself, Cassandra sped ahead with her palms pushing forward. The intense light of her *shen* was blinding her to the outside world, holding her in a profound vision of ecstasy and power as she ran to evade her pursuers. Though her senses were overstimulated on the outside, inwardly she felt the peace of Mount Wudang radiating from her like an aura, a perfect culmination of *jing*, *qi*, and *shen*. Time seemed to stop for a while. Then the light faded and her body became still.

The next thing she knew, Cassandra was sitting in Svetan's car.

Chapter 16

Cassandra could no longer see the light or feel the *qi* in her fingertips. Instead she felt the rumbling of a jeep engine below, and she saw the concerned, bewildered faces of Loukas and Devora on opposite sides of her. They were packed into the back seats of the jeep, while Brazhnikov sat in the front passenger seat, occupying as much of its ample room as he could. Devora's brother Svetan, the monk, was driving.

"Where are we? What happened?"

"I've never seen anyone run so fast in my entire life!" exclaimed Devora.

"We'd better not be dealing with spirits here," the monk declared firmly. He held his index finger up at Cassandra, though he kept his eyes on the road.

"Relax, brother," Brazhnikov told him. He reached into his knapsack pocket, which was empty, and then jumped up in his seat. His eyes opened wide like a fish. "We're going to have to stop at the convenience store."

"We don't have time!" cried Loukas, who, to Cassandra's great relief, held his painting of Zhen Wu on his lap.

"What a weakling, the way you whine all the time," chided Brazhnikov. "You want my protection? I need my fuel."

"We also need to stop to get our *diamonitirion*," explained Devora. "That's the entry pass pilgrims must bring onto the ferry. It's a very important document. You can't get to Mount Athos without it."

"I'm familiar with the *diamonitirion*," Loukas replied with a sigh. "I just never thought I'd actually need to use one."

"You never wanted to come to Mount Athos?"

"No. Not while I was married, anyway."

As Svetan made a sharp left turn he interrupted them and

called to Cassandra.

"What's your name, boy?"

"Me?"

"Who else?"

"Tell him," prompted Brazhnikov with a wink.

"George," she answered, thinking of her brother.

"And how did you come to be Greek Orthodox?" the monk asked.

She bit her cuticle. She wasn't prepared to lie twice.

"My family...came to Greece years ago...from China. But I wasn't—"

"George's family and I go way back," Brazhnikov interjected. "I took *Kung Fu* classes from his mother, Yan-Mei, who was baptized Greek Orthodox in Athens."

Inwardly the mythologist shuddered to think of Master Yan-Mei as a mother figure. But the lie was sensible enough that she could play along. She smiled and nodded as Brazhnikov expounded on his extensive dealings with the Zhang family. He had lied so naturally she wondered how much of it was true. Their banter got quicker as more and more Bulgarian phrases seeped in. But eventually their dialogue closed, like an elegant book, coming to the conclusion of nothing more than tacit solidarity among compatriots. The jeep's engine hummed more softly as they stopped at a traffic signal.

After the bumpy ride, they came to a gas station. Next to it was a convenience store with a large service window. Pilgrims from all over the Orthodox world—Russia, Serbia, Finland, even India—lined up at the window to receive their *diamonitirion*. The streets were sanded with summer dirt, while in the distance a band of French tourists stood about holding maps and arguing over directions. After turning off the engine Svetan got out of the car and stood in line at the window. Meanwhile, Devora ran into the store to fetch a case of Coke for her companion. The smell of the old jeep was strangely comforting as the three of them sat in silence.

Loukas broke the silence: "Leon, I'm still worried about us

trying to bring Cassandra into Athos."

"What, the disguise? You don't like the way she looks?"

"No, not just the disguise," the artist explained. "I mean, come on, as an Orthodox believer you can't be comfortable breaking the rules like this, can you?"

"I told you before, Adrian. Cassandra is as much *yang* as you or I. Her presence as a woman will not disturb the peace of Athos."

"That's not the point!" he insisted, shifting his hands emphatically and trying not to shout.

He knew it was prudent not to pursue the matter any further, though it was a stretch for him to accept a new interpretation of the rules. He felt like one of the people Jesus had compared to "old wineskins," incapable of holding any new ideas just as old wineskins cannot hold new wine without bursting. The wine stains on his shirt only emphasized the analogy. Caught in an inner dilemma, he kept quiet and furrowed his brow, trying to let it go.

"Are you okay, Adrian?" asked Cassandra.

"You're not the only one who can see things beyond what the eyes are capable of seeing," Brazhnikov said to Loukas in a more amicable tone. "Isn't that why we're all here?"

"It's okay, it's okay," Cassandra said, helping him ease his forearms back into rest upon his legs.

"I'll be fine, Cassandra," he said, taking a deep breath to relax his body.

"It's George, remember?" she said.

Loukas softened his brow and chuckled softly, somewhat in a state of disbelief. If he was to get through their mission, he would have to acquiesce. He would have to become like the new wineskins instead of the old. He drew in another quick, deep breath and affirmed her disguise: "Right. *George*."

The monk and his sister soon returned to the car. "Here are your passes," said Svetan as he handed them out.

"Why only four?" asked Loukas.

"You think Devora is coming with us? Bah! Then who would

drive the car back to Thessaloniki? No, she is not coming. We'll get on the ferry by foot."

The monk led them on a short walk to the ferry dock. As they checked their documents, Cassandra adjusted her ponytail to make sure it looked boyish enough not to draw attention. Brazhnikov and Devora kissed goodbye, and the three of them followed the monk aboard the ferry without delay. They found seats on the top deck under a large blue-and-white-striped awning designed for shading pilgrims from the sunlight. Unfortunately, the morning sun was still low enough that its blinding light still struck them from the side. Nevertheless, the deck was bustling with eager pilgrims, young and old, bound for the monasteries of Mount Athos. Not wanting to speak too much, for fear that her voice might give her away, Cassandra watched the billowing of the Greek flag at the back of the ferry, which darted into the Aegean Sea, leaving a curved triangle of white waves to trail behind them.

"George!" called the monk after a time.

"Yes?"

"You have the perfect name for a guest at Moni Zographou. Do you know why?"

"Because of Saint George?" she said, trying to stay in character. "Mr. Brazhnikov told us all about the icon of Saint George. How it wasn't painted by human hands."

"Saint George was a miracle worker of his time. We have many icons of him, some of which are in bad need of repair. But now there is hope. Leon has brought us a new miracle: our very own iconographer." Svetan clasped Loukas's shoulder as a show of confidence and solidarity.

"With God as my witness," the artist said humbly, too tired to assert his lack of iconography training. He looked up at the sky and made the Orthodox sign of the cross with his right hand.

"Adrian, look there!" Brazhnikov interrupted, reaching out towards the peninsula with his hand like a probe. "That is Moni Panteleimon, the Russian monastery. The first time I came to Mount Athos, I stayed there. My Father brought me there when I was thirteen." They all stood up and approached the railing to get a better view.

"Why didn't you stay at the Bulgarian monastery?"

"Because my father was Russian."

"No kidding."

"But, I never lived in Russia."

Svetan muttered something in Bulgarian to Brazhnikov, which apparently upset him and caused an argument to ensue in that language. Loukas supposed that Svetan had a negative opinion of Russians and wanted Leon Brazhnikov to know it, or maybe that he didn't want his sister getting involved with someone of Russian descent. But neither the artist nor the mythologist had the slightest idea what the argument was about.

Loukas tuned it out by studying Moni Panteleimon: there were at least five floors of tan brick walls, which stretched out two hundred yards or more and the impression of a modest castle. On the top were stunning green and red roofs, as well as green cupolas with onion domes, each marked proudly with the Orthodox cross. He would have loved to paint such a tranquil scene. If there was any good thing to come out of being abducted from Mount Sinai, it was getting to extend his pilgrimage. The anticipation of reaching Zographou and seeing the icons was thrilling.

Cassandra, too, was lost in thought. Now that they were standing, Cassandra could fully observe Svetan's long, black cassock and the black cap atop his head. In their humble simplicity, these monastic garments faintly resembled those of the Taoist monks she had seen on Mount Wudang. She even sensed a similar, peculiar combination of zeal and tranquility between the Wudang monks and the Orthodox pilgrims surrounding her.

The mythologist thought about Zhen Wu and his attempt to teach her. How unprepared she had been for the harshness of Taoist training! In a way, the training itself was a kind of monasticism, a seclusion from the rest of the world in order to devote oneself to a single-pointed goal: cultivating the Way.

But she was unsure exactly what it would entail. At least, she figured, spending time among the Athonite monks would let her soak up the spirit of monasticism in preparation for the austerities of her training to come. Just as myths from cultures across the world shared universal similarities, the two religions had more in common, she felt, than many would care to admit.

Moni Zographou was an inland monastery not visible from the ferry. When they arrived at the dock, a caravan of dusty cars picked them up and drove them up the mountain to the monastery's entrance. The air was getting hot, and they rode with the windows open. Brazhnikov and Svetan had apparently made amends. Both of them chatted with the Bulgarian drivers as though they were old friends. Everyone could feel a certain awe and excitement about their ascent.

"Once you get to your rooms," Svetan explained, "you will have some resting time. Pilgrims may do as they please, get acquainted with Zographou, venerate the icons, look around. At four o'clock you will come to the kitchen and help prepare the *trapeza*."

Cassandra figured that the word *trapeza*, Greek for table, meant the dinner for the entire monastery. It made sense they would have to work to earn their keep.

When they arrived in front of the monastery's tan, rustic gates, Svetan told them that he would be dusting bookshelves in the scripture hall if they needed him, then he promptly disappeared. One of the other monks, a young recluse with few words and even less eye contact to offer, led them inside and up to their rooms. Brazhnikov opened a small door, which Loukas had thought was a broom closet, and rolled the silver suitcase inside, presumably taking it as his bedroom.

The silent monk led Loukas and Cassandra into a spacious room with light blue walls and eight empty bunks. He pointed with the back of his hand to indicate that this was the room where they would both sleep. Then he drifted back into the monastery corridor like a breath into the air.

"Well, *George*, which bunk do you want?" joked the artist.

"Doesn't matter, I guess," answered Cassandra. She climbed into the highest bunk farthest from the door and lay down with her arms spread. "I'm going to rest for a while."

"Okay."

Loukas went downstairs and explored Zographou for an hour. He encountered a few monks, but no other pilgrims. Everyone maintained a solemn countenance, and no one seemed particularly interested in talking. He visited the church, venerated the icons, and admired the exquisite, colorful frescoes on the walls of the church's nave—a 16th-century iconographic depiction of the *Last Supper*, an even older icon of the Transfiguration, and finally the twenty-foot-high fresco of the Resurrection on the back wall.

Outside the church there was a stone well, surrounded with beautiful red and white mosaics of the four gospel writers. There was even a rope with which to pull up pure water from the well to drink. As Loukas sipped the well water, he admired the tan exterior of the monastery with its rustic brown window shutters. Everything around him drew his spirit into the sublime tranquility of Athos. When he felt ready to rest, he returned to the room.

"Hi," Cassandra greeted him, still lying down and staring at the ceiling.

"Hi," he said smiling, surprised she would greet him first. "How are you feeling?"

"Good," she answered. "Peaceful."

"Me too."

Loukas crossed the room and placed his leather carrying bag on the floor next to a full-length window, which overlooked a hilly field of grass. As Loukas looked beyond the glass, he saw a narrow cobblestone path wind its way around the mounds of grass like a serpent, as if its pavers had worried little about making it straight. Instead, the artist imagined, the pavers had trusted in a higher power able to see the design from overhead. Indeed, each curve of the path appeared unpretentious and aesthetically perfect from the window's bird's-eye view.

"Mount Athos is a beautiful place, don't you think?" she said.

"I agree." He turned his head toward Cassandra, and his expression grew concerned.

"What's wrong?" she asked, sitting up on the bed.

"Do you feel anything else besides beauty?"

"What do you mean? What is greater than beauty?"

"Holiness, for one. God's love of mankind. Mount Athos is a deeply spiritual place."

"Hmm."

"I've felt the holiness of Mount Athos ever since I stepped off the ferry," Loukas explained. "It's as though my heart is a cup overflowing with joy. My heart is at peace, and yet it is strong and vigorous, full of the grace of God. I feel like I've come home, like I'm among family, even though the monks here don't talk much. I can't imagine being here on Athos, and not being able to feel this."

"What makes you think I can't feel it?"

"How can you feel holiness if you don't believe? In God, I mean."

"I believe," Cassandra asserted. "Just not the same as you believe."

"What do you believe?"

"I don't need a god with a face in order to feel what you feel. I open my mind to the myths of the world, and I let them inspire me. Even gods inspire me. But I keep my mind empty so I can continue to receive."

"Your mind is empty?"

"Yep. Yours is overflowing. Mine is empty."

"Does that mean you are open to learning about Christ?"

Cassandra froze. Being peddled religion always put a bad taste in her mouth.

"Forgive me," Loukas apologized. "I don't mean to push religion on you. It just makes me sad that you are here and aren't able to appreciate what Athos means to the Greek

Orthodox."

"Oh, but I do appreciate it. Really, I do. Mount Wudang, in China, is also a deeply spiritual place. When I went there, I could feel something beyond beauty, beyond form. In our culture we revere what is sacred. In Taoism, we call this 'the Way'."

"So, you do have a religion!" Loukas smiled. At least some religion, he felt, was better than no religion. "Tell me about it."

"Well, it's complicated. The only way I can understand it is through mythology. When I read myths, they are more than stories. They show us the meaning of life and the nature of our humanity. Myths teach us about our collective unconscious, about who we are and where we are going. I don't know enough about the Taoist religion to call it my own, but when I study mythology, my mind is open. I can even get lost in reading story after story and never want to leave."

"It's easy to lose yourself to myths," Loukas replied. "But where do they lead in the end? How do you find what is real?"

The mythologist plopped herself back on the bed and sighed.

"Questions for another time," Loukas said softly, returning his gaze to the window. He watched a trio of brown sparrows fly gracefully around the curved cobblestone path below him singing sweet hymns to the Athonite monks. Even the birds seemed to appreciate the holiness of the mountain.

"She does feel something," he thought to himself. "But what, I wonder?" He smiled and appreciated her presence with him on Athos.

"You know, Cassandra," he continued, "last night when I said the religions should never mix, I didn't mean people of different religions should never mix. Of course, we should. We do mix. At least, I do. And I do try to learn." He noticed Cassandra's breathing was getting slower and more relaxed. "Anyway, I'm sorry I got so upset. And for making you upset. Are you listening?" She was either sleeping or reluctant to respond. Loukas grinned and crossed his arms as he glanced at the mythologist. Her stillness only added to the peacefulness of the room. "Sweet dreams," he whispered.

The lighting in the room was low, and a faint smell of vanilla soothed the artist's senses. An icon hanging on the wall adjacent to the door stood out to him. It was a miniature facsimile of the *Sinai Pantocrator*. How he longed to gaze upon the original again! But Brazhnikov stood in his way, keeping it locked away in the silver suitcase. Then again, he wondered, perhaps now that they were in a safe place, the Bulgarian would keep his promise and show him the beloved *Pantocrator*.

"Adrian Loukas!" Brazhnikov's abrasive voice boomed as he stepped into the room.

"What?" the artist answered. A sinister smile spread across the Bulgarian's wide face.

"Come with me."

Brazhnikov was holding a full-sized icon of Saint George in his hand. It was faded with several streaks of paint crumbling off of the surface. The icon was in such disrepair that Loukas could barely feel the saint's austere serenity when looking him in the eyes. The *Saint George* had a gaudy, gold-leaf frame, which stretched vertically from Brazhnikov's knee level up to his shoulder.

The Bulgarian winked and turned away, leading the artist into a large room with a long, rectangular table. The long side of the room had windows all the way across, out of which Loukas could see the same field as in his own room. Brazhnikov laid down the Saint George next to a blank wooden canvas, on which Loukas presumed he was to paint his replica. Once again, the thought of painting thrilled the artist, and yet, something about the way Brazhnikov's eyes shifted made him feel a little devious himself.

"Get me my brush."

......

Cassandra woke to the persistent ringing of her cell phone. "Stavros!" she answered. "Yes, I know...No! I'm not saying no! It's just...But I do love you!...I'm in the middle of something really important...I can't explain...Mount Athos...In a monastery...I don't know...Please, let me call you tomorrow...I said I don't know!...Please don't say that!...Ok...Bye."

The conversation did not end well. She felt her mind filling up with anxiety and discouragement. As much as she loved getting lost in the myths she studied, romantic love was a story in which she had trouble placing herself. She knew countless myths about lovers, and most of them involved death and tragedy in the end. The idea of loving one man forever was fraught with risks and pressures. She feared what might happen if marriage were to lead her to an unhappy ending. If only her mother were there, she thought, to hug her again and wish for her happiness.

As she set aside her phone, the conversation she and Stavros had had ran through her mind in an endless loop, exhausting all her energy.

"Energy," she said to herself. "Energy is what I need."

Indeed, as Zhen Wu had taught her, energy was the core of who she was—a never-ceasing interplay between *jing, qi,* and *shen*. These concepts from the immortal's scroll were fundamental to her understanding of the Way as the source of that energy, the source of myth. The more she learned, the more she realized how essential it was for her to tap into that source separately from anybody else, especially from Stavros, or from any lover. If she could not do this—if she could not find strength in her own mind—then the torturous myth of romantic love would trap her in a never-ending story with no hope of escape. She needed to know herself, to master the story of her life as independently as she could before giving it over to a life of marriage. Stavros would need to accept this.

"Who am I?" she asked herself. "What is my story?"

Then she remembered Master Zhang. The world is aching. You will show Greece the Way. The story of her destiny was begging her to proceed, and yet she felt nothing but unease.

She had failed Zhen Wu. Maybe, she thought, this was why Master Zhang didn't recognize her at the train station. Maybe he could sense that she wasn't strong enough to complete the training. Her only consolation had been the hope that the monastic serenity of Mount Athos might calm her nerves and improve her preparedness for returning to Zhen Wu. But if anything, being on hiatus from her usual life made her even more on edge than usual. She worried about Jason.

"Please, keep him out of trouble," she spoke out loud, nearly approximating the gentle tone of a prayer. She sat on the bed cross-legged and covered her face with her hands. "I have to go back and complete my training," she resolved.

She massaged her eye sockets with her palms and groaned cathartically. Then she climbed down from the bunk and took in the atmosphere of the room. Pale blue walls soaked up tranquil light that poured through the three oak-framed windows. The room was silent; she could hear no extraneous noises like the buzzing of power cables or the humming of refrigerators.

The warm scent of vanilla that wafted in through the door made her smile. She massaged her eye sockets again, then blinked her eyes hard. Even the texture of the oak bed frames was soothing to her touch as she rubbed it. This was the peace of Athos, she presumed. Finally, she noticed Loukas's carrying bag. Upon inspecting the bag, she found Zhen Wu's portrait inside.

"Let's go."

Cassandra carried the portrait in its sack down the stairs and out the monastery door, finding a large patio with a fountain in the center. Surprisingly, no one was in sight. Suddenly she heard a loud gong sound ringing through the entire monastery grounds—it was the semantron, alerting the monks it was time to begin the afternoon prayer.

"Perfect. They'll all be occupied."

She walked around the side of the monastery and found the hilly grass area with the cobblestone path she had seen from her room. The path led to a small outdoor alcove, which shaded her from the midday sun. Sitting down under the arch of the alcove, she decided this would be a suitable spot for her return to Zhen Wu.

As she rescued the marble slab from its leather bag, she caught Zhen Wu's eyes with her own. He seemed to be sizing her up, trying to motivate her with an austere, warlike expression like her old *Kung Fu* teachers used to make. She recalled how these stern looks were still, like a brazen statue, yet could erupt into movement with shouting critiques at any moment without warning. Oftentimes without needing to berate the student, a *shifu's* look alone was enough to stir up the fear of failure.

During her earliest lessons, Cassandra found this method to be the worst of all motivators. But after she improved her skill, she got used to it, and even appreciated it. Her modest inner satisfaction grew to meet those stern looks with confidence and esteem for the *shifu*. And like this icon, whose stone face should have been unable to shift as she looked, the teacher's look would eventually dawn a new meaning. A tough visage became an expression of respect and approval. The face, like an icon, begat an invisible smile.

In that instant, her heart relaxed. She was ready to see where the myth would take her. She felt patient and calm inside, and her mind was empty. Using her hands she folded her right foot over her left ankle in a lotus position. Then, holding the image of the Taoist Immortal's face close to her eyes, she released her grip on her current reality and slipped back into time.

Chapter 17

Jason Yin and his new friend Sophia found themselves approaching Omonia, Athens's roughest neighborhood. It was just after midnight. From the windows of dilapidated townhouses, restless locals blasted all kinds of irreverent music. Bits of newspapers lay torn about in the streets, glued to the cement by the previous night's rain and shredded by the trampling of pedestrians. There were no sidewalks. All traffic, from ragged autos to rustic bicycles, skidded seamlessly through the same dingy, lumpy roads.

"Jason, wait!" called Sophia, feeling her shoe caught in a gutter. She bent down to try and pull it out, but couldn't free herself from the gutter's oddly shaped opening.

"Let me see," Jason commanded, feeling heroic. He pulled up the low-hanging flaps of her royal blue gabardine coat, took her ankle into his right hand and pulled on her shoe with his left. He repeated the motion swiftly six times before the girl stopped him.

"You're hurting me!" she cried.

"Hold still."

"I am!"

She tensed her leg and her whole body to show him she was still. She also scowled, making her displeasure known.

"No, no, not still, like you're unable to move. I mean still, like letting someone else move you and not resisting. Relax. Haven't you ever done Tai Chi?"

Sophia relaxed. Jason squeezed the side of her shoe with all five of his feisty, exacting fingers, and guided her foot out.

"See?"

"Xie xie," she thanked him in Mandarin.

"You're welcome," he replied, switching emphatically back

to Greek. He retrieved her shoe from the gutter and handed it to her to put on.

"But why did you say that?"

"Say what?"

"Why did you ask me if I had done Tai Chi? What do you know about Tai Chi?"

"My *Kung Fu* teacher makes us do it sometimes. He says Tai Chi is how you become relaxed and also active. It's the secret to great power." Jason held up his fists to explain what he meant: "You see, if you're too tense, then anything you hit will hurt. But if you're relaxed, you have a kind of softness. Soft—but strong! Like when Master Nikos is teaching you a new move, he says hold still, and then he takes hold of your arms and legs and puts you into the correct position. If you resist him, then it doesn't work. You have to yield. Do you understand?"

"Yield? You mean, like acquiesce?"

"Maybe." Vocabulary was not Jason's strong suit. "Master Nikos says you do that in fighting too. When your opponent comes at you with his fist, you have to yield. That doesn't mean give up! It means you take his move, bring it around, and then give it back to them even stronger!"

"So, you mean deflect?"

"Maybe."

"My mom gave me this."

Sophia pulled back the collar of her shirt to reveal a silver-stringed necklace. Pulling on the strings, she fished out a flat, circular black and white pendant that she treated with reverence.

"It's the *yin-yang*!" the boy exclaimed.

"Are you even Chinese, laundry boy?" she chided. "It's not the *yin-yang*. It's the *ba gua*. See?" She polished the pendant with her dainty thumb and then revealed its carvings. "There are eight symbols, called trigrams, and they are placed around a circle. Each trigram is made up of three lines. Some lines are broken, others are unbroken. Look at the first one—all three lines are unbroken. This is the trigram of Heaven. See the one next to it? Two lines are unbroken, and the third one is broken. That one is Wind."

"But what do they mean?"

"They're from the I Ching. You know, the *Book of Changes*. They tell how the universe moves. Everything is changing. Strong things with unbroken lines always get broken, and broken lines always go back to unbroken. Nothing stays the same. Everything in nature is transforming; everything is giving and taking, pushing, and yielding, like you said you do in Tai Chi." Sophia made hand movements that reminded Jason faintly of Tai Chi exercises he had seen.

"I meant, what does the whole thing mean? The *ba gua*?"

"Oh," she sighed, disappointed at having to explain something so rudimentary. "Ba means eight, so the *ba gua* are the eight combinations of lines. Broken and unbroken. Each *gua* is three lines. That's why they call them *tri*-grams."

"That's so easy! There has to be eight of them because two to the third power is eight."

"What?"

"It's not hard to understand. When there are three slots and two possible outcomes for each slot, then there are always eight combinations."

"Quit making nonsense, laundry boy!" she joked, covering the *ba gua* with her hand as if it were a game.

"Hey!" He shouted, grabbing her hand and trying to remove the pendant.

"What are you doing? Hey! It's around my neck!"

"Ha-ha! You have to *acqui-ness!*"

"It's *acquiesce*."

"I knew that."

"Hey!" a male voice called. "Children!"

Jason and Sophia turned around to find an armed security guard approaching them. He wore a black, bulletproof suit and carried a stick.

"You all need to clear out of here. We're roping all these

streets off."

"You're roping them off?" Jason echoed. "Why? What's going on?"

"We're not letting anyone pass through."

"But it's a free country!"

"Not today, *kinezaki*."

Jason's entire body jumped. He squeezed his hands tightly into fists as he shouted.

"WHAT DID YOU CALL ME?"

The Greek security guard had no idea what that particular word implied, or of Jason's history with it. *Kinezaki*—"little Chinese"—was the word strangers often mumbled to each other whenever Jason passed them in the streets. It annoyed him that his mere existence seemed to trigger either a remark about his Chineseness or a discussion of some other Chinese person. Wherever he went, it seemed, he couldn't avoid hearing this word—*kinezaki*.

They would sometimes shout as he approached: "Let the *kinezaki* through!" Or else, they would look at each other and make a casual remark as if he were too dumb to hear them: "The *kinezaki* is coming. Where are his parents?" Even laundry customers, whom he was obliged to treat politely, would use it: "The *kinezaki*'s here!"; "Give the money to the *kinezaki*!" It was a word the boy absolutely detested. The more he had to take it without being able to fight back, the more the anger built up inside him. "They don't get it," Jason would think. "Don't they know that a boy might want to be called a boy, not a little Chinese?"

At the present moment, Jason stood with his body square against the body of the security guard, who was slender and not exceedingly tall. He watched carefully how the guard would react to his outburst in defense of being called *kinezaki*. He squinted his eyes and bent his knees slightly as if to prepare to strike.

"Did you hear what I said?" shouted the guard. "Get out of here, *kinezaki*. Both of you!" The guard held his hands out thinking to casually push Jason and Sophia out of the street, not realizing he was provoking a boy who would not stand for being brushed away like an inconsequential child.

"You can't get rid of me, you pig!" the boy shouted, raising his fists in the air and making a tumbling motion with them.

"Come on, Jason, let's just go," pleaded Sophia.

"We're not going anywhere! Not until THIS dumb guard apologizes for saying *KINEZAKI!*"

"*Kinezaki?*" he repeated, more disparaging than confused. Then he raised his voice back, accenting his words with sharp Greek intonation: "I say *kinezaki* because you're a *kinezaki*, eh? Get out of here, *kinezaki*! Tell your friends to go home!"

Jason's mind snapped. Though his aunt Cassandra may not have realized it, the boy's ears were all too attuned to the controversy of the riots in Athens: *Greece for the Greeks! Immigrants go home!* When he wasn't thinking about it, the anger was dormant. But when prejudiced sentiment was thrown in his face, even if it wasn't intended in the way he took it, it erupted like foul ash from a rumbling mountain peak.

"You will NEVER tell me to go home! DO YOU HEAR ME?"

Jason charged at the guard and delivered a swift butterfly kick into the air.

"Jason, what are you doing?" exclaimed Sophia. "Run!"

"I'm not running anywhere!" Jason trumpeted with vigor and clarity in his voice. "I'm not going home, Sophia! And neither are you!"

Two other security guards promptly came to the scene. Sophia tried to explain what had happened as a misunderstanding. She knew that she shared his biraciality, and also a longing to reconcile the dual identity of being a Chinese-Greek in the day and age of the riot, but now, being confronted by the guards, her high hopes seemed to fade.

Though she spent less time in the streets than Jason, she had faced her own kind of discrimination. And though the word *kinezaki* had never bothered her before, the guard's condescension as he called out the name made her sympathetically outraged. In such a neighborhood where crime was rampant and hate-crime the norm, this attitude was to be expected, as was the unfortunate result. The nice boy with the tiger shirt was transformed, in an instant, into a crusading monster.

"We'll never give up!" Jason declared. The guards took him by his flailing arms and restrained him. Given his size, it was not hard to do, even with his unusual knack for surprise strikes. "Two Chinese dead! And what do we get? We want justice!"

Sophia surrendered to the guards more readily, and followed as they led her through Omonia, carrying Jason between them. She felt rightly worried about Jason's fate, and yet she stood calm. She knew it was the nature of all things to change. A peaceful place may suddenly become a violent one and a virtuous crusader may, through his actions, become an ill-fortuned rebel. Just as the I Ching had taught her, everything was constantly changing. The only way to find peace was to accept the changes, and realize that the future of these things, too, would lead them to further change.

Just like the pattern of broken and unbroken lines in the *ba gua*, everything good and valuable was vulnerable to break, and everything broken—like the trouble she would be in when her parents found out where she had been—was able to be fixed. As she followed the guards, Sophia listened patiently to their footsteps and their chatter, waiting for the perfect moment to offer an apology.

Unfortunately for the well-mannered Sophia, no such moment would come that night. From the cavernous alleyways of nighttime Omonia arose an impetuous clamor, like the opening to a symphony which lacked all tonality and structure. The first sound was a deafening bomb explosion. Shouting immediately erupted in Chinese.

The clearest phrases that Sophia and Jason could make out were "You took our lives!" and "Death will be avenged!" These threats were met with vitriolic yawping by Greek townsfolk, from which racist slurs could be detected. An amorphous crowd began spilling into the boulevard, advancing toward Jason and Sophia. Sensing another potentially devastating riot, the guards held them back from the action.

"See, I told you!" screamed Jason. "It's a free country! You'll never keep us away!"

A second explosion went off and sent fire and smoke into the street. The instigators began banging together sticks to make a ruckus. It was a kind of parade of Chinese Greek outrage at the two deaths that their community had suffered earlier that week. As the riot grew louder and nearer, the three guards frantically tried to pull the two children in the opposite direction. However, when they managed to retreat from the main street into an alleyway, a flood of Greeks arrived, bringing with them noise and terror.

Men and women ran with clubs, sticks, and makeshift shields. One olive-skinned man with a bloodthirsty scowl on his face even held a camo-colored pistol as he ran, which caught Jason's attention particularly. Pistols were illegal in Athens. Jason had never seen one used before. For a split second he thought this man resembled Master Nikos, but he quickly realized it wasn't. Nothing about any of these people seemed to share his *shifu's* mastery of calmness and confidence. Instead, it was pure hatred, fear, and chaos.

"STOP! EVERYBODY, STAY BACK!" the guards demanded, but to no avail.

The crowd charged toward them from the west like a stampede. The mob was hot-headed, fierce and energized. Then, from the east came the other side—a rioting throng of Chinese Greeks assembled in a close-knit echelon, raising sticks, fists, and flags as they approached the opposing crowd.

Jason, Sophia, and the three guards stood in the middle, equidistant from both masses, suspended in the terrible anticipation of what would happen when the two forces met.

"I could die here," Jason realized. He stood near Sophia and was glad not to be alone. "No. I won't die. I have to protect

Sophia. I have to stay alive."

Chapter 18

Cassandra Yin struggled to let go of the agitations that consumed her. Back in Athens, riots against Chinese immigrants were threatening her family's way of life. She knew Chinatown wasn't safe, and she especially worried about her mother. She hoped that Daphne was making sure she took her pills, that George wasn't overworking himself with deliveries and neglecting to spend time at home, and that Jason was staying away from trouble, even though she knew very well his penchant for finding it.

These agitations were, according to Zhen Wu, like sandbags in a pulling cart; they were extra weight that—if she refused to unload it—would burden and exhaust her forever. Without mastering the worries carried inside her mind, she could not hope to influence the rest of Greece. Zhen Wu taught that change in the outer world begins with change in one's own mind, a realm in which Cassandra was only beginning to understand. Eventually, as her *shifu* explained, she would need to let go of the cart altogether. This was the beginning of the Way.

Cassandra's second arrival at Mount Wudang was much smoother and more natural than her first. The transition between worlds was strange, but no stranger than any of the ancient myths she knew by heart. She was getting used to the power of icons to transport their viewer to the place and time of the saints. She knew time was valued differently inside the icon as compared with time in her present day, and that the day she had spent on Mount Wudang during her first visit was only a number of hours back in Greece. But as far as she could gather, time within the world of a saint passed at the normal speed. If she spent days, months, or even years inside the icon it would feel as long, despite the fact that little time would have passed in her real life.

As Cassandra reacquainted her senses with China again, her apprehensions dissolved. All that remained was her emotional burden dragged from home. The world is aching, she thought. And yet, that world as she knew it did not exist where she now stood. The twenty-first century was not yet a seed in the earth, not even an embryo in the gods' design. This was Zhen Wu's world, four hundred years before her own. However long she had to stay as a guest in this world, she would persist. Whatever the Taoist Immortal might ask of her during her training, it didn't matter. The training was necessary for self-knowledge; she had to learn the legend of her own destiny. And she had all the time in the world within the icon to learn it.

......

Zhen Wu's monastery, called Nanyan Palace, was situated on the side of a precipitous cliff overlooking a lush forest valley. Her first night there was not entirely uncomfortable. She met Sai-Lu, one of the chief Taoist priests, who made her a home in a small, rustic dormitory one floor below the main temple. He gave Cassandra a simple, black cassock and cap—the same as he wore—a pair of black shoes, a string to tie her hair up, and linens for her wooden bed.

Sai-Lu took her through all the monastery's practical spaces, which he referred to as 'mansions': a washroom, a laundry chamber, a common dining area, a library, herb and vegetable gardens, a room for medicines and acupuncture, and various altar rooms containing red and gold painted statues of Taoist deities and large scripture books. Each mansion had its history and its rules, which Sai-Lu explained in long and exacting detail. His voice was pleasing to listen to. In the center of Nanyan Palace was the main temple, where at various times throughout the day—determined precisely by the positions of the stars to the earth—all monks and priests would congregate for about thirty minutes for meditation, incense burning, and chanting.

Cassandra felt the Taoist rituals at Nanyan Palace to be more efficient than those of the Greek Orthodox church. Not once did she find herself idly counting the candles on the hanging candelabra or counting the number of *yin-yangs* painted on the ornately engraved wooden ceiling. Never was she bored by too much theology and speculation. Every ritual had a purpose, and every incantation activated a special feeling within her that quickly concluded.

She sat on her knees, like the other monks, upon a mat made of woven bamboo strips. The chants, though simple, were quite pleasing to her. They consisted of mythological names of deities, the life-principles they represented, as well as practical formulas for self-control. Musical accompaniment included bells, gongs, and a hollow, fish-shaped wooden block called the *muyu*, which was struck with a wooden mallet at certain times to produce a more upbeat cadence. Cassandra caught herself chanting quietly during her routine activities each day, using the words to empty her of all other thoughts.

She trained daily with Zhen Wu, her new *shifu*. Each day she began with Wu Chi practice. This was particularly difficult to do, since it meant silencing even the lingering resonances of the chanting. And in the rare moments she could manage that, the constant drumming of the *muyu* still pestered her for attention like a nagging child. But as her thoughts and feelings softened, she learned how to numb her mind comfortably. She tuned in to her own heartbeat and observed the blood pulsing through her head, chest, groin and limbs. In stillness she could slow down this pulsing if she focused hard on it, but Zhen Wu cautioned her against doing so. Wu Chi was about experiencing, not experimenting.

One time, he had her practice Wu Chi in what he called 'eagle stance', in which she held her arms out to each side and allowed them to droop slightly. Another time he had her stand on one foot and balance with her arms straight up and opposite knee raised. Yet another time it was a kind of inverted plank position that western yogis might call a 'downward-facing dog'. Every position he gave her was to improve her ability to still her mind and body. Oddly enough, the more uncomfortable the position, the easier this became. But in order to find stillness she had to convince herself she could hold the posture without straining.

She learned—through her own experimentation rather than Zhen Wu's instruction—that she could convince herself to relax by imagining her body being baked into a giant pan of jello, held in place by a soft, gelatinous ocean rather than by muscular exertions. The problem with this visualization, however, was that the visualization itself was a thought that disrupted her stillness.

It wasn't until after two weeks of these exercises that Cassandra gave voice to what had become a nagging a question. "Will I be learning any exercises other than these different forms of Wu Chi?"

To this question Zhen Wu laughed coldly and said no words. Then he walked away and left her in the training pavilion alone, not returning for three full days. Not even Sai-Lu knew where he had gone. Cassandra struggled not to feel distressed. With Zhen Wu gone, why was she not fading back into her own world? Was she stuck here? She tried several times desperately to force herself to disappear from Mount Wudang and return to Athos, but with no success.

She anxiously started questioning the other monks, but most of them gave few words and left her even more confused. After she accepted that nothing could be done, she kept her mind off her worries by exploring the gardens, perusing the library and admiring the altars, particularly the one with a bronze Lao Tzu statue across from the common dining area. When the days felt long she heeded the sage advice from a monk she met called Hui-Lum: "Chew your rice slowly, and take small bites. If you rush one meal, you will wait an eternity for the next one." This wasn't true, of course, since meals at Nanyan Palace were always punctual and there was always enough food, but the exercise of chewing mindfully became one of her comforts during this strange waiting period.

When Cassandra was able to resume her training, Zhen Wu doubled her practice time to eight hours a day and restricted her to only one form of Wu Chi: the form he called 'horse stance', which turned out to be the one that Master Zhang had taught her originally. He did this, she figured, partly to make her feel humbled, and partly to teach her not to ask questions. Giving pupils exactly the opposite of what they wanted was a classic Chinese test of dedication.

What she learned in the weeks to follow, however, was how much she hated being talked down to. Zhen Wu treated her like a child, as if she knew nothing, as if she would continue to know nothing until the end of time! She began noticing that all the time spent not in training—in her room at the start and finish of each day, in the washrooms, in the dining area, in the temples—these lovely intervals seemed to pass with a devastating quickness. Holding onto these moments felt like grasping at candles that were melting in her hands, consumed by a hungry flame too quickly for her to enjoy their light. Even sleep seemed to pass instantaneously, while the long hours of her training seemed like daily eternities.

Eventually she came to accept that she truly knew nothing. She let herself forget why she was there, what the training meant and who she was doing it for. The nothingness of Wu Chi was all that was necessary to know. Each time she reported to Zhen Wu for her daily training, she knew that all he required was that she empty her mind. She began appreciating the immortal's punitive doubling of her training time, since it took her at least the first few hours to quell her internal protestations.

"I've already mastered this! Can't we get on with the real exercises? Why do I need so much Wu Chi?"

As soon as she managed to get that part of her mind still, the other parts usually followed suit. Occasionally she wondered if spending less time on the exercises would have somehow been more efficient, since she wouldn't waste as much time worrying about the time she was wasting. Unfortunately, this kind of circular reasoning only slowed down the passing of time by heightening her frustrations.

One night, toward the end of her second month at Nanyan Palace, she came to her chamber in the evening and noticed her left heel was bleeding. Sai-Lu took her to the medicine room and mixed together some dark-leaved herbs in a jar of molasses-colored liquid. After a few moments he fished one of the leaves out and used it to paint over her wound with the liquid. Sai-Lu then laid Cassandra face-down upon a cushioned bed, which was much softer than the wooden bed she slept on. He placed tiny acupuncture needles on her entire back side, including the heels.

Sai-Lu kept her company for several hours until the color vanished from her heel and the wound was gone. It was interesting how he talked more than any other monk, and yet he never seemed to say anything important. His musical way of speaking functioned more for expressing his energy than communicating information. She wondered whether the medicine and the needles really did anything or whether it was all the placebo effect. Sai-Lu's friendly smile and melodic voice were as soothing as any remedy he gave.

There was also a second time when her heel got wounded. Zhen Wu had made her take the horse stance on top of a nine-foot-high outdoor wall that separated the pavilion from the vegetable garden. The wall's edge was narrower than the length of her shoes, which made balancing difficult. Nevertheless, she persisted far longer than she believed she could. Initial disbelief was, in fact, the only real obstacle to her completing a stillness exercise.

When Zhen Wu finally asked her to step down, her legs began to shake. Slowly she straightened her knees, and then lifted her left leg up to flex her stiff ankle. But the weight of her body all on one exhausted leg was too much. She slipped and fell from the wall into a cabbage patch. Miraculously, nothing was injured except her heel, which was scraped and bruised from hitting the wall. Sai-Lu took her in and applied the same remedy of molasses-colored liquid to her wound, smiling and laughing as he treated her. Cassandra laughed too, joking that she felt like Achilles, and that if it weren't for her heel she would already be an immortal.

When summer came, Zhen Wu told Cassandra she was finally ready for a test. Cassandra nodded and waited as her *shifu* sized up her courage. After a few minutes he took her through Nanyan's main temple and out the back side, where the ledge overlooked the valleys of Mount Wudang. From there, they climbed down three flights of rickety stairs that had previously been roped off. The stairs led to a bridge-like scaffolding that wrapped around the cliffside for nearly a quarter mile, along which various altar chambers were carved into the mountain.

A few of these chambers contained monks prostrating in ritual prayer. Others contained lonely statues of ancient gods. At the end of the scaffolding there was a large room with a dirt floor, enclosed by stone walls and a stone roof. The room was illuminated by sunlight through a wide, rectangular window, out from which a stone plank stretched out overlooking the valley. Cassandra couldn't figure out what such a plank would be used for, since it didn't lead anywhere. She was sure Sai-Lu could give her a lengthy lesson explaining it.

"Drink this," the Taoist Immortal commanded. He pointed to a pool of water in the corner of the room. "It is water collected from the Well of Sweet Dew."

Cassandra knelt down and drank the water, which lived up to its description without disappointment.

"Now, give me your palms facing up, and hold these incense sticks between your thumbs and the sides of your hand so that the tip points at the sun."

She held out both hands with palms up, and Zhen Wu rooted the incense sticks firmly in the webbings of her thumbs. The sticks felt thin and frail, as though a strong wind could blow them away from her with ease.

"Do you see that stone plank?"

"Yes." She was already looking at it through the window.

"Climb out onto the plank. When you get to the very edge,

you will practice horse stance. Continue holding these sticks in your hands. Do not drop them! You must stay in horse stance until both incense sticks are completely burnt out."

"But won't they burn my fingers when the sticks get too short to hold?"

"Everyone feels pain," he answered. "Do not fight it—experience it, use it. You will not be allowed to come off of the plank until the sticks are gone. Understand?"

"What happens if I drop them?"

Zhen Wu looked at her angrily.

"If you drop the sticks, you will drop yourself from the plank as well."

"What?"

Zhen Wu looked at her coldly once more and then left the room. Anxiously she watched his smooth, masterful gait until he was far enough around the scaffolding, she could no longer see him. Once again, the desire to give up and go home overwhelmed her. She missed her mother, Jason, and everyone dear to her and dreaded the thought of dying before ever seeing them again.

"If I die here, will I die in my real body?" she wondered. But the body she saw herself in was her real body. The world around her was completely formed, just as it had been when she entered Saint Theodora's icon with Loukas. The room overlooking Mount Wudang's southern valley was as real as her home in Athens. She thought back to the wound in her heel and felt the echo of its pain again; her body was real and all pain was the same. Below the plank was open air and a green valley floor at least five hundred feet down, which she felt would not cushion her nearly as well as the cabbage patch. There was absolutely no way she could let herself fall, or else she would certainly die.

"What if I leave instead?" she said to herself. "I can just as easily do the exercise somewhere else?" But as the thought arose, she remembered what happened the last time she questioned Zhen Wu's instruction. He gave her exactly the opposite of what she asked for, which only made things harder. No, there was no option to modify the exercise. Zhen Wu surely was watching her from somewhere, noticing every fault and weakness in her thinking.

"I must complete this training," she encouraged herself. She climbed out the window and stood on the plank, squatting low upon the wooden structure. "Don't look down. Only forward."

Cassandra held up her palms still with the incense sticks up and slowly walked along the plank. She could feel the incense sticks trembling in the wind as she moved. When she finally made it to the edge of the plank, the tension in her body eased.

"Okay," she thought. "The hardest part is over. Movement is difficult. But standing still is easy. I've practiced it every day for months!"

Still, she couldn't help feeling unprepared. Learning a skill in the abstract was one thing, but applying it in a way that risked her life was something else. As she got into horse stance at the edge of the plank, she took a deep breath and sighed. Birds in the distance darted from tree to tree. The summer heat made her sweat. "All I have to do is wait until the incense sticks are completely—"

A deathly chill swept through her. Zhen Wu had not lit the incense sticks! Had he forgotten? Was she supposed to light them herself before getting out onto the plank? She hadn't noticed if there was anything to light them with in the room. Perhaps noticing that was part of her training, which she had now failed.

At this point, her fear was so strong, she knew she could never make her way back across the plank without slipping. Without keeping the stillness she had found, all hope would be lost. She was stuck there, and her incense sticks were cold. Part of her even surmised whether this entire exercise was actually a test of her stupidity in waiting for something to happen that could never possibly happen. After all, what kind of teacher expects the impossible?

"It's impossible," she griped, surrendering to the hopelessness of her situation. "I will wait until the end of time for these incense sticks to burn. No, I will surely fall asleep first and fall to my death. Either way, my life is over. My life will be nothing."

Like a zebra thrown to the hyenas, Cassandra surrendered her body to death. "Death is the natural order of things," she reminded herself. "All living creatures have predators. Mine is time."

She remained motionless in Wu Chi state for the rest of the day. Thanks to her training, her body managed not to shake, with one exception. Her eyelids twitched as she struggled against the temptation to open them and look down. Her mind remained mostly subdued from thoughts that weren't useful to the exercise, however, some still took hold of her. She caught herself breathing heavily through her nose as if to sniff for incense, hoping that somehow the sticks would have miraculously started burning. Several times she tried to imagine herself trying to light the sticks using her own bioelectricity—first stirring up *jing*, the seminal essence inside her kidneys, and then letting it flow through her body as warm *qi* and radiate outwardly as fiery *shen*. However, the more she tried, the less she believed she could do it.

She felt the air grow cool. It was night. And then it was morning again. She felt the sun's heat faintly thereafter, but mostly she continued to feel only what was inside of her. Fewer and fewer mental protestations came to challenge her. She treated every thought and sense impression that occurred to her objectively, as a doctor would treat a patient. When she felt her stomach growl, she acknowledged it, prescribed it a regiment of waiting in stillness, and then sent it on its way. When she felt the wind blow and the sticks twitch between her fingers, she allowed those sensations to happen without judging them. She tried not to control her movements, only to be fully present to them. Time passed until she was no longer sure how much time had even passed. Was it possible she had been there for days? Weeks? Months? Even in an alternate world, the passage of time was just as long and harsh and cruel as ever.

"I have to check," she decided. "I have to open my eyes and at least see whether the incense sticks have changed." But as she wiggled her eyes barely open, the light from the sun was so bright and strong, she had to shut her eyelids back and could not see anything. "Just like Semele," she thought. "Blinded by the light of Zeus in his uncreated form." Instead, she squeezed her fingers against her thumbs: the sticks were still inert. They still felt cold. The smell of incense was absent. "Maybe a blue cloud will come and save me," she thought without much hope. She had no other recourse.

For a brief moment, she felt as if she had left her body. She couldn't see anything, and yet she felt like she was moving about, hovering above the plank and the valley.

"What am I?" she wondered as she explored her out-of-body experience. She felt energized, but there was something more—she was energy! She was free of the weight and burden of her physical form. And yet, this freedom came at a terrifying price. Zhen Wu had warned her about it on the first day— he had explained that when an aspiring student is ready to advance a level, she must face a demon. While out of her body she began to sense this demon's presence. She could feel it flying toward her, seeking her, hungering for her! Somehow, she knew the demon was near, and the danger was imminent.

As she returned to her body a smell came to her. But it wasn't the smell of incense. It reminded her of the smell of holding snakes and lizards taken from their cages, and yet the smell was right in front of her. Something was breathing on her, sending her subtle gusts of foul-smelling wind into her face. She felt the heat of the sun on her eyelids and the strange breath on her eyelashes. Then, she felt a shadow come over her.

Without thinking she reacted. She opened her eyes and activated her muscles. There, in front of her was a beast she could not have imagined, one she didn't even believe existed outside of mythology. It was a human-sized, white dragon.

Cassandra froze in shock. The dragon was about her own height from head to foot, though with much bigger bones. Its wingspan was even longer, and its tail lashed back and forth, adding an additional dimensionality to its threatening physique. The dragon kept itself in constant motion, flapping its wings and sending its reptilian stench in her direction.

"Demon!" she shouted at the dragon, not sure exactly why. Then she began speaking an incantation she had learned in the temple. It was difficult to make eye contact with the beast, since its shadow continually blocked and revealed the sun to her eyes, but she persisted.

The dragon was not fazed. It let out a puff of smoke from its nostrils and gave a nasty hiss. Cassandra could not deny the fear she felt, but she had no means of assuaging it. Her mind filled up with terror, and her whole body trembled. She continued to chant the incantation, this time shouting it at the top of her lungs.

At this, the hovering dragon let out a fire from its mouth like a blowtorch. It missed her, but she could feel its heat on her face. She stopped her incantation and closed her eyes, trying to get back into Wu Chi state.

"I don't know if Wu Chi will work, but it's the only exercise I know. It's the only thing Zhen Wu would teach me!" She held out her hands again with palms facing up, pointing the incense sticks toward the sun.

This time, the dragon unleashed a full explosion of fire right at her. She felt her hands burned and singed in the fire, so much that they went completely numb. The rest of her body, too, lost all feeling as she swooned and lost consciousness.

Cassandra woke up in the medicine room with both Zhen Wu and Sai-Lu standing in front of her. Her hands were bandaged and still felt like they were hot as a furnace, but the rest of her body appeared to be fine. Neither of them would tell her how she survived the fall. Instead they were quick to commend her for completing the exercise until the incense sticks had burnt completely.

"The dragon is not out here," Zhen Wu explained. "It's

inside of you."

"That's comforting," Cassandra responded. Using sarcasm to express her own discomfort was, ironically, comforting. "But then how do I know if what I'm seeing now is real? How do I know you, or Sai-Lu, or this room or anything I see on Mount Wudang is real?"

"You don't have to know," the *shifu* answered. "All that matters is that you respond to what you perceive in a way that is harmonious with nature. All things exist as a harmony of opposites. You're a mythologist, right? You understand that you have a duality of opposites: light and dark, active and receptive, positive and negative. Well, the opposite of you is this dragon. Learn to master it, and you will master the *yin* and *yang* within yourself. That is the Way."

From that point onward, the immortal's lessons were far more stimulating, albeit infinitely more arcane. He taught her to hold an 'energy ball' in her hands and let it expand and contract slowly in order to manipulate her *qi*. He taught her several moving sequences of Tai Chi focusing on maintaining fluidity and relaxedness. He taught her the mental discipline of breathing evenly as she shifted her weight, as well as how not to hold the breath while changing directions. He taught her the eight palm formations of *Ba Gua* Zhang, making her walk along the edges of a giant circular *ba gua* diagram on the floor thirteen feet in diameter. Once Cassandra mastered each individual palm of the *ba gua*, Zhen Wu taught her to alternate between them using what he called the 'swimming body change'. All the while, thoughts of the white dragon both terrified and motivated her. "The next time I meet my dragon," she thought, "I will be ready."

......

At the end of Cassandra's first year on Mount Wudang, the monks threw her a celebration. They served sweet yams with rice and sang a special blessing for her. Hui-Lum even let her take his place drumming the fish-shaped *muyu* during that day's chanting. It was hard to believe she had been away from her own world for so long.

Questions of reality were wearing upon her: "Was my other world a dream, or am I dreaming now? How can I know what is real?" She occasionally questioned Zhen Wu's motives. Maybe, by keeping her from questioning anything, he was somehow trapping her there, feeding his own ambitions by sucking the consciousness from her. Then again, by all objective comparisons, her life in Nanyan Palace was far more pleasant than her life in Athens. There were no family problems and no financial worries, no political dramas and no violent predicaments. No longer did she feel the need to escape. Nevertheless, whenever she thought of her family, she missed them gravely.

She imagined trying to describe to her mother what she was doing on Mount Wudang. She had no idea where to even begin. Her father had supposedly visited the mountain once during his youth, but Cassandra couldn't imagine his experience would have been comparable to hers. Words could not convey it—nothing she could say would make it real for others in her family.

She then thought of what it would take to explain the riots in Athens to the Wudang monks, and this made her all but burst into tears. Two Chinese had died, and for what? To make an inch of headway in a battle to change a Greek law? In her new life in Nanyan, there was not even a concept of law, let alone a reason to die for it. If a monk failed to follow one of Sai-Lu's many hygienic ordinances there would be no dire consequence. Everyone cared about each other and about the community as a whole. Any refusal to give way to another person's request would appear petty and pointless.

Then again, she reminded herself, Mount Wudang is a culturally homogenous place. How would things be different if Greek refugees came and asked to share the mountain with them? Would there be conflict? Violence? Coexistence was a true puzzle.

Another year passed at Nanyan Palace. No answers were

revealed, but Cassandra learned to delight more deeply in her progress. Her training days seemed to pass more quickly, and her kinship with the other monks deepened. Hui-Lum, she discovered, was a bit of a prankster. Sometimes he would steal the sugar spoons from the tables and demand solutions to his riddles before giving them back.

She also learned that Sai-Lu was a skilled spearman. After weeks of prodding, Cassandra even managed to get Sai-Lu to give her a few lessons. Unfortunately, her skills with the spear were nothing compared to her knack for storytelling. All the monks would listen to her and hang on her every word. Sometimes she would make up the story as she went. Having an audience of such mindful listeners made her talents thrive.

One day, when winter's frost had covered the roofs and gardens, a new monk called Aisha showed up at the monastery and took the second bed in Cassandra's room. Aisha was a Persian soothsayer, recently exiled from her kingdom for trying to warn the prince of a bad omen.

"Bad omens are always unwelcome," Aisha explained. "One shouldn't offer them unless asked. I learned that the hard way." The Persian's story was complex and suspiciously embellished, but Cassandra loved hearing it and eagerly shared her own.

During her visits to the herb garden Cassandra found a unique camaraderie with an apothecary priest called Laughing Daisy. According to Sai-Lu, Laughing Daisy was an immortal, which meant he always went barefoot. Laughing Daisy had taken a vow to never speak a word. His only way of communicating—which he shared with Cassandra most readily—was by laughing out loud.

By the end of Cassandra's sixth year, Zhen Wu finally took her back to the plum tree he had shown her during her first visit. Sai-Lu and Aisha came too.

"Do you remember this tree, Cassandra?" Zhen Wu asked.

"Of course. You grafted a betel nut branch onto the plum tree and told me to wait for it to produce plums for fruit."

"Look now, and see what it has grown."

It was the height of spring again. The mythologist pulled

back the leafy plum branches and found the betel nut branch.

"What do you see?" asked Aisha.

"It looks exactly the same," she said, disappointed.

"And why should it look any different, hmm?" shouted Zhen Wu. "It's a betel nut branch."

"But you said—"

"Cassandra, forget this branch. Forget your training. You will never change into something you're not. Are you a plum tree? No. You're small, like a betel nut. You're nothing. You'll never know the Way."

Immediately she suspected something was not right. Her *shifu* did not sound like himself. He was known to be strict, yes, but he had never made insults. No one on Mount Wudang would say such a thing. Except, maybe, one's own self-talk. In that instant the body of Zhen Wu raised from the ground and transformed into the same white dragon that was her demon.

"Do you see something?" asked Aisha. "Are you having a vision?" Aisha and Sai-Lu could not see the demon. To them, the *shifu* had simply disappeared.

"It's my white dragon."

"Take this!" called Sai-Lu. He handed her his spear. "If it really is the demon you see, you must defeat it yourself. We cannot help you." Aisha began pronouncing incantations, but Sai-Lu promptly made her stop.

"What do I do?" Cassandra demanded. Sweat bedewed her forehead and moistened her armpits. "I've never fought with a spear before!"

At this question, Sai-Lu was uncharacteristically silent. Aisha, too, had no advice to give. Neither of them could see the dragon. Only Cassandra could master the demon within herself.

Chapter 19

Brazhnikov, still in his purple suspenders, hovered over the Loukas's shoulder with interest - far more than he had shown in his Chinatown apartment while Loukas had painted the portrait of Zhen Wu—but the artist wasn't bothered. The light from the window flattered his painting, and Brazhnikov's shadow, at least, didn't get in the way. Loukas even accepted the Bulgarian's offer of a can of Coke, which he set aside while working.

Loukas's approach to replicating the icon was completely different from the one he'd taken with Zhen Wu. He used a dark background with silver undertones, all brush strokes converging in the center of the painting, where Saint George's circular halo was outlined in gold. The saint's curly, brown hair framed the space where the face would be drawn. Saint George wore golden armor covered with coins, rings, jeweled flowers, and an Orthodox cross which hung on a silver chain from his neck. In his olive-toned hand he carried a silver spear that came to a point on the upper left side of the painting. The overall feeling radiating from the image was that of undaunted courage. Saint George was the protector of Moni Zographou, its patron saint. Loukas set down his brush and paused. He was quite pleased with his work.

"You know," the artist said as he rubbed his eyes, "I've seen many icons of Saint George before. He is often shown pointing his spear at a dragon. Do you know why?"

"Sure, I do. It's part of the legend. He fought the dragon off while...it was to protect the people of his hometown of... in this one Saint George has already slain the dragon." It was clear Brazhnikov didn't know the story. For the first time since Loukas had met him, his conscience prevented him from lying.

"There's also a little depiction of a princess in the background," added Loukas. "Her name's Sabra, and her father was King of Silene, a city in Libya. According to the legend, a dragon lived nearby. A terrible and hungry dragon, who rampaged through the city in search of people to eat. To get rid of the dragon, the King had to give one person each day to the dragon as a sacrifice, rather than let the whole town be terrorized. So, each day he would cast lots in order to choose a random townsperson, and that person would be fed to the dragon. For a while, it seemed to work. The dragon stayed away, and the King was pleased."

"But then, as more and more victims died by the evil dragon, the people became outraged. 'We need to fight the dragon and defend ourselves,' they said. But the King of Silene was stuck on his plan. He said, 'No. None of us is strong enough to defeat such a demon'. Until one day, something happened that made the King change his mind: his own daughter Sabra was chosen to be sacrificed. 'Never!' said the King. He was angry. He wouldn't feed his daughter to the dragon. 'I've heard your suggestion,' he said to the people. 'None of us is worthy of fighting the dragon, so we have to pray for divine intervention.'"

"I know how the story ends," Brazhnikov interrupted. "Saint George heard the King's prayers and rode in on his white horse to slay the dragon and protect Sabra and all the people of Silene." He took a quick drink from his can of Coke. "You know, adding the princess would improve your painting tremendously."

"Yeah, right."

"Not too large of course, but, you know, make her just visible enough for someone to see who is really looking." Brazhnikov made a joking gesture with his hands to indicate a woman's breasts.

"Sacrilege!" replied Loukas sarcastically, trying to play along.

"What sacrilege? You iconographers are such prudes."

Loukas and Brazhnikov laughed and drank from their Coke cans. Then Svetan the monk entered with a newspaper and a look of consternation.

"I hate to intrude," pleaded Svetan, "but there is some news you should know, in case you haven't read about it." He held the newspaper so Loukas and Brazhnikov could read the headline.

"Two Greeks were killed?" reacted Loukas.

"Yes, last night around midnight. The riot was started by Chinese dissidents in Omonia. They fired grenades and caused a violent uproar in the streets."

"Did the Greeks fight back?" inquired Brazhnikov.

"You can be sure they did. But two were killed. There is also a child in critical condition."

Loukas's face softened, and his voice came out in a horrified whisper. "A child?"

"Yes, Lord help us, a twelve-year-old child," answered the monk. "But maybe this is a sign. Maybe this is the breaking point, and things will change. I think sometimes it takes the death of an innocent child to make us see the error of our ways. The riots, I mean."

"But you said the child is still alive, right?" asked Brazhnikov.

"According to the newspapers, yes."

"What was a child even doing out in the streets at midnight?" asked Loukas, nearly in tears. Painting always made him emotionally vulnerable.

"It doesn't say," said Svetan. "All it says is that a twelve-year-old child, a Chinese-Greek, is in critical condition due to a bomb blast."

Loukas was speechless. He thought of Jason, Cassandra's nephew, who had been taking photos of a riot when they had first met! The thought of Jason—or any such boy—being killed by a mob made his soul mourn for the cruelties of man. "Where was Saint George to protect that child?" he lamented in his head.

Brazhnikov appeared disturbed by the artist's sudden dejection. "Svetan, leave us," he said in Bulgarian. "Our painter still has work to do, and I don't think your news is helping."

Svetan nodded and left the room, taking his newspaper with him.

"Adrian, get a hold of yourself. You need to finish Saint George. You need to paint his face!"

Loukas breathed deeply and wiped three tears from his cheek. "Okay." He stood up and stretched his legs. Paint drops of all different colors spotted his light-brown collared shirt. He looked out the window at the grass field with the curved cobblestone path. Clouds now filled the sky, and the light from the window was not as strong as before. A light drizzle appeared to fall. Somehow, he felt, God was crying over the tragedy of the riots. And if there was one solution, one person who could save them, it was his Savior, the Christ, Jesus of Nazareth. Crossing his arms, Loukas turned to Brazhnikov.

"First, you can show me the *Pantocrator*."

Brazhnikov stepped ominously toward Loukas and whispered, "I said for you to paint the face now."

"Relax, man, I just want to see it for inspiration."

"What are you trying to pull?" His temperament had changed so drastically from their earlier camaraderie that it left the artist confused.

"Alright, alright. I just thought, maybe, since we're getting along now—"

"We're not getting along. You're trying to get out of your promise."

"I never technically promised to paint this. You forced me, remember?"

Brazhnikov sucked in his belly and reached into his pants, pulling out a sheathed jade dagger. He did not remove the sheath but gripped the dagger's handle with his gargantuan hand, pressurizing the artist with his eyes.

"I remember. The question is, do *you* remember?"

Loukas stood his ground. He kept his arms crossed and stared back into the Bulgarian's swampy, gray eyes. About fifteen seconds passed before the Bulgarian released his grip. He scowled and shook the sheathed dagger lightly in front of the artist's face.

"When I come back, the Saint George had better be finished."

Loukas kept silent, internally relieved. Brazhnikov snatched both his and Loukas's Coke cans and left the room.

"Fine," he said out loud, drawing the sign of the cross with his right hand.

The clouds outside were even darker, and the rain started to pour. Faint sounds of thunder roared in the distance. Through the window he also noticed a person sitting in a covered alcove across the field. "Cassandra?" he wondered. It certainly looked like her. "What is she doing out there? Oh well, at least she's keeping dry." Loukas went to the door to close and lock it, and then he grabbed the silver suitcase. To his dismay, it was once again locked. He tugged on the zipper and looked for other ways of getting it open, but found nothing.

"Damn." He would have to finish the Saint George quickly if he wanted to abscond with the suitcase.

Wasting no time, Loukas went back to his painting and finished the face. Then, a mischievous thought occurred to him. "I know I shouldn't paint the princess," he said to himself. "But maybe I can still paint the dragon. Just a small dragon in the background, to help tell the legend of Saint George." He studied his painting, looking for the most aesthetic and symbolic place to add the dragon. "It must be painted white," he decided, "to show it has been defeated." Smiling, he grabbed a fine brush, dipped it in white acrylic, and added the dragon, placing it up in the corner where the silver streaks met the gray background. When he finished, he stood up and marveled at his own work. "Perfect."

A flash of lightning lit the sky, followed by a cataclysmic thunder. Loukas darted toward the window to see if Cassandra was safe. When he got there, he couldn't believe his eyes. Cassandra was standing in the rain with her eyes closed like a zombie, looking up. Hovering above her was a white dragon—

the very same dragon he had just painted!

"Am I imagining this?" he wondered.

Sometimes his heightened concentration made him daydream vivid depictions of what he had painted. But that was not the case—the dragon was real and vicious. It circled around Cassandra and teased her with hisses. Cassandra, however, remained in a trance, as though still asleep. Loukas's palms moistened with sweat as he squinted through the downpour to try and see better. As his mind searched for an explanation, it came to the only logical conclusion it could manage: he had created the dragon by bringing it into being from the unseen world through his painting. He was responsible for everything the dragon did and, God forbid, anyone the dragon harmed.

"I have to get down there and help her."

Loukas dashed to the door and unlocked it, then he stopped.

"I've let the *Pantocrator* out of my sight too many times already. I'm not leaving without it again."

As fast as he could, he lugged the heavy suitcase out of the room and down the monastery stairs. Its wheels got caught on the stairs a few times, which hindered his pace, but adrenalin made him persevere. He had to get out of the monastery, away from Brazhnikov, who he still wasn't sure he could trust, and toward Cassandra, whose life was in danger.

As he passed through the gates, the rain hit him like a waterfall spilling out of nowhere. He pulled the silver suitcase across the difficult cobblestone terrain, around the side of the monastery where the grass field was. He had to switch arms frequently to manage the weight of his prize.

"I hope this suitcase is waterproof," he suddenly realized. "Ah yes, there are alcoves beside the field. I can dry off there." He regrouped and redoubled his efforts. He pulled the suitcase by its middle handle with both hands and hobbled along as fast as he could. When he got to the field, both the dragon and Cassandra were gone. In their place, a crowd of monks stood around a wheeled stretcher.

He pulled into the nearest alcove and hid the suitcase in a dry spot. Then he raced out into the field to where the monks stood.

"What happened?" Loukas screamed, looking at the stretcher. On it, a body was laid with a white sheet covering it. The body was petite, and his perceptive eyes could tell it had adult female proportions. "Cassandra!"

"You'll have to keep your quiet," one of the monks told him.

"But how did she—I mean, he—die?" the artist whispered aggressively.

"It appears young George was bit by a large animal. It's quite a mystery."

"Did you see the animal?" he questioned.

"No, no animal. Father Maximos just found him lying here. Now, quickly. We must bring him in from the rain."

Loukas fell to his knees. He watched the Zographou monks wheel Cassandra's body away, helpless to follow them. If he did, he would have to face an apparent truth: he had painted that white dragon into existence and was responsible for Cassandra's death.

"Damn my painting," he cursed. "Damn these eyes and all they've seen!" He buried his face in his hands. Rain drenched his hair, neck, and clothes as he knelt in the grass. "Damn my slowness. I tried to save the *Pantocrator*, but I killed my friend."

He looked toward the alcove where the silver suitcase stood. It appeared dry. Then he looked across to the alcove where Cassandra had been. To his horror, his painting of Zhen Wu stood against the wall under the far alcove. She had been looking at it while the rain came. His own painting, it seemed, was the cause of her even being outside and in the place of danger. Everything, it appeared, was his fault.

As the thunder rang again, the artist repented to God.

"Lord, save her, and I shall never paint again."

Chapter 20

Cassandra woke up on the bed in the medicine room with acupuncture needles stuck all over her. Her hair was still wet from the rain.

"What happened?" the mythologist asked. Her head was throbbing.

"Don't you remember?" responded Aisha. "You saw your demon. Your white dragon."

"You fell into shock," said Sai-Lu, placing his hand on her forehead. "You've been unconscious for nearly an hour."

Then Cassandra remembered. It was like a scene from her own personal myth. The dragon appeared before her, and all she had to defend herself was Sai-Lu's spear. After dodging the dragon's lunges a few times, she grounded herself in a horse stance, drew back the spear and hurled it at the dragon in the air. Amazingly enough, the spear had hit the dragon right in the belly! Unfortunately, it didn't pierce the dragon's rough hide hard enough. The white dragon pulled the spear out with its mouth and snapped it with its teeth. After that, it started to rain. She couldn't remember anything more.

"These things take time, Cassandra," Sai-Lu tried to assure her. "Mastering your demon is no easy task."

After her treatment was finished, Cassandra went with Sai-Lu and Aisha to the dining area. It surprised her to find Zhen Wu sitting at one of the large, round tables. A tan old woman with round cheeks and long, straight, white hair sat next to him. The table was set with plates, glasses, and chopsticks, and food was abundant: black rice, curried eggplant, lion's mane mushrooms, yams, and other fine delicacies. Hui-Lum poured wine from a flask that was oddly reminiscent of old Greek pottery.

"*Shifu*? What are you doing here?"

"Sit down, Cassandra. We will not train today. Instead, we will all feast together."

Cassandra and her two companions thanked him and joined the table. Zhen Wu then introduced his guest:

"This is the Venerable Sage Lao Tai-Tai." The name meant 'old woman' in Chinese. "She is visiting us from Purple Cloud Palace, over on the northern slope of Mount Wudang. She is an old friend of mine."

"It is an honor to meet you," said Aisha in her soft Persian accent.

"I am honored as well," said Cassandra.

Lao Tai-Tai spoke, "I believe Zhen Wu has told you all about his journey to immortality. No? Then I will. I met him when he was still a young man. He left home at the age of fifteen to seek enlightenment in the mountains. He trained in all the Taoist ways of meditation, martial arts, and asceticism. Then, after forty-two years, he perfected the Way and became a Taoist Immortal."

"How did he perfect the Way?" Cassandra asked.

"Not with impatience, Cassandra," Zhen Wu answered. "It was Lao Tai-Tai who first helped me. When I came to Nanyan Palace I saw her out by a well, sitting with a large bar of iron on her lap. She was scratching the iron bar with a small metal file. I asked her what she was doing, and she said she was filing down the iron bar to make a sewing needle. I was only a boy, and so I asked her: 'Why do you want to spend so much time filing down a large iron bar just to make a needle?' Lao Tai-Tai's answer was very instructive to me. She explained that there is no shortcut to immortality. Some ways of doing things may seem quicker, like starting with a smaller piece of iron, but in the end there is only one Way. It is the way of persistence."

"You filed an iron bar all the way into a sewing needle? Incredible!" exclaimed Aisha.

"And Zhen Wu learned to do the same," the old woman explained, "except not with a bar of iron. The piece he would file down over those long forty-two years was his own ego."

"How did he do that?" the mythologist asked.

The white-haired Lao Tai-Tai replied, "Your *shifu* realized one day that he had mastered all the exercises, and that there was nothing he couldn't do, no fight he could not win. When he was training, he felt strong and secure in his destiny of immortality. But when he wasn't training, he felt there remained impurities inside of him that were obstacles to perfection. True, he had learned to be still and to pacify all the evils and passions within his mind, However, these passions would always come back to haunt him. They were the impurities of his soul.

"So, to purify his soul, he went down into the north foothills where there was a river of clear water and decided to wash his organs in this river. He took a knife and slit his belly open. When he did this, black water spilled from his gut, and his organs fell into the river. Zhen Wu bathed in the river and became purified, but when he went to put his stomach back inside of him, it resisted. Instead, his stomach transformed into a giant red turtle. His intestines also resisted, and so they transformed into a giant red snake. To this day, the demon turtle and snake travel together and sabotage seekers of the Way. Lucky for us, now that Zhen Wu is a Taoist Immortal, he will live forever in order to protect Mount Wudang from their evil influence."

"The turtle and the snake from your portrait!" Cassandra observed. "Do you mean, *Shifu*, that the turtle and snake are your demons, like the dragon is my demon?"

"You could think of them that way," Zhen Wu answered. "But try not to. These demons were inside me. But after I cut them out and purified myself, they were no longer my demons. In fact, you could say that the turtle and the snake are me and I am them. They are as immortal as I am. Ha-ha!"

Everyone at the banquet laughed along with him, enjoying the food and wine as if nothing outside the present moment existed. Cassandra felt happier than she had felt in years.

The feast reminded her of her old life—not her schooling or her struggles to assimilate, but the parts of her life that felt most real: family, food and company while celebrating special occasions. She thought back to the last time her family had thrown an event like this. It was on her brother George's thirtieth birthday. There was wine, gifts, and loads of laughter. It was the last time Cassandra had seen her mother with a carefree smile on her face. Alas, it now seemed no more than a myth.

After the impromptu banquet in the dining hall, Cassandra asked to follow Lao Tai-Tai back to Purple Cloud Palace and train there for a year or two. Zhen Wu accommodated her wish and gave her a new black robe made of thicker fabric for the winter.

"The north slope gets chillier than here," he explained.

What began as a year of training with Lao Tai-Tai turned into several years of personal reflection and devotion. She learned to move and breathe more evenly and study Taoist philosophy. She helped Lao Tai-Tai cultivate an herb garden on a terraced slope of the mountain, and even learned to brew alchemical potions. One time, Lao Tai-Tai's great-grandson—a silver-haired man said to be more than a hundred years old— showed Cassandra how to wield a sword. She didn't like it, but thanked the peculiar old sage anyway.

Upon her return to Nanyan Palace, the monks and priests welcomed her back with enormous exuberance.

"Let's have a party!" exclaimed Hui-Lum. Aside from the monks' eagerness to break their strict regimen on her behalf, the thing that surprised her most was how Aisha had changed. She seemed so much older, calmer, and wiser than when they had first met.

"I could say the same about you, Cassandra," said the Persian, handing Cassandra a mirror.

It was the first time she had seen a mirror in over eight years. Tiny wrinkles had emerged near Cassandra's eyes and on the edges of her mouth.

"Holy hell! How old am I?" she shouted carelessly, silencing the room. The silence was broken by the barefooted immortal, Laughing Daisy, who came over and smashed the mirror in front of her, cackling like a madman. Cassandra thought to herself, "I've come to live in such a fantastical world of crazy immortals and Taoist legends. How can I ever leave?"

But Cassandra knew she would have to leave eventually. She had to face her demon. At the end of her twelfth year, she decided to leave Nanyan Palace and summon the white dragon alone. She climbed to the highest point on Heavenly Pillar Peak and waited. Night came, and a shimmering full moon lit the sky. Sure enough, the dragon appeared.

"I have waited twelve years for you," Cassandra told the dragon. For some reason, she said it in Greek.

"No. I have waited for you," the white dragon seemed to say. Its voice echoed so loudly in her mind that she wasn't sure it had spoken aloud at all.

The dragon circled around Cassandra in a counterclockwise formation, which she mirrored with her own stride. It was just like walking around the *ba gua* circle. When the dragon got close, she quickly used the 'swimming body change' to evade its grasping claws. Frustrated, the dragon unleashed a fierce, orange plume of fire from its mouth. Cassandra did not back away. Instead, she lunged toward the dragon, wrapping her arms around its body and hugging it tightly. This made the dragon especially aggravated, as the added weight made it difficult to fly. But Cassandra stuck to the dragon like glue, and when the dragon leapt off of the side of Heavenly Pillar Peak, she clung onto its belly still.

The angry dragon clawed at her while flying, trying to shake her off of his belly. Cassandra managed to hang on. Instead of clawing back, she reached her mouth up to the dragon's ear and whispered to it. She whispered a phrase in Greek she had learned long ago and would never repeat to anyone, a phrase from the depths of her unconscious. As the dragon heard her, it slowed down its wings and came to a landing. Cassandra could tell the dragon's eyes were pacified and its nostrils were softening. She rubbed the dragon's belly with her hands, and then mounted its back. "Let's go."

The dragon leapt into the sky with a smile on its face. As she rode the dragon, she admired the verdant forests surrounding Mount Wudang and recited a chant of gratitude for her teachers and friends. She felt they were a part of her, as was the dragon. Everything was a part of her story. All things in the inner and outer world converged in the identity and soul of Cassandra Yin, the Chinese-Greek, the legendary mythologist who would bring balance to the East and the West.

The view of Mount Wudang from above was heavenly. She could see Nanyan Palace in the distance as she flew westward, her heart set on home. After a while, she felt herself yawning. She closed her eyes and leaned back on the dragon's back. They were moving quickly through the air. Strangely, however, with her sleepy eyes closed she felt as though she were lying on a bed with wheels, being rolled away into the night.

Then, all was dark.

......

Jason Yin and his friend Sophia stood frozen amidst a harrowing face-off in Omonia. The mob of angry Chinese-Greeks stood strong and vengeful, demanding that the referendum to ban all immigration be quashed. Some were recent immigrants with barely any depth of contact in Athens, while many were second and even third-generation citizens who had long grown tired of being treated as foreigners. A few of them were old enough to have known the wars and fought beside the rest of the Greeks in patriotic duty, but most were young and working-age, able to arouse energy and dynamism to the cause.

Despite their individual stories, each rioter contributed solidarity and conviction, vulnerability and responsibility for their risky actions. They demanded justice for the killing of the two Chinese earlier that week. They were prepared to take an eye for an eye.

Opposite the rioters was an equally angry mob of Greek reactionaries. Among them, some were hard-core nationalists who touted the proposed immigration ban and had rioted against the Chinese before. Others were sympathizers who believed in dialogue and only took to protesting in order to denounce the violence they were seeing. A few were simply oblivious to the reasons for the conflict and wanted a piece of the action.

As a combined total, the mob scared Jason, for it both revealed and expressed the warring factions within his psyche: the one part that wanted his Chinese side to be loved and constantly expressed, and the other part that wanted to forget being Chinese and assimilate to the Greek identity. It was a war of motherland and fatherland, of change and resistance, and of future and past.

The three guards stood with Jason and Sophia determined to keep the twelve-year-olds safe. They stood their ground, exchanged code words with each other to form a plan, and then nodded to affirm it. The two sides were getting closer. Jason could feel the heat of the conflict and the smell of hatred.

Before they were near enough to clash, the guards used their beating sticks to break the window of the nearest building. They lifted the children in through and out of harm's way while the riot ensued. Sophia pulled her dark-blue hood over her head and held her eyes and ears closed the whole time. Jason squinted his eyes and watched through the jagged edges of glass.

It was nearly ten minutes until police backup arrived and the riot could be contained. Men in dark suits with full-body transparent shields emerged from armored vehicles and lined up to face the rioters. For a brief moment, there was a clearing in the street between the two sides, and Sophia suddenly cried out.

"My necklace!"

"What? Where?" asked Jason. He remembered her showing

him the silver-stringed necklace with the round pendant. It had a black-and-white engraving of the *ba gua* on it.

"It's on the ground." She pointed to the street. "It must have fallen off."

"We can go and get it when it's safe," said the guard that held her, "and then we'll get you home."

"Please, no!" she shouted. "My father gave it to me on the day he was deployed. He said it was a symbol of how all things in the universe change and return to balance, just like he would come back someday."

"Come on, now," consoled the guard, "it will be okay. You have other things to remind you of your father."

"It's not the same. That *ba gua* is my faith. My lifeline!"

"I'll get it for you," shouted Jason as he slipped away from the guard that held him.

"Jason, be careful!" the girl cried.

"Get back here, *kinezaki*!" called the guard as he stood up and chased the boy around. That name—which Jason hated—only spurred on his determination to keep his distance. A blast, fired from the riots, sent dust through the air into the building.

"I'm almost there!" Jason exclaimed. He leapt through the broken window and darted into the street to fetch the *ba gua* necklace. The first two guards rushed toward the window to grab Jason. The third guard, who had remained with Sophia, now stood up to follow what was going on.

"Jason, don't get too close!" called Sophia. "Remember Icarus!"

The mayhem of the street was dizzying. Jason retrieved the necklace without trouble, but then stood there, paralyzed by distress.

"Jason, hurry!" screamed Sophia in tears.

As the guards reached Jason and stood on either side to protect him, he could hear the voices of the angry mobs beating upon his brain like a hailstorm. All the familiar refrains stormed through: Greece for the Greeks! Chinese, go home! He even heard a few angry outbursts directed at him personally. All of this was torture to the poor boy. It made him unable to move on his own.

Suddenly, the olive-skinned man with the camo-colored pistol appeared. He was the man Jason briefly thought looked like Master Nikos, except his face had a wicked and distorted expression. The man raised his pistol at the guards and fired. The bullet ricocheted off the wall of the building behind them. When the guards drew their guns, the man lowered his pistol slowly. He detached a grenade from his belt and gripped it in his hands like a juicy, ripe orange. Then he ignited it and threw it past the two guards and into the building where Sophia and the third guard were hiding. It exploded, and flames filled the building. Jason looked back at the smoke that poured from the broken window and screamed.

"Sophia! No!"

The first guard immediately shot the man, while the second guard ran into the building looking for Sophia. A collective groan ran through the crowd, followed by a swell of discontent. Jason watched the building erupt in flames and squeezed Sophia's necklace in his hand. This was the danger his grandmother had warned him about. It made him sick to his stomach, and also angry.

He stared at the fallen body of the olive-skinned man. The man's pants were also a camo design—not elegant and peaceful like the *yin-yang*, but full of meaningless green and brown splotches that had no pattern, no balance, and no comfort. Like those incoherent splotches, the riots gave him no clarity as to whether he was Greek or Chinese—they only filled his mind with chaos. His only hope was for the twisted game of violence to end. Perhaps, he thought, there was an overseer somewhere who could guide both sides into balance, like the dark and light sides of the *yin-yang*.

"God, help us!" Jason shouted, only to keel over seconds later as his stomach emptied itself onto the sidewalk.

Soon, more backup arrived, and the energy died down. As

the first guard escorted the queasy Jason to his police car to drive him home, the second guard emerged from the building carrying a wounded Sophia in his arms. Jason could barely see her through the smoke and darkness, but he knew it was her, and he knew she was alive.

"Thank you, God." the boy whispered.

Two Greeks were killed. And a girl was in critical condition.

Chapter 21

It was a day of devastation for both Jason and Loukas. When Jason woke up the next day, his mother comforted him in bed, saving her rebukes for later. His father and grandmother, on the other hand, let him have it.

"But where's Sophia?" he protested. "She needs her necklace back!"

As he held the pendant in his hand, he rubbed it with his fingers and wished for her recovery. Worrying about her, at least, helped him take his mind off of how much trouble he was in. He could not believe that Sophia was meant to die. Amidst his gravest fears, he still had hope.

Neither had Loukas believed it was Cassandra's fate to die. But he could not deny what he had seen. He had tried to save her, but by the time he reached her she was lying on a stretcher with a sheet over her body. Death was all around him, he felt, recalling the newspaper that Svetan had shown him. Two Greeks were killed in a riot, and a twelve-year-old girl was in critical condition.

"Maybe Svetan was right," he thought. "Maybe this will be a wakeup call for everyone, and the violence will cease."

Something inside of Loukas was also in critical condition. During his life of forty years he had always felt a yearning to see what could not be seen. His soul's most vigorous impulse was to peer beyond the veil of what was apparent and express the unseen, which usually meant painting it. Now, more than ever before, his passion for iconography fed that impulse, since he had learned from Master Yan-Mei to cross this veil with the body as well as the eyes. Within the last three days he had entered the icons of Saint Macarius of Egypt and Saint Theodora the Empress. He had met the saints in their own times and places. He had also feasted his eyes on the *Sinai Pantocrator*, the icon he adored more than any other, and witnessed Master Yan-Mei steal it from Father Feyzal's keeping.

But the things he saw were short-lived. In his passion for restoring the fading icons and retrieving the stolen *Pantocrator*—which he hoped to enter and meet his Savior—he had led Cassandra into danger. His gluttony for the unseen had caused her death. With that death, so too his personal longing to paint met its devastating end.

Still in mourning, Loukas returned to the monastery thoroughly drenched by the rain. He dried himself off, borrowed a change of clothes from Svetan, and visited the church. It was empty, and yet the presence of the saints in the icons and frescoes that adorned the colorful interior filled his heart with comfort. In his faith, at least, there was room for redemption.

The pilgrimage would end, and the truth of his purpose would be revealed. Loukas made the sign of the cross and knelt before an icon of a golden-crowned Mary holding the Christ Child. In the Child's hand was a spherical orb, painted blue like an earth globe with a black equator across the middle. On the top half of the globe there was a golden sun, and on the bottom half a silver crescent moon. Indeed, Christ held the aching world in his hand. In his eyes, Loukas saw how Christ felt the world ache.

With a sudden jerk, Loukas broke eye contact with the Christ Child. "I am unworthy of your love. I am unworthy of meeting you. I am unworthy even painting you." He wept for several minutes, letting his crying voice reverberate throughout the empty spaces of the nave. "Forgive me. Lord, have mercy!"

When he opened his eyes, he spied something different on the left side of the nave. His portrait of Saint George had been hung, like an icon, on the wall opposite the Christ Child.

"It can't be," he thought. "I am not an iconographer. They

should never allow my work here." He went over to the painting and stared it down, wishing it weren't real. In the church's cave-like setting, lit by candles from above, Saint George seemed mysterious and aloof. Once again, the artist averted his eyes. "I am not worthy of any of this."

"Adrian Loukas," whispered a resonant voice from behind him. Brazhnikov stood at the door of the nave. "Forgive me for disturbing you. I've come to apologize."

Loukas wiped a tear from his eye and reluctantly invited Brazhnikov to join him in front of his *Saint George.*

"We missed you at dinner," the Bulgarian said casually. But Loukas was not in the mood for small talk, or any talk for that matter. Brazhnikov apparently did not know that Cassandra was carried away on a stretcher, and Loukas wasn't in the mind to explain what had happened.

"I was held up."

"Don't worry, Adrian. I gave up my dagger. Svetan has it now."

"And?" Loukas asked sharply, expecting something more.

"And I've come to tell you that I will be serving my sentence here for the crimes I have committed. The stealing of the icons, I mean. And the kidnapping, the threatening, well, you know it already. I'm even giving up drinking."

"You're sorry? Is that all?"

"That is all, and that is everything," Brazhnikov said sincerely. "I am sorry."

"What do you mean when you say you are serving your sentence?"

"I've arranged to sell all my possessions and become a monk here at Zographou. I will take Jesus as my only *shifu*, and I will never leave again."

"You've...what?"

"And don't worry about the *Pantocrator*. The silver suitcase is safe. I sent it along with the other stolen icons back to Mount Sinai. Father Feyzal should receive it in a few days."

"I...don't know what to say." The news was so unexpected

that the artist was lost for words.

"You've done a fine job with our *Saint George*, by the way."

"I'm not so convinced," the artist sighed. "I didn't exactly follow the rules. I added a little dragon in the background."

"Hmm." pondered Brazhnikov. "If you're not happy with it, I'm sure Svetan will allow you to redo it."

"But that's the thing," the artist protested. "I feel as though this pilgrimage has taught me something very difficult."

"What's that?"

"I should never paint again."

"What in the devil are you talking about?"

"*Saint George* will be my last painting." Loukas nodded to himself as he reinforced his thoughts. "My work has caused too much suffering, especially for..." He trailed off, unable to speak about Cassandra. "And my divorce? Well, that's another nail in the coffin. When I go home, I will pray to the Lord for guidance and ask how to start my life anew."

Brazhnikov nodded with his eyes closed. He placed his large, warm hand on Loukas's shoulder. "You and me both."

The two of them stood facing the icon for a few minutes in silence. Eventually, Loukas let his eyes wander onto the nearby fresco of the Resurrection. It was the scene of the ultimate miracle—Jesus of Nazareth conquered death by appearing to the disciples after being buried in the tomb. It was the central event of the Christian religion, and its twenty-foot-high commemoration on the back wall certainly did it justice. In fact, everything in Zographou's church was visually exquisite, from the frescoes to the icons, and even the ornately carved chairs that lined the side walls. Part of him envied the Bulgarian for getting to spend the rest of his life there.

"You know, Adrian, there is another option."

"What do you mean?"

"Why wait until you get home to pray? Saint George is right here. He can give you the guidance you need."

Loukas turned back to face his painting of Saint George. The saint's gold-plated armor shimmered in the candlelight.

"Wait a second!" the artist cried in alarm. "The white dragon is gone. Where did it go?"

"That seems like another question you should ask Saint George himself. Go on. Enter the icon."

"But my painting is not an icon."

"You don't need to repeat yourself, Adrian. There are many icons of Saint George here to choose from. Look around."

The artist held his breath and looked around. It was an intriguing idea, and the more he considered it the more it felt like the right thing to do. He would go to Saint George directly and ask for guidance. The only question was which icon would be best suited for his visit with the saint.

"Which one should I choose?" he asked.

As Loukas perused the icons around him, the largest one of all stood out. It was as tall as his own height and stood on an altar three feet high. The saint's face was long and narrow, twice the size of a normal man's head, with deep, melancholy eyes that penetrated the soul. The face was complete with a perfect continuum of flesh tones and shading, and yet somehow there appeared to be no layering to the painter's technique at all. To the observant artist, it was as if all of the paint for the face had been applied all at once by a single imprint. Loukas smiled, as he knew this could not have been done by human hands.

"This one," said the artist as he identified the holy icon.

"Your perceptions never fail," confirmed Brazhnikov. "This icon is the jewel of Zographou, the one painted by God Himself. If you enter the icon, you will surely get the guidance you need."

"Will you be here when I come out of it?"

"Of course."

"How can I trust you?"

Brazhnikov made the sign of the cross with his right hand.

"As I said, I will never leave."

Loukas released his breath and made eye contact with Saint George. Soon enough, he felt himself entering the icon.

......

Saint George dwelt in a world beyond wonders. The sky was black as pitch, and yet the saint's golden armor gleamed brilliantly. Silver streams of stardust shimmered in the saint's presence. Around his solemn face was an aura of heavenly knowing. Loukas knelt before him.

"Your soul bears much trouble, my son," said Saint George tenderly.

"I must confess my sins," the artist explained. "I fear that I have caused another's death. Not directly, but through my painting, and my slowness to come to her rescue."

"Tell me more," invited the saint.

Loukas held nothing back. He poured out his words as he purged himself at the saint's feet. From the incident of his abduction, to meeting Cassandra, to painting Zhen Wu and also Saint George himself—all of it tumbled out in an irrepressible stream of consciousness.

"I don't see anything sinful with painting."

"The painting wasn't the sin. It was my ego. When I learned to use icons to pass into the worlds of the saints, I thought I could also develop the power to bring the saints back to us. I secretly dreamed of bringing Jesus back to us through the icon of the *Pantocrator*. Oh, my vain thinking! He would never have needed my help to come. Instead I brought forth an evil, white dragon into the world, and this monster killed my friend, Cassandra. I confess, this was my fault. Help me repent, please! Help me do right by this poor woman's soul."

"The powers of the supernatural are not for human beings to control. You already know that. Even the saints cannot control them. Neither you nor any other painter can bring things through the veil without God's intervention. Do you think God would have allowed it if it wasn't part of His plan?"

"Are you saying that Cassandra was meant to die?"

"We're all meant to die. Do you think you could have

saved her?"

"Well," the artist sighed. This was the hardest part of his confession. "I saw her in danger, and I should have run to save her. I should have been there to help her! But I was distracted by thoughts and worries, and instead of leaving right away I tried to take the silver suitcase with me. I was obsessed with recovering the *Sinai Pantocrator*. But carrying the suitcase was too difficult. I was too slow. Sure, I could have come back later, after I knew Cassandra was safe, but I refused to leave it. By the time I got there, they were wheeling Cassandra's body away."

Saint George looked at Loukas with soft eyebrows.

"Your heart is pure. You are not responsible for Cassandra's death, if indeed she has died."

"Oh, thank God," the artist uttered as he prostrated himself again.

"But Providence has involved you in her story. This is part of fate's grand design."

"What should I do?"

"Go to Cassandra's family. Tell them all you witnessed, and listen to their grief. Be a soft ear for them, a shoulder to cry on."

"I can do that," the artist agreed, overwhelmed with gratitude that his repentance could be so straightforward.

"And honor her memory using one of your spiritual gifts."

Loukas froze.

"You mean...painting?"

"Yes. Paint her. Paint her!"

Saint George's vehement command seemed to make the golden armor vibrate.

"But...I can't. I can never paint again."

"Tell me. When was the last time you painted something purely from your heart, not because you wanted something or because you were forced to, but because God made your soul yearn to express His essence?"

Loukas thought back to his pilgrimage to Mount Sinai.

"It was my *Sinai Sunrise*. When I started to paint it, I felt that I was capturing the essence of God's power and glory. For a while, it felt effortless, like the image was being driven through me from the other side of the veil. But then I lost focus and ruined it. Oh, I was so vain!"

"Wrong! Your vanity did not paint the *Sinai Sunrise*. Your vanity only tries to take the credit for it. Adrian, be at peace. Look to the iconographers of the past. Did any of them write their names at the bottom of the icons? No. Take any icon in any old church, and most likely its human creator is now completely anonymous. The mortal vessels who mixed the colors and applied the paint are lost in the dust of history."

"Like me."

"Not yet, my son. You are not lost in the dust of history. You are the living history. Look at yourself and remember. Your image and likeness are the very same as the One who created you, who put you here on this earth to paint and who gave you the fortitude to carry out your destiny."

"How can I possibly live up to such a destiny?" Loukas protested wearily. "Painting the image and likeness of God is beyond my humble talents."

"Then maybe you are setting your ambitions too high. You are not an iconographer, remember."

Loukas laughed. Finally, someone had relieved him of that burdensome expectation.

The saint continued. "You are not meant to paint God, or even the saints. Your art is not meant to be praised or venerated throughout the centuries like an extraordinary masterpiece. It's not iconography that you aspire for. No! You are meant to paint the ordinary, and nothing more."

"The ordinary," the artist repeated.

"Paint the ordinary sunrise, but paint it so that God's essence reaches us through it."

It made sense. "Yes. Yes!"

"Paint the ordinary person, the humblest of all souls, one who is most in need of God's love. And give your painting away. Do you understand?"

"I do," the artist nodded. "Cassandra once told me she always kept her mind empty. She sees virtue in being empty—even empty of the belief in God—because emptiness makes her capable of receiving. That is Taoist philosophy, I think. My cup is overflowing with God's love, I told her. But I think no person can be completely empty. Even in someone whose heart is empty of faith and religion, there is still the image and likeness of God. That is what I will try to paint. I will paint Cassandra in this image and likeness. And I will give my painting to her family in Athens. They deserve closure, at the very least." His heart was brimming with divine inspiration. He could see Cassandra's face in his mind's eye. Everything was becoming clear.

Saint George held out his golden spear and touched Loukas's shoulders with it one after the other. "Your gift is great, and your heart seeks solace. Seek, and you shall find."

Loukas thanked Saint George and stood up. Looking up he admired the magnificent, dark sky. He placed his palms together at his heart and said a prayer. Then he looked back at the sky. The longer he looked, the more bits of silver dust he saw, which were streamed into the glowing night's sky. Saint George's face and armor also glowed and electrified the night like the aurora borealis. Way up in the distance, there was something else: a little white dragon hurtling through the sky.

"Impossible!" he exclaimed, though he struggled not to smile. It was the same dragon that he had painted himself in his own *Saint George*, except now it was here instead. The dragon hovered tamely and morosely around the venerable saint as if it were a ghost. For a split second, when Loukas squinted, he thought he saw Cassandra riding upon it. "How strange." He rubbed his eyes, and then the dragon vanished. Perhaps it had gone back to his own painting, he surmised, or had simply returned to the space behind the veil of the uncreated forms. Whatever the case, the artist was ready to let it go.

It was decided. He would spend one night at Moni Zographou, and then leave to complete his pilgrimage.

Chapter 22

Cassandra Yin woke up on the stretcher with a sheet still over her face. Removing it, she found herself in complete darkness. The air was damp and smelled strongly of incense. She clapped her hands to sound an echo, and then reached out her hands to feel around. Testing the ground with her feet, she realized it was made of cool stone, like that of the inside of a cave. She could hear a faint sound of trickling water, which she decided to follow.

"Hello? Is anybody there?"

The mythologist crawled on her hands and knees to better navigate the cave without eyesight. The sound of the water gradually became louder, which made her hopeful of finding an exit.

While crawling she thought of many myths related to trudging through the darkness: first, Theseus and the labyrinth. She imagined herself searching through King Minos's labyrinth, hunting down the minotaur. She reached dead ends and retraced her steps several times. However, with the exception of the sound of running water, the cave was quiet. No such monster lurked within it. Cassandra wondered if that meant she had conquered her demon and mastered it for good.

"Can anyone hear me?" she called as she kept crawling.

The second myth she thought of was that of Sun Wukong, the legendary Monkey King. Sun Wukong lived in a village of monkeys near a stream with a waterfall. One day the monkeys started asking themselves where the water came from, and they looked up the waterfall to see it spilling out of a cave. They proclaimed that whoever could climb up into the cave and follow the rushing water to its source would be their king.

Sun Wukong's first act in the legend was to enter the cave and make a home for all of the monkey's inside it, earning him the title of Monkey King. As Cassandra crawled towards the trickling water, she imagined reaching its source and finding something there worthy of accreditation. Quickly, however, she dismissed that unlikely outcome from her mind.

"Hello?" she continued to call, getting no response.

Her thoughts moved on to Plato's *Allegory of the Cave*. This myth told of a society of people dwelling in a cave never knowing the beauty and truth of the outside world. They believed the cave itself was the only reality. Such a cave-dweller, Plato conjectured, would not only denounce the existence of a world outside the cave, but if he ever emerged from the cave, he would dismiss it as an illusion and cover his eyes. The meaning of the myth was that people who live their entire lives in caves, metaphorically speaking, would prefer to climb back into the cave and live out the rest of their existence in darkness, rather than open their eyes and experience a brighter, more colorful world.

Cassandra imagined herself trying to explain the *Allegory of the Cave* to the Greek public from the pulpit of a national stage. If she had the whole country's attention, she thought, this would be a revelatory myth to tell. It could help the Greeks learn to recognize the 'darkness' of their view of immigrants and the need to rise into a higher reality: the reality of the Way, in which opposing forces of *yin* and *yang* could coexist and not struggle against one another.

She would explain to them that the world outside the 'cave' was one like Mount Wudang in China, where people cared more about each other than about following rules and protecting one's own interests. Certainly, there were societies on earth who would deny that any lifestyle was preferable to their own, or even that another lifestyle was possible. If ever a peaceful reality were in sight, certain people—powerful people—would fight and cause riots for the chance to make everyone close their eyes again and return to the darkness of the cave.

"On second thought," she considered, "the *Allegory of the Cave* may be too abstract to persuade a general audience. I would need to choose a myth that everyone can see and understand." The mythologist continued to contemplate as she crawled.

The cave's passageways alternated between wide and narrow. Some were tight channels she had to slip through like a misshapen coin into a slot, while others were cavernous rooms that had to be explored carefully so as not to mistakenly end up where she began.

"Whatever myth I tell will have to reach deep into the collective unconscious and speak to a universal truth."

A falling stone interrupted her thought. Then the squeaking of a rat pierced through the quiet. The trickling water was getting louder. She figured that it must be only one cavernous chamber away. As she got closer, she looked down and saw faint traces of light emanating from a hole near the ground. Squatting down as carefully as she could, she wriggled through the hole and stumbled around the corner. At last she had escaped the darkness, and now found herself standing at the entrance to someplace else.

"Welcome," greeted a female monk in a brown cassock. She was robust with long, silvery hair. Next to the monk stood a short, very muscular woman in an identical brown cassock. She was Chinese, and she wore her black hair up in an infinity-shaped bun. Cassandra quickly checked her pocket for her glasses—which, miraculously, were not broken—and put them on.

"Master Yan-Mei?"

"Yes, Cassandra," she answered. The *shifu's* deep, grainy voice echoed against the cave wall behind her. "And this is my friend, Mother Helen."

Cassandra greeted Mother Helen with a bow. Next to them, a miniature fountain was carved into a stone pedestal, which contained medieval Greek inscriptions. A small icon of *The*

Resurrection was placed behind the fountain and illuminated with an incandescent light.

"Where are we?"

"We are still in Athos," explained Mother Helen. "Except we are underneath it." As she lifted her hands to point further into the cave, Cassandra could see bracelets with wooden charms of the Orthodox cross on both of Mother Helen's wrists. Her silvery hair seemed to shine in the darkness of the cave like a secret gem begging to be discovered.

"Come in," invited Master Yan-Mei. She fitted a brown monastic cap over her hair and led Cassandra into an open cavern the size of a large amphitheater. "This is one of Greece's greatest secrets. We call it Moni Bardous, our monastery in the dark."

Cassandra could not believe her eyes. Moni Bardous was built entirely inside an underground cavern below Mount Athos. Its walls were painted with religious frescoes and adorned with gold-plated icons and cherry oak-framed lighting fixtures. Cavernous passageways opened up into rooms, chapels, a dining area and a large cathedral. The ceiling was vaulted so high it did not even give the impression of being underground. Nuns moved busily carrying all kinds of supplies: bibles, chotchkies, religious figurines, musical instruments and important-looking, embroidered linens. Everyone was joyously greeting each other as they walked by. Some were even singing.

"It's a women's monastery!" Cassandra exclaimed.

"There is no need to state the obvious," shushed Master Yan-Mei. "Come with me." Master Yan-Mei took Cassandra through a hallway painted mahogany brown and into a cozy bedchamber. The walls inside the chamber were made of uneven, differently-sized rocks, which gave the impression of being in an old castle. She laid a pile of Cassandra's clothes on the bed, which had been fetched from Moni Zographou, though the mythologist did not know when or how.

"You will stay the night here, and tomorrow we will go

back to Athens." The *shifu* did not smile. "I believe you have something that is mine."

"That is true," Cassandra responded, trying to sound unintimidated. Zhen Wu's stillness training made this much easier than it used to be. "Your painting of Zhen Wu is a safe place. You will get it back when you return the icons you have stolen."

"Thank you." In an instant, Master Yan-Mei's voice turned sweet as she took off her cap and set it on a table next to an icon of Saint Augustine Zhao Rong, the Chinese martyr.

Despite the dim lighting in the room, the gold-plated icon seemed to glow. Cassandra studied Master Yan-Mei's face, which suddenly seemed warmer and less threatening than before. The *shifu's* black eyes were peaceful like a still night beneath a watchful moon. Her large-knuckled hands were soft like the feet of a lamb and moved slowly and gracefully as she spoke. She resembled Master Zhang both in looks and in mannerisms. Seeing the *shifu* in this new light, Cassandra questioned whether this kinder, more sympathetic, more vulnerable side to her was true, or whether Master Yan-Mei was only behaving this way because her company was Chinese. After all, when dealing with Loukas, a foreigner, she had been manipulative and cruel.

Master Yan-Mei pointed at the wall opposite Cassandra's bed. "Adrian's work is exceptional, don't you think?"

There hung Loukas's painting of the Taoist Immortal, just as Cassandra remembered it. Like the icon of Saint Augustine Zhao Rong, it seemed to emit a glow amidst the darkness.

"Does he know where I am?" the mythologist asked.

"He thinks you are dead."

"But how did I get here?"

"I could tell you that," the *shifu* answered, inviting Cassandra to sit in a small wooden chair with a faded orange cushion. "But you may have an unfavorable opinion about the answer."

"Not so," she said proudly, sitting up straight against the wooden back of the chair. "Thanks to my gracious teachers, the Taoist Immortal Master Zhen Wu, the Venerable Sage Lao Tai-Tai, Master Sai-Lu, Master Hui-Lum, Master Aisha the Persian, the Laughing Daisy Immortal, and many others, I no longer have a mind for opinions about anything."

"Good," Master Yan-Mei answered. She lifted two blue ceramic teacups from a shelf and placed them on the table in front of them. "I rarely answer people's questions for that reason."

"I've spent the last twelve years training in a Taoist monastery on Mount Wudang."

The *shifu's* eyes lit up. "Hmm. Twelve years." She reached for a blue, octagonally shaped teapot and filled their cups with hot oolong tea.

"So, please tell me. How did I get here? Did you bring me here from Zographou?"

"Yes."

"Why?"

"You put yourself in danger by taking Zhen Wu's portrait outside with you. Fortunately for us, your mistake was to our advantage. We faked your death and brought you to Bardous to keep you safe from your demons. No one except Master Zhang and myself knows you did not die."

"How long was I asleep?" Cassandra asked as she blew on her steaming tea.

"Not long. It is still the same day as it was when you entered the portrait, but it is night."

"My family must be worried sick."

Cassandra had not yearned for her family's presence in what felt like many years. Jason, George, her mother, Daphne—all of them had been alive yet dormant in her mind while she lived on Mount Wudang. She thought about her father, who would have been proud of her *Kung Fu,* and of her grandparents back in the Xi'an of her childhood. She pictured all her departed relatives in photos on the living room shelf, some stone-faced with the pains of the past, others smiling with the hopes of the future. She smiled as she remembered Peony the cat, who made the household complete. Now, with the flood of sensory impressions filling up her twenty-first century mind, all the feelings erupted like lava from a volcano.

"I need to make a phone call!"

"Remember patience." Master Yan-Mei held up one hand, urging patience. "Soon enough, you will be with your family again."

Cassandra took a slow sip of tea and then sighed deeply.

......

Back in Moni Zographou, Loukas, too, thought of his family that night. His father, mother, sister Jeanne and her fiery preacher husband, nieces Kira and Susannah, little nephew Saul—they all held a place in his heart. He prayed for them while sitting upright on his bed with palms together.

He also prayed for his wife, Sharon: "May she find peace with the Lord, wherever she is, and love, wherever she chooses to be."

Everybody knew Loukas was on a pilgrimage, and they respected his need for time away to figure out his life. The artist had always had his eccentricities, but all of his family members loved him. Not one of them—including himself— had imagined his uncomfortable trip across the Sinai desert on a camel would end with him reposing in a Bulgarian monastery in Greece. As Loukas bowed his head he thanked God for each person and each event that led him to Athos. All was peaceful in his heart.

......

After Cassandra finished her tea with Master Yan-Mei, she prepared to sleep the night in Moni Bardous. She changed into a comfortable yellow gown and beige sheepskin slippers provided by Mother Helen. When Master Yan-Mei came to check in with her one last time for the night, Cassandra asked the question she had been wondering for a long time.

"I'm confused about Master Zhang," Cassandra began. "When we were at the train station, he acted like he had never seen me before. He seemed to not even recognize me. Why is that?"

"Don't be silly. That is the only time he has ever seen you."

"But we trained together that same morning, and also the day before that. Master Zhang was teaching me Wu Chi and some verses from the *Tao Te Ching*."

"That can't be true. Unless...no, never mind. Li-Kuo has not trained you."

"How do you think I knew to look for the painting? Master Zhang was the one who asked me to find it for you because it was stolen. Why would he send me after the painting and not tell you about it?"

"My brother does not keep secrets from me." The *shifu's* tone was gentle, yet uncompromising. Cassandra's manners forced her to acquiesce on the matter, but her mind continued to search for answers.

"Where is Master Zhang now?" she asked.

"*Είναι στο φως*," Master Yan-Mei answered, suddenly switching to Greek.

"What?"

"You probably don't understand that expression. 'In the light.' We use this phrase to refer to the men's monasteries above ground. Master Zhang is up there, so we say he is 'in the light.' But when we are down here in Moni Bardous, we say that we are 'in the dark.'"

"*Στο σκοτάδι*," Cassandra translated. "In the dark."

"Exactly. No one must ever speak of Bardous, especially while in the light."

"I understand. You're using the expressions 'light' and 'dark' for the upper and lower monasteries of Athos. They are symbols for male and female, just like *yin* and *yang*."

"Symbols, yes. But remember, there is a knowledge that goes deeper than symbols. This knowledge is the origin of all symbols, forms, energies, and the entire natural world. Do you remember what it is called?"

"I do," Cassandra answered, thinking of the Way. "Unfortunately, I cannot name it." According to the *Tao Te Ching*, as she had learned, the Way that could be named was not the true Way. "If I could, then it would lose its power."

"Zhen Wu has taught you much." Master Yan-Mei smiled. "But there is one great *shifu* who could teach you even more. He is the one who will take you to the end of your destiny."

"Who is he?"

Master Yan-Mei's face cast a smile so bright that a halo of *shen* seemed to radiate around her. "He is the only true immortal. Next to him, the others are like little babies not yet weaned from their mothers' milk."

"Another immortal?"

"His being is so eternal that we call him the Alpha and the Omega, the Beginning and the End. When you receive him, your soul will finally feel the holy rapture of perfection."

"Tell me his name."

"It is good that you have opened your mind, Cassandra. I will tell you. His name is Jesus of Nazareth."

Cassandra felt uncomfortable. She was stupefied—it felt like a ploy to convert her. Not wanting to appear impolite, she tried to change the subject.

"I am grateful to you also, Master Yan-Mei, for leading me to Zhen Wu's painting."

Master Yan-Mei's brow softened with increased concern for the mythologist. She folded her aged hands in her lap and spoke softly.

"If you want to complete your knowledge the Way, you will do well to open your heart to Christ."

Cassandra couldn't believe it. At least Loukas, when he approached the subject of Jesus, had been sensitive enough to stop. But Master Yan-Mei seemed to be trying to instruct her against her will. The *shifu's* presence was soft on her, like water, and yet it engulfed her with a blatant ulterior motive.

Cassandra looked down at her yellow gown and nervously pleated its fabric between her fingers.

"With respect, *Shifu*, I don't—"

"Do you think by training we will ever reach perfection? If we live on earth and train forever, do you think we will ever achieve the perfect balance of *yin* and *yang*?" Master Yan-Mei let her right hand float up in front of her to draw a *yin-yang* in the air. "We will always have imperfections. The world will always ache."

"I think part of training is to teach us to use our imperfections in order to become better," Cassandra countered.

"True, but training does not teach us to love our imperfections, Cassandra. That is the key. Christ is about love, not training."

"Are you saying training is pointless?"

"No, it is not pointless. But it is also not eternal. The Way itself is eternal, even though the world we live in, which follows its pattern, is not. Taoist masters like Zhen Wu might extend their lives for as long as they train, but they will never be sure they have found immortality. A veil of innocence covers their eyes—they lack the final revelation that would make life on earth complete: the truth of God's love for us and the eternal heaven that awaits us beyond our mortal deaths. Jesus himself said, 'I am the Way.' Follow the Way to eternity, Cassandra, and you will realize that Christ is its destination."

The *shifu* folded her hands on her lap and became still and quiet.

"But there's no...I don't know what to..." Cassandra pressed her fluffy slippers together and squeezed her fists.

Master Yan-Mei studied Cassandra's shifting eyes and unstable posture. "You're upset."

"I'm just not sure what's real anymore."

"Hmm. Maybe I should not have told you so much. I should have waited until you were ready."

Cassandra tried to hide her rolling eyes.

"It's okay, Cassandra," the *shifu* assured her. "You don't have to listen to me. Maybe what I am saying sounds like more myths and falsehoods to you." She stood up and cleared the empty teacups from the table. "Or, blame the holy bards of Bardous for filling my mouth with hot air!"

"Are you making fun of me?"

"Of course not," she grinned. "I only mean to remind you that you are still young. You have many stories to live before you get to the end. But no matter what you do, beware of your own mind. Empty it, yes, but also do not resist filling it. Let your heart be filled when the Way brings you an experience of love. Hold onto it. Who knows? Maybe you will find love soon. Anything is possible."

Cassandra looked over at Zhen Wu's portrait. She had spent twelve years emulating his knowledge of the Way. It was a beautiful time in her life, and she would never forget it. Likewise, she could never think to abandon her own undying quest for the Way within her. If she had to choose between the foreignness of the Orthodoxy and the myth of self-discovery that was dear to her heart, there was no contest.

What did Master Yan-Mei know about Cassandra or her search for love? No amount of reasoning could convince the mythologist she needed religion to fill her heart with love. She could follow the Way if she wanted, or abandon it. It was her choice.

"Thank you for your opinions, Master Yan-Mei. And for keeping me safe." Cassandra stood up and bowed cordially, secretly trying to shake off the residual discomfort of the conversation.

"You are welcome," nodded the *shifu*. "Now, you should sleep. Tomorrow we will go back to Athens." She left the chamber and closed the door.

As Cassandra laid her head to rest, so did Loukas in his own dormitory. The sweet and pious voices of the Athonite monks singing throughout the night—both in the dark and in the light—soothed their souls. Above ground, a spread of crisp nighttime stars illuminated the sky and made everything visible. Underground, inside the cavernous Moni Bardous, the cool air of the earth's interior purified the hearts of monks and pilgrims alike. Together, the worlds of heaven and earth, cave and mountain, female and male, light and dark, *yin* and *yang*—all the dualities formed from the original Way were brought to rest, at least for one night, in the peaceful, sacred repose of Athos.

Chapter 23

The Yin family was not unaccustomed to hardship. Their fourteen years in Greece were rife with problems, and no one bore the brunt end of these difficulties more than the grandmother, the matriarch. Most days she did not leave the apartment. The longer she lived in Greece, the more it intimidated her. With the exception of some aspects of Chinatown—the hanging lanterns, the smell of the outdoor market, and of course people speaking Mandarin—it still felt foreign.

Now that the matriarch was growing old in age, and the family was somewhat self-sufficient without her, a sickness born of the soul was catching up with her. As she sat on the couch next to her son George, she held her cane in her hand and pressed it into the floor, as if she was weighing a long decision about whether to get up. Then she released her grip on the cane and closed her eyes. She attempted to swallow but instead bent her head down to vomit.

"Hold on, mom," George comforted her. He held a large, round, orange bowl under her. "We should get you some tea to help keep the food down." He shouted to the bedroom: "Daphne! Come out here and make us tea!"

While they waited, the matriarch cursed her daughter-in-law and turned on the television. After a minute, Daphne appeared. She wore a sandstone towel around her hair and a beige towel around her body, which was bare and clean as a whistle.

"What were you doing in there?" George asked frustratedly. "We could hear the shower stop ten minutes ago."

"I've been waiting on your mother hand and foot all week. Can't I take my time?"

The matriarch fixed her eyes on the television as she inwardly criticized every aspect of Daphne's answer. For the last fourteen years, Daphne had failed to show she was submissive enough for her traditional standards. Being a mother to Jason only made her less of a fit for the mold.

"Next time we'll get Jason to do it," George said mindlessly as he watched the television. His voice was so loud, his wife winced. "Jason!"

"Let him rest, George," Daphne argued. "He's been through enough. I'll do it."

The television was playing a special news broadcast. A new anti-immigrant demonstration was happening in downtown Athens. Over a thousand people were gathered at the Theater of Dionysus, where a bombastic speaker took the center stage and rallied their support for the immigration ban. George was infuriated.

"Scoundrels! We once did laundry services for this theater. And now they allow those skunks to take it over? I say, we're not going to let them kick us out of Greece."

As they watched the news, Daphne sauntered in with the tea. She served it in silence until George yelled at her again.

"Why don't you get the boy up? Make him vacuum. He needs chores to do."

"He's not well, George."

"What's wrong with him? He's not sick. I don't understand why you let him miss school. He needs routine. He needs discipline."

"How can he concentrate on school after what he's seen?"

"It serves him right. Now he'll stay out of trouble because he understands what trouble is really like."

Daphne kept her tone reasonably restrained for her mother-in-law's sake as she argued back: "If you would only look at your son as he cries in bed you would understand." Then she went back into the bedroom to get dressed.

George shook his head. "And who let that cat out?"

Someone pounded on the door.

"Daphne!" called George. After she failed to appear, he got

up and answered the door himself.

In walked a short, swaggering man of thirty who wore a black leather vest and tattered, green khakis. His hair was curly and well-oiled, and it was long enough to stick out around the sides of his black baseball cap, which he wore with the brim to the back. He had three gold rings pierced in his left ear and two in his right. His arms contained a patchwork of tattoos, including an angry pit-bull, a tree with vein-like roots, and a modified *yin-yang* in the shape of a heart. He jolted to the breakfast nook with his hands in his pockets.

"Where's Cassandra?" the man shouted hotly. "Is she here?"

"What are you doing here, Stavros?"

Now that the Yin family had a guest over, etiquette obliged them to switch to Greek.

"She's been ignoring me for six days. Six days! Is it because I didn't give her a ring? Is she that upset?"

Stavros paced around the room and stopped to stare down the hallway. George tried to excuse himself so as to get his mother to the bedroom for privacy.

"I will not hide in the bedroom," refused the matriarch, adjusting her gray bandana. She set down the orange bowl and hid it behind the side of the couch. "I'm not dead yet."

"Cassandra's not here," George said to Stavros. "In fact, she didn't even come home last night."

"What do you mean, she didn't come home? I've been trying to call her, but her phone is off."

Daphne entered and greeted Stavros.

"Daphne, where's Cassandra?"

"She called me the day before yesterday. She said she was going to Thessaloniki to help a friend with an emergency."

"And what about mother?" George protested. "Cassandra should be here taking care of her."

"I can take care of myself," scowled the peevish matriarch.

"I know all her friends," Stavros insisted. "No one's seen her. She said she was on some mountain or something. What's that about?"

"Look, man," George said as he approached Stavros, putting a consoling hand on his shoulder, "I agree with you. Cassandra should be with you. She should just say yes. It's about time she got married and assimilated. If she doesn't, those skunks might try to send us back to China."

George's mother groaned.

Suddenly Jason burst into the living room. "WHY IS EVERYBODY FIGHTING IN HERE?"

"We're not fighting, Jason," his mother said, trying to comfort him. "We're just worried about Auntie."

"Why? Where is she?"

"Probably getting herself into trouble," George muttered. "But *you* know all about trouble, now. Don't you?"

Jason hid his teary eyes in his sleeve. Daphne comforted him and sat him down at the breakfast table. Then the boy pointed to the television.

"What are those people doing?"

"Maybe we should change the channel," suggested Daphne.

"No!" refused Jason as he leapt up to grab the remote from the armrest next to his grandma. "This is my country too, and I won't let you keep me in the dark."

A news flash came upon the television: "We're here at the hospital with the family of twelve-year-old Sophia Zikopoulos, who was left in critical condition after a riot explosion in Omonia two nights ago. Doctors say she is gaining strength and will make a full recovery. Her father says it was nothing short of an act of God that saved—"

"I'm sick of this," shouted George. He snatched the remote from Jason and turned off the television.

"Hey! That was my friend!"

"Your friend?"

Jason pulled out the girl's *ba gua* necklace from his pocket.

"I need to give this back to her!"

He leapt out of his seat like a grasshopper and reached for the remote in his dad's hands. He managed to press the on button.

"What do you want to watch that for?" his father griped. He turned the television back off and held the remote out of the boy's reach.

"I want to see Sophia."

Jason went to the television set and manually turned it back on.

"What do you think you're doing?" George threw down the remote without turning the television off.

"You're always hiding things from me, Dad. How come I never get to go to China or read about China? How come I never get to go to church or learn about God? How am I supposed to know who I am?"

George raised his voice even further to deal a long-winded rebuke in Mandarin. During this tirade the grandmother chimed in a few times but was unable to gain the floor without her son talking over her.

"Maybe you should leave," Daphne urged Stavros. "We'll call you as soon as we get word about Cassandra."

"And why does Stavros always have to leave?" challenged Jason.

"It's not a good time, Jason," his mother explained.

"Listen while I'm talking to you, boy!" George interjected. He struck the boy on the side of the head, causing him to bury his head back in his sleeve. As Daphne came to comfort him, there was a pause.

"I think I will go," said Stavros politely. He swaggered toward the door. "Thank you for the tea."

Before he could touch the doorknob, another visitor knocked, causing Jason to look up. Daphne brushed Stavros aside and opened the door. It was Adrian Loukas, newly shaven, wearing a wrinkly but clean set of clothes and a backpack. In his arms was the Yin family's missing cat.

"Peony!" shouted Jason. He ran over to take his cat.

"I found her outside your building," explained Loukas. "I hope you don't mind."

"Who are you?" questioned George. "How did you know

she was ours?"

"This is Adrian!" the boy exclaimed. "He's a world-famous painter. And, he solved Auntie's riddle!"

"What are you talking about?" demanded Stavros. "I've never met this guy. How does Cassandra know him?"

"Do you know where Cassandra is?" asked George. "What is she up to? Why hasn't she called?"

"Unfortunately," Loukas began. He drew a long breath. "I have some bad news. I think it would be easier if everyone sat down." He handed Daphne the blue backpack with the rest of Cassandra's belongings. "Cassandra and I were chasing after thieves who had stolen some very important paintings."

"That's nonsense," reacted Stavros. "Why would she do that?"

"It's a long story. But it led us to Mount Athos, where the monasteries are. It's a peaceful place, and no one suspected any danger. Cassandra went out on her own and took one of my paintings with her. She fell asleep in an alcove next to the painting, which was also stolen." The artist stopped. He had rehearsed this speech, and yet somehow the words he had planned did not feel right. He thought it best to get right to the point. "Cassandra was attacked by a wild animal. She died."

"What do you mean, 'attacked by a wild animal'?" cried George.

"And where were you during this time?" demanded Stavros. He stepped towards Loukas with cold suspicion in his eyes.

"I went out to look for her," the artist explained, avoiding direct eye contact with Stavros. "But by the time I got there, it was too late."

"You're lying!" accused Stavros. He shoved the taller man, Loukas, against the wall with both his hands. "Tell us where she is!"

"Stop!" commanded George. He raised his firm hands to fill the space between Loukas and Stavros.

Stavros threw up his hands, but backed away and began

pacing around the room with his hands on his head. "This doesn't make any sense."

George interrogated the artist. "If she's dead, where is her body?"

"The monastery is taking care of it," Loukas explained. "Here's their number." He offered a white, folded slip of paper.

"What am I supposed to do with this, hmm?" cried George. "Listen to more lies about monsters in the woods?"

"Why aren't the police handling it?" asked Daphne, also becoming upset. "Instead, they send us a painter to tell us? Are you even sure she died?"

"Quiet!" shouted the matriarch in Greek. This was the first Greek word the Yin family had ever heard her say in her own home, and it shocked them all into silence. The matriarch stood up slowly from her seat and leaned on her cane, speaking in the best Greek she could manage: "I am...disappointed. Yesterday...I call Cassandra. But...no answer. Today...I call Cassandra. But...no answer. What meaning? Bad...very bad."

"Yes," agreed Loukas, "that's what I am trying to explain—"

"Go home!" the matriarch commanded. "You respect...our family. You respect...our problems."

"I'm sorry, I'll go," the artist conceded.

"You!" The matriarch pointed at Stavros. "You...go home!"

Stavros was shocked but tried to stay polite. "Xie xie," he thanked them using the only Chinese phrase Cassandra had taught him, and then left. Loukas also left the apartment, but said nothing.

Daphne's heart raced with fear. She knew her mother-in-law didn't care for her, and that it was mostly because she was a foreigner. Sometimes she didn't even feel like family, though she had been married to George for fourteen years. The matriarch made eye contact with Daphne briefly, but then she looked down and lowered herself back onto the couch using her cane. It was clear no one else needed to leave the room. Daphne was relieved, and also a little touched. For the first time, being family was more important than being foreign.

Daphne's implicit inclusion in the family conversation made her heart weep with thanks.

"You should rest, mom," said George, switching back to Mandarin.

"Tomorrow morning," the grandmother declared, switching back to Mandarin, "we will find Cassandra. Today we will not know the truth. We will rest. Our hearts will be sad. We will hope for the best. But we will also accept the worst."

The Yin family nodded and honored the matriarch's wishes. Jason shed a few tears, and the television droned on in the background, still broadcasting news about the demonstration at the Theater of Dionysus. George reached for the remote control to turn it off, but Jason stole it away again as he gasped, pointed at the television, and screamed.

"Look, it's Auntie! She's on TV!"

Chapter 24

After leaving the Yins' apartment, Adrian Loukas caught a quick flight from Athens back to Cairo, where his pilgrimage had begun. Though his room had been cleaned out and overtaken by other pilgrims, all of his belongings were held safely for his return. The only room available for the night's stay was a tiny bedchamber with a half-moon shaped window too high on the wall to see anything except the sky. Between the bed and the window was only the thinnest sliver of floorspace, but fortunately he didn't need much room for his final act of the pilgrimage: painting a portrait of Cassandra Yin.

The artist sat at the head of the bed and held a letter-sized canvas in his lap. It was a plain, modern-style canvas made of natural fibers, stretched around a wooden frame. He spread out his acrylic paints and brushes on top of the bedspread gingerly before closing his eyes and visualizing Cassandra's face. She had a round forehead with a widow's peak, bright, black almond eyes that twinkled like the North Star, a round but proportioned nose, and soft, gray, unadorned cheeks. Her ears were small like a child's, while her jaw and chin were mature and pronounced. Loukas recalled her hair tied up the way she had it on Mount Athos, but he decided to paint it the way he imagined her hair would look if allowed to fall naturally, long and wavy, without effort or restraint.

He considered Cassandra's smile. Since he had met her, the mythologist's deepest, most sincere smile seemed to occur while she told the myth of Semele and the uncreated light. Loukas recalled in his mind how her smile folded dimples in her cheeks and moved subtle shadows beneath her eyes. It made her entire head lean back and to the left, as though relaxed in the thought of a happy moment. This face, the artist was certain, was the one he wanted to paint—the face that revealed Cassandra's essence, beyond the veil of forms.

Slowly the artist added lines and colors to the canvas. Smaller paintings required everything, more or less, to be treated as a detail. Each line—from the sagacious curves of her temples to the lines that pursed her upper lip—had to be precise down to a fraction of a millimeter. Fortunately, all was faithfully stored in the artist's visual memory, from which no image or likeness could escape.

While working, the artist made no contact with the outside world. He kept to his bedchamber, scarcely looking up at the clouds through his window. From time to time he munched on crackers and dates from his suitcase, but all of his energy and concentration went into his art, which he dedicated to Saint George and to the Athonite way. For though Cassandra was no pilgrim, her expression was the essence of embracing the journey of self-discovery. Hers was a smile laden with paradoxes—it was so childlike and free that it lacked all presumptions to know, to seek, or to act self-righteously. And yet it boasted a kind of hidden integrity which yearned to understand, to discover, and to be virtuous. Her face was a universal symbol for the magnificent ordinariness of human life.

Then the artist noticed something that shocked him. During the entire process, he had not thought about Cassandra's Chineseness—he just painted her the way she was. And yet, being Chinese was a vital part of her character. Her Chineseness was not merely something foreign to him or to the Orthodoxy, but something precious and near to her soul.

More importantly, it was no barrier to her openness to learning ways outside her own. To the newly awoken Loukas, Cassandra's face represented exactly the purpose for his changed heart. Believer or not, she was the image and likeness of all he held dear. In it he discovered that faith was something universal, beyond borders, beyond culture, and beyond ethnicity. No Greek could claim to own it. The world, and all its God-given glory, existed to be shared with those alike and different. In the eternal scheme of things, she was his equal, his companion, his friend.

When the portrait was dry, Loukas kissed the forehead and said a prayer. "Tomorrow," he resolved, "I will give this painting away. Then I will be ready to go home." Night came and stole the light from his half-moon window. Finally, he would sleep.

......

The Yin family couldn't believe what they were seeing on the television. A crowd of twelve hundred Greeks rallied around the outdoor stage of the Theater of Dionysus. Above them, dozens of thick, splotchy clouds filled the sky, looking like a herd of faceless sheep. In addition, three news-reporting helicopters hovered around, vying for the best camera angle from which to record the event. All attention was fixed on the presenters on stage—until an unexpected mythologist made an impossible entrance.

Cassandra Yin flew into the scene on the back of a white, winged dragon and landed masterfully in the center of the stage. The dragon's feet thumped the ground hard, sending a whirlwind of dust to chase the rally's leaders into the grandstands. The crowd was shocked—even those viewing from home could hear their cries of confusion and fear. As Cassandra dismounted the dragon, which then launched itself into the sky and out of sight, her white blouse remained unmarred by the dust. She stood to face the people of Athens, and all eyes turned towards her. All faces leaned in to hear what she had to say.

"Fellow Greeks, and fellow friends, I have come to share a story with you."

She looked out at the crowd and tried to calm her nerves. The last time she gave a speech was to defend her dissertation, and there weren't more than ten people in the room. Now she was speaking to an audience of hundreds, and the sight of it was more than a little daunting. She looked up to the sky and reminded herself that she now had experience mastering demons far more threatening than a human crowd. Before speaking again she drew a slow breath and centered herself. She relaxed her knees and grounded her feet as if to enter a state of Wu Chi. In a state of timeless ecstasy, she waited for intuition to feed her the best myth.

"This is a story I think you all will like very much. It's the story of…"

The crowd had fallen silent. Her mind was empty and still, and her intuition was lucid. Her words would be powerful, she knew, and yet she was free from any desire to take advantage of this power. She would have been content to go home and spend a carefree day with her family instead.

Nevertheless, her intuition told her she was on this stage for a reason. Like Master Zhang had told her on the day they met, the universe had brought her there for a reason. The world was aching, and Cassandra Yin was to show all of Greece the Way. In that moment, as she looked up at the sky, she knew that all the myths of the universe—the symbols and ancestral memories of the collective unconscious—were at her disposal to tell. She drew them effortlessly into her mind like a placid lake receiving many streams flowing from all directions. Then she began.

"It's the story of Jason and the Argonauts. Except…" Moving smoothly and gradually like her *shifu* had taught her, she animated her storytelling by adding expression with her arms. "The Argonauts I'm talking about—are my own family."

The crowd chuckled pleasantly. They were hooked by the mythologist's charm. Cassandra reached into her pocket to retrieve her wallet and pulled out a photograph.

"This is my nephew, Jason," she explained, showing it to the audience. "He was born at the meeting place between two mighty rivers near the mouth of the Aegean sea.

"The first of these rivers was protected by a goddess called Daphne. Daphne was the keeper of all the memories of the past—she treasured all Greek traditions, from songs to myths to ancient family recipes for cooking *pastitsio*—all these things fed her mighty river and made it roar with passion and pride. But the second river was a mighty tributary of yellow water that flowed from the East. None of the Greeks from the first river knew where the water came from—not even Daphne— but they knew it was protected by a wandering horseman called George.

"One day, Daphne was washing clothes in her river, when George rode in on his horse. 'What are you doing here?' asked the goddess. The humble horseman replied, 'I followed the river up from its mouth. You may not know this, but each night I ride my horse to visit your river. What a beautiful and mighty river you have! I asked all the people who live here to tell me which goddess protects this river, and they told me that you, Daphne, were the goddess. So, I have come now with the sun as my witness in order to meet you.' Daphne was flattered but she also had questions, for she didn't know who this horseman was or what he wanted with her river.

"Daphne said to the horseman, 'First, tell me your name. Then, tell me by what spirit your river was blessed. You must tell me this, because I will never let my river become polluted by foul waters.' He answered, 'My name is George, and I come from the East, but I want to make my home beside you, if you will let me. My river has been blessed by the spirit of Love, which turns all waters pure.' The goddess was intrigued by his answer. 'Then let me drink from your river to test its character,' she said. She dipped her hands into the yellow river like a cup and drank the water. Then, her belly began to quiver.

"'Are you all right, great goddess?' asked the horseman. 'I hope my humble waters are to your liking.' She beamed a beautiful smile and said: 'Your river has enchanted my heart and filled it with love, dear George.' But before she could say anything else, her belly swelled like the leathery skin of a blowfish, and she realized she was pregnant. 'What a fortuitous meeting this has become!' exclaimed George. 'Surely a child born from the love of our two rivers meeting will be cherished by all. He will be loved by your people and my people alike!'"

Cassandra paused to look at Jason's photo again. She let her posture sag a little, and then held it up to the people again.

"When Jason was born, I got to visit him in the hospital that same evening. I was sixteen, and Daphne let me hold him in my arms. Then, I saw his jewel-like eyes, and I looked into them. Just as a prospector sifts through river sands looking meticulously for traces of gold, I searched through Jason's beautiful face for a resemblance to my own. 'Will he look like me when he is older?' I wondered. 'Will he take after his father George, who brought his dark eyes and black hair from the East? Or will he take after his mother Daphne, with sandy hair and eyes as clear as a mountain stream?' I held Jason close to me and rocked him in my arms. I sang to him and saw him smile. That was the first moment in my life when I felt true love. Whenever I look at this photograph, I remember that moment. When you look at the faces of your children, I am sure you also remember the first time you held them and felt their love—the purest, most innocent love there could ever be between people on earth.

"Friends and citizens of Greece, it is time for us to realize that we are all the product of the meeting of two mighty rivers. Mother, like motherland, is a river filled with the cherished purities and traditions of the past. Father comes to her from outside the family and asks to pour his own waters into this river to create something new: a precious child. Listen to me! You are this child. We all are these children. You may say 'Greece for the Greeks', but the Mother Greece you inherit is already changed by the mixing of generations. The fact that you are brought into this world means that she has changed forever and looks only to the sea. Father has added something new. You may say 'Immigrants, go home', but the father whose river we also inherit is already here. You may believe that immigrants are not a part of you because you have none in your family, but I say: look around at the sea of people who are your neighbors in Greece and beyond its borders. A river born from the meeting of many streams can only move forward. Someday—as inevitably as dyes will mix in a bowl of water—our families will mix together and will create children like Jason. But they will come with the spirit of Love, and they will not be impure. The only thing that could possibly pollute our river is our fear of letting it be touched by other rivers. I ask you to let go of this fear. Instead, let us fill our river with love."

In that moment, Cassandra felt a breath of release. Her training was complete. She was speaking on the national stage just as Master Zhang wanted her to do, responding to the aching of the world by showing all of Greece the Way. With the power of her inner dragon, she manifested the full extent of her knowledge for all to see and hear.

And yet, telling this story felt no different than telling any story. She was the same storyteller she had always been, and Greece was the same audience. The collective unconscious, too, was unchanged by her success. Cassandra stood in the same threshold between alternating cycles of history as every woman and man has stood before the masses seeking change. And the truth was clear—the ebb and flow of activism would forever be subject to fierce and deflating natural consequences.

Every word she said had been said before, everything she did had been done before, and no matter how well she might succeed every shortcoming would inevitably repeat itself again due to the cyclical nature of time. *Yin* and *yang* were the immortal gods of destiny. There was no new combination she could hope to create. All existed as it had always been, never more and never less. There she stood, a timeless myth-bearer for all of humanity, filling the same old news stories with the same old headlines.

Suddenly, a cloud appeared and covered the sun. The

faces of the crowd started to shift. Some looked at her with skeptical bewilderment, while others rolled their eyes with apathy. Somehow, she had lost their respect. She could not feel the warmth of her own *shen* or the energetic qualities of her *qi*. Her soul felt inert and powerless. Somewhere amidst the crowd, she sensed Master Zhang was watching her, but she couldn't locate him. He was mixed into the masses like a lone white grain of sand in a muddy basin. Then, her eyes caught those of a surly dissident who pointed his finger at the photograph and shouted angrily.

"I know that boy!"

Cassandra tried to focus back on the stillness of her mind. Like turbulence added to a pool of clear water to stir up mud from the bottom, her fear of what this man might say stirred anxiety and defensiveness from the depths of her heart. The man continued:

"He's the *kinezaki* who ruined my shirt!"

"You're right," chimed another dissident. "He's the laundry delivery boy! What a troublemaker!"

"I've got a real bone to pick with that *kinezaki*," a bellicose woman shouted. "He tore my mother's wedding gown when he stepped on it!"

Cassandra was heartbroken. The complaints continued.

"He's the boy who teases my dogs whenever he walks behind our fence!"

"What an arrogant child! He demanded a tip from me when I already told him no!"

"Send the *kinezaki* away! Greece for the Greeks!"

All at once the crowd burst out into protests. The old refrains returned with an added fierceness. Picket signs that had rested on the ground during Cassandra's speech were swiftly raised again. Ears that had hung on her every word were instantly overtaken by mouths that hungered for blame and accusation.

There were also some who spoke up in Jason's defense: "He's only a boy!" "Leave the *kinezaki* alone!" But even these remarks were devastating to Cassandra—they should never have needed to be said. The innocence of Jason's childhood name was stained for good. The blows were dealt, and the wounds were deep. The more the shouting from all sides continued, the more it ripped the mythologist's heart to shreds from every angle. She felt herself in shriveling up a wasteland of the worst of both *yin* and *yang*.

Quickly, the police arrested the mythologist for disturbing the peace. But her story wasn't finished. Greece kept aching, and its people longed for the Way.

Epilogue

"I'm proud of you, little sister," said George Yin as he threw down a newspaper onto the breakfast table. The front headline read: *Rogue Mythologist Stirs Hatred.*

"I just spent the night in jail. Can't I eat my spanakopita in peace?"

"We should have a banquet." George squeezed his sister's shoulders from behind and gave her a loving shake. "Daphne, get in the kitchen now! We're making a feast tonight!" He paced around the living room rubbing his hands enthusiastically. "We will invite all the neighbors. The Chens, the Hans, the Mings—everybody! Is there anyone you want to invite?"

They heard a knock on the door. George went to the door and held his hand on the doorknob, taking his time to answer it as he finished his thought.

"I wish I knew how to contact that fellow who posted your bail, some guy called Zhang. They told me his given name was Li-Kuo, I think. But who is he? Do you know? Not a customer. I've never heard of him. Whoever he is, we have to get him a gift. Do you have any ideas?"

The door knocked a second time, and George opened it. It was Adrian Loukas, back from Egypt to make an important delivery on his way home. His brown hair was nicely combed, and he wore a clean, purple collared shirt.

"You again? What are you doing here?"

Loukas still couldn't believe it. He had seen Cassandra's body rolled away on the stretcher. And yet, she had appeared on television later that day! There she was, alive and sitting in front of him.

"You're the painter, right?" Cassandra's brother confirmed. "Well, of course you are! Look what you're carrying!"

Loukas hid the face of his painting behind a cloth and started to greet Cassandra. But George interrupted him.

"Daphne! Come out here, we have a visitor!"

When Daphne didn't come, George went into the bedroom to hunt her down.

"I can't believe you're alive!" the artist exclaimed. "And what did I read in the news? A mythologist stirring hatred? That sure doesn't sound like you."

Cassandra wasn't in the mood for his playful banter. "Don't believe what you read in the headlines." She took a bit of spanakopita and chewed it without a hint of a smile.

"Right. Because the headline is just a myth."

"And don't mock me," she griped.

"I'm not mocking. How are we to know what is real and what is myth? When I saw you there with that dragon, I was shocked. I didn't think dragons even existed."

"Wait a second. You saw the dragon in the theater? But, how could you?"

"At the theater? No, I meant on Mount Athos. I saw it coming to kill you, and so I ran out. But when I got to you, they were rolling you away."

"Hmm," she said, dejected. "Maybe we're both delusional."

"Are you okay, Cassandra?"

"I'm not sure."

"Well, I may be able to cheer you up. I brought you a—"

"None of the things we experienced really happened. Right? The icons. The paintings. They were only dreams."

"What? Why are you saying this?" asked the artist. This was not the kind of welcome he had expected from her.

"This entire week to me has been a long and confusing dream. Would you believe I entered your portrait of Zhen Wu?"

"No, because it's not an icon."

"I can't make sense of it at all."

"Sometimes things don't make sense. We have to accept them by faith."

"Faith?" Her face cringed with disgust. "You sound just like Master Yan-Mei. Did you know she was the one who faked my death? She stowed me away in another monastery."

"Which one?"

"Oh, god! That's even stranger. She claimed it was a secret women's monastery built inside the caverns beneath Mount Athos."

"Really?" Loukas was pleasantly intrigued. "I'll be damned. What's it called?"

"Moni Bardous. Master Yan-Mei is apparently a monk there, or something...but no! None of that is real!"

Loukas reminisced in cautious admiration of the enigmatic thief. "Well, if Master Yan-Mei is real, and if she does run some kind of apocryphal monastery beneath Athos that nobody knows about, then I'm sure she would keep the secret far from me."

"A secret, yes. Good point, Adrian. That means we need to forget all of this. What we saw in the icons, I mean."

"How can we forget it? These experiences renewed my faith in everything, including humanity." The artist took a breath and paused. Cassandra seemed inconsolably perturbed. Loukas worried his visit wasn't timed well. "I can step out and give you a moment if you want," he said.

"No. I'm fine."

"Then why are you so bent out of shape?"

"Because I hate the way they are portraying us in the news. I hate it! I hate the way it has exposed my family, especially Jason. You wouldn't understand."

"Maybe not," he admitted. "But what can I do?"

"Nothing."

"Nothing?"

"I'm done dreaming of a future in which children and immigrant families can go through life without being targets of fear and discrimination. Those dreams are dead to me."

Loukas looked down and sighed, searching his feelings for something to say. For him, the dreams and the hopes were just beginning.

"Besides," she continued, "they were all illusions of western culture."

"What are you talking about?"

"In Western mythology, dreams tell the future. They promise us hope and prophecy, which is a lie. But in Eastern mythology, dreams tell the past. They reveal to us how history moves in cycles and always repeats itself. Whatever problems may happen, even if we fix them temporarily, the problems will come back over and over again because that is how the world has always been. Whatever we do to try and influence the outcome will only stir the pot and make things worse. See?" She pointed vehemently at the newspaper headline. "It says, *stir hatred!* It would be better just to leave the pot alone and let the world take its course."

"How can you say that? Do you really think God would put us here to take sides and never learn to love each other?"

"I already told you. I have no god."

"Then what about your intuition? Surely, you must have faith in something. Don't you?"

"My intuition tells me to look at history. Things have never changed. That means, they never will."

"Are you being serious? I can't tell."

She kept silent.

"Hmm. Maybe you're right," he said facetiously. "Or else... no, that's nonsense."

"Or else, what?"

"No, no, you wouldn't believe me."

"Tell me."

"Or else...maybe we can change history."

"Change history?" she said skeptically.

"Change the past in order to change the future."

"How could that even be possible?"

"By the power of an image, maybe. Imagine that a picture of someone is like a veil, a window. They may seem to be a certain way on the outside, but behind the veil is their true likeness. When you hold the image of their face in your mind—like an icon—you can see them in a new light, beyond the veil, and you can forgive what they might have done in the past. Maybe then you can see history in a new perspective."

Loukas uncovered his portrait of the mythologist and showed it to her.

"This is for you. I painted it last night when I was in Cairo."

"Thank you for your kind gesture." She stood still. "But I cannot accept it."

"I see." Loukas covered the painting back up. He scratched the collar of his purple shirt and nodded to himself. "I'll just leave then."

George emerged from the hallway and filled the room with his booming chatter.

"Daphne's not feeling well. I think she ate some bad shrimp. Oh, Adrian! Aren't you going to show us your painting?"

Cassandra crossed her arms and turned away. Loukas showed the portrait to George.

"This is beautiful. This is fantastic! Who is it? Cassandra, did you see this painting?"

"I don't want it," she said, crossing her arms.

"Please excuse her," George pleaded. "She's not feeling well."

"Well, someone in your family should have it," suggested Loukas.

"I know!" shouted George as he swiped the painting from the artist's hands. "We will give it to that rich fellow who bailed you out of prison, Cassandra. What was his name again? Oh, yes. Li-Kuo Zhang. Is that okay with you, little sister?"

"Fine."

George thanked the artist several times and returned to his bedroom, shouting the news of the gift to his wife.

Then Loukas smiled and said, "Well, at least we know one thing was real: Master Zhang. I was almost starting to think you made him up. But if he posted your bail, then he has to be real, right?"

"He did seem real on the day I met him. But then...it was so strange. At the train station he acted like he didn't recognize me. Was I just a ghost to him?"

"Or was he the ghost?"

"Don't be silly. For *him* to be the ghost, there would have to be an icon of me...somewhere."

Cassandra held her breath for a moment. If the Master Zhang that trained her had been from the *future*—if he had come to her through Loukas's painting of Cassandra, just as she had come to Zhen Wu through his portrait—that would explain why the Master Zhang at the train station didn't recognize her. He had not met her yet! It was an intriguing thought, perhaps worthy of legends. But, not wanting to get lost on the world of myth again, she tried to shake off the idea.

George burst into the room again.

"Mr. Loukas, you should come to our banquet tonight in Cassandra's honor! We will have plenty of food and wine to feast on. Of course, if you don't speak Chinese, you might not understand much."

Cassandra gave her brother an aggravated stare. George picked up on her signal and excused himself from the room.

"You shouldn't come," she told him. "It's really more of a family event."

"You're right," said Loukas. "I will leave you alone. Unless... no, that would never work."

Cassandra feigned a smirk.

"Someday, years from now, I will enter your portrait...and show up to you as a ghost from the future!"

"Quit it, Adrian."

"I'm sorry. I'm making you feel worse."

"Yeah, you are."

"Forgive me. But how can you just forget the extraordinary adventure we've had? Doesn't it mean something to you?"

"Of course, it does. It means that I don't want anything extraordinary anymore. I don't want to become so full of stories that I hide from what goes on around me. I just want an ordinary life."

"I see. You want to be empty."

"Yes. Now you understand."

After her words, there was silence.

"Okay, I'm going."

......

Loukas left the Yin apartment without looking back. He knew without a doubt that the mystical moments he experienced with the icons were real, even if Cassandra chose to forget them. They were the miracle he needed for his life to restart. For him, the sights he had seen were like an elixir of life—filling his field of vision with all that was holy and true. And for that reason, he knew he no longer needed iconography to see proof of his life's providence. He didn't need icons to stay in relation with saints like Macarius, Theodora, and George—his faith alone was sufficient. He didn't even need the *Sinai Pantocrator*. Like photographs etched into the tablet of his memory, what he saw would last eternally.

As he retraced his memories of the past few days, he realized that something was amiss. "Miracles happen for the unbelievers," a priest once told him, "so that they might believe." But why, then, had God revealed the miracle of iconography to Loukas, the believer? It made more sense to him that Cassandra would have needed this miracle in order to find faith. And yet, she seemed to know no need for faith at all! She had no concept of God. And yet, who could deny the purity of her spirit? How could the artist fail to see that behind her smile was the soul of an angel? That in her unpresuming nature to remain empty of such things as religion, she was perhaps even more full of the Spirit than he? "A full cup cannot receive its fill," he reflected, remembering a proverb he had heard from somewhere, "but an empty cup can."

Loukas focused on the portrait of Cassandra in his mind's eye. Something about her still intrigued him, even baffled him—something that neither his religion nor his common sense could explain. She had a way about her that was beyond what he could put into words or pictures. Her presence was patient and unassuming, yet creative and cunning when applied to a problem. She had physical stamina and strength, yet also softness and humility—by her stillness alone she could entrain the heartbeats of those around her. Her mind was fluid like water yet rooted in principles; her heart was passionate like a fiery dragon, yet sober like a newborn lamb. Without ambition for herself she had accepted the highest calling of any woman or man—to heal the wounds of chaos between East and West. With little more than superficial knowledge of spiritual lore, she had come as close to meeting God face-to-face as he ever had—maybe even closer!

The more he reflected on it, the more he realized that the greatest miracle of all had been the mythologist herself. Before he met Cassandra, his mind had been like the old wineskins, unable to receive new wine in the form of a fresh perspective. To revive his soul, he needed to follow Cassandra and learn from her—a Chinese-Greek chained to the duality of her heritage—how to transcend the past in the ultimate test of human character and endurance.

"If it's true that only an empty cup can receive," Loukas thought, "then maybe Cassandra's emptiness is her way of receiving the miracle she needs so she can believe." For a moment, Loukas's soul lit up, thoroughly inspired, and joy entered every bone in his body. "Then again," he wondered, feeling his joy subside, "if she allowed herself to believe in something, then wouldn't she lose her emptiness? Wouldn't she lose her ability to believe in anything? If she let herself be filled, wouldn't she become like me, like the old wineskins?" He shook his head, unable to fully comprehend this thought. Instead he prayed for Cassandra.

May she remain young in spirit, like the new wineskins, forever able to receive.

......

After the artist left, Cassandra fell into her bed and cried.

A few hours later she went for a jog around Plato's Academy Park, and then cleaned herself up for the banquet. "I won't let my mind dwell in the past," she reminded herself. "Or in the future. I'm setting my sights on the present, where my family is."

She put contacts in her eyes and makeup on her face, which she had not done in several years, and put on a blue and silver dress that she kept in the back of her closet. Stavros, too, dressed elegantly, which did not come naturally to him. He offered her a shimmering ring of diamond and onyx as he reissued his proposal of marriage, which Cassandra gleefully accepted.

The family set up as many chairs as could fit in their humble apartment so all their guests could join them. They feasted on steamed white rice, roast suckling pig with hoisin sauce, seafood and cabbage rolls, red and plum wines, and a dessert of peach lotus buns glazed to perfection. Sharing food and drink with loved ones to celebrate a momentous occasion was a tradition that had existed since the dawn of time. It made them forget minor squabbles and embrace their love for family and friends. None at the table struggled with one another, but balanced their quirks and imperfections like the dual colors of the *yin-yang*, working and alternating in perfect harmony. The banquet was the event that made even the myths feel real, because it was ordinary, and therefore timeless.

Cassandra thanked all the guests for coming and her family for preparing the food. George raised a glass of wine to toast his sister's valiant effort to show Greece the Way. When they had drunk the wine, they filled their glasses again, never tiring of the moment's ecstasy. Jason, too, had his fill, not of wine but of hope for his family's future. Before that evening, he had never seen so many happy faces in his own home! He took as many photographs as he could. And he never needed to ask permission, for their smiles came effortlessly and welcomed his capture on film.

As the night was winding down, a guest took a photograph

of the entire Yin family, which they would keep in a golden frame to admire later. No one would forget the day of Cassandra's engagement.

It was a day that made her mother happy.

Photo: Theatre of Dionysus, Athens

Derek Olsen is a world-traveler and interfaith philosopher based in Tacoma, WA. He has given occasional talks in association with the Unity Church and currently teaches high school English, drama, and humanities.